SARAH PIRTLE

To the ones who keep making it through the heartaches in life and have decided to choose their own fate, this one's for you.

Content Warning

Some of the topics in this book may be triggering for some readers, Trigger Warnings are listed out in the back of the book. Please be aware that trigger warnings may contain spoilers, but as always your mental health matters. Please read with caution.

Xo, Sarah.

Playlist

Ghost Town - Benson Boone
Intrusive Thoughts - Natalie Jane
Halo - Alexander Stewart
Changes - XXXTENTACION
My Stupid Heart - Walk Off The Earth
Lose Control - Teddy Swims
Please Notice - Christian Leave
Can't Take My Eyes Off Of You - Craymer, AllVAWN
Down On Me - Jeremih, 50 Cent
Mind On You - George Birge
Nobody's You - Dylan Brady
Thinkin' Bout Me - Morgan Wallen
Belong Together - Mark Ambor
Take Me Back To Eden - Sleep Token
Locksmith - Sadie Jean
Figure You Out - VOILA
Soulmate - Chanin
Too Sweet - Hozier
In The Stars - Benson Boone
Young and Beautiful - Lana Del Rey
I Was Made For Lovin' You - KISS
Perfect - Atlus
Wish You The Best - Lewis Capaldi
Gonna Love You - Parmalee
Go Get Her - Restless Road
Only For You - Tors
A Bar Song (Tipsy) - Shaboozey
Nothing Left But Leavin - Austin Williams
How Do I Say Goodbye - Dean Lewis
Stargazing - Myles Smith
Wildest Dreams - Taylor Swift

Prologue

Sawyer

10 years ago. . .

"Sawyer, you're so lame. Where is your costume?" my younger sister, Taylor, asks from her bedroom as I stop in the doorway to see when they'll be ready to go.

"I'm an off-duty hockey player. You're just unobservant." I smirk at her, and she rolls her eyes.

"Whatever. You're still driving tonight, right?" She leans closer to the mirror as she continues to dab some gray shit on her eyelids. Her three best friends, Shane, Leah, and Lauren are all scattered around her room putting final touches on their costumes as well.

"Yes. When the hell are you going to be ready?" I look down to check my watch. We're supposed to go to the haunted trail, like we do every year, before going to their senior class Halloween party at the McCallum property. At the rate they're getting ready, we might not even make it to the party before midnight.

I still can't believe they're seniors already. It seems like just last week the four of them were sitting at the kitchen table working on their 6th grade class project—the thing that brought them all together in the first place.

"I'll be ready when I'm ready." She scowls at me.

"You know, you should really switch costumes with Lauren." I nod to where Lauren stands dressed as a devil. I'm sure there was some *adorable* strategy behind them picking their cat/mouse and angel/devil costumes, but I simply don't care enough to ask.

Being three years older than Taylor, it's no surprise we grew up doing everything together. What shocks most people is to find out that we still do. A lot of times with siblings you expect them to grow apart the older they get, but that wasn't the case with me and Tot. Since I was a senior their freshman year of high school, I felt like it was my duty to lookout for her and her friends, who in turn, have become my friends as well.

"If I were going to switch costumes with anyone, it would be Leah." Taylor smiles at me sarcastically, bringing my attention to the angel in the room.

"Nah, Dove's costume suits her best of all." I wink at Leah, noticing the way her cheeks turn red as she rolls her eyes at me. Over the years I've grown the closest to Leah. I'm not sure how it happened or when, but the two of us just clicked. She's always the one I've felt most protective over too. Taylor is what a lot of people would call *unhinged*, whereas Leah— she's the gentlest soul I've ever met in my life.

My Dove.

God, she looks beautiful. With her brown locks, porcelain skin, and a smile that could relight the sun if it were to ever dim—all things that match her personality perfectly.

I've viewed Leah as one of my closest friends for as long as I can remember, but I've been looking at her in ways that push the bound- aries of our friendship for longer than I should admit. When she tucks a strand of her long brown hair behind her ear, turning to look in the mirror once again, I regain my focus and realize just how long I've been standing here staring at her.

"Hurry up. I don't want to be standing in line all night." I look back at Taylor and tap the top of the door frame before disappearing downstairs. I can hear Taylor groan as soon as I walk away and then their giggles echo through the hall at what I'm *sure* was a sisterly jab at how much of an annoyance I am to her.

When they finally come running down the stairs my eyes immediately land on Leah. It's like an involuntary response to her presence for my eyes to find her. She has on a simple long sleeve white dress, fitted on the top with a silk skirt that flows right along her thighs, knee high white socks with sneakers and her long brown hair is set in loose waves—why she always covers up her natural curls with hand crafted ones has always been a mystery to me. The wings and halo only add to her already angelic persona.

"Hello? Earth to Moose." Hearing the nickname the four of them gave me years ago brings my mind back from wandering. Taylor waves her hand in front of my face, making me aware of how fiercely I was just staring at Leah. *Again.*

Shit, I have to stop doing that.

"What?" I snap, glaring over at her.

"Take our picture." She presses her phone against my chest. My face drops in annoyance as I open the camera app.

"1...2...3..." The camera shutters several times before I hand it back to her. "You better like one of them cause I'm not taking any more."

"Rude." She glares at me. "JJ would let me check and make sure I liked it," she mumbles under her breath—referring to our older brother, JJ, who hasn't lived at home since he went off to college for nursing two years ago.

"Well, JJ isn't here, so you get to deal with me." I smile back at her before grabbing a piece of paper from the counter.

"Dove, come here." I nod Leah over to me, handing her the paper. "Read this out loud," I whisper in her ear. She glances up at me and I give her a wink, loving the small giggle that falls from her lips when I do.

"Shotgun!" Leah smiles as she turns the paper around.

"Dammit, Sawyer!" Taylor groans as I finish putting my jacket on and snatch my keys from the counter.

"Let's go!"

When we pull up to the haunted trail, I'm pleased to see the line isn't too long to get in. We're always in there far past the temperature dropping and I'm left with four iron deficient girls whining about being cold by the time we get back to the truck. Because God forbid, they wear jackets over their costumes because it doesn't *"fit the vibe"* as Taylor always claims.

When we're almost up to the entrance I see Leah wrap her arms around herself and her jaw chattering fiercely.

"Cold?" I shove my hands into my pockets as I slide up next to her.

"Freezing," she chatters through her teeth. I shake my head and chuckle as I come to a stop, making her steps halt right along with mine.

"Here, take this." I slide my arms out of my denim jacket and hold it out in front of her.

"Can't. It'll break my wings." She turns around, letting the feathers that line her angel wings brush along my now bare arm.

"Alright, trade then." Her eyebrows knit together in confusion.

"What?" she laughs.

"Yeah, give me the wings and you can wear my jacket." I take a step closer and motion for her to give me her wings.

"Oh, I can't wait to see this," she snickers, pulling them off and sliding her arms through my jacket. She rolls her lips to keep from laughing when she sees me struggle to get the elastic straps over my broad shoulders.

"Here, Moose, let me help you." She rolls her eyes playfully, walking behind me to pull them the rest of the way up and adjusting the straps. The tingle that runs down my spine from feeling her slender fingers brush against my back catches me off guard, but when she walks back in front of me and brings her fingers to her lips to keep from laughing, I push the feeling aside.

"How do I look?" I clear my throat, holding out my arms to strike a pose.

"Totally angelic." She shakes her head, clearly being sarcastic.

"Looking good, Sawyer." Someone says from beside us. When I look over, I see one of my old classmates practically trying to undress me with her eyes. I glance back down at Leah to gauge her reaction—though I'm not entirely sure *why*—but she's not even paying attention. She's looking in the opposite direction and for some reason, that bothers me.

Something that feels a lot like disappointment settles in my chest over the simple fact that she didn't scowl at Angela for hitting on me in front of her.

Am I actually mad that she isn't jealous?

Why would she be though? We're just friends, and she has no idea how I feel about her. I shake away the feeling, ignore Angela, and I throw my arm around Leah's shoulder.

"You *look* ridiculous," she giggles as we walk closer to the entrance of the trail.

"Are you warm?" I ask, as she hugs the jacket closer to her body.

"Very. Thank you." When she smiles up at me, I can feel the warmth from it spread through my entire chest.

"Then it's worth looking a little ridiculous. Let's go, it's our turn." I nod towards the entrance as she takes a deep breath, nodding in agreement. Leah is *not* a fan of spooky things. She will watch any movie in the world, but if it has a jump scare in it, she's immediately out. So, the fact that she continues to come to the haunted trail every year is a true testament to her commitment to her friends and their traditions.

Well, *our* traditions, I guess.

When we reach the front Taylor, Shane, and Lauren all turn around and face us.

"There you guys are. We lost you for a minute." Shane locks eyes with Leah first, then tilts her head and looks at me.

"Glad you decided to dress up after all Sawyer," she snickers, drawing attention to the wings I'm now wearing. Taylor and Lauren both laugh, and Taylor quickly snaps a picture of us just before the ticket attendant calls for us to go through.

"Come on, Le." Taylor waves her over to link arms with her and the four of them walk through the entrance together.

The beginning of the maze is basically a small shed with worn out tarps covering both the entrance and the exit. As soon as we walk through, a strobe light flashes and a clown pops out of the corner, making all the girls run out screaming as fast as possible. I can't help but laugh as I walk behind them through the tattered fabric hung on the threshold to the maze.

I hear them scream again in the distance and follow the sounds until I can see them, but before I can catch up, the actress dressed as the girl from *The Ring* starts speed crawling towards them and the girls start falling all over each other. I snicker at how ridiculous they look until I see them all scatter, and Leah falls to the ground. I'm already walking a little faster to get to her but when the girl starts crawling towards Leah, causing her to scream louder than I've ever heard someone scream before, I'm there in a matter of seconds.

"Come on, I got you." I bend to help her back to her feet.

"Sawyer, thank God," she sighs, dusting herself off. "I'm gonna kill them for leaving me like that." We make it around the next corner with only a scarecrow hanging on our right, but as soon as we turn again a chainsaw starts in the distance, prompting Pinhead and Michael Myers to pop out of the field. Leah screams as she backs into me, and I instinctively wrap my arms around her. She turns to bury her face in my chest as the sound of the chainsaw gets closer and closer. She frantically grabs my T-shirt, digging her nails into my sides as she screams.

"Sawyer!" Something happens in that moment that completely alters my brain chemistry, and my heart skips a beat. Suddenly I feel the magnitude of her presence, and it's nearly enough to knock me on my ass.

I tighten my grip around her, lifting her feet just barely off the ground, hurrying past the loud noises and masked men. When we're finally at a clearing with no one else around, I place her feet back on the ground and our eyes lock, making it hard to catch my breath. Her nails are still digging into the skin around my ribs and her bright green eyes are locked on mine with panic and adrenaline still dancing behind them wildly. The scent of warm vanilla wafts around me as she turns her head to take in our surroundings. I close my eyes and breathe her in, feeling time slow down around us.

Why is this happening? Why now?

Time catches back up to me when she turns around and I do my best to ignore the tension in the air.

"Don't worry, Dove. You know I've got you." I squeeze her arms gently and she nods vehemently, backing out of my embrace.

"Let's get out of here." I can't help but laugh when she swats her angel wings out of the way to hide behind my left arm, keeping a death grip on me until we're safely out of the maze and I hate it when she finally lets go.

The only thing on my mind the whole ride to the McCallum's land was Leah. The way she felt against me, her nails in my skin, the way she smells, the way I loved hearing her scream my name. I never thought someone's world could change in one night, but in one simple *moment*, mine has. The girls file out of my truck and run straight over to the drink table, filling their cups before yelling *"Cheers!"* and tipping them back.

They all ease into the night—talking with their classmates, playing corn hole and beer pong—while I give myself some distance and time to think. In an effort to talk myself *out* of seeing Leah as anything more than a friend, I find myself doing just the opposite, and when they start dancing around the fire, I can't take my eyes off of her. The light from the flames illuminate around her like the angel that she is, making everyone else fade away.

So pure, sweet, and innocent. My Dove.

Only she isn't mine. Not in the ways I want her to be.

So why can't I think of anything other than having her in my arms again, or having my name fall from her perfect lips.

"What the *actual* fuck are you doing?" Taylor's voice tears me from my thoughts, making my heart beat even more erratically than it was before.

"Shit, Taylor. You can't just sneak up on someone like that." I warn, checking my surroundings and trying to slow my heart rate.

"If I'm following your gaze correctly, you're staring *really* intensely at the *wrong* person." She leans in trying to follow my line of sight.

"And who might that be?" I level her with a glare.

There's no way she could tell who I was staring at.

"Um, Leah. Duh."

Shit. Maybe she could.

My jaw flexes and my gaze settles on her once again when Taylor says her name. The smile on her face as she laughs with Shane, and the way she swings her hips back and forth to the music has me lost in thought all over again.

"Are you fucking kidding me, Sawyer? You can't." Her voice is pitchy and aggravated, but she doesn't specify *what* exactly it is I can't do. Though I'm assuming she means literally anything.

"Why not?"

Not the question I meant to ask, but okay.

"She's one of my best friends, Sawyer. And she's one of yours too. If you *do* something or *start* something with her that doesn't work out, you'll lose her. And since you're *my* brother, I'll lose her too. And I will *ne-ver* forgive you if you cause me to lose one of my best friends just because you're thinking with your boy dick." She wags her index finger at me and pins me with a stare that travels straight to my soul.

"We're just friends, Tot. So just…chill out. Okay?" My jaw ticks as I try to convince her *and* myself that it's the truth.

"Really, Moose? Cause friends don't look at friends the way you were just looking at Leah." When she walks away, I look back in an effort to find Leah, but she's no longer dancing in the same spot. Instead, she's standing awfully close to Justin McCallum and every bone in my body is telling me to go snatch her up and keep her by my side the rest of the night.

Holy shit, am I actually jealous right now?

When she looks my way and smiles, I fear Taylor might have been right. Because I'm definitely not looking at her as a friend right now.

"Fuck," I mutter to myself. Closing my eyes I try to contemplate what the hell I'm going to do about this newfound fascination I have with my sister's best friend.

My best friend.

"Hey, Moose!" I know it's her before I even open my eyes, but when I do I feel my heart skip a beat. Her long brown hair swooshes back and forth as she spins to stand next to me, sending her vanilla scent soaring through the air again. "We're all going to Flapjack's tomorrow morning to cure the inevitable hangovers that are to be had, you're coming too." It's a statement more than it is a question, and I feel an odd sense of pride knowing she wants me there.

"Yes ma'am." I chuckle, saluting her. She rolls her eyes and laughs before grabbing my hand.

"Come on, I need someone to dance with. Lauren is a little handsy tonight."

Lucky her.

"I don't know, Dove. I'm not sure I'm up for it tonight." She turns around to face me with a pout. She says nothing. She simply pleads with her plump lips jutted out sadly.

God, what I would give to know what they would feel like against mine.

"Fine." A devilishly sweet smile spreads across her face when I agree, and she turns to lead me over to where people are still dancing.

The moment her hands land on my shoulders and she starts moving her hips back and forth, I'm done for.

I want my sister's best friend in the most sinful ways, and I can't do a damn thing about it.

Morning comes faster than I wish it had, and I've fought myself every hour over whether or not I should be going to breakfast with Leah and whoever the hell else is supposed to be there. But of course, if it's for Leah, I'm going to show up. Throwing on a plain black hoodie and a pair of blue jeans I head out the door so I'm not late.

The entire drive to Flapjack's I try to convince myself that what I was feeling last night was a fluke, making up any and every excuse I could for why I was looking at her like…like I *shouldn't* have been looking at her.

I've all but convinced myself that it was a one-time thing when I pull into the parking lot, but as soon as I catch a glimpse of her through the diner window that foundation crumbles. Because my breath catches when she tosses her curly brown hair over her shoulder, and I find myself wondering if she still smells like vanilla.

It definitely wasn't a fluke. Of course it wasn't, she's been the only thing on my mind since she landed in my arms—and for much longer before that if I were just freaking honest with myself.

My heart races and my palms begin to sweat as I look down to see a text from her.

DOVE

You're still coming right? I feel mean telling people they can't sit beside me if you're not gonna fill the seat. LOL

She's scanning the diner when I look back up, likely wondering when I'm going to walk through the door. A smile finds its way onto my lips knowing she's waiting for me. I close my eyes, trying to prepare myself to go in and act platonically with her.

I can do this. Dove and I have been friends for years.

Images of me pulling her chair closer to mine, wrapping my arm around her, and whispering in her ear that I've been haunted by the feeling of her hands on me last night flood my mind, making my eyes fly back open.

Yeah, I can't do this.

There's no way I'm walking into that diner without it being painfully obvious that I want her in all the ways I shouldn't.

One night. One simple moment changed everything and decided my fate.

I have to put some distance between us before I do something I'll regret and fuck everything up. Not only between *me* and Leah, but potentially Taylor and Leah as well.

Fuck.

I can always blame my not showing up on needing to head back early for training. That gives me at least until the holidays to see if distance will help me shake the feeling of wanting *more* with her. Maybe then we can continue on like normal and I can put all of this behind me.

ME

Sorry Dove, not gonna make it. Maybe next time.

Oh, how terribly wrong I was… About all of it.

BRÜMANS
Every cup is full of love
RATED #1 IN NASHVILLE

Chapter 1

"Ms. Gates. What are you going to be for Halloween?" Liliana asks from her desk. I've taught kindergarten since I graduated college and I have loved every sticky, slimy, chaotic moment of it. However, after five years of teaching I am convinced all six-year-olds are the same—unfiltered little humans who lose their ever loving shit over some fruit snacks.

"Well, I thought about going as a teacher, what do you think?" I bend to her level, smirking at her playfully.

"That's definitely a scary costume," Deaton yells from a few seats over.

"*Scary?* You guys think I'm scary?" I gasp, letting my jaw hang open as I scan the entire classroom.

"Only when Rocco brings in frogs from outside," Liliana assures me, giving Rocco a *very* sassy look. When I look his way Rocco just smiles up at me, showing off his missing two front teeth.

"That's fair. I do get pretty scary when Rocco brings in frogs, but that's just because I'm scared *of* frogs." I shudder at the thought, making the whole room burst into a fit of giggles.

"What about you, Liliana. What are you going to be?" I turn my attention back to her and she folds her hands on top of the table.

"I'm going as an angel." She smiles sweetly, "My daddy said my sister should go as a devil because she's bad as..." she leans forward and whispers, "H-E-L..."

"*Okay!*" I clap my hands together, cutting her off. "I think we got it."

Lord have mercy, these kids. Filterless, all of them.

"You know, that's funny. My best friend and I went as an angel and devil one year when we were younger." I tilt my head as I look at Liliana, remembering the Halloween Lauren and I went as angel/devil opposites while Shane and Taylor went as cat/mouse opposites. We had the best time picking out and putting together our costumes that year.

Fall has always been my favorite season. The leaves changing colors, the temperature dropping making the air a little crisper, and the fact that I can finally pull out all my favorite sweaters are all the reasons I fell in love with the season. October was my favorite month in particular when I was in grade school simply because of Halloween. My friends and I always loved dressing up and going to the haunted trail before grabbing food from a drive-thru and riding around town blasting our music way louder than necessary. Then we would go home, snuggle up on the couch and watch scary movies. Well, they would watch, I would shield my eyes for almost the whole thing.

Funny how things change so much when you grow up.

"Which one were you?" I'm pulled from my thoughts by Liliana's voice. She narrows her eyes waiting for my response.

"The angel, definitely." I wink and she nods her head in approval.

"Good." She winks back at me, making me laugh just as someone knocks on my door.

"Knock, knock." My heart stops momentarily when I see Jackson standing in the doorway.

"Hey, Jackson—uh, Mr. Morris. Everything okay?"

"Yeah, yeah. Everything's fine. Do you have a minute?" I nod and glance at my assistant, making my way towards the door.

"Go ahead and grab the sensory bins, I'll just be a minute." I step out of my classroom with Jackson and shove my hands into the pockets of my jumper anxiously.

"What's up?" I take a deep breath and let it out slowly, trying to not make it noticeable how nervous I am. Jackson is one of the other kindergarten teachers in this hall, and one of very few guys I've ever dated.

Tried dating? Went on a date with? Whatever.

We went out once on Taylor's birthday, only talked about work, and after that it was just...awkward. We never really talked about going out again and kept things strictly professional between us.

I will admit I was a little bummed that things didn't go any further than they did. Jackson is handsome in a...*scholarly* way. He has light brown hair, green eyes much like my own, he's only a few inches taller than me—probably five foot eight if I were to guess—and stays in good shape, though he's not super muscular like the other guys I'm used to being around.

He wears khakis almost every day to work—that I pray he has multiple matching pairs of—and different prints and colors of button-down dress shirts, with the same square-framed glasses that are set on the bridge of his nose. But good looks aside, he always seems to be happy, and his students love him, so I've always gotten a good vibe about his personality too—which is what I'd hoped to learn more about on our date that flopped.

"Listen..." He peeks into my classroom before looking back down at me. "I know it's been ages since we first went out, and I don't know if you've been seeing anyone else?" He pauses for a moment, so I shake my head to answer.

"Ok. Good. Well, I was wondering if you'd like to go out with me sometime? Again." The smirk on his face as he nervously adjusts his glasses causes me to blush. "I realize that we didn't talk about much outside of things related to work, and that was probably the *worst* possible thing to do on a first date."

Was he just crawling around in my brain or something?

"No matter how out of sorts I may have been that night, I don't love the way we left things. So, I would love a second chance to take you out. Maybe just the two of us, this time?" I bite down on my lip as I contemplate his offer. Maybe the group setting wasn't the best idea for a first date. Before I can stop myself, I'm overanalyzing every interaction of ours from that night. The clearing of his throat is what snaps my attention back to him.

"Um…yeah. I just uh… Sure, yes." The words tumble out of my mouth most ungraciously and his left brow shoots up towards his hairline.

"Don't let me twist your arm or anything, you *can* say no," he laughs.

Oh my gosh, could I be any more awkward?

"You're not twisting my arm. I would love to go out sometime." I meet his gaze to reassure him of my decision.

"Okay then." His smile grows wider. "Can I call you later with a more concrete plan?"

"Of course. That sounds great." He begins backing away and I hear a high pitch scream come from my classroom, causing me to nearly jump out of my skin.

"Okay, well I'll let you deal with that." He points to my classroom. "But I'll call you." I barely catch him winking at me before I nod and head back into my classroom. When I walk in my assistant is frozen in place and Rocco has a *lizard* dangling over Liliana's head.

Why is there always one reptile obsessed child in my class?

ME

Breaking news. Jackson asked me out again.

TAY

Wait, The same guy you brought to my birthday?

SHANE

Ohhh. He was cute, Le! But didn't you say he was like, hella boring though? 😟

ME

Nooo. 😣 I SAID all we talked about was work. But I don't think that will happen again. But what if it's awful? Maybe I should tell him no. I can say something came up.

RUBY

If it's awful then you know you're not compatible and you move on. 🙆 It'll be fine babe. 😊

LAUREN

Honestly, Le. Go. You're 28 years old. You should put yourself out there. At this point, what do you have to lose? And if he's still boring I'll just come proclaim my love for you in the middle of your date and get you out of it.

ME

Again, I didn't say he was boring! And I've put myself out there plenty...

LAUREN

Oh, baby cakes. No... You haven't.

ME

Fine, I'll go. But I'll have you on speed dial.

TAY

Sorry to change the subject, but is everyone still making it to Sawyers party tomorrow?

SHANE

We'll be there!

LAUREN

I might be late, but I'll be there.

RUBY

Yes ma'am! Hendrix is so excited to meet a real hockey player.

ME

Yep. See you tomorrow.

I adore my best friends, and I admire how much time and effort Taylor has put into throwing this *Welcome back to Nashville/Congratulations on getting traded* party, but I'd be lying if I said I haven't been thinking of a way to get out of it since she told me it was happening. Sawyer *used* to be one of my best friends and I held him in such high regard that no one could say an ill word about him to me. Until he lost every bit of my affection and loyalty when he stood me up my senior year of high school and continued to pretend like I didn't exist every day after that without even a hint of a reason why.

I lock my phone and toss it into my bag just as class is dismissed for the day. I think I'll go home, curl up on the couch and watch *10 Things I Hate About You.*

For no particular reason whatsoever.

Chapter 2

Taylor and Tucker's new house is absolutely stunning. It's not *massive*, per se, but the open floor plan makes it feel immensely spacious. Which might just come in handy since I have a feeling I am going to be finding strategic ways to avoid the man of the hour for the better part of the evening. There are balloons everywhere and enough food platters to feed an army—or by the looks of it, Tank, Tucker, and Max. Seriously, if someone doesn't remove them from the kitchen there will be no food left for anyone else.

"Do your wives not feed you?" I slap my hands on the top of the oversized kitchen island. Tank is bouncing Poe on his chest in a baby carrier, and all three of them look over at me, then back down at the almost empty platter.

"Taylor wouldn't let me in the kitchen today while she cleaned the house. I'm starving," Tucker says over a mouth full of food before snatching another crescent wrapped sausage from the tray.

"You look like starved shelter dogs. For the love of God, pace yourselves, gentlemen. This event just started, the person it's for isn't even here yet, and other people are hungry too," I playfully scold them, grabbing the last pig in a blanket with a smirk on my face.

"Yes, Mom," Tank groans, making me roll my eyes.

"She keeping everyone in line in here?" The familiar sound of Sawyer's smooth voice washes over me, causing a pit to form in my stomach. I suddenly wish I was as invisible as he's made me feel over the last ten years.

My heart is hammering against my chest, my feet unwilling to turn around and face the man standing behind me as my eyes bounce between the guys. Tank, Tucker, and Max all shoot anticipating glances my way, but when I subtly shake my head Tank picks up on it and wipes his hand on his blue jeans before extending it to Sawyer.

"Hey man, I'm Tank. I think I was dangerously drunk the last time we met." Leave it to Tank to break the tension just by being Tank. Sawyer laughs and reaches across the island to shake his hand.

"Right. Taylor's birthday party. No, I remember. Good to see you again." The warm scent of cedar surrounds me as he nearly brushes against my arm, making the breaths I'm already struggling to catch that much harder to take. Then I feel Sawyer's gaze land on me.

"Yeah, I was insinuating that *I* didn't," Tank mumbles to himself and I have to roll my lips together to keep from laughing.

I finally take a deep breath and turn to face Sawyer, doing my best to show my indifference towards him. To prove how unaffected I am by the way he took our once cherished friendship and drove it straight into the ground. But when I catch those deep, sapphire eyes already on me when I turn around, my plan flies out the damn window.

"Hey, Dove." His smile acts like a dagger to my heart, but I can't ignore the warmth from the wound spreading through me at the same time. My throat bobs as I swallow past the emotions threatening to choke me up.

"Hey, Moose."

More like, hey asshole.

It's like my mind factory reset and I was transported back to high school. The sense of longing for him that I've actively shoved down for the better part of ten years comes crawling back up to the surface.

Not today, hormones. Get it together.

He chuckles when he hears the name and slides his hands into the front pockets of his dark gray slacks. He's paired them with a dusty-blue dress shirt that's tucked in, the top two buttons are undone, and his sleeves are rolled up just past his forearms. His long brown hair looks as though he just stepped out of the shower and ran his fingers through it, the curls tousled in a perfectly messy way.

Freaking kill me. He looks delicious.

"You look great." His gaze slowly glides over my body causing my cheeks to warm instantly. I have on a simple white turtleneck paired with a navy-blue overall dress, my hair is thrown up into a messy bun with a few stray hairs framing my face and my favorite pair of gray booties.

"Thank you." I tip my chin up confidently, refusing to give in and tell him how great he looks too. He turns to face me head on, making my breath catch in my throat when he does.

"Could we go somewhere to talk? I'd really like to catch up." *Ugh, is he serious?* I can feel my nostrils flare as I draw in a breath— acting as if I'm contemplating my answer— then I quickly respond.

"Hmm. No." His jaw flexes the way it always does when he's frustrated, and I feel the corner of my lips turn up in a smirk.

"Come on, Dove. I–" Before he can finish whatever he was about to say, Taylor enters the room, and magnetically draws all attention to her.

Thank God.

"Pizzas are here!" she announces, placing the boxes on the opposite end of the island.

"Fucking finally," Tucker sighs, walking her way.

"Little ears." Tank covers Poe's ears while he scolds Tucker. As if Poe could actually repeat anything he hears at this age.

I snatch my phone off the counter, hurry to the spare bathroom and lock the door behind me before resting my head on the door and letting out a shaky breath.

"Shit," I whisper to myself, fighting back the sadness I feel washing over me. The last time I saw Sawyer—on *good* terms—was my senior year of high school. He was one of my best friends, and regardless of the secret crush I harbored for him all throughout high school, I never let it get in the way of our friendship. I knew liking your best friend's older brother was a big fat to-don't, but once he and I actually formed a friendship of our own, I was scared of losing more than just my friendship with Taylor—I was scared of losing him as well.

Jokes on me though because in the end, I lost him anyway.

Man, I wish Tucker had built a secret escape door in this bathroom. Because I would really love to disappear right now.

I jump at the sudden buzzing of my phone in my hand but when I look down and see Jackson's name flash across the screen, I can't help but smile and welcome the distraction.

"Hello?" I bring the phone up to my ear, tucking my other hand in the crook of my elbow.

"Hey there. Is this a good time?" *You have no idea.*

"It's a great time, what's up?" I find myself fidgeting with the decorative towels hanging on the rack to give myself something to do in the small space since I can't pace like I normally do while on the phone.

"So listen, my sister just told me about a margarita tasting event at Casa Taco next Thursday, and it made me think of you." He's silent for a moment as I chew on my bottom lip.

Aww. He thought of me.

"If it's not somewhere you think would be good for our first date… Second date? Second first date? Then I will plan something else. Otherwise. How about I pick you up at seven?" I hesitate for a moment before looking up in the mirror, remembering the encouraging words— somewhat depressing, but encouraging nonetheless— that my friends gave me about giving this another shot. I have to put myself out there and move on from the fantasy that has lived, unwelcomed, in my mind for so long that it's kept me from giving anyone a real chance.

"I love Casa Taco. That sounds like a *perfect* second first date."

"Okay then. I'll pick you up at seven next Thursday." I can almost hear his smile through the phone.

"I can't wait. Bye!" I hang up the phone and take a cleansing breath, smiling as I lock my phone and turn to unlock the door. Maybe things are looking up afterall. As soon as the door swings open, I suck in a startled breath.

"Found you, Dove." Sawyer is leaning against the door frame, completely blocking the exit with his burly frame.

There's a reason we call him Moose. The man is massive.

Six-foot-four with muscles that look hand carved... Not that I care.

"Jesus Christ, Sawyer. You almost gave me a heart attack." My hand flies to my chest as I try to catch my breath. "You know they have like two other bathrooms, right?"

"But *you* were in this one. And I was looking for you." He smirks and I cross my arms over my chest, hating the way my stomach still flips at the sight of him.

"Why?" I clip, making it clear I'm not interested in talking to him.

"Look, I know you're mad at me, but I still wanted to give you this." He pulls a ticket from his back pocket. "My first game is next Thursday, and I want you there." I take the ticket and glance down at it then back up at him.

"Sorry, I have plans that night." He scowls at me, and his eyes drop to the ticket.

"With who? Everyone else said they were coming." He nods toward the area of the house where literally *all* of my friends are.

"Why does it matter?" His jaw flexes again, making it harder to pull my eyes away from his strikingly handsome features.

"Is it a date?" His eyes narrow on me and I rear back, shocked by the insinuation. The tone of his voice takes me by surprise because I would almost think he sounded *jealous* if I didn't know any better. But I know better, and there's no chance in hell that's what I'm hearing.

"Welcome back, Sawyer. Good luck at your game." I slide the

ticket in his shirt pocket, tapping it twice before I push past him, only stopping when he catches my arm in his hand.

He pulls me back and a small gasp escapes my lips as I look down where he has me in his grasp and then back up at him. Something flashes in his eyes before he quickly blinks it away, so I wait a beat for him to say something, but when he doesn't I pull away and rejoin our friends in the living room.

I refuse to be the one who gets walked away from—again.

Chapter 3

Sawyer

I've always been known as the guy who goes after what he wants. Whether it was a date with the head cheerleader my sophomore year of high school, or the top spot on the hockey team, when I wanted it, there was nothing that could stand in my way of going for it. That persistence is what landed me the title of team captain in both high school *and* college, and the reason I was one of the top draft picks when I graduated college.

Serves me right that the one time I held back and *didn't* go after what I wanted, I lost one of the most important people in my life.

It didn't take long for me to realize I made a risky decision when I cut all contact with Leah, but I'm just now realizing how badly I fucked things up with her. She's nowhere near the same girl she was ten years ago, just like I'm not the same guy I was.

But Leah always has been and always will be *my girl*, and I'm done acting like she's not.

If I could go back in time and tell my sister to keep her opinions to herself and take my shot with Leah, I would. I barely made it two months without talking to her, but still, I tried. By the time Christmas rolled around, I was ready to throw in the towel and tell her everything, but when I got home that year, she didn't even look my way. Taylor and the girls have religiously spent December 23rd together since middle school, and being in the same house as her that year when she basically pretended I didn't exist, was torture.

Once they all went off to college, holidays didn't quite look the same, and I lost my last sensible reason to be around her. When I finally tried reaching out again, she made it very clear she wasn't interested. I couldn't even blame her; I handled things like an absolute asshole. I tried reaching out several more times throughout the years, but every text has gone unanswered and any time we are around each other—be it a wedding or a birthday gathering—she's just polite enough to get through the evening.

I was determined that Taylor's birthday party a couple of years ago would be my chance to apologize. But not even five minutes into being at that damn karaoke bar, I saw her with somebody else, and it felt like my heart had been ripped out of my chest and was standing across the room. How do you open up to someone about your past mistakes and ask for forgiveness while they're on a date with someone else?

Simple answer. You don't.

Though I did do my best to ensure she wouldn't be taken for long.

I slid the ticket to my game into her bag before she snuck out of the party the other night and I'm still holding out hope that she'll find it and show up.

Getting traded to the Nashville Badgers and being back home feels good. Even if Taylor is the only family I still have here since my parents moved to Colorado. Nashville always has been and always will be home to me.

I'm thirty-one years old, have been playing hockey for most of my life, and this season may very well be the last one before I hang up my skates. I'm undoubtedly in the best shape of my life, but there are moments lately when I stop and reflect, and my heart just isn't in it anymore. When I think about what I'll do next, I always come up empty. I've lived and breathed hockey since I was old enough to hold a stick, thinking about being done officially is…haunting.

So, if there's a possibility this is going to be my last season, I'm going to make it the best one yet. When we get out on the ice to start warming up before the game, I find myself more distracted than usual. My eyes keep shooting over to the section Leah should be in. I see Taylor and the rest of her friends file in right before the puck drops, and Leah is nowhere in sight.

She really isn't coming.

"You waiting on somebody special, Clark?" Dom grabs my attention as we get in position for the puck drop.

"Nah, man. Not tonight." He gives me a knowing look but doesn't pry.

My focus is shit for most of the game, but we still come out with the win—which is a silver lining I suppose.

"Hey Clark, good game tonight. You coming to celebrate with us?" Devon—the goalie for the Badgers for the last five years— asks as I throw my bag over my shoulder.

"Thanks man, I think I'll pass tonight."

"Bet." He holds his fist out and I bump it with mine. As soon as I make it back out from the locker room, I see Taylor and her entire group of friends hanging out waiting for me.

"There he is!" Taylor slaps my arm as she beams up at me. "You did great tonight."

"Bullshit. I was so off my game it was embarrassing," I scoff, running a hand through my hair.

"Bullshit is a bad word." A small voice emerges from within the huddle of people behind Taylor.

"Hendrix Landry, if it's a bad word then *why* are you repeating it?" I peek around to see Ruby with her face in her palm while Tank looks like he can barely contain his laughter.

"Sorry about that." My eyes widen with my apology. Tank waves a hand, dismissing me. "I'm glad you guys were able to make it tonight.

Sorry you caught me on an off night." I force out a laugh, looking around the arena one more time.

She's not here, dickhead. Let it go.

"You wanna go eat? Or are you too cool to hang out with your little sister and her friends?" Taylor rolls her eyes dramatically.

"When have I ever been too cool to hang out with you and your friends?" I scoff, not missing the ache in my chest from the absence of a certain friend. "Sounds great. I'm starving."

"How long have you played hockey?" Hendrix acts like we've been best friends for the entirety of his life, dipping a French fry into his ketchup as he strikes up a conversation with me. We ended up at Spur's diner, knowing they would likely have the room to seat all nine of us without an atrocious wait time.

"Since I could walk, probably." He nods as I take a bite out of my burger.

Holy shit, I've missed this place.

"I started playing soccer when I was like, three." He leans forward to take a sip from his milkshake.

"Right on. What position do you play?"

"I play everywhere, but I like being the goalie." The spark in his eye when he talks about soccer reminds me a lot of myself at his age. Lighting up any time I got to talk about hockey.

"Are you any good?"

"Oh yeah, the *best*," he says confidently.

Man, I love this kid already.

"He says ever so humbly." Ruby's head appears on the other side of Hendrix, interjecting as she rustles his hair.

"So, Moose. How's the new place?" I turn to face Taylor who is putting her burger away like a true savage.

"You seriously have to stop calling me that," I grumble, making

Taylor roll her eyes. "It's nice though. I'll have to have you guys over sometime once there aren't boxes in every corner of the place."

"If you need any help Tucker can help you." She hikes a thumb behind her at Tucker who laughs at the sight of her.

Jesus, she's acting like this is her last meal.

"Sure man. I'd be happy to help. But I don't do pillow fights."

"Yeah, that's our thing, sorry man." I bark out a laugh when I see Max raising his brows playfully at Tucker.

"Oh, my," Shane giggles, widening her eyes at Taylor.

Looking around the table everyone seems so happy—so content with their lives and surrounded by the people they love the most— and all I can think about is how much I wish Leah was at this table with us.

So, I do something I haven't done in years.

ME

Wish you were here tonight, Dove.

I watch as the text goes through, keeping my eyes glued to the screen as I see it change from *delivered* to *read*. I hold my breath, waiting to see those three little dots appear, but they never do. Next thing I know her *"do not disturb"* notification pops up on the bottom of the screen.

Ouch.

I tilt my head back, letting out a frustrated breath as I lock my phone and slide it back into my pocket.

"What's the matter?" Taylor tilts her head when she looks at me.

"Nothing. Do you know why Leah couldn't make it tonight?" I try my best not to sound *too* invested in the answer, when in reality I'm desperate to know.

"Oh, I think she's at a margarita tasting with her co-worker." She glances over at Lauren for confirmation and Lauren simply nods her head in agreement.

I sit back a little more relaxed knowing she wasn't just blowing me off. Not that it wouldn't be some well-deserved karma.

"So, are you going to this haunted trail thing too?" Tank asks, taking a drink from his water glass.

"What?" I shoot a confused glance at Taylor.

"Of course he is! I was going to tell you, I swear. We all talked about it and we're going back to the haunted trail this year. I mean, it's perfect since you're back home now and we get to officially add Ruby and the guy's as honorary haunted trail members." She grins, looking around the table and before I can stop it, my mind travels back to that one night.

Her nails in my skin.

My name on her lips.

Her scent surrounding me.

"I'll be there."

"Are you okay?" Jackson grabs my water glass from the table and slides it to me.

"Yeah, I'm okay. Just…went down the wrong way."

Someone dig me a hole to crawl into, because I'm pretty sure I'm in the process of dying from embarrassment.

"You sure?" The way he's caressing my arm as he makes sure I'm not going to continue my gasp for breath makes me feel like I'm in good hands. I nod my head and take one last sip of water as he leans back into his seat. He only waits a moment before he continues our conversation.

"Okay, let's see…What's your favorite season?" The way Jackson flawlessly eases into a new topic of conversation has me smiling at him in appreciation.

I have a good feeling about giving us a second chance.

A chance to move on and put my feelings—bitter or otherwise—of Sawyer to rest and start something new with some*one* new.

LAUREN

How did the date go?

SHANE

Yesss. Tell us everything!

ME

It was great actually 😊 He did NOT like the margaritas but I told him that's because he hasn't tried Shanes.

SHANE

🍸 🍹 🍷

RUBY

What elseeee?

ME

He's really sweet. We talked about so much more than work. It was nice. I have no idea what happened the first time we went out but this time was so much better.

TAY

Speaking of sports, Sawyer was asking about you tonight. I think he missed having you there.

I hate the way my heart squeezes from the thought of him missing me. The text I got while in the middle of my date with him saying as much really did it for me too.

After typing out: "Of course he did. I'm fucking delightful." I realize I'm also a little too buzzed to be having conversations about Sawyer in the group chat and I delete it.

ME

Hope you guys had fun at the game. I gotta go to bed so I can sleep off some of this alcohol before school in the morning.

LAUREN

Night night boozy baby.

SHANE

Drink lots of water. Night!

RUBY

Friday nights are hands down my favorite night of the week because it's girls' night. We switch out who hosts every week, the husbands and kids all hang out at whoever's house we *aren't* at, and we get a few hours of uninterrupted girl talk. No matter what kind of week I'm having, I know I can count on Fridays to turn things around.

Lauren is hosting this week while the boys and babies are at Tank and Ruby's.

"Okay, so do we want to all meet at the trail at like six tomorrow?" Taylor asks, twisting on her barstool.

"We will probably be there a little early to do some of the activities they have for Hendrix's age, but we can meet up with you guys at the trail when it's time to go in."

"Max said he will stay outside with the kids because he quote: *doesn't need to go to jail for choking a clown to death.*" Shane air quotes before grabbing a chip and popping it in her mouth. "He doesn't do well with jump scares."

"See, it's not just me!" I point out, bringing my margarita glass to my lips.

"Okay, but...he has like, *reasons* for not liking jump scares. Like... *war* reasons," Shane mumbles, as if she doesn't want Max—who *isn't* here—to overhear us.

"Well now I feel like an asshole for making the comparison so thanks for that." I plop down on the stool next to Taylor, grabbing a chip from the bowl.

"Okay! So, Max will stay with the kids, but everyone else goes in." Taylor swiftly changes the subject, giving me an idea.

"Do you think it would be okay if I invited Jackson?" I avoid eye contact from any of them for a moment, but the second I look up the room fills with dramatic looks and flirty *oooh*'s from my friends.

Jackson and I have been out a couple of times since the margarita tasting and things have been going surprisingly well—outside of the fact that I'm not sure I've felt *the* spark yet. I don't know how long it usually takes to feel that spark everyone talks about, but I do know that I don't want to give up on something that I haven't given a fair chance. My friends are nothing if not observant as hell, so I know they'll be able to get a read on the situation and tell me if something is off.

"Yes! Bring him. I want to meet him again." Shane claps her hands together excitedly.

"Duh, of course!" Lauren chimes in.

"So, things are getting pretty serious with you two then?" Taylor's tone catches me off guard. She's the main one out of the five of us that is usually encouraging us to go all in, to take chances and, for lack of a better term, *get it*.

"I don't know about it being *serious,* it's only been a couple of weeks but it's going *well* I guess..." Taylor nods silently and I glance around for help from the other girls, but they simply shrug like they don't know what's going on either. "It's a haunted trail, Tay, not a marriage proposal. I think it'll be fine." I laugh, making her shake her head and reach for another chip.

"No, yeah. I know. I just meant I'm glad you're feeling good about him. That's all." When she smiles at me it doesn't quite meet her eyes and I can't help but wonder what's going through that sweet, chaotic little mind of hers.

"Speaking of marriage proposals." Taylor perks up again, "Tucker and I have set a date for our wedding."

"Finally! You got me all excited about being sisters-in-law like forever ago. Make it happen already," Ruby groans, leaning over to squeeze Taylor.

"What's the date?" Shane sing-songs, shimmying in her seat.

"June first."

"Thank God. A summer wedding." I throw my arms around her letting out a sigh of relief. I hate when big events happen during the school year because I'm never able to give them the attention they truly deserve.

"You're welcome." She winks at me, finally acting a little more like herself. "Okay, who wants to look up bridesmaid's dresses?" she sings out excitedly.

We spend the rest of the night huddled on the couch looking at different dress styles suitable for a summer wedding, making plans for after the haunted trail, reminiscing on the past, and telling Ruby how much we wished we'd known her when we were kids. A well-rounded girl's night that was very much needed.

Chapter 5

Sawyer

"Hit the showers," Coach yells as practice comes to an end. "I want to see that same power at this weekend's game." There's a collective exhale when Coach finally calls it a day because he was working us hard as shit today. Dom—one of our goalies—actually stops on the way to the locker room to lay on the ice to cool down.

"Dom. Get your ass up before you get freezer burn on your face like some old ass ice cream." Matty slaps his ass with his stick as he skates off the ice, leaving Dom grumbling to himself by the goal.

I waste no time hitting the showers since I still have to get home and change before we head to the trail tonight. A bunch of the guys are talking about going out for drinks tonight and seeing what kind of trouble they can get into, bragging about the girls who are constantly throwing themselves at their feet. Whereas I, on the other hand, haven't hooked up casually since college and haven't lasted longer than a single post-game drink in *years*. The appeal just isn't there anymore. I don't want casual hookups, or someone who only wants to be with me because of my name or status. So, I left that part of the game behind me when I signed my contract with the NHL.

"Got any plans tonight, Clark? Some of the guys are going out, maybe see if we can find a slutty nurse or something to take home.

You in?" Devon gives me a hopeful stare while Javier and I exchange glances.

"Nah man. I've got plans already but uh, good luck with that." Swinging my bag over my shoulder I pat his arm and shoot Javier another glance.

"Javi..."

"Dev, you always pretend like you don't know I've been married for ten years. I have my own little spawns to take trick-or-treating tonight, so I'll pass—again." Their voices fade as I make my way down the hallway towards the parking lot. I appreciate the effort he's putting forth to try and include me—even if it's not my scene—and though the idea of finding someone to take home *is* appealing, my sights are set on an angel tonight.

I climb in my truck and grab my phone out of my bag to turn it back on when I notice a bunch of unread messages.

> **MAX**
>
> Hey, wanna meet us at the bar for a drink before we go to this haunted corn field?

> **TANK**
>
> It's called a haunted TRAIL, grandpa.

> **MAX**
>
> I'm literally only five years older than you.

> **TANK**

> **TUCKER**
>
> Stop fighting in front of the new guy. You're gonna scare him off.

> **TANK**
>
> If he's related to YOUR bride, I doubt he scares easily.

ME

Sorry, I just got out of practice. But you would be correct. Being related to Taylor gives me an advantage of not being spooked easily. I'm down for a drink. What time?

MAX

Tuck and I are here working and Tank is heading over in about an hour. How's five?

ME

Sounds good. See you in about an hour.

For as long as I can remember I've only been friends with people on whatever hockey team I was on. From high school, up until I moved to Nashville, it's been eat, sleep, breathe hockey twenty-four-seven. I'm starting to get a glimpse at what it will be like to have friends outside of the sport and I'm honestly grateful for that. Maybe they'll be the ones to help me figure out what happens *after* hockey.

"Welcome, soon to be brother-in-law." Tucker's voice hits me before I'm even through the threshold at Chattahoochies. Max pops the top off a beer and holds it up, placing it at the empty spot next to Tucker—that I assume is for me. I slide onto the stool and thank Max for the drink before turning to Tucker.

"Are you ever actually going to marry my sister? It feels like you two have been engaged forever."

"Shit, I would have married her in the backyard the night I proposed, but after these two—" He waves his beer between Max and Tank—who is now walking up beside me. "Decided they needed to marry their women within *days* of proposing, she made it very clear there needed to be a *thoroughly planned wedding*." He air quotes. "Well, guess who's now getting married in his own backyard?" He's silent as we all stare back at him.

"Correct. Me." He finishes off his beer before setting the bottle down on the counter.

"Wait, you guys finally set a date? When?" Max looks appalled that he's just now hearing about it as he looks over at Tucker.

"Down boy, we just decided yesterday. We're getting married June first at our house. Consider this your official save the date." He drums on the bar, and I can't fight back my laugh.

"You know better than that, right? She's probably got five different samples of *legit* save the dates and invitations you'll have to choose from." I raise a brow at him as his smile fades.

"Just let me have hope that this can be simple, please," he pleads, making the rest of us laugh.

"Still wanna talk shit about our super-fast marriages *or?*" Tucker flips Tank off while Max clears his empty bottle from the counter.

"What about you, hockey star? Anyone special in your life you'd consider enduring numerous painful hours of looking at floral arrangements for?" Tucker redirects the conversation, tipping his chin up at me.

"Hmm. Maybe." I don't think now is the time to dredge up my past and how I'm trying to fix ten year's worth of damage with the only girl I've ever felt time stop with.

"*Okayyy.*" Tucker raises a brow at me.

"Don't wanna jinx it." I click my tongue before finishing my beer.

"Alright, I gotta go." Tank eyes the clock before taking a sip of the water he hasn't touched until now.

"Already? Dude you *just* got here." Tucker holds his hands up in confusion but Tank shrugs it off.

"Ruby and the Hen want to get there early to do things like bobbing for apples and shit. I don't know, but I'll catch up with you guys there." Tank slaps Tucker on the back and waves bye to Max and I before rushing out.

"Big family guy?" I nod my head to where Tank is already walking out the door.

"You have no idea." Max raises his brows and knocks on the counter before walking to the other end of the bar to wait on someone that just sat down.

"You'll learn soon enough how tight knit of a group you're

running with. We might not all be blood, but we're a family, nevertheless. And we put family first. Always."

"I can get on board with that."

The crisp fall air and the smell of bonfires burning around us is nostalgic in all the best ways. I can already hear the screams coming from the haunted trail as soon as I step out of my truck and with that sound come memories from my childhood that I've done my best to hold onto—not wanting to forget a single detail.

I check my watch and look around in an effort to find a familiar face, and that's when I spot Tank and Ruby with Hendrix and Poe by the pumpkin patch. I walk over and say hi, earning a high five from Hendrix as well as a *very* detailed story about how he's the best apple bobber probably in the universe. Ruby's phone goes off as soon as he finishes his story.

"Everyone is down at the trail waiting for us," she announces.

Why the hell is my heart racing all of the sudden?

I take a deep breath, trying to calm my nerves about seeing Leah again. After the way she acted at Taylor's house I wouldn't be surprised if she didn't even come simply because I'm here—but she can't avoid me forever.

I'm back for good now and it looks like we'll be running into each other more often than not since I've been adopted into the guy portion of this found family. Before we can start down the hill Max comes around the corner with a bundled-up Cece in his arms.

"Hey pretty girl! You look so cozy." Ruby is absolutely gushing over her, pinching her cheeks and tickling her through her fuzzy jacket. By the way Tank is looking at Ruby while she talks to Cece I have a feeling Poe won't be their last baby.

"Say *hi Aunt Rubes*." Max talks in a high-pitched voice that I would *never* expect to hear from him as he waves Cece's hand for her. Then

Hendrix starts in on the baby talk. If there's one kid on this planet that was born to be a big brother, it's Hendrix. When Cece tries saying Hendrix's name with a big grin on her face, I can't help the smile that comes across mine.

"Okay, little people with me. Grown people, go try not to punch a clown in the face." Max grabs Poe's stroller and Hendrix runs over to stand beside him as Ruby crosses her arms over her chest and levels Max with a glare.

"I feel like there's a story we're missing about you and a clown?" I'm pretty sure Max audibly growls before walking in the opposite direction and Ruby's hands fly up in mock defense.

Tank, Ruby, and I start walking down the hill again and he drapes his arm around her, kissing her temple.

"So, you've been to a lot of these? Taylor mentioned you guys used to come here a lot when you were younger," Ruby asks.

"Yeah, every year since the girls were in eighth grade up until they graduated." I remember those days so vividly it hurts sometimes.

"Bummer you guys stopped; it seems like such a fun tradition." Ruby keeps talking about how it makes sense that we wouldn't though since everyone went away to college, but when we round the corner and my eyes land on Leah, I tune everything else out.

I find her almost immediately and, as always, she looks perfect. She's wearing a tan knit sweater, dark blue jeans, and brown riding boots. Her long brown hair is straight down her back tonight and there's an absolutely infectious smile spread across her lips.

I can never help but smile when I see her.

She's so beautiful that I physically ache just to be near her.

Then Tucker moves one step to the left and I notice it isn't one of the girls she's talking to and smiling at. Her fingers are intertwined with the guy who has somehow put himself in a position to earn her smile, her laughter, her touch. Upon closer examination I realize it's the same guy she was with at Taylor's birthday party.

This motherfucker, again?

"Oh, Jackson made it too!" My head snaps in Ruby's direction.

"Jackson?" I try not to let my tone reflect the way I want to toss him so far into the corn maze he never finds his way out.

"Yeah, they work together but they've been out a few times so maybe they'll be more than coworkers soon." Ruby shoots a hopeful look over her shoulder before making her way down the hill to join the rest of the group.

She was on a fucking date that night. Coworker my ass.

I look back over to see them cozied up in line together and I know my smile is long gone because I'm biting down so hard to keep from cursing it feels like my jaw is fixing to break.

"Shit." I look over to see Tank still standing next to me. "The girl you were talking about earlier. It's Leah, isn't it?" he asks, his eyebrows raising in surprise. I blow out a breath and nod. *No reason denying the painfully obvious.*

"Yeah. It's Leah…" As much as I don't want to look back over and see her with someone else, I can't seem to stop myself. She's still talking with her friends and smiling so big her eyes squint the wider it gets.

"Since when?" This time when I answer I don't take my eyes off her. I can't. Like a tragedy you can't look away from, my attention is hers.

"Since always." As if she can feel me willing her to look my way, she turns around and our eyes lock.

I hold my breath—trying to gauge her reaction from seeing me—and my heart cracks a little when her smile falls. Then she simply turns around and continues as if I'm not even here.

Which somehow feels worse than any other reaction she could have had.

Chapter 6

Sawyer

"Fuck," I murmur, rubbing a hand down my jaw. "Have they been together since Tot's birthday?" Tank chuckles at Taylor's nickname and I turn to face him, making him clear his throat.

"Um, I don't think so. From what I can tell he hasn't been around again until tonight. I mean, from what I know at least."

What kind of fucked up karma do I have that this motherfucker shows up every time I plan on talking to Leah?

Whether they've been together this whole time or not, I'm not letting anything stand in my way when it comes to telling her how I feel about her this time.

How I've *felt* about her for too damn long.

Then if she wants to blow me off and continue dating the guy who looks like Egon Spengler, then so fucking be it.

"Is it too early in our friendship to ask for a favor?"

"We're friends?" Tank raises a brow at me.

"I'm hoping my desperation sways your answer in my favor."

"Alright but quit hitting on me. I'm happily married." I bark out a laugh and he waves two fingers. "Let's hear it."

When we make it to the bottom of the hill Ruby is quickly tucked beneath Tank's arm again, Shane is linking arms with Lauren and, as always, Taylor is acting like a cruise director.

"Okay, Tucker and I will go first, then Shane and Lauren. Moose, you can go with Tank and Ruby after Leah and Jackson." About the same time, I glare at the back of his head, *Jackson* turns around and looks up at me. His smug grin wavers as realization hits him.

Ah, so he remembers me.

"Moose?" The snarky tone to his voice makes me want to thunder kick him across the field.

"Only to these four." I glance at the girls and give Leah a wink, causing her eyes to widen in surprise before she shifts on her feet.

"Nah, dude. I'm definitely calling you that from here on out." Tank leans forward and claps my shoulder, making me chuckle.

"Well, hey, I'm glad you could make it." Jackson wraps his arm around Leah pulling her in closer.

Showy little ferret. Stop touching my girl.

I wonder how smug he'll be once I steal my girl back right out from under him.

"Let's go!" Taylor squeals, gripping Tucker's arm so tightly he sucks a sharp breath in through his teeth.

"Claws away til we're home, Darlin'."

Ah, gross.

A second later they disappear behind the cloth covering the entrance.

When it's finally our turn Tank gives me a nod, we walk in, and the strobe lights start just like always. They've extended the entrance and added more jump scares from the looks of it, but the rest is pretty much the same. The nine of us are bunched together so tight I can smell the mixture of body spray and the lack thereof.

There's fake cobwebs, torn tapestry, and costume blood in every inch of the small entrance, but as soon as the same creepy ass clown pops out from the corner, all the girls take off screaming. They're out in a matter of seconds leaving Tank, Tucker, and I lagging behind laughing.

"Why do they come if they're so fucking scared of this shit?" Tucker laughs as Tank grabs a mask off one of the mechanical dummies.

"No clue." Tank subtly hands me the mask before we leave to catch up with the girls.

"Hurry *up*. We're gonna get murdered out here or something." Taylor waves Tucker over dramatically.

One benefit to coming to this maze every Halloween for five years straight, I've memorized every little detail and pattern of the actors. No matter how many new employees there may have been over the year, the routine is still the same. Every jump scare has the girls shrieking and the more Leah grabs onto Jackson, the more I want to shove him into the corn and hope for a real life *Scarecrow* moment to occur.

When we get to the area that has been cut to look like a cross-roads, the chainsaws start up and several groups cross each other, trying to find the path *away* from them. Tank shoots me a playful grin before dramatically scrambling our group with fake screams, giving me the opportunity to slide the mask we took from the entrance on. I wait for my chance to snatch Leah from the group and take off running down the empty path behind us.

She's kicking her feet wildly, like she stands a chance at escaping my grasp, and in an effort to keep her from screaming anyone's name but mine, I cover her mouth with my hand. When she bites the inside of my palm it sends a wave of excitement straight to my dick that I try to ignore. When I find an opening big enough, I dip into the corn stalks and spin her around to face me. Her breaths are coming so quickly I think she might be seconds away from passing out. Her eyes grow wide just as I remove the mask and reveal my face.

"Gotcha, Dove."

"Sawyer?! What the *hell* is wrong with you? You scared me to death!" Her small hands slap at my chest repeatedly and I can't help but smirk at her failed attempt to hurt me.

"Something funny?" She stops her assault on my chest and huffs, glaring up at me.

"No. Nothing at all." I hold my hands up defensively.

"Fantastic. Now if you'll excuse me, I have a date to get back to." She rolls her eyes and turns to walk away from me, but I grab her wrist and pull her back because I did not go through all of that just to let her walk away.

She trips over an unearthed root beneath her feet and falls into me with a gasp. I wrap my free hand around the nape of her neck and let my fingers glide through her soft brown locks as if on instinct. Her eyes bounce between mine and it takes more restraint than I realized it would to not lean in and kiss her. To tell her everything I've never had the chance to say without uttering a single word. I swallow past the urge to do so, pulling my gaze from her lips and smirking.

"You know, the last time we were here you screamed my name similarly to how you did tonight." She visibly swallows and as much as I hope I'll get a smile; she rolls her eyes instead.

"The only difference is I'm pretty sure I was *glad* to see you the last time we were here," she scoffs, but makes no effort to remove herself from my grip.

"You saying you're not glad to see me, Dove?" I slowly move my hand down around her neck as her eyes frantically search my face.

"Quite the contrary, actually." She's trying to appear unphased and it makes me want to prove that she *is* that much more. So, I press my luck and lean in closer, bringing my lips to the shell of her ear.

"Then why is your heart beating so fast?" I feel her shudder against me, and if I was a betting man, I'd bet there were goosebumps covering her arms right now. I barely catch her eyes fluttering back open when I pull back before she swats my hand away and stands up straighter.

"Probably because you scared me, you Sasquatch."

"C'mon. You know you're safe with me, you've always known that," I remind her, seeing any hint of desire disappear.

"No. Maybe I *used* to feel that way. But I don't know anything about you anymore. Come to think of it...maybe I never did." She's careful not to trip again when she takes a step back, and I miss her the second she's out of my reach.

"Leah..." My voice is low as she turns to walk away.

"I have to go, Sawyer. I'm not going to leave my date wondering where I am."

Fuck.

If she meant for that statement to hurt the way I think she did, then mission fucking accomplished.

"Will you ever give me a chance to apologize?" When she turns around this time there's a calmness about her that terrifies me.

"I don't need an apology, Sawyer. I need to move on. Just...let it go."

How the fuck can I let something go that I've never even had to begin with.

I remain silent because what the fuck do I even say to that? She must take my silence as acceptance because she gives me a tight-lipped smile and disappears from in front of me—leaving me simultaneously empty and full of regret. She may think I've quietly agreed to let her go, but she's sorely mistaken. That's the one thing I will *never* do.

Leah Gates will be mine, and I don't care what bridges I have to burn to make it happen.

Chapter 7

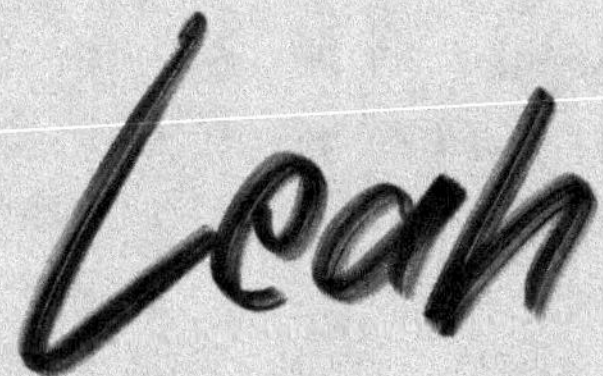

What the fuck is happening?

No, like seriously. What the hell was that?

Sawyer snatches me into some corn stalks, and I suddenly start to forget every reason I have hated him for the last ten years?

His stupid muscular arms.

And stupid swimmable blue eyes.

And the way he smells like a *man* in all the best ways.

It took me *years* to be able to smell anything cedarwood scented and not spend the rest of the day missing him.

Stupid Sawyer Clark and the way he makes me feel things I have no business feeling for him.

The worst part about all of this is that I can't even run to tell my best friends about any of it because they have absolutely no clue what happened between us all those years ago. Nor do they know that I've liked Sawyer for far longer than that.

Liked Sawyer. Past tense. I don't still like him. I *can't* still like him because I've spent too much of my time hating him.

"There you are." The sigh of relief as the words come out of his mouth make me snap out of my Sawyer-filled haze and smile. "I was about to start retracing my steps to try and find you." Jackson walks over to me and wraps his arms around me.

"You worried about me Mr. Morris?" I bat my eyelashes at him, making a huge smile spread across his face.

"You bet I was. I was mostly worried you had disappeared on me before I got the chance to do this." He leans in and within seconds I can feel my heart beating through my temples. His lips land on mine, and in the middle of chainsaws roaring to life and horrified screaming, Jackson and I are having our first kiss.

He shifts slightly to take my face in both of his hands as his lips glide across mine, making me melt into his touch. He pulls away and I'm left a little speechless because I had not expected that even a little.

"I'm keeping you close the rest of the night, because I plan to do *that* again." He winks at me causing my cheeks to flush instantly before taking my hand in his and leading the way towards the exit. I hear someone squealing behind me and as soon as I turn to see the teenage rag doll running past us, something else catches my eye.

Sawyer is standing about ten feet away from us looking downright lethal.

He just got a front row ticket to Jackson kissing me, and some dark part of me is a little happy that he did.

If he thinks he can just cruise back into town, hand me a ticket to his game and whisk me away into some corn stalks to remind me of *the good ole days* and all will be hunky dory, then he's got another thing coming.

You don't get to break someone's heart—unknowingly or otherwise —and expect time to do the dirty work of apologizing for you. He may want to apologize now, but *I* want *him* to know how it feels to hurt the way I did when he let all my calls and texts go unread. So, if it's my attention he's wanting, then he's gonna have to work a hell of a lot harder than this to get it. But one thing is certain when I see his hands balled into fists and his jaw so tight it looks painful—I definitely have *his*.

"You okay Sweetheart?" I feel my mom's hand wrap around mine, snapping me out of the state of shock I am in over the text that I just received.

I had picked up my phone to respond to a text Jackson had sent me when I was on my way over here a little while ago—since I had forgotten to before coming inside—but as soon as I hit send another one popped up and all but knocked the air out of my lungs.

I have dinner with my parents every Sunday so we can fill each other in on what's happening in our lives. Usually, the conversation flows from the moment I walk in the door until I'm walking back to my car, but right now I couldn't form a coherent sentence if I wanted to—and Mom notices.

"I'm sorry, what did you say?" I shake my head as if that will somehow make all the thoughts swimming around my brain disappear like an Etch A Sketch. She gives my dad a knowing look before glancing back at me with a raised brow. For some reason my stomach drops, and I feel like I've been caught with my hand in the cookie jar or sneaking back in the window past curfew—neither of which have I ever done.

"Everything okay? You seem awfully distracted tonight." She takes another bite of her food and I realize I've been twirling my fork on the tablecloth for God only knows how long. I quickly drop it onto my napkin and reach for my water, trying to think of a valid, albeit fake, reason I could give her for why I suddenly got so silent.

"Yeah, just a busy week ahead at work. You know how the kids get before fall break." I lie.

"Sweetheart, you are a terrible liar." My eyes grow wide at my dad's comment and my mom snickers. "Does this happen to have anything to do with a certain Clark boy moving back home?" My head swings back in her direction and my mouth pops open. I hold her stare as she raises a brow at me, and I clamp my mouth shut again before letting out a sigh.

Mom has always been able to see right through me.

Dad may know when I'm lying, but Mom always knows *why*.

She's the only one who ever truly knew how I felt about Sawyer, but she never gave me a hard time about it. I assume she mentioned it to my dad of course, because they were both there for me when he basically disappeared from my life. Mom and I had deeper conversations about my feelings while watching *10 Things I Hate About You*—which was my favorite movie long before it felt so relevant in my own life—more times than I can count, while Dad would just tell me to get my shoes on and take me for ice cream or iced coffee before driving around in a comfortable silence with me. Windows down, music up, and spirits lifted—that was Dad's expertise. When I'd reached a point of thickening my skin and told Mom I didn't want to talk about it anymore—that I was done crying over a friendship that was likely one sided anyways—we never spoke of him again.

Until now, apparently.

"No," I snap, a little embarrassed that that's *exactly* what's wrong with me. "Besides, I'm seeing Jackson and things are going well with him. So, I'm just focusing on that right now." When I lift my head again her eyes are full of concern, but she nods, and we drop it.

"So, tell me about Jackson. I want to hear all about him." She folds her hands together and smiles at me, causing me to blush as I think about the kiss we shared this past weekend. When my dad notices he simply grumbles and reaches across the table.

"That's my cue to leave." He reaches for a cookie but my mom swats his hand away.

"Allen Gates, you know you can't have that until you check your insulin." Dad rubs his hand like he's shocked by my mother's actions —as if it's not the same one she gives him every time he tries grabbing a treat before checking his blood sugar levels.

"Yes, Dear, I know." My parents are grossly in love, and I can't help but laugh when they get on each other's nerves like this.

The rest of the evening is spent talking while *Sweet Magnolias* plays in the background. We've both binged every season, but who doesn't love a comfort show as background noise while you chat?

When I finally get back in my car to leave and grab my phone to start my playlist for the drive home, the breath is sucked from my lungs all over again when it opens straight to the text I was reading at the dinner table.

MOOSE

That kiss should have been mine.

"Ms. Gates, my pumpkin didn't turn out right." Liliana's head falls back dramatically as she groans.

"What's the matter with it?" When I reach her side of the table and see her orange construction paper cut into an unidentifiable shape, I have to place my fingers over my lips to stifle my laughter. "Oh…" I tilt my head, trying to find a way to make it work. "It looks like a—"

"It looks like troll hair," she interrupts, glaring up at me like I am somehow at fault for this mishap. "I might as well call it Poppy the deformed pumpkin." This time, I can't hold back my laughter no matter how hard I try. This girl is the most dramatic six-year-old I have ever taught and I love her all the more for it.

"I was going to say it looks like a gourd, which is close enough." I do my best to encourage her, but she is *not* having it. "Just finish the project sweetie, I'm sure your mom will love it." I pat her shoulder and walk over to the next table to see how the other students are doing with their projects before checking my watch.

Five minutes until dismissal.

"Okay, everyone finish your projects it's almost time to go!" When

I clap my hands together the kids begin scrambling to gather their backpacks and are lined up at the door within two minutes.

"Okay, why don't you guys move that quickly any other day?" I tease them, making them all giggle and bounce up and down in place. After wishing everyone a good fall break and finishing cleaning up my classroom, I grab my bag and head home.

I have big plans for a self-care evening and I'm not going to think about anything school related while I soak in a bubble bath and drink some wine. I blast my music the whole way home to get myself out of work mode—leaving my phone on do not disturb so I don't have to worry about notifications ruining my vibe. About the time I turn off do not disturb mode, kick off my shoes and drop my bag in the entry-way, I hear my phone go off several times.

JACKSON

Hey, you must have left on two wheels, I looked for you after dismissal but couldn't find you. 😅

GIRL GANG GROUP CHAT

TAY

Sawyer is coming to Thanksgiving this year!
Everyone cool with that?

SHANE

The more the merrier. It's not like I'm making the turkey.

LAUREN

True that. I'll bring an extra pie.

MOOSE

> You can't ignore me forever, Dove. Please just talk
> to me.

The fucking audacity of this guy.

"Ughhhhh!" I toss my phone onto the couch, grab the bottle of wine from the fridge—not bothering with a glass—and head straight to run my bath.

How is it possible that in the fifteen minutes it takes me to get home from work I receive enough texts to make me reconsider a *Xanax* prescription. I soak in the tub until my bottle is empty, the water is cold, and my fingers look like raisins. Once I'm wrapped in my favorite plush robe, with my eye masks in place and I'm snuggled into my couch, I finally pick my phone back up. Thankfully there aren't any *new* notifications, so I click into the group thread and text back a thumbs up emoji, apologize to Jackson and then stare at my message from Sawyer for at least half an episode of *Gilmore Girls* before I finally type out a response.

ME

> You underestimate my ability to pretend you don't
> exist. You should be familiar with the act. You are an
> expert after all.

I roll my eyes and scoff as I press send and within seconds another text comes through.

MOOSE

> Do I need to prove to you just how real I am, Leah?

Heat rushes to my face and for some reason my thighs start sweating, causing me to toss my phone to the other end of the couch. As if being far enough away from it will make my heart stop racing and cause the text that's currently on my screen to not be real. I close my eyes in an effort to clear my mind of Sawyer, but instead images from Halloween flood my mind.

His hands on my waist, in my hair and around my neck.

His lips against my ear.

The mention of me screaming his name.

My eyes fly open and I burrow deeper into my fleece cocoon, wishing I'd never responded to his text in the first place.

I haven't been able to get the text he sent me while I was sitting at dinner with my parents out of my head, no matter how hard I've tried. Now he goes and says shit like this?

I'm still pissed at him.

I still want him to know how it feels to be so blatantly ignored you wished you actually were invisible.

So why does everything he says lately make me feel like he can't see anything *but* me.

Freaking. Sawyer.

Chapter 8

Sawyer

It's the week of Thanksgiving and the fact that I've gone almost an entire month without talking to Leah is about to drive me crazy. Sure, we went *years* without speaking to one another, but being back in the same city as her is making it a hell of a lot harder to pretend I'm still fine with that arrangement.

I finally got a response from her via text, and because I can't shake my uncontrollable need to flirt with her, it was a one and done reply.

We have a game in Minnesota tonight then we fly back home tomorrow for the holidays and I'm holding out hope that I'll finally be able to get her to hear me out.

"Pink tape, Clark? Really?" Matty snickers as we sit in the locker room taping our sticks before the game. "I'm just as committed to my pre-game rituals as the next guy, but that's a pretty bold statement you're making, very *Legally Blonde* of you."

Not the first time I've heard that one.

"Some things just stick man. I like my pink tape. But you don't have to act like a *Vivian* about it." His mouth drops open when I hit him with my stick.

"Oh my god, you actually know the other chick's name?" He barks out a laugh, making me roll my eyes. "I didn't take you for the rom-com type, Clark."

"What can I say? There's a lot you guys don't know about me." I rip the tape with my teeth and secure it around the blade, lifting a brow at Matty. "Like that I have a sister who made me sit through both of those movies about thirty times *each*. But I'm not the one who started the name calling, am I?" I raise an accusing brow at him.

"Alright, slow down. It's my girl's comfort movie. It's just fresh on my mind." Javi, Devon, and I all share a look and laugh when Matty starts getting overly defensive of his *Legally Blonde* knowledge.

"We're all secure men here, Matty. It's okay." I give him an encouraging nod and clap his shoulder before leaving the room.

Being on the ice has been my escape for as long as I can remember. The feeling I get when I'm gliding across the ice, the way it feels when a play is executed flawlessly, knowing that you've won a game when the final horns go off, it's a rush unlike any other. Winning against the team I just traded from is just an added bonus.

"Good game, Clark. You're still a bitch for trading though." Carson, one of my old teammates, slaps my back with his stick and holds out his fist.

"You can say you miss me, Carson. I won't tell the missus." I wink at him, and we bump fists before he skates off, shaking his head and mumbling something I can't quite hear over the excitement on the ice.

"Clark! You're coming out with us tonight. No excuses!" Rooney yells directly in my ear, throwing his arm over my shoulder as we walk back to the locker room.

As much as I want to say no, go back to the hotel, crash before our flight home tomorrow and leave the guys to celebrate without me—I've only been out with them once since joining the team, so I feel an obligation to at least *try* to get to know them better.

Before I know it we're at the same pub I used to frequent when I played here. Though we only came in after *winning* games, I keep watching the door to see if any of my old teammates walk through it.

"You waiting for someone, Clark?" Javier slides onto the barstool next to me, bumping my shoulder with his when he sits down.

"Not necessarily." He raises a brow at my vague answer. "Some of the guys used to come here after games—wins, mostly—but I just keep wondering if some of them will show tonight." It's strange, not knowing how to feel being back in the state I've lived in since college, playing against the guys I called teammates for so long. I thought I would miss being here, or at least the normalcy of the life I'd built for myself here. Regardless, I don't regret the decisions that were made that brought me back home to Nashville.

"Was it weird? Playing against them tonight?" I run my hands over the label on my beer bottle, surprised when I realize that it wasn't.

"Not really. I wasn't sure how I'd feel during tonight's game to be honest. But I guess my focus stays on the game and the team I'm *on*, not the team that I *left*." I shrug it off, hoping my statement came across the way I meant it and not like I'm a flake that doesn't care about loyalty to his teammates.

"So why did you trade? If you don't mind my asking." We turn around on our stools to face the bar when the bartender places Javi's loaded fries on the counter.

"I liked the Badgers jerseys better." His eyes cut to mine with a French fry an inch away from his open mouth and I bark out a laugh. "I'm kidding! Obviously. Just uh…personal reasons. When I weighed my pros and cons, the pros landed me back in Nashville," I assure him as he finally takes a bite of his food.

"Respect," he says over a mouth full of food.

The rest of the evening Matty, Javi, and I talk and get to know each other a little better while some of the other guys get a little more drunk and leave early with some girls that I'm almost certain followed us here from the rink.

Matty and Javi are both fully committed to their girls—Javi being married and Matty in the process of asking his girl to marry him, apparently. They're just the kind of no-nonsense guys I find myself gravitating towards more often than not.

"How did you and your wife meet Javi?" We moved to a table shortly after Matty joined the conversation to keep from having to look around Javi every time the other was talking. Matty leans back and folds his hands behind his head as he settles in for the story.

"I was good friends with Maria's brother. She was dating some other dude for a while but when she was single again, she asked me to go to lunch one day and the rest is history. Thankfully it all worked out because I was running the risk of getting my ass kicked by her brother otherwise."

"A risk you were more than willing to take," Matty chimes in.

"Yup. I'd take it a million more times too if it meant I ended up with Maria. She's the kind of woman that's worth risking it all for, ya know?"

Yeah, I know the type. I'm just too dumb to have taken the chance with her when I had it.

"Speaking of— I'm heading back to the room for a phone date, fellas." Javi waves the waitress over and we all pay our bills before heading back to the hotel.

It was nice getting to spend time with some of the guys tonight after the game, and I hate that I've put off doing so for this long.

TOT

Are you bringing anything for Thanksgiving dinner?

ME

Was I SUPPOSED to be bringing anything for dinner tomorrow?

TOT

No...

ME

Then why would I mess up the system and bring something? I'd hate to run the risk of having too many cans of cranberry sauce. 🤭

TOT

You ever wonder why Mom never taught us how to cook when we were younger?

ME

Besides the fact that I lived at the rink and you cried like she was asking you to shave your head every time she asked for help in the kitchen? No idea, Tot. That Marilyn sure is a mystery.

TOT

You're insufferable. 🙄

ME

And yet you still invite me to your house for holidays because you love me.

TOT

🙄 See you tomorrow Moose.

ME

Your face is going to get stuck like that. See you tomorrow Tot. 😜

TOT

And you're worried about MY face…

Chapter 9

Spending holidays together has been a tradition Shane, Taylor, Lauren, and I have tried to uphold ever since we were in grade school. If we couldn't see each other on Thanksgiving due to having to spend it with our *actual* families, we'd see each other the day after, and we made a pact to always spend Christmas Eve eve together as long as we were all in town. It's been over ten years and we've successfully done so—even with spouses and babies coming into the picture. Ruby has also officially become part of our family and I love how much it keeps growing.

"Mr. and Mrs. Gates we're so glad you could make it." Taylor squeezes my mom and dad as soon as we walk through the front door of her and Tucker's house.

"Taylor, sweetheart, please call me Loretta," Mom insists.

"I'll try but old habits die hard so forgive me if it takes a few times to get comfy calling you Loretta." Taylor smiles brightly as she takes her coat.

"I'm Tucker, it's a pleasure to meet you both." Tucker offers his hand to my dad and brings my mom in for a hug.

"Would either of you like a glass of wine or some sweet tea?" Taylor offers.

"We have beer as well if that's more your speed," Tucker chimes in, holding his beer bottle up.

"Now you're talking." My dad nods and the two of them head for the kitchen.

"Tea sounds wonderful." Taylor links arms with my mom like they're the best of friends, handing me my mom's coat as the two of them walk to the kitchen together.

"Sure Tay, I'll hang these in the laundry room," I call after her, holding our coats out. "And yes, I *would* like a glass of wine." She turns around and sticks her tongue out at me like we're in middle school and I can't help but laugh.

"I could grab you that drink." Sawyer's smooth voice echoes from behind me and I feel my heart flip inside my chest. I roll my eyes and turn around to see him standing at his six-foot-four, perfect height, his long brown hair perfectly messy, and a long sleeve gray thermal shirt hugging his body in all the right places. It really pisses me off that he has the audacity to walk around looking so damn dreamy all the time.

"I'd rather dehydrate, thanks." I glare at him and give him a sarcastic smirk, but he simply returns it with one of his own. Letting his eyes roam over my body before settling on my face again. When he leans in closer I feel my breath catch in my throat.

"You're being really stubborn; you know that right?" Regardless of the way his proximity is making it difficult to focus on anything other than how good he smells, I'm surprisingly able to gather myself long enough to form a coherent sentence.

"At least I'm being *truthful*." I raise a brow, challenging him to try and argue with me. His jaw begins to tick, and his eyes grow darker.

"I don't think you're ready for my truth, Dove."

"Says who?" *Oh my god what am I, in middle school?*

"You still dating the teacher?" he asks, with contempt filling every word. My brows knit together, wondering why that's relevant to him telling me whatever *truth* it is he thinks I'm not ready for.

"Yes."

"Then you're not ready." With a wink he walks away leaving me utterly confused and frustrated. I should have turned and walked away the second I heard his voice. I should have hung up our coats and joined everyone else in the kitchen and paid him no mind. Then I wouldn't be sitting here wondering what the hell he can't tell me just because I'm dating Jackson—and utterly desperate to find out.

UGHHHHH. Freaking Sawyer.

"Let's go around the table and say what we're thankful for!" Shane exclaims from her seat at the oversized dining room table.

I didn't have to try too hard to avoid conversation with Sawyer tonight since the guys stayed in the kitchen most of the night while the girls were in the living room chatting and fawning over Cece and Poe. But as my luck would have it, I wound up sitting right across from Sawyer for dinner—which just feels like some kind of cruel karma at this point.

How the hell am I supposed to act like he doesn't exist when he's literally all I can see?

Everyone else is seated beside or across from their significant others with Hendrix and Cece heading up each end of the table.

"Ohh I love that idea!" Taylor claps excitedly, looking around the table to encourage everyone else's participation. I know both Shane and Taylor are married—well, one is married, and one is getting there —but I'm pretty sure their soulmates are actually each other.

"I'll go first." Shane clears her throat before taking a sip from her water cup. "I am thankful for the family that I've found since moving back to Nashville." She reaches across the table and grabs Max's hand —who is looking at her like she hung the moon and all the stars.

"Holidays are a lot less lonely with family, and though I've always known my girls would be there for me... I'm thankful for you, Max, and the family we're starting together." Max winks at her and I'm pretty sure Shane wipes a tear from her eye just as I finish my four– *fifth?* Glass of wine.

The rest of the group goes around saying what they're thankful for and when it gets to Sawyer my stomach twists. His gaze is set on me in a way that feels like he can see straight into my soul. Like all my sins and secrets are on full display, and he looks completely intrigued by them.

"I'm thankful to be back home for good. That I no longer have to miss the things I did while I was away."

"Things?" I'm shocked to hear myself say the words I had *no* intention of letting past my lips. "What *things* did you miss while you were away, Sawyer? Huh?" I finish pouring myself a fifth...sixth, maybe— fuck if I know—glass of wine.

"Leah..." Sawyer's steady voice is no match for the absolutely manic tone of mine.

"Because we know it wasn't the people. I mean, you clearly have *no* problem just up and leaving those behind and without a damn reason *why* at that."

"Leah." His voice is more assertive this time, but with all the alcohol and decade's worth of pent-up rage simmering out of me, I don't think I could stop yelling at him if I wanted to.

"How could you do that to me? You never showed up for breakfast, you left for college, and you left me on *read* or sent me to voicemail for *months*. I thought we were *friends*, Sawyer. You were mine, but clearly, I meant less to you than I ever thought." Sawyer's fist slams against the table, making me suck in a startled breath.

"Dammit Leah, you meant *everything* to me. That's *why* I had to leave the way I did."

"Watch your tone, son." My dad says from somewhere around the table.

I'm pretty sure my heart falls out of my ass when those words leave Sawyer's mouth and I realize that I'm literally crying in front of my parents and every single one of my friends during Thanksgiving dinner.

I would be thankful to disappear into thin air right about now.

With everyone's eyes wide and mouths hanging open, the silence is so deafening that I'm pretty sure I could hear a leaf fall off a tree outside. Until Hendrix—God bless his soul—speaks up.

"Dammit is a bad word."

"Not now Hen," Ruby whispers from beside me.

"I'm so sorry." I scoot my chair back from the table and rush upstairs—likely to die of embarrassment. I never lose my temper, and yet I just unleashed every bottled-up emotion I've had towards Sawyer for *years* in front of *everyone*.

What the hell is wrong with me?

I'm halfway up the stairs when a hand wraps around my bicep and I spin around to see Sawyer looking up at me.

"Please don't go, Dove." The pain in his eyes almost has me turning to walk closer towards him. That is, until my senses kick in, and I remember he's the one that put us in this position to begin with. Making all the sadness I was beginning to feel turn back into anger.

"How dare you ask that of me when *you* were the one that left first."

"I told you, I *had* to leave things that way." The muscle in his jaw flexes, giving his face a hard appearance. A shocking contrast to the gentle hold he has on me still.

"Why?" I challenge, hoping he'll give me some explanation that will douse the fiery anger I've been holding onto in regard to him.

"I told you why." I shake my head at his answer.

"No, you didn't. You may have given me a strikingly vague reason five seconds ago about why you left the way you did. But that doesn't excuse the *years* of hurt and confusion you put me through by doing so. So now is your chance. Tell me why." I cross my arms over my chest, giving him the floor to say what needs to be said. He looks around, letting his mouth pop open and shut a few times before it closes for good, and he shoves his hands in his front pockets.

"I had to learn to let you go when you left, Sawyer. Now it's your turn. Let me go." The pain that flashes through his eyes could damn near break my heart—if it wasn't already broken.

He has no idea how many years I wished for him to look at me the way he is right now. Like he can't stand the thought of losing me.

He finally releases my arm and I rush to the spare bedroom, locking the door behind me.

After weighing the pros and cons of jumping out the second story window to be able to leave undetected, someone knocks on the door.

"Leah, Sweetheart. Unlock the door." I almost immediately start crying when I hear my mom's voice on the other side. I take a deep breath in hopes of composing myself and unlock the door, but the moment I see the genuine concern in her eyes my lip begins to quiver all over again.

"So, it has *nothing* to do with a certain Clark boy moving back home, huh?"

"I'm fragile right now, Mother. Please don't make jokes." I choke out a laugh and turn to walk to the foot of the bed before falling back on it. I feel a dip in the mattress when Mom sits down beside me, her cool hand brushing through my hair comforting me the way only a mother can.

"You know we have to make jokes, or we will end up drowning in our tears." I remember when my mom told me that the secret remedy to heartbreak was a rom-com. So you can laugh and cry all at once until one day, you're left with only the laughter.

"I can't control myself around him, Mom. I'm still so mad at him but I..." I bite down on my lip so hard to keep the next part of my sentence in that I can taste the blood that's been drawn from the sensitive flesh.

"But you still love him." I shoot up from the bed and rush to close the door.

"Mom! Do you want a megaphone? Sheesh."

"Oh, Honey. If anyone doubted the way you felt about him before, they're likely clued in now," she laughs.

My head drops as I stare at the light wood grain floors in Taylor's spare bedroom, wishing that tonight hadn't happened.

That I hadn't drank so much.

That he hadn't looked straight at me with those sapphire blue eyes when he said he was thankful to be home.

That he didn't *still* affect me the same way he did ten years ago.

"I don't love him. I hate him." My eyes burn and my throat feels dry, and I force the words out. "I hate him for not showing up that day for breakfast. I hate him for leaving and ignoring me, but never telling me *why*. I hate that I loved him for so long and he never saw it. And I hate that he's *finally* looking at me the way I *always* looked at him." I focus on the warmth of my tears running down my face, embracing my emotions before I pack them back up in their little box so I can face my friends again.

"Because it's too late. He waited ten years too long to apologize, and now I don't want to hear it."

"There's a fine line between love and hate, Leigh-Ann. Make sure you know with absolute certainty what side you're standing on before you lose him again. If you need to hate him, then I'll understand. But *I* love you too much to see you hurt like this if there's a chance you could trade all of this hurt for happiness." I shake my head as she caresses my cheek, wiping away the rest of my tears.

"I was on the other side before, Mom. Look at how that worked out for me. Maybe I'm just not meant to be in love." My voice is such a low whisper I'm not even sure she heard me until I see the sympathy in her eyes.

Just as she looks as though she might say something, a soft knock sounds at the door and I push off it, turning just in time to see Shane peek her head in.

"Hey you. Everything okay in here?" Her eyes bounce between me and my mom as I quickly wipe away the tears that have stained my cheeks.

"I'll let you two girls talk. I'm going to go find your father and make sure he's not into dessert just yet." Mom gives me a reassuring wink before standing up.

"He was definitely eyeballing Ruby's homemade brownies before I came up here." Shane tells her, making Mom shake her head.

"This man will be the death of me." The soft smile that plays at her lips is a dead giveaway that she's not the least bit angry. When she's finally gone Shane slips in and shuts the door, following me to the bed to sit down.

"Wanna tell me what that was all about?" She pulls a water bottle from behind her back and hands it to me, making me laugh.

"What has happened to me? Are you the only levelheaded one left?" I laugh, unscrewing the top to take a sip.

"Starting to look that way. Even with Ruby in the group now, she leans a little more on the unhinged side," Shane laughs. "Probably all of those mama bear instincts that make her not give a shit." We share another laugh, but when it's silent again Shane takes my hand in hers. "If you don't want to tell me what's going on, then I'll respect that. But I know you and Sawyer used to be close—like, really close—until you weren't. Losing a friendship like that has to be hard, and you shouldn't have to go through it alone."

My phone buzzes in my pocket and when I pull it out to see who it's from, tears resurface in my eyes.

> DAD
>
> Car's warmed up and ready to go. Just say the word.

"I didn't go through it alone." I smile, earning a confused look from Shane. "But I'll keep what you said in mind. Coffee date tomorrow?"

"Yes!" she immediately agrees. "Brüman's at nine?"

"Sounds like a plan." She pulls me in for a hug and when I finally let out a full breath, it feels as though there's been a weight lifted from my shoulders.

Not telling my three best friends what really happened between Sawyer and me was one of the hardest things I've ever done. No matter how much support I got from my parents, sometimes you just need your girls. Because they're the ones that will trash talk, prank call, and help you rebound from the guy who broke your heart.

Since he's my best friend's *brother*, it always felt a little too messy to bring them into the middle of it, but we're grown now and that's about to change.

Chapter 10

I can't explain what it is about the smell of a coffee shop that puts me in a good mood as soon as I walk through the door. The rock music playing through the speakers just loud enough to catch your attention, the sound of the coffee machine whirring every few minutes, and the smell of your favorite pick-me-up drink being made is just overall the best combination if you ask me.

"One iced mocha latte, and one iced vanilla latte." Shane and I walk up to get our drinks and find a table tucked into the corner of Brüman's and settle in.

"If they ever shut this place down, I think I might die. No one else makes a latte like Clara." Despite the cold weather outside Shane and I stay true to our iced beverages.

"Okay, so. What is new with you?" Shane asks, pulling the sleeves to her wool sweater down over her hands before tucking them under her chin. I give her my best *are we really beating around the bush with this* stare, but she shrugs it off innocently.

"I'm serious! I meant what I said— if you don't want to talk about...*that*, then we can talk about anything." I roll my eyes playfully, appreciating Shane's willingness to respect personal boundaries.

"No, we can talk about *that*." I imitate her over exaggeration of referring to what happened between Sawyer and me as a *that*.

"Oh, thank God." She practically melts in her seat with relief. "I was really trying to play it cool but I'm lowkey dying to know what the hell happened with you two."

"Me too, if I'm being honest." I lean back in my seat and let out a sigh. "Do you remember our senior year class party? It was on Halloween night at the McCallum's ranch. I mean, it was an empty field at the time but…"

"Oh my gosh, yes! I thought Lauren was going to throat punch a guy for trying to grind on her at that bonfire," she snorts before taking a sip from her coffee.

"As she should. Anyways, that same night Sawyer had been acting a little different around me. He was…" My words tail off as I absent-mindedly get lost in my thoughts from that night.

"Patience is *not* my strong suit, Le. He was what?" Shane presses. My cheeks flush as the next words come out of my mouth.

"He was acting as interested in me as I had always been in him." Her mouth hangs open like her jawbone no longer has the capability to keep it shut. She casually regains her composure and clears her throat. Wrapping her hands around her coffee cup she leans in closer to me.

"You had a thing for Tay's brother, and you never told us?!" Her voice becomes pitchy at the end of her sentence.

"What was I supposed to do? Be like *Hey Tay, I'm helplessly in love with your brother, hope that's not weird for you.*"

"In *love with?*" She's shouting now and seems to give zero fucks who can hear her.

"Umm, a little louder please, they didn't hear you at *Chatta-hoochies!*" I slump down in my seat while Shane looks around the coffee shop—politely smiling in apology for her outburst.

"In love with?" she whispers.

"I mean, it started as a crush, of course. I met him when I was in what…sixth grade? But by the end of it we'd become best friends and…yeah. I'd fallen pretty damn hard for him." She nods her head like she's taking it all in but doesn't say anything for several seconds.

"I feel like I broke you. Did I break you?"

"No. No. Just processing." Another minute goes by as her eyes are closed and her head is still shaking.

"Shane?"

"I'm almost there." I take the time to sip on my latte while she continues *processing*.

"You know that was only like half the story, right?" Her eyes shoot open, and she brings her straw to her lips.

"Continue." She waves a hand, giving me the floor to tell the rest of what happened.

"So *anyway*… Halloween night when you guys *abandoned me* in the haunted trail—"

"Our instincts kicked in, don't blame us because yours didn't." She holds a finger up as she argues her defense. I roll my eyes and continue.

"Sawyer swooped in and saved me from getting attacked by the girl from *The Ring*, and it almost felt like it was at that moment that something shifted between us. I wasn't sure if it was the hopeless romantic in me just making it up, or if maybe it was something *real*. Then we danced at the bonfire together and again, it just felt *different*. I don't know… It sounds so stupid when I say it out loud, but he didn't feel like just my *friend* anymore. I wanted to ask him about it the next day after breakfast at Flapjack's but…"

"He never showed," she finishes for me. The tone of her voice matches the sadness in her eyes—perfectly mirroring the way my heart feels from revisiting the memory.

"That's not even the worst part. He ignored me for *months* after that. The amount of texts and calls that went unanswered by him is embarrassing. I went through my five stages of grief over it and when I finally reached acceptance over the fact that I'd lose the only guy I've ever loved *and* my best friend—"

"Hey!" She glares at me.

"*One* of my best friends… I was just done with it. When he finally tried talking to me a few months later I just couldn't do it. I swore I wouldn't let myself get hurt by him again or whatever excuse he had come up with for why he left things the way he did with us."

"When was that? That he tried to talk to you again?" The look on her face is curious, like she's trying to connect dots that I can't even see.

"I think he said Hey to me at Christmas that year and I ignored him in an effort to give him a taste of his own medicine. After that I would get random texts here and there, but I never replied. I was trying to move on from him and it wasn't until he showed back up here that I realized ten years' worth of rejection was just me being in denial."

"So, do you still have feelings for him? Because not to be *that* friend, but what about Jackson? You guys seem to be doing really well." The guilt from almost forgetting about Jackson hits me when she asks.

"I don't know how I feel about Sawyer if I'm being honest. I want to hate him so much for everything that happened, and I kind of do. But it doesn't change the fact that I still have *fond* feelings for him as well. They just get skewed when I'm around him and I end up…"

"Yelling at him across the table during Thanksgiving dinner?" She smirks behind her coffee cup turning me a lovely shade of red, I'm sure.

"If we could just wipe that from all our memories, that'd be swell." I hide my face in my palms, letting the hair from my ponytail fall in front of my face. Shane pulls my arm to get me to look back at her.

"If you ask me, it was long overdue. You still didn't answer my question about Jackson though." Her nose scrunches, as if she hates bringing it up again.

"Jackson is great. We have so much fun together and it's honestly so different than the first time we went out. I have no complaints." Her eyes narrow on me again.

"The tone of your voice is telling me a different story." I let out a heavy sigh and remember why Shane and I always got along so well—we're more alike than we even realize.

"I don't know. Maybe it's because he asked me out literally the *day* before Sawyer walked back into my life and everything has been so... intertwined."

"Ew."

"Not like that." I roll my eyes at her. "I just mean my positive feelings towards Jackson are always getting trampled over my negative feelings towards Sawyer."

"*And* the not-so-negative feelings," she adds.

"Oh my god. I'm one of those messy girls, aren't I?" I whine. "Maybe I'll just become a nun." Shane starts to giggle and throws her straw wrapper at me.

"You're not becoming a nun. You're way too hot to stay single forever."

"Thank you?" I say more as a question.

"Do you want my advice?" she finally asks, taking another sip from her half-finished latté.

"I'm practically begging for it."

"Focus on Jackson. You can decide whether or not you're ready to hear Sawyer out, or if you want to keep ignoring him. But this thing with Jackson is new and there's an opportunity there to have fun and experience something exciting. So, if it's something you *want*, focus on that."

"Do you think it's childish of me to keep giving him the cold shoulder? Sawyer, I mean."

"I don't think you ever act childish, Le. I think you got hurt, and you never got an explanation or an apology and sometimes, whether we want to admit it or not, it makes us harbor bitter feelings. *He* seems ready to have the conversation, but what matters is, are *you?*"

"I don't know," I whisper, letting my mind whirl through all the possibilities that our conversation could end with. Because what if he had begun to notice the way I would look at him and it freaked him out. What if he just outgrew our friendship and didn't know how to tell me. But he said I meant *everything* to him? What did that mean?

"Well, my mama always said, *When in doubt, don't.* If you're not sure, then there's no harm in holding off until you feel more sure of things. The last thing you want to do is jump into a conversation you're not ready to have and end up even more hurt than you already are."

Maybe Shane is right.

Maybe I just need to focus my attention on Jackson and see where things could go with us. The way it was *meant* to be before Sawyer stormed back into town.

Chapter 11

Sawyer

What kind of an idiot blurts something like that out at the dinner table? During *Thanksgiving* no less. I didn't wait ten years to tell Leah she meant more to me than anyone else sitting around that table by blurting it out in frustration, but dammit the way she was acting like our entire friendship was one sided was pissing me off. I've been waiting for so long for her to give me just five minutes of her time so I could explain to her just how *in it* I was—which was clearly way more than she ever realized. Then she did—she gave me the chance and I blew it.

I hesitated because I didn't want everyone on the other side of the wall to have a front row seat to the conversation.

After everything that's transpired between the two of us, I'm beginning to worry that my affections for her *will* be one sided, but it doesn't change the fact that the feelings are still there—and by the way my stomach twists every time I see her, they're not going away any time soon.

"You good, man? You're pumping those dumbbells like they stole your lunch money," Tank asks, tipping his chin towards my arms. They're red and the veins in them look like they'll burst at any moment from me losing count of my reps. The guys invited me to their day after Thanksgiving workout, and I have to admit, it's been nice working out here—the gym is empty outside of the four of us.

"Just distracted I guess." I place the weights back on their rack and reach for my water bottle, finally feeling the burn in my arms from overdoing it.

"Wanna talk about it?" He lets out a deep laugh when he sees the hesitation on my face. "I'm not telling you to pull up a couch and pour your heart out. I'm just saying I'm here if you need to." My eyebrows jump to my hairline.

"Honestly, I'm just not used to having guys I can talk to about the real shit."

"Well, while we can be all fun and games when we want to be… we know who we can go to with the real shit," Tucker chimes in, racking the weights on the bench press.

"I think I fucked up with Leah," I admit, rubbing a towel along my neck. All three guys turn to face me in various stances.

"When? Last night?" Max furrows his brow.

"Yes, but no. Before that. This is like a ten year in the making fuck up and I don't know how to recover from it." Tucker whistles, bringing my attention to where he's leaned against the squat rack.

"Damn bro. What the hell did you do?"

"Basically, I did exactly what Leah yelled at me for last night. I stood her up and didn't return her texts and calls for two months."

"Is that really that big of a deal though? You were in college, right? Surely, she'd understand if you were busy." I can appreciate the effort in trying to ease my mind about how I handled things—since they have no idea how the relationship was between Leah and me.

"Not when we talked every single day for *years*. It was a pretty obvious blow when I didn't answer any more. She would always call to tell me what happened on her favorite TV show, or about a new book she picked up and loved or I would text her when I found a new coffee place around campus I enjoyed. Neither of us ever missed a call or text. She has every reason to be as mad as she is at me."

"So…what happened though? We know what you did. But *why* did you do it?" Tank asks. My eyes bounce over to Tucker involuntarily before I look back at Tank, but it's long enough that everyone notices.

"Well, I know *I* didn't do anything. I didn't even meet you until like two years ago," Tucker says defensively.

"Taylor caught me looking at Leah a little too fondly during the senior bonfire and threatened me not to *go there*. She said I would ruin my friendship with her and possibly theirs if it didn't work out. I thought I could just go back to seeing her as a friend if I put a little more distance between us but—"

"You don't strike me as the type that does what his little sister says. Respectfully." Max holds his hands up in mock defense.

"I'm *not,* usually. But I couldn't get what she said about losing Leah out of my head."

"But you lost her anyways?" Tucker concludes, making me sigh.

"I didn't say it wasn't stupid." I smirk sarcastically.

"So, why not just tell her now?" Tucker, Max, and I all turn our heads to face Tank who looks genuinely curious. "What?"

"What a great idea, Einstein. I'm sure he hasn't thought to do *that*." Tucker whips Tank's leg with his towel, making him jump back.

"Words hurt, Tucker." His hand falls to his heart dramatically, before extending it towards me. "I'm just saying, there are other ways to explain himself. He could text her or email her or shit… write her a letter."

"Yes, a letter. Please tell me, brother, in your experience how well does *that* method work out?" Tucker tilts his head at Tank who flips him off.

"I don't want to say what I need to say if it's not in person. I need to see her face when she hears why I did it—and how I feel."

"I respect that." Max finally rejoins the conversation. "And I admire you for not giving up on what you want now. I stupidly walked away from someone I should have been fighting for because I thought I was doing what was best for her. Luckily, she took me back once this guy finally talked some sense into me." He hikes a finger over at Tucker who is giving me a shit eating grin now.

"So basically, I'm your guy for all this relationship stuff."

"Even if I plan on yelling at your future wife for putting her nose where it didn't belong?" His grin falls immediately as he salutes me.

"It was nice knowing you, pal."

"You'll find your moment. Keep playing the long game, bud. She'll come around eventually." Max claps my shoulder. "Let's go, lunch is on me."

"Thanks, Dad." Tank gives Max a goofy smile as we all grab our things and head to Chattahoochies for lunch.

"Switch!" Javi calls as we're skating across center ice.

This team came to play tonight, but so the fuck did we. Matty appears just in time for me to pass the puck to him and he slaps it straight into the top of the net. The crowd is going absolutely wild and when I look across the ice, I see Devon skating like he's trying out for the figure skating team, making me bark out a laugh.

"Another win in the books, boys. Let's go out and celebrate!" AJ yells across our small huddle on the ice.

As always, I'm tempted to go straight home and go to bed, but I will admit I'm beginning to enjoy the after-game celebrations. Matty, Javi, and I always get to hang out and enjoy a beer before heading out a little earlier than everyone else—so with that in mind, I agree.

Imagine my surprise when we meet up on Broadway and Javi and Matty are nowhere in sight. I check my texts and see they've both informed me they'll be going home tonight to spend time with their families.

Fantastic. Now I'm babysitting the rowdy bunch.

All the younger guys from the team are all rallying on where to go

—while I plan my subtle disappearance—when I see Matty running up to us.

"I thought you weren't coming out tonight, Gallagher." We bump knuckles as he pulls a woman under his opposite arm.

"When my girl says she wants to go out, out is where we go."

"Which is going to be *where* exactly?" As if on cue Devon pops up beside her to answer.

"Line dancin' little lady." He winks at her, and I think Matty mentally chokes him.

"She's not available, DJ." Matty pulls her closer to himself, making me laugh.

"Not until we hit the dance floor at least." She lifts a brow at Matty as we all start walking towards Knockin' Boots Line Dance Bar & Grille.

As soon as we walk through the door the energy is electric. The smell of burgers on the grill hits me first and my stomach begins growling its demand for one. We grab a table right off the dance floor furthest from the band in an attempt to still be able to hold a conversation as the music plays. Our first two rounds of beer come and once we've all eaten to our satisfaction, some of the guys start to hit the dance floor.

"You dance, Clark?" Matty yells, leaning closer to hear my answer.

"Oh yeah. I would wipe the floor with all of you," I admit, making him rear back as his brows reach his hairline.

"Big talk, prove it."

"I don't dance without a partner," I argue. Matty leans over to whisper in Lyssa's ear, and as soon as she smiles at me, I know I'm not getting out of whatever is about to happen.

"Then let's dance, Cowboy." She holds her hand out and I shake my head at Matty.

"Don't blame me when your girl falls in love with the swagger." I dust the shoulder of my shirt for show, making Matty bark out a laugh as he holds up three fingers.

"Scouts honor."

Lyssa and I walk over to the dance floor and as soon as the next song starts, we fall in line with everyone else. It's fast-paced but the majority of people on the floor seem experienced enough to stay out of each other's way. We spin, dip and glide across the floor until both of us are laughing so hard my cheeks hurt.

She stands on her toes and yells into my ear, "Damn, you *are* really good at this, Cowboy."

"Thank ya ma'am." I tip my invisible hat to her.

"I think I'm ready for another drink, how about you?" I nod and spin her once more allowing her to lead the way back to our table.

"Alright, alright, we get it. You can dance," Matty says jokingly as Lyssa sits down on his lap. I hold my hands up and give him a cocky smirk.

"Told ya." We finish one last beer while I explain that my dancing is *not* a natural gift, but a direct result of my parents' line dancing with me and my siblings every chance we got growing up.

"That's so fun! And by the looks of it, it's a tradition you'll be able to pass down to your kids one day as well." When I look over at Lyssa her face is as white as a ghost. She begins rubbing her neck like she doesn't feel good, and I can see every sign in the book that she's about to throw up.

"Umm, Lyssa, you feeling okay?" I make eye contact with Matty and nod to Lyssa. When he catches a glimpse of her, concern washes over him as well.

"Shit, baby. Let's get you outside." We all stand to walk out since we've already paid our bill when Matty turns to me.

"I'm gonna pull the car around so she doesn't have to walk that far. You cool to hang with her while I do?"

"Of course. We'll be right outside." Matt runs out the door and I wrap one arm around her as her body feels almost limp. We're halfway to the door when her head shoots back upright.

"Shoot, I forgot my phone," Lyssa mumbles.

"I'll grab it." I prop her up against an empty bar stool near the exit and head back over to the table to retrieve it.

I'm almost there when someone not so gently bumps into my shoulder. I know that Nashville is a crowded place, but there's nothing that pisses me off more than someone not having the common courtesy to *not* run directly into another person. I turn around, ready to put whoever it is in their place, until I see those familiar green eyes boring into mine.

"Sorry 'bout that." Leah has me leveled with her stare when an arm wraps around her waist, pulling her closer. It's only then that I tear my eyes away from hers and see who she's with.

I feel my blood turning to lava as her perfect hips sway back and forth watching her walk out of here with fucking *Jackson*. He's still facing the exit, but I have the mind to chase after her and throw her over my shoulder to make sure she doesn't go home with him when I hear Lyssa call me from across the room.

"Sawyer! I'm dying over here." I see Leah glance over her shoulder once more between Lyssa and me before walking out the door, tucking herself further under Jackson's arm.

My hands involuntarily ball into fists when I think about where they're going to end up when they leave here, but I do my best to push those thoughts out and make my way back over to the bar to take Lyssa outside like I told Matty I would.

"Thank you," she mumbles as we get out into the cold fresh air. When a gust of wind blows by I see her whole body shake and since I'm used to the cold and didn't bring a jacket I gently rub my hands along her arms to keep her warm.

"Let me guess, a jacket didn't match your outfit?" I smirk as she looks up at me and half smiles.

"How'd you know?" She rolls her eyes.

"I don't think I've ever seen my sister wear a jacket unless it's snowing outside." We share a laugh as Matty pulls up to the curb.

"Don't tell me you fell for the swagger, Lyss," he jokes as I move my hands from her arms.

"Nothing like that. But maybe buy the girl a jacket that will match everything she owns." I wink at Lyssa as she melts into Matty's side, resting her head on his shoulder.

"We gotta get home." The noise that comes out of Lyssa next is one I know I should get far, *far* away from. "Thanks for looking out for her man." Matty nods at me.

"Don't mention it. That's what friends are for."

Chapter 12

I finally took Shane's advice and shifted my focus solely to Jackson. We planned a barhop so we could try new drinks together, listen to some good music and just all around, have a good time. I was really excited and very optimistic about things between us since I was pretty confident we wouldn't run into anyone we knew to spoil our evening. Not to mention, I couldn't contain my laughter when Jackson stood up from our table at *Knockin Boots* and tried to convince me to dance with him. Then I looked up—and all the air was sucked out of the room when I saw Sawyer dancing with some other girl.

She was a little taller than me, had long blonde hair set in loose waves, and was wearing the hell out of a pair of Wrangler jeans. They glided across the dance floor, smiling and laughing, like they were the only ones in the room. The moment my stomach dropped at the thought of them together, I knew my plan was going to fail. You know, the plan to move on with Jackson, try to forget about Sawyer, and not have to talk to him?

Yeah, that plan—not looking so good right now.

"Okay, okay. Maybe you're right. I have some work to do before we're ready to hit the dance floor," Jackson laughs, snapping my attention back to him.

I have to will myself not to look back at the dance floor again while Jackson continues talking, but when he gets up to go to the bathroom my restraint finally breaks, and I immediately wish it hadn't. Because they're no longer on the dance floor but they're side by side headed for the door.

"Ready to hop again?" I turn to face Jackson, slapping a smile on my face before nodding in agreement.

"Let's do it." If I'm going to give this thing with Jackson a fair chance, it's time I put my game face on and ignore Sawyer the way I used to.

Only, that doesn't happen. Not even a little bit.

Instead, I see him heading back to their table for something and when Jackson and I walk past him, I bump right into his arm.

He turns around, clearly annoyed by the lack of respect to his personal space, but his expression changes almost immediately when we lock eyes.

"Sorry 'bout that." As if on cue, Jackson slides his arm around my waist, and I see Sawyer's face harden almost immediately. When his date calls him from the bar, I glance between the two of them, then walk out the door. I'm fully aware that I'm on a *date* right now and have zero right to feel any kind of way about Sawyer being on one of his own, but I'm only human and I *do* feel some kind of way about it.

It was a lot easier to ignore Sawyer's existence all together when he lived a thousand miles away, but it's going to take a little more work now that he's here and showing up at every damn place I go.

After visiting every bar we could get into and trying countless drinks together, Jackson and I call it a night and head home. When we pull up to my house, he informs the driver he'll be right back before hopping out behind me to walk me to the door.

I live in a quiet, older neighborhood—seeing as how I inherited my house from my gran when she passed away. I've done a lot of work to the little two bedroom, two bath house to make it into my own little oasis. The red brick house with stairs leading up to the small front porch—that's just big enough for a couple of rocking chairs—has black shutters and white trim, much like it was when Gran still owned it. The inside is completely updated though, with a mix of bohemian and mid-century decor and I can't imagine living anywhere else. I have so many good memories with my gran in this house, living here is like having a piece of her with me always.

"I had a lot of fun tonight," Jackson says, nervously tucking his hands into the front pockets of his blue jeans. I wrap my arms around myself, hugging my oversized sweater to keep from getting a chill.

"Yeah, me too." I bite down on my bottom lip as the tension in the air begins to grow. He pulls his hands from his pockets, untucking mine from my sweater to hold them. My heart rate picks up as my eyes bounce between his. Just as I think he's going to lean in to kiss me, he pulls my hand up to his lips and presses a kiss there instead.

"Goodnight, Leah."

"Goodnight, Jackson." My lips roll together then turn up in a smile as he rushes back down the porch steps, and the car pulls away.

I take a deep breath before walking into the house and kicking my shoes off at the door. I waste no time putting my favorite pajamas on —an oversized hoodie and some sweatpants—and crawling under my coziest blanket on the couch.

SHANE

How was the date?

ME

It was great. We drank, we laughed, we ended up at the same establishment as Sawyer while he was on a date.

SHANE

Yikes.

ME

One question. What is up with the universe??

SHANE

So what happened? Did you talk to him?

ME

Sort of... I may or may not have accidentally on purpose ran into him on the way out. 😬 Jackson didn't see it happen though.

SHANE

😬 So then how was the rest of the night with Jackson?

ME

Meet me in the group chat.

ME

What does it mean when you've been on like five dates with a guy THAT IS IN HIS THIRTIES and he has only ever kissed you once?

TAY

How was the date, Le?

ME

It was great until he kissed my knuckles goodnight.

RUBY

Weird...

ME

Like, he kissed me that night during the haunted trail and seemed REALLY optimistic about doing it again and...hasn't?

LAUREN

Maybe he's secretly gay?

TAY

Maybe he got a little too   excited

SHANE

Maybe he's just really stupid?

ME

Not a single one of those responses was even
remotely helpful.

LAUREN

Mine felt kind of valid, but okay.

RUBY

Maybe he's just trying to take it slow? Since things
were so rocky in the very beginning maybe he just
doesn't wanna mess things up. 🙊

SHANE

Maybe he's just really nervous? Maybe he's working
up to it and then freaks out.

TAY

Maybe he's celibate.

ME

OMG what if it was a bad kiss? 😰 Anyone want to
go cat shopping with me tomorrow?

SHANE

Stop that right now. You're not getting a cat.

LAUREN

OMG. You are NOT a bad kisser Leah. However you
ARE totally a cat gal. I'll go with!

TAY

Awww kitty!

ME

Is it too much to want a guy to know what he wants
and just freaking go for it? 🙄

RUBY

Pretty sure that's all any woman wants, babe. You're
not asking for too much. I swear.

ME

Says the woman married to a man completely
obsessed with her.

LAUREN

Yeah, where can I get one of those?

SHANE

Well, we all found ours at a bar...

TAY

Oh my gosh, you're right.

I'm two episodes of Gilmore Girls in, and about to pass out on the couch when my phone goes off again.

JACKSON

Guess what.

ME

What?

JACKSON

I got us tickets to the Badgers game tomorrow.

OH. MY. GOD. WHY?

I am moving to Mars. No, the sun, then I won't have the ability to come back.

I internally scream, placing my hands on my cheeks as I stare at my phone screen and try to think of a way to politely tell him I won't be doing that, but I come up empty.

It feels rude to turn down a perfectly planned date night just because I'm playing a risky little game of avoidance with my feelings, but *why* did it have to happen in the middle of a silent crisis I'm having with their best defenseman?

Deep breath, Leah. You can do this.

ME

No way!

JACKSON

I remembered you saying you enjoyed hockey on our second first date so I thought you'd enjoy it! Maybe teach me a thing or two about hockey. 😬

ME

That was so thoughtful of you Jackson. Can't wait.

JACKSON

Same. Goodnight, Leah.

Since my eyes are barely staying open at this point, I love his message and lay my phone down before drifting off to sleep. No matter how much I joke about dying an old cat lady with the girls, I'm still not giving up on dating. Maybe he *is* just trying to take things slow, but I'm not going to be able to stop thinking the kiss was bad until he kisses me again.

If he ever kisses me again.

Chapter 13

Leah

I can't remember the last time I went to a hockey game. The sound of pucks on the ice, the energy, the smell of beer, popcorn and stadium nachos all have me feeling nostalgic. I've got on my favorite cable knit sweater that is the same color green as the Badgers' jerseys, a pair of dark-blue jeans, and my white Converse. For the first time in forever I wore my hair natural and much to my delight, the curls are actually acting right tonight. Then there's the matter of my glasses since I slept in my contacts last night and my eyes were *not* having it with them today. But I'm going to embrace them because I feel really cute tonight.

"Here we are," Jackson says, ushering me into our aisle. We are so close to the ice that every way we turn we have an unobstructed view of the game.

"Fancy meeting you guys here," a familiar voice says from down the aisle. I look up from searching for my seat number and see Shane smiling at me before Taylor's head pops out from beside her.

"What are you two doing here?" I glance back at Jackson, but from the slight look of disappointment on his face I can tell he wasn't expecting them to be here. I lean in and give them both hugs as Taylor answers.

"We come to every home game we can make it to." My brows knit together and a pit forms in my stomach.

"Oh, I didn't know." Shane's mouth pops open to say something but before she can the crowd starts cheering—Taylor included—when the Badgers skate onto the ice to start warming up. Shane and I share a glance, but she shrugs and starts cheering with Taylor.

"I'm going to grab a drink; do you want anything?" Jackson offers.

"I'll take a Diet Coke, thanks." He takes off up the stairs and I turn back to face the ice. I clap to show my support, recovering quickly from feeling left out since my friends haven't invited me to a single game they've *apparently* attended. Regardless of whether or not I would have come, they could have at least invited me.

My eyes scan the ice, watching player after player pass the puck, make their shots and then like a beacon of light in the ocean, bright pink tape on a hockey stick catches my attention.

Number thirteen.

Sawyer Clark.

Using the same pink tape that he's used on his hockey sticks since high school.

When he skates past, Taylor whistles and hollers at him. "Let's go, Moose!"

He glances over and his gaze lands on her immediately—he's probably familiar with where to find her since she comes so often—then he rolls his eyes and looks away.

Before he makes it too far, he turns around and does a double take. There's no mistaking that he's looking straight at me when he flashes that gorgeous bright smile my way. My cheeks heat instantly, and I offer a soft smile back at him, but as soon as those damn butterflies that only come to life when I look at Sawyer Clark begin to flutter around, the memory of him with another girl comes to mind, and they die on the spot. When I finally refocus, he's already back to his warmups.

"I think he's missed seeing you." Taylor doesn't look at me when she says it, but there's a hint of sadness in her voice that makes my heart sink.

"Yeah…" I glance at Shane, and she gives me a wink of encouragement.

"One Diet Coke." Jackson's voice has me shaking off the melancholy feeling and joining him on the other end of the aisle. When we sit down, he wraps one arm around my shoulder, and we make light conversation about the different warmups and why they stretch the way they do. When I glance over at him the look on his face reminds me of some of my kindergarteners trying to retain information and it makes me laugh. He looks at me and begins to laugh too.

"What?"

"Oh, nothing. You just look like one of my kinders trying to remember all the different sounds the letter *a* makes." I giggle and he pulls me closer to him, planting a kiss on my temple.

"It's a lot of information to take in, give me a break." When he finally stops and I look back up, we're barely a breath away from each other and my chest tightens with anticipation.

His throat bobs when he swallows and his eyes land on my lips for a moment, my heart rate picking up just before the announcer comes over the loudspeaker and the game starts. Jackson sits back in his seat and clears his throat, keeping his arm around my shoulder as the teams are announced and take center ice for the puck drop. As soon as the game starts, my inner sports fan comes out in the fiercest way. I'm cheering, yelling at the ref, and biting my nails so much I'm really glad there's no polish on them right now or I'd probably choke on it.

"Wow, you weren't lying. You *really* like hockey," Jackson laughs as I'm on the edge of my seat watching Sawyer and Garcia pass the puck back and forth. Then number twenty-four comes up out of nowhere—completely wide open on the goalies unattended side of the net. Sawyer slaps the puck over to their forward, Rooney, and he makes the shot.

"Let's go!" I jump up from my seat and glance over at Shane and Taylor to share in our excitement.

When I sit back down, intermission is starting and I'm able to take my first deep breath since the game began. We watch the guys skating around until the Jumbotron starts showing all the celebrity look-alikes and our eyes stay fixed on it instead.

Jackson leans over to crack a joke about the Mr. Peabody look-alike when the Jumbotron switches to the kiss cam. The old couple at the beginning makes the entire stadium *Awww* and when I look around to see if I can spot where they are in the crowd, I'm able to quickly find them in the section next to us. Jackson and I share an endearing look then I hear the crowd going absolutely *wild*—specifically my best friends. I look over to see Taylor and Shane screaming and acting like complete fools. Then they point to the screen, and I'm slightly mortified to see my own face, right next to Jacksons.

My eyes are wide when I turn back to Jackson, but he simply smirks and takes my face in his hands and kisses me. The crowd grows louder as his lips move over mine and when we pull away, I'm sure my face is as red as a tomato. I hide behind my hands, unable to wipe the grin off my face, but when he moves them for me and points to the Jumbotron, I glance at the screen and they have one of those silly kiss cartoons playing, which of course, makes me laugh even harder.

I hide my face with my sweater sleeves again as Jackson holds me close, planting softer kisses on the top of my head. A moment later I hear something crashing against the plexiglass on the ice below us and my head snaps up.

Sawyer.

"Keep your fucking hands off of her!" He practically growls as he slaps the glass, eyes locked on Jackson.

WHAT?!

His jaw tightens before he skates away, and I'm left frozen in my seat. My mouth pops open but I have no words. None that would ever make what just happened make sense at least. I look over at Taylor and Shane out of the corner of my eye and, as expected, their mouths are both hanging open. I feel more heat rush to my cheeks and when I turn back to look at Jackson, he has a confused and almost angry look on his face.

"Want to tell me what that was about?"

Um…Wish I freaking COULD.

"I have absolutely no idea," I answer honestly.

The rest of the game Sawyer is playing so aggressively I am just waiting for the ref to send him to the penalty box. When the final buzzer sounds, I exhale and release all the anxiety I had been holding onto the entire third period.

"Can we go somewhere to talk?" Jackson whispers in my ear. I nod in agreement as he leads us through the crowded building until we make it outside.

"What's going on between you and Sawyer?"

Right to the point, shit, okay.

"Nothing is going on between me and Sawyer." I cross my arms defensively, unsettled by the look on his face. He takes a deep breath, running a hand through his hair. "You don't believe me?"

"I want to. But I mean, come on Leah. That wasn't nothing." I suppose he's not wrong there. That was definitely not *nothing*, but it's also not what he's more than likely thinking it is.

"Clearly he's lost his mind," I scoff, but Jackson just stares at me like he's searching for something.

"So, it's just a coincidence that the first time we ever tried to go out, he told me not to bother getting too friendly with someone that didn't belong to me? Which, by the way, seems *pretty* aggressive."

"He did what?" I ask through gritted teeth.

"I got the message loud and clear, and I backed off. That's why I never asked you out again after that night. But then he seemed to disappear, and I thought maybe it was just some weird joke or something, so I asked you out again… And now? He's threatening me in the middle of a hockey game because I'm here with *you*."

Sawyer is the reason Jackson never asked me out again after that night?

I hear him talking, but all I can focus on is the burning desire I have to choke the shit out of Sawyer.

"Jackson, I swear to you I haven't spoken to Sawyer since I graduated high school. Outside of greetings in front of friends and at weddings, he hasn't been part of my life in *years*." He adjusts his glasses and slides his hands into his coat pockets.

"Well…it's clear you've been part of his. Or at the very least he's wanted you to be."

"But I *haven't* been!" I croak, getting more upset and confused by the second.

"I believe you, Leah. But I do think someone needs to tell him that you're not *his*." I take a deep breath and try to calm myself down.

"I'll talk to him and just tell him to mind his own business. I am so sorry about tonight, Jackson." He shakes his head and smiles at me.

"Did you have a good night?" he asks, placing his hands on the back of both of my arms.

"I did. It was a lot of fun." I smile up at him as he tucks a strand of hair behind my ear, leaning in until his lips are brushing mine as he speaks.

"Good. I did too." Then he kisses me again and it's a feeling I could really get used to. Even though Sawyer's face is all I can see when I close my eyes.

I'm definitely going to have to talk to him soon. I can't keep seeing his face when I'm making out with another guy. That just feels… dirty.

Chapter 14

Sawyer

There are plenty of moments in my life when I regret the decisions I make. The mohawk I tried to get away with my freshman year of high school, not telling Leah how I felt about her, then *telling* Leah—even if it was vaguely—how I felt about her during Thanksgiving, are all things I regret.

However, telling Jackson the woman stealer to keep his hands off my girl, is not one of them. I've been waiting for Leah to come to one of my games since I started playing this season, and when I saw her here tonight—I had never felt so excited.

Seeing her in the stands with a sweater on, that was a perfect match for the color of my jersey, with her curls framing her gorgeous face when she smiled and jeans that hugged her in all the right places. She was in her most natural state—which has always been my favorite look on her—and she was absolutely breathtaking. I was already planning out what I was going to say when I found her after the game—then that god forsaken kiss cam found her first and I had a front row seat to the harsh reality that she still isn't mine.

I could have jumped into the stands and ripped his arms off after he pulled her in for that kiss. My heart twisted and my mind spiraled and I remembered I have only myself to blame for the position we're in.

But I am done waiting around for the right moment to tell her how I feel. This shit is getting old and I'm tired of playing the waiting game. So tonight, instead of looking for Taylor and Shane like I do after every game, I head straight out the back doors to my truck.

I'm going to get my girl, and there's *nothing* that's going to stop me this time.

Except maybe her not being home.

When I pull up to the curb, I notice her car isn't in the driveway, the porch light is on but none of the other lights in the house are. I hop out of the truck and run up the steps and knock on the door.

Nothing.

I knock again, going as far as peeking through the window behind the rocking chairs to see if I can catch any movement.

I swear to God if she went home with that guy.

I jog back to my truck, my face growing hotter by the second as I picture her with him. His hands on her perfect body, her hair on his pillow, her lips around his—

Fuck! Why have I been waiting around like an idiot to talk to her while she's out here falling in love with some other dude?

I pick up my phone and dial Tank's number before pulling off towards my next destination.

"Hello?" The genuine confusion in his tone makes me do a double take that I've dialed the right number.

"Tank, It's Sawyer." I can hear him laugh immediately when I identify myself.

"Yeah, man, I know. I have your number saved. I'm just not used to getting phone calls. Everything okay?"

"Not fucking really. I think Leah went home with that guy, Jason."

"You mean Jackson?" he corrects.

"I literally could not care less what his name is right now." I hear him snicker but I'm too distracted to say anything about it. "She's not at home and I think I may have pissed her off so badly that she went home with him."

"Well Leah never struck me as the type to go have revenge sex, maybe she just *wanted* to go home with him. What the hell did you do, exactly?" My teeth grind together with immense force when I hear him suggest Leah having any kind of sex with someone that isn't *me*.

"Can you just... I don't know, talk me down or something. Because I'm about to pull some real crazy shit and hunt this guy's address down to find her."

"Well now don't do that...yet. You never told me what you did that you think pissed her off so bad to begin with." I let out a defeated sigh, knowing just how insane this makes me sound.

"I may or may not have seen them kiss on the Jumbotron at the game tonight."

"Oh?"

"And may or may not have threatened him afterwards because of it." Silence fills my truck as I wait for Tank's response.

"Tank?"

"Hold on. I'm trying to think of all the wild shit me, Tucker, and Max have done for our girls to see if this tops any of them."

"You almost murdered my ex in a motel room. I think you'll always win, babe." I hear Ruby's voice float into the receiver and my eyes almost bulge out of their sockets.

"Thank you for the reminder, Honey." Tank's voice is more distant, like he's holding the phone away from his mouth.

"Jesus, dude. At least I know I called the right person."

"So why did you need to find her? To apologize, break the guy's nose, or finally tell her how you feel?" I hear Ruby gasp in the background, and I scrub a hand over my face with a laugh.

"All of the above?"

"Why don't you try to blow off some steam first. If you still feel like you need to hunt him down after that give me another call and we'll find the unlucky son of a bitch together."

"Thanks man. I'm about to do just that." I hang up the phone and throw my truck into park before rushing the sidewalk to my sister's house.

I knock on the door and roll my neck as I pace back and forth on the front porch, waiting for someone to answer. When the door opens my sister's eyes grow wide when she takes me in.

"Sawyer, what are you doing here? No more innocent bystanders to threaten?" The sarcasm in her tone that I usually retaliate from with a jab of my own, rubs me in all the wrong ways tonight.

"Taylor, not now. Do you know where Leah is?"

"Are you serious, Moose? She's probably at home, or at Jacksons if you didn't scare him off after that shit you pulled tonight."

"*Fuck!*" I yell, making her roll her eyes. If there's one person used to seeing my temper, it's Taylor. She's been on the sidelines during some of my most heated moments on the ice and has become completely unphased by me getting worked up like this.

"Haven't you done enough already? Just leave her alone, Sawyer," she says quietly, almost pleading in a way.

I've always had a soft spot for Taylor—she *is* my little sister after all—my Tator Tot, and I've protected her, stood up for her, and been best friends with her for her entire life. But I'm done backing down just because she thinks she knows best.

"Don't fucking start with that bullshit. You do realize that *you're* the reason shit is the way it is with me and Leah, don't you?"

"*Me?* What the hell do I have to do with this?" she squeals, the look of shock on her face making me furious.

"Is that how you're gonna play it then? Pretend like you have no idea what part you played in me disappearing from Leah's life and making her *hate me* for ten. Fucking. Years!" I yell, watching as the color drains from Taylor's face.

"Sawyer, I'm serious. I don't know what I did. Please tell me." I run my hands through my hair, pulling on the wavy strands before letting out a manic laugh.

"The senior Halloween party? You basically threatened to hate me forever if I ruined your friendship with Leah, if I tried anything with her."

"Sawyer, I was drunk off my ass at that party! I did like six shots within the first fifteen minutes of being there, I don't remember saying *any* of that! I *barely* remember you even being there that night."

"Don't lie to me just to save your own ass now." I stop and glare at her, coming to the slow realization that she really didn't know.

"I'm not *lying!*" Tears start filling her eyes and I start to believe that ten years' worth of pining, regret and wishing I could have a do-over of that night, were all the result of a drunken comment she doesn't even remember making.

"You liked Leah?" She sounds so surprised. I don't know how she couldn't see it though; I hardly ever took my eyes off her.

"She was one of my best friends, Taylor! The way I felt about her was unlike anything I've ever felt for another person. I knew if given the chance I could have really…" I stop myself before the rest of that sentence slips out, because Taylor isn't the one I want to be saying this to. "But instead, I was too scared of ruining your friendship—and mine—with her if she didn't feel the same. So, I just disappeared instead. I stood her up, I stopped answering her calls and texts… I stopped being *me* for her, and she's hated me ever since."

"But why? Why would you stop talking to her? Why not just stay friends with her?" Taylor shakes her head, panicking as she realizes the magnitude of why Leah and I have been less than friendly all these years.

"Because being friends with her and nothing more would have killed me. Because I knew eventually, I *would* cross that line, and if she didn't feel the same—if it didn't work out—you would have been right. Drunk or not, you made it clear that we might lose her if I went there. Because at least the decision I *did make,* let *you* keep your best friend. Even if I lost mine."

"Sawyer," Taylor chokes out, with tears spilling from her eyes.

I've always hated seeing my sister cry. I was the first one asking who I needed to beat up whenever she was upset back in the day. I still don't like it now that I'm the reason for her tears, but tonight's conversation was a necessary evil. Something that was long past due.

"We're adults now, Taylor. It's not a crush that I'm unsure about, I've thought of nothing but *her* for ten years, while she went on hating me. I'm done worrying about losing her friendship—because I haven't had it since that night. I trust you two will be fine regardless of how she responds to my feelings. The next time I see her, I'm telling her how I feel." I turn to walk away, my heart hammering behind my chest as I fight the urge to still track down this asshole's house and find her.

"Sawyer!" Taylor's voice cracks as she calls after me. I turn around to see her still crying in the doorway and sigh. "Are we good?"

Taylor and I have never been in a serious fight. Sibling disagreements, bickering, and fighting over who got the remote first, sure. But nothing as serious as what we discussed tonight. I know she's not the one to blame, her comment may have prompted my decisions, but she really isn't as involved in this as I've always made her out to be.

"We're good, Tot. Just—don't say anything to her if you see her before I do. She needs to hear this from me." I nod, watching as her lips roll together to let a tear finish rolling down her cheek. She nods back quickly and dips back inside.

Between the adrenaline that's been pumping through my veins and the high from winning the game tonight, I'm absolutely *beat*. I may not be tracking Leah down tonight, but the next time I see her— the next conversation I have with her—is going to determine the rest of my future.

Chapter 15

Leah

When Taylor asked if I wanted to come over for an impromptu girl's night after the game, I was a little hesitant. Mostly because I knew she was probably going to ask me about Sawyer's outburst tonight—for which I have zero explanation—not to mention I have work tomorrow and I'm not normally up past nine on weeknights, but after the mention of Tucker making Mama Marilyn's cookies for us, I was sold. I'm sitting in the kitchen in my sweats, throwing back chocolate chip cookies like they're some kind of problem-solving tequila or something when someone knocks on the door.

"You expecting someone?" Taylor's brows knit together, and Tucker shakes his head, as he continues mixing more cookie dough.

"Be right back." She smiles and disappears into the living room. The door opens and I hear the muffled sound of voices, though I can't make out who it is or what they're saying.

I give up on my sad attempt at eavesdropping and look back at Tucker and can't help but snicker. He's wearing black sweatpants, a plain white T-shirt, and a black apron while he makes homemade chocolate chip cookies.

"What's so funny?" He tips his chin at me as I push my glasses further up the bridge of my nose.

"You just look so...domesticated." I wave a hand up and down and he looks down before he shrugs.

"I'd love to argue with you, but I'm afraid you might be right." I put another cookie in my mouth—not bothering to keep count of how many I've had at this point—and grab my glass of milk off the counter.

"So, you okay? Taylor doesn't typically demand comfort cookies unless it's something serious." Tucker smiles at me, and I'm immediately comforted by his checking up on me.

"I'm...not sure." I take a deep breath, settling back further on my barstool.

"Wanna talk about it?" He begins scooping dough onto the baking sheet, glancing up at me only long enough to gauge my reaction.

"I don't know. It's something Taylor isn't exactly clued in on yet, so I'd hate to put you in an awkward position with the information." He sets the bowl down, keeping the scoop in one hand as he puts all his attention on me.

"Well, I appreciate that. And while I won't pretend that I don't want to know what it is you're needing to get off your chest so badly —because let's face it, I'm nosey as shit—I won't pry. But I'm always here if you need to talk." He picks the bowl up, but before he gets back to work scooping more cookies out, he looks up at me again.

"And so is Taylor. Whatever it is you haven't told her, I'm sure she'll be understanding about it. She loves the four of you girls probably more than she loves me most days," he laughs, lightening the mood as my sight becomes blurry.

"As if. That girl is scary in love with you." I take the oversize sleeve of my hoodie and wipe my eyes, bumping my glasses out of the way when I do.

"And she's scary protective over you. She loves you with the same ferociousness she protects you with."

"Thanks, Tuck." I smile, earning a playful wink from him. He turns around and places the baking sheets in the oven and sets the timer before starting to clean the counters. Just about that time,

Taylor walks back into the kitchen with tear-stained cheeks and Tucker is immediately at her side.

"What happened, baby? Who was that?" He's standing in front of her with his hands on her arms as I stand up from my barstool to walk closer to them.

"I'm fine, Tuck. I promise. It was…" Her eyes cut over to me and I raise my brows in anticipation.

Who the hell just made my best friend cry?

"It was Sawyer." Her eyes never leave mine as she answers Tucker's question, making a lump form in my throat.

"Well, I'm gonna kick *his* ass the next time I see him," Tucker says, pulling Taylor in for a hug. Meanwhile, I am standing here insanely confused by what could have possibly been said between the two of them to make Taylor cry. Taylor never cries, she makes people cry and Sawyer is always the one to threaten anyone that upsets her. Or at least, he used to be.

"It's nothing like that. No ass kicking necessary." She gives him a playful eyeroll. "Can you give us a minute?" Tucker glances between us, nods and kisses her forehead before walking out of the kitchen.

"*Sawyer* made you cry? If you don't let Tucker kick his ass, then I'll freaking do it." Taylor motions for us to sit so we walk back to our barstools, and each grab another cookie from the first batch—that's almost gone now.

"That image alone is enough to put me in a better mood," Taylor laughs, and when I picture my five-foot-five self trying to take on the guy we call *Moose* for all necessary reasons, I can't help but join in the laughter.

My phone vibrates on the counter causing both of us to look down. My stomach drops when I see Sawyer's name pop up on my screen. I roll my eyes and grab it, planning to turn it face down to ignore him, but Taylor grabs my hand to stop me. When I look up there's a weird look in her eyes I can't quite make out.

"I know you're mad about what happened tonight, and believe me,

I would be too. But if he's reaching out, maybe you could hear him out?"

"Why?" My eyes narrow on her and she shifts in her seat.

"Just, I don't know. Maybe he has a reason for acting so nutty." She tries to roll her eyes like she doesn't know the answer, but Taylor can't lie to her friends to save her life.

"Do you know the reason, Tay?" Her lip begins to quiver, and I have to do a double take to ensure my eyes aren't playing tricks on me.

"I watched you guys go from being best friends, to you hardly looking in his direction for the last ten years and I tried to mind my own business about it, which you *know* is hard for me. I wasn't sure if something happened to cause bad blood or not, and I think part of me was scared to find out the truth and have to pick between my blood family, and my chosen one."

"Taylor, what are you talking about?" She takes a deep breath and starts over.

"I don't know why you have avoided Sawyer for so long, but would you just consider talking to him? Just one conversation, and if you don't want to speak to him again after that—I'll stay out of it. I think he may have something to say that you need to hear." My heart rate picks up and I get the weird feeling I'm either about to throw up or pass out.

Seeing Taylor be so invested in Sawyer and I talking again, and hopeful that we will clear the air between us, makes me feel guilty for keeping things from her for so long concerning Sawyer. But if I open up to her *now* I'm not only admitting to a long time crush I had on her brother while we were in grade school, but I have to admit that he broke my heart when he cut me out of his life—without a single clue how much he's meant to me— and that *that's* the reason I haven't been able to get over it and forgive him. Even after all these years.

Because Sawyer Clark still holds more of my heart than I ever wanted to admit. But I'm starting to see I may be left with no choice than to do just that—admit it.

The only question is, who do I tell first?

Do I tell Sawyer and run the risk of being rejected? Getting my heart broken for the second time by the same man.

Or do I tell my best friend, and hope that if everything goes to shit, I'll still have her support to lean on.

"Tay… I have something to tell you." She sits up a little straighter, nodding her head as her expression turns more serious.

"I can't believe you never told me." We're tucked into the corner of her oversized couch, covered with blankets with an empty cookie plate on the coffee table beside us. Tay rests her hand on mine on the back of the cushion between us as we face each other.

"I just didn't know how you would react. I didn't think you'd be *mad* necessarily, but I did know it might make things awkward. If you knew the way I saw him. I don't know. It's just so messy, we were friends, but I liked him as so much more, then he just disappeared on me, and I had to act way less hurt by that than I actually was." I groan, resting my head on the cushion, watching as Taylor chews on her bottom lip. "What?" I ask, sitting up when I realize she hasn't said anything for a while.

"Nothing." She shakes her head, but clearly there's *something*.

"Tay, come on. What is it?"

"I just think you guys should talk. I *know* you don't want to. But I'm serious Leah, I think you need to hear him out." I narrow my gaze on her.

"Why? What did he say tonight?" She shakes her head, looking down at her nails.

"I told him I wouldn't say anything to you." I contemplate asking her until she breaks, but I don't want to do that to her. Taylor is the very one that will say whatever she wants, whenever she wants no matter what anyone else thinks about it. This is obviously important if she's keeping it in. She gave him her word and I get her wanting to respect that.

"Okay. If he tries to talk to me again, I'll hear him out, but I'm not seeking him out first."

"Thanks, Le. I'm so sorry that I wasn't able to be there for you when you were hurting." Her eyes gloss over and I squeeze her hand.

"You don't have to apologize. It was my choice to keep the way I felt hidden from you guys. I just honestly can't figure out what I feel about him anymore. It was a lot easier to ignore his existence when he didn't *live here*." She chokes out a laugh and swipes a tear from her eye.

"Well, maybe you won't have to continue ignoring him forever. Maybe you guys can find closure." I smile and nod, not missing the way my heart sinks at her words.

Closure.

There's something about *that* word that packs a finality that I don't think I want to have with Sawyer.

Do I want answers? Yes.

Am I afraid they'll hurt me even after all this time of trying to build a Sawyer-proof wall around my heart? Also, yes.

But I know it needs to happen.

Chapter 16

Staring at the notes app on my phone to make sure I've completed all my Christmas shopping is stressing me out more than usual this year. Normally I have all my shopping done by December first, ensuring everything is ordered with enough time to account for any shipping delays, so I don't show up to Christmas empty handed. What a nightmare that would be.

I take pride in my early planning and preparedness execution every year—except for this year. Because *this* is the year I have a new name on my list and I don't know how, or if I even *want* to shop for it.

Sawyer. Freaking. Clark.

I know he'll be there, but what I *don't* know is if I'm supposed to get him something. Or if he'll get *me* something. Because what if he gets me something but I don't get him anything? Or worse. What if I get him something and he doesn't get me anything?

My brain literally cannot handle another thought about this right now.

I lock my phone and toss it in my desk drawer, rubbing my temples ineffectively trying to rid my oncoming migraine.

"Hey-yo." Jackson's head appears in the doorway to my classroom, and I involuntarily groan. "Uh-oh. You okay?" He sticks his bottom lip out in a pout.

"Just a migraine, nothing that teaching kindergarten for five years hasn't prepared me for," I tease. "Or maybe that's what has caused them," I add under my breath.

"Do you need to cancel tonight? We don't have to go out if you're not feeling well. We can reschedule," he offers, smiling up at me from where he's bent down in front of my desk chair.

"No, I will be okay. No need to reschedule." I give him a reassuring smile and when he grins ear to ear, I can almost feel it putting pressure on *my* frontal lobe.

"Okay then. I'll pick you up at six?" I nod in agreement, and he bounces to stand back up. "See you in a bit." I can't even appreciate the wink he gives me because all I can think about right now is laying my head on this cool desk until the kids get back from lunch.

As always, Jackson was at my house to pick me up at five minutes 'til six. He's nothing if not punctual, I'll give him that. When we pulled up to the steakhouse, I felt a little underdressed but seeing as how he's still in the same khakis and sweater he wore to school today, maybe I'm just overthinking it.

"Good evening, I'm Michael and I'll be your server tonight. What can I get you started with?" I've barely picked up my menu when I spot the photo of a raspberry margarita front and center.

"I'll take the raspberry margarita, on the rocks, with a sugared rim." I smile politely at the waiter, earning an unsolicited wink from him that makes me grimace.

"A woman that knows what she wants, I like it." His gaze lingers on me a little longer until Jackson starts to order and snags his attention.

"I'll have a beer. Whatever is on draft. Oh, and can we get some fried pickles?" Jackson wags his eyebrows at me as the waiter nods and walks off.

"That was weird..." I lean over the table, watching as Jackson looks around cluelessly.

"What was weird?" My brows knit together and I'm shocked that he didn't pick up on the inappropriate way the waiter was just looking at me.

"No, maybe it was nothing." I shake my head. "Nevermind." He smiles at me and changes the subject as I see our waiter out of the corner of my eye staring at me from across the room.

Why don't you focus a little less on me and a little more on getting my tequila to this table, Michael.

"I mean even *you* know that no one wants to be paired with Janice for that." I look over at Jackson, completely lost as to what the hell he's talking about because the gaze that's settled on me from across the restaurant is making the hair on the back of my neck stand up.

"Here we are, fried pickles, one raspberry margarita, and a Coors on draft. Are we ready to order?" Jackson orders his food first, but as soon as he's done the waiter turns to me and I'm immediately uncomfortable again. His gaze falls from my face to what is very obviously my chest, before giving me a suggestive look that makes my lunch threaten to make a second appearance today. I manage to get my order in without asking him what the hell his problem is, but as soon as he's gone again, I contemplate asking for a different server.

Throughout the rest of our dinner any time the waiter checks on us, his focus is primarily on *me*. I begin to ignore him completely, trying to get the point across that I'm uninterested, but when he asks us about dessert and calls me sweetheart right in front of Jackson, I snap. I let my fork clatter onto my plate and level him with a stare.

"None for me. I'm quite ready to get the hell out of here, thanks." The chill to my tone surprises even me, but even that doesn't seem to get the point across. He simply offers to get our check for us and retreats to do just that, but not before giving me yet *another* wink.

Does this guy have a twitch or something? What the hell is wrong with him?

Jackson must *finally* pick up on the fact that this guy is bothering me, because he glances over his shoulder then back at me and shrugs.

"Ah, I see what you were talking about. Of course he's checking you out though, you're beautiful." He reaches across the table and takes my hand in his, giving me a reassuring smile.

"Yeah well, he should cut it out. Plus, he's doing it *right* in front of you. Like, hello, we're *clearly* on a date." I roll my eyes and see his brows draw together in confusion.

"Should I say something to him? Do you want me to?"

Is he serious? The date is literally over *at this point. Why even bother?*

My mouth pops open before I quickly snap it shut again, offering him a soft smile instead.

"No, don't worry about it. Excuse me a minute, I'm just gonna use the ladies' room." As soon as my back is to him my face morphs into utter disbelief.

He literally couldn't care less that this guy is practically looking down my shirt and flirting with me right in front of him during the entirety of our date. It's not like I want him to stand up and clock him or anything but like…he should care, right?

Well, there's only one reliable source to get that answer from. The counsel.

I pull my phone out of my clutch and open the group chat, typing as quickly as my thumbs will let me.

ME

Hypothetically speaking, what would your husbands do if a waiter was not no subtly checking you out and flirting with you while you were on a date?

SHANE

Not so subtly meaning????

ME

Practically losing his eyeballs down my shirt while I ordered. Calling me sweetheart and winking at me so much I'm beginning to wonder if it's a nervous tick.

TAY

Guy would be losing his eyeballs one way or another.

RUBY

Possible assault charges.

SHANE

Yeah, he wouldn't have a job or the ability to see anything for much longer.

LAUREN

Why am I here for this?

ME

See, that's what I thought. SOME kind of reaction other than saying "of course he's looking because you're beautiful"

ME

Lauren–Because I wasn't going to start a whole other group chat just because it was a relational question. Duh.

LAUREN

Fine. Also, barf. The least he could do is throat punch him.

SHANE

He actually said that?

TAY

We already know Tucker isn't afraid to break someone's bones over unwelcome flirting. Let us know if you need back up.

I mean, even Hendrix would say some shit to that
guy. What a wank.

Thank you, counsel. Going back before he thinks I'm
taking a shit or crawling out the window or
something.

Well, at least I'm not crazy to think he should have had at least a *bit* more of a reaction to the way our waiter was acting.

"I can't tell you guys how thankful I am that we moved girls night up this week, I couldn't wait 'til Friday to pour it out," Lauren says, pouring a gracious serving of Shane's famous margaritas into her glass.

"I hear that. I'm still not over my catastrophic date Monday night." I roll my eyes, earning disapproving grumbles from some of the other girls.

"Did I tell you guys that Zander and Tana are sleeping together now?" Taylor joins in. Shane gasps dramatically from her end of the island.

"TOENAILS?! Shut the fuck up."

"Yes, toenails. I don't know whether or not they deserve each other or if I should still do her a solid and warn her," Taylor snickers into her drink.

"Shit, let it play out and then bring the good popcorn when you tell us about it. We all know that girl can't keep her mouth shut about her personal life," Ruby says.

Tana lived with Taylor for a *very* short period of time before Shane moved back to town a few years ago and was one of the nastiest humans to ever rent a room from anyone—at least that's what Taylor tells us. Going as far as clipping her toenails in the kitchen.

Barf.

However, she ended up getting a job in Taylor's department last year and come to find out, she has no boundaries and no filter in *any* area of her life. She has been the source of many a girl's night stories. And now apparently, she's dating Taylor ex-situationship that was nothing less than a walking red flag.

Thank God Tucker was done letting Tay ignore the fact that they were *made* for each other and swept her off her feet and out from under Zander.

"Okay well there's that. Lauren, you go. Pour it out baby." I shake my head and give her the floor since she seems more on edge than usual.

"*UGH,* okay. We have this new guy who came in from New York, right? And since he apparently made millions selling some of the most upscale homes and penthouses there, he thinks he's like, the *god of real estate* or something and wants to tell everyone how to do their jobs. Like, excuse me *Mr. Real Estate*, I'm pretty fucking great at my job already. Sit down." She tosses the rest of her margarita back while the rest of us stay silent, staring at her.

Normally when Lauren pours it out it's because her parents are on her ass about something, her client ended up having to pay closing costs they weren't expecting, or the nail salon didn't have her favorite dip powder. But I've never seen her *this* worked up over any of that stuff.

"Who is he?" Ruby decides to be the brave one and asks. Lauren groans in disgust.

"*Fitz.* That's it. He just goes by Fitz. Like *Elvis* or *Prince*. How pretentious is that?"

"*So* pretentious. What a wank." Taylor rolls her eyes in agreement.

"I should just call him Lucifer. It's more fitting and keeps the one name brand going for him." Lauren smiles devilishly.

I can't tell if she's angry, being sarcastic, or lethally serious right now.

"Who's name is Lucifer?" Tank asks, swiping his keys from the island, holding Poe in his car seat as Hendrix runs past him to the door.

"New guy at my work," Lauren answers simply.

"Poor guy, his parents really set him up for failure. Have fun ladies. See you tonight, Honey. Wait up for me." He kisses Ruby and gives her a wink before heading out for guy's night at Max and Shane's.

"Anyway," Lauren pops a chip in her mouth as soon as the front door closes and dusts her hands off. "Enough about the *Satan of real estate*, tell us more about this dumb ass date you went on."

"I don't know. I mean, you guys got pretty much all the details when I text you from the bathroom, he was just so passive when the waiter was literally trying to eye-fuck me." I shudder at the thought. "I mean, he barely got out *Hi, my name is Michael* before his eyeballs were on the girls." Taylor stands up straight, no longer leaning casually over the island as her face grows more serious.

"His name was *what?*"

"Michael..." *GASP!* "Oh my *god!*" My hand flies over my mouth.

"Where did yall eat?" Taylor asks for clarification.

"The steakhouse off 11th. I forgot the name of it." Taylor beats on the kitchen island.

"Son of a *bitch*. It was him!" Taylor yells. Michael is one of Taylor's more terrible exes, that is truly a piece of trash. "Tucker is gonna kill that guy one day, mark my words."

"Well, someone needs to tell him he's a piece of shit and *clearly* it won't be Jackson." I roll my eyes as all the girls burst out laughing.

Chapter 17

TAY

You should come to the game with us tonight!

ME

Idk Tay. After last time do you really think that's a good idea?

TAY

Well I don't think we have to worry about Sawyer doing anything embarrassing if you're there by yourself. And if you get uncomfortable and want to leave then you don't have to stay. No biggie. 💀

TAY

I just figured you could use a fun night out. You looked so happy at the last game. Until you know, my brother got fucking FERAL.

ME

It was a lot of fun…

ME

Okay. I'm in.

TAY

Yay! Pick you up at 6!!

Chapter 18

Sawyer

It's been almost a week since I went looking for Leah after my last game and wound up talking to my sister instead. Not that I don't love getting to talk to my sister, but I've got a lot of shit to get off my chest and she's not the one I need for that.

I've been doing my best to put as much of my focus into tonight's game as possible, but I'm not sure how successful I'm going to be in doing so.

Because the girl of my dreams is in the stands again tonight.

She's wearing a green sweater dress and a pair of short black boots. Her hair is curly—my favorite way to see it—and the radiant smile on her face is one I've missed more than I ever thought a person could miss a smile.

I'm hesitant to look around too closely, worried I may find that she's here on a date again. But when I don't see any *Ghostbusters* lurking around her, I make the assumption she came with Taylor tonight and continue warming up.

I lose count of how many times I have to tell myself to stop looking up in the stands after the puck drops. I need to keep my focus on the ice and get the win that my team deserves. Rooney, Matty, and I are all in sync tonight and when Roons passes the puck to me I waste no time slapping it right inside the top corner of the net. I stop dead in my tracks when I hear one very distinct voice cut through all the other noise.

"Way to score, thirteen!" My heart leaps when I see Leah cheering, eyes trained on *me*. I'm tempted to abandon the entire game just to go pull her into my arms and tell her I've waited my entire career to hear her cheering for me. But with only two minutes left in this period, I force myself to stay put and finish the game out strong.

I spent most of the game trying to think of a way to get Leah alone, and as soon as humanly possible, so I can finally talk to her. I've been dying to see her ever since the last game, and if I have to wait another minute to be near her, I'm going to lose my fucking mind.

ME

Can you come to the locker room?

DOVE

Why???? 😖

ME

Please.

DOVE

I'm not sure that's a good idea. I'm not even supposed to be back there.

ME

Running out of time, Dove.

My heart is hammering so hard in my chest I can almost hear it. My knee bounces up and down relentlessly as I wait to see if she'll show up or leave me hanging.

"Sawyer?" I hear her whisper through the barely cracked door.

She has always been a much better person than I am, though.

"No need to whisper, Dove. It's just us." I smirk, standing from the bench underneath where my jersey hangs. When she steps into the space completely, I take a minute to admire her up close.

"Oh my gosh, Sawyer!" I can't help but smile when she turns her head away from me, holding her hand up to shield her eyes.

"What's the matter, Leah? Don't like what you see?" I have on my hockey pads, but I've stripped out of my jersey already. When she splits her fingers open and peeks through them, I bark out a laugh.

"Take it in, Dove. There's no one here but us." I hold my arms out and wink at her. She huffs and turns to face me completely, no longer feeling the need to hide from me, apparently.

"Is this what you needed me for? To parade around shirtless in the locker room?" When her brow arches the bite to her tone and the little bit of attitude she's giving me, makes my dick twitch.

"No, it wasn't." She stumbles backwards as I stalk closer to her, closing the distance between us until my body is pressed firmly against hers.

"Sawyer, what are you doing?" Her breathless tone makes me want to forego answering her and kiss her until neither of us can feel our lips anymore. But I *somehow* refrain.

"Truthfully? Trying like hell not to kiss you right now." A small gasp escapes her lips while her cheeks turn bright red. "But that's not why I asked you back here. I wanted to apologize."

"For what?" She clears her throat. Her head is tilted up to look at me, her nose nearly brushing my own from how close I am keeping her.

"So many things, Dove. But I guess I'll start with how I acted at the last game you attended." My jaw ticks as I remember seeing her kiss someone else.

"You must have *really* hated seeing Jackson kiss me." Her voice is low, as our eyes connect and suddenly my apology takes an intense turn.

"You want to know what I hated, Dove?"

"Sawyer... I didn't—"

"I hated not showing up for you at Flapjacks that day. I hated not talking to you every day after that, and not being able to tell you about my days—good or bad, I always wanted to share them with you. I hated that I lost my best friend and I hate that we lost ten *years* together. I hate that I waited so damn long to finally say fuck it and tell you how I really feel about you. I hate that that sneaky little weasel made it to you before I did, and I *really* hated that you wore your hair natural for him."

"You like my curly hair?" She blinks a few times, her eyes wide like she's still processing the rest of what I just told her. I smirk, tucking a piece of hair behind her ear.

"Are you kidding? When your hair is curly, and you have your glasses propped up on that perfect nose of yours while getting lost in one of your favorite books or watching one of your favorite movies— that's my favorite version of you. I could stare at you for the rest of eternity and never stop finding new things to adore about you." Her chest rises and falls more quickly now, her breasts brushing against my bare chest with every breath. I'm dying to wrap her legs around me and let my hands glide beneath her dress to see if she wants me as badly as I want her right now.

God what I wouldn't do to know what her body feels like beneath my touch.

"I—" I hold my finger up to her lips, letting my eyes fall to them before I meet her gaze again.

"You don't have to say anything. I can see how hard that perfect brain of yours is working right now while you process. But I was going crazy not telling you how I felt. I'm sorry I handled things the way that I did back then. I thought my reason was valid, but regardless of that reason, I shouldn't have treated you that way. Our friendship was *never* one-sided, Dove. I just needed you to know that."

Leah jumps when she hears commotion outside the locker room door and looks at me with panic in her eyes. I give her a reassuring wink and open the door.

"Thanks for bringing me my backup shirt, Dove. I would have hated wandering around outside without one." Matty and Rooney stand up straight and clear their throats, nodding at Leah as she walks out of the locker room.

"Uh, yeah. No, you're problem." My brows knit together, and I roll my lips together to keep from laughing. "I meant no problem or you're welcome." She shakes her head, her cheeks growing redder by the second. I can't contain my laughter any longer and finally let a laugh slip.

"See if I ever answer your texts again, asshole." She rolls her eyes before glaring at me and tossing her long brown hair over her shoulder.

"You will." Her eyes grow wide when I wink at her prompting her swift exit down the hallway. I let Matty and Rooney make their jokes about what was going on before they showed up while I get dressed, and when I finally leave the rink, I feel lighter than I have in *years*. I'm nowhere near done making up for lost time with her, and I still have so much I want to say to her—but this is a start. The fact that she even came to the locker room to begin with feels like a major step in the right direction for us to finally start over.

Chapter 19

I've never personally experienced my heart stopping but being pressed against a wall by Sawyer's shirtless body, while he tells me he's trying not to kiss me, definitely made me feel like it skipped a few beats. I would have thought I was having an out of body experience if I hadn't been so responsive to his touch. I was already a puddle for him before he ever opened his mouth to tell me everything he hated about being apart and apologizing for the way things ended between us.

I hate that I had to rush out when his teammates showed up, I hate that when he said he was trying not to kiss me all I wanted was for him to do it anyways. I hate that every time I'm around him I lose all control of my own thoughts, but what I hate even more is that as soon as I was on the other side of that door, it hit me that I'm still dating Jackson and guilt over everything I was thinking and feeling about Sawyer crept into the deepest parts of my mind.

Oh my god, I'm a horrible person.

Just as I'm rounding the corner to exit the long hallway that leads to the locker room, I see a familiar face heading in the direction I'm coming from, and the guilt grows stronger.

Her long blonde hair bounces in perfect rhythm with her steps as she gets closer to me and I'm suddenly curious about *who* exactly she's looking for. Hoping like hell I'm wrong about who it is.

"Hey!" I stop and turn to face her.

"Hi there." She smiles and stops a few feet away from me.

"You look really familiar, have we met before?" I know playing dumb isn't the best route to take in this situation, but I can't currently bring myself to ask her straight out what I want to know.

"Well, if you come to many of the games you've probably seen me on multiple occasions. I'm always here watching my boyfriend."

"Boyfriend?"

"Yeah! Are you dating someone on the team too?" She glances down the hallway towards the locker room then gives me a curious glance.

"Oh, no. I was just…taking something to a friend of mine. Sawyer Clark?" I say his name as a question, hoping to find an answer to my unasked questions through her response.

"Oh! So you know Cowboy?" she squeals.

Cowboy? She gave him a nickname? I wonder what he calls her? Beautiful blonde goddess with an ass worth worshiping?

"Cowboy?"

"That man could dance a lady right down the aisle, am I right?" she giggles. My mouth pops open but no words come out.

Is he actually dating her and thought it was okay to say the things he just said to me? Am I that much of an idiot that I didn't think he would have someone in his life he was serious about? I mean I even *saw them* together so how did I forget about that already? Probably because my brain stops working any time I'm within five feet of this man. He was probably just saying what needed to be said so we could coexist without me freezing him out at Christmas this year.

Say something before this gets awkward.

"Well anyways," she drags out.

Too late. It's awkward.

"Maybe I'll see you at the next game. We should sit together! My name is Lyssa." She holds her hand out and I accept, still in a state of shock and barely able to even say my name.

"Leah." I force a tight-lipped smile as a toothy grin spreads across her face.

"Leah and Lyssa, sounds like a destined friendship to me." She winks and it takes everything in me not to tell her how much I already hate her. "See you around, Leah." She struts down the hallway and I can feel my entire body deflate. Just when the walls I've spent ten years building around my heart to protect it from Sawyer start to come down just the slightest bit, they shoot right back up when I realize he may very well be playing me while in a relationship with someone else.

Bitch YOU'RE in a relationship—I think—get it together.

I've come to the conclusion that I don't think I'll ever be ready to talk to Sawyer. Not until my brain and body stop acting like a complete hoe every time he looks at me with those swimmable blue eyes.

TAY

Who wants to drag the guys out line dancing this weekend? I got some cute new boots I want to break in.

SHANE

Oh yay! It's been AGES since we've been dancing!

RUBY

Didn't someone almost get into a fight one of the last times we went out?

LAUREN

Have you met the men you guys have decided to marry? Of course someone almost got in a fight.

I'm so in though. Let's fucking go.

Yassss.

😈 That's what I'm talking about.

I'll take any distraction I can get from sitting at home and thinking about all the ways I want to bury Sawyer under the ice he plays on every week for making me feel things for him again.

Everyone who knows me knows I'm the quiet, responsible, levelheaded type—until me and Tequila get together. Then I'm Leah 2.0 and she's fun as hell. Tonight, I need Leah 2.0. I'm standing at the bar watching all my friends dancing and it's no wonder the guys are always seconds away from getting into fights when we go out. I would be too if I had a wife that looked as hot as my friends always do.

"Okay, do we see any potential for a dance partner?" Lauren asks, as we slam our shot glasses down on the bar.

Jackson said he wouldn't be able to come with us tonight, so I'm on the prowl for a dance partner for the night. We scan the room in every direction before I spot a couple of guys standing at a pub table glancing our way.

"Holy shit. Yeah, actually." I cut my eyes discreetly in their direction and Lauren gives me a flirty glance.

"Damn Le, you're not playing around. Those are some *Yellowstone* looking cowboys." Her remark makes me physically wince, though she doesn't seem to notice.

"Oh, you know Cowboy?" Yeah, I knew him way before you did, bitch.

I hate myself for being bothered by this.

Lauren turns around and adjusts her bra to push her boobs up higher in her fitted red top and fluffs her hair.

"Let's go catch us some cowboys." She winks and I toss my curly hair behind my shoulder and nod as we make our way over to their table.

"You boys sure are dressed to impress." Lauren gives them a seductive look that has *me* hot for her.

Damn, she's good.

"Thank you, ma'am," one of them says, tipping his cowboy hat.

"Do your dance moves live up to the image though?" The way she asks the question would have any man with an ego desperate to prove himself.

"Let's see for ourselves, shall we?" He offers his hand, and she follows him onto the dance floor. I fix my eyes on the guy left standing as he lets his gaze drift over my body. I have on my favorite stretchy jeans that make my hips and ass look phenomenal, if I do say so myself, and a solid black corset top with thick tank straps that accentuates my waist *and* my breasts.

"How about you? You gonna earn your right to wear that hat?" His lips turn up into a sly grin and he nods.

"After you, Sweetheart." We join everyone else on the dance floor and I catch a shocked glance from Shane before Taylor looks at me and howls. I don't typically do couples dances, I'm more of the group dance type but for tonight, I'm going to let this guy dance me around this room until I can't take another step.

When my partner, who's name I have not cared to get yet, spins me again, I whip my hair around and just as I stand upright an arm wraps around my waist and spins me in the other direction. I spot Jackson walking through the door, having just enough time to make eye contact and smile at him before I'm spun in the opposite direction. Partner stealing happens every now and then during these dances so I'm not too surprised by the trade off and am able to keep my steps consistent, but it's the voice I hear next that sends a shiver down my spine and has my feet almost rooting into the ground.

"You've gotten better at this, Dove." The dance is so fast paced, I don't have time to stop, so we just keep moving and talking between spins. "But I don't care too much for someone else's hands being on you."

"Well that's too bad, what would *Lyssa* think about you having *your* hands on me, *Cowboy?*" Sawyer dips me just as the music stops and the smirk on his face has me glaring at him.

"Well, since she's dating Matty I don't think she'd really give a damn." I feel my face get red as soon as the words leave his mouth.

Oh my god. She's Matty's girlfriend. Not Sawyers.

When he lifts me from the dip we're standing chest to chest, making me tilt my head to look up at him.

"Oh." *I'll just go crawl under a rock and die now, thanks.*

Sawyer brushes my hair off my shoulder and leans down to whisper in my ear, making goosebumps breakout all down my arms.

"You sound a little jealous, Dove." He stands back to his towering height and I try to slip my mask of indifference back on.

"As jealous as someone who *threatens* someone else's date for kissing them?" His face hardens and his nostrils flare while his jaw ticks furiously.

"I'm not afraid to admit I'm the most jealous motherfucker there is when it comes to you, Leah." His use of my real name in lieu of my nickname has me more aware of how serious he is right now. I swallow hard, my mind spinning from the tequila hitting me now that I'm standing still.

"Jackson is here, I have to go." His grip tightens on me, stopping me from moving, and for the first time since he got back, I actually don't want to walk away. I want to stand here and hear him out. I want to see if he's really changed, and I want him to prove to me that he means it.

"No." He spins me around, keeping us moving with the rest of the crowd on the dance floor until we're on the opposite side of the room. "I'm not letting you go so easy this time, Dove." I see him scan the perimeter then he turns and leads the way off the dance floor before pulling me down a hallway in the back of the restaurant.

"What are you doing, Sawyer?" I'm practically running to keep up with him, as he keeps a firm grip on my hand. He turns to face me and backs me into the exposed brick wall, and even though I should be annoyed that I keep finding myself in this position with him, the rate at which my heart is beating begs to differ.

He takes a deep breath, towering over me. "I know you hate me, Leah. You've had every right to. I've acted like an asshole and screwed up in more ways than I can even count, but I am *done* pretending like you're not mine." He tucks a stand of hair behind my ear, letting his knuckles caress my cheek and down my neck until they're resting on my collarbone while goosebumps shoot down my arm. My eyes flutter shut, savoring every electric feeling from his touch.

"But I'm *not* yours, Sawyer," I whisper, finally dragging my gaze up to meet his.

"Is that so?" He slides his hand down to my chest, as I will my heart to beat slower.

It doesn't.

"Then why does your heart feel like it's about to beat out of your chest, *again*? The same way it was racing when you were tucked away in the corn stalks with me." His other hand runs along the length of my arm, clearly bringing attention to the goosebumps there as he smirks.

"We both know you've always been mine, Dove. It's just a matter of time before you accept it and let me prove to you how sorry I am for fucking it up for us all those years ago." His nose brushes the tip of mine, and I take a deep breath in trying to steady myself.

His signature cedarwood scent surrounds me and I can feel the warmth of his lips so close to mine, if I were to lift my head even the slightest bit, I would finally know what it feels to kiss Sawyer Clark.

"Let me know when you lose the boyfriend, Leah. You were never supposed to be with him anyway." Suddenly the warmth of his presence is gone and he's walking away. Leaving me standing alone in the hallway.

Speechless.

Breathless.

And more turned on than I've ever been in my entire life.

Shit.

I run my hands through my hair, leaning my head back on the wall behind me as I try to compose myself. Things with Sawyer have always been intense—only tonight, instead of being angry with him, I wanted to give in to him. I wanted him to wrap me in his arms and show me just how sorry he is—the way he keeps saying he's going to.

But once again, he walked away.

Only this time, I want to chase after him.

Chapter 20

Sawyer

I deserve a damn medal for walking away from her tonight. Feeling her heart race against the palm of my hand, seeing the way her pupils dilated as soon as we were a breath apart, and the fact that she didn't go running for the hills the minute I had her alone was enough to make me want to break and kiss her right then and there.

She's only partially right about not being mine. While *she's* still entertaining the idea that dating *khakis* is going to work out, I know they won't last. Because as I sit here watching her from across the room while she talks with him at the bar, she can't stay focused on him for longer than a minute before I see her eyes land on me. Where they should be.

I've never been a very patient man, but for her I'm fucking trying to be.

I don't just want her quick glances and stolen moments tucked into the corner of a corn maze or a bar we both end up at. I want every smile she has to offer and to be the one that makes her head fall back in laughter. I want to hold her hand as we walk down the street and wrap her in my arms when she's cold and isn't wearing a jacket—because she's *never* wearing a jacket. I want to see her cheering me on in the crowd at every one of my games and spend Sundays watching her get lost in a book or making lesson plans, or whatever it is she does now. I want to get lost in the taste of her and prove to her that no one else will ever know her the way that I do.

I won't be the one to break while she's still seeing someone else, but that doesn't mean I won't be doing everything I can to get her to break first.

"We're heading to Spurs, you coming?" Tank comes up and asks as I finish off my beer. I watch as Leah and Jackson join the rest of the group and if they're going, there's no way I'm *not* going.

"Yep. Let's do it." I clap my hands on the thighs of my blue jeans and stand to leave. When we get outside, I get the absolute pleasure of watching as Leah's cheeks turn the perfect shade of red when she turns around to see me standing right behind her. I give her a wink and it's like I can hear the very moment she stops breathing.

"Hey, you okay?" Jackson asks, tugging on her hand. She spins to face him again, quickly slapping a smile on her face.

"Yeah, great!"

I'm about to join the other guys of the group— because, well this guy makes me want to punch a hole through cement and the others *don't*—when he leans down and kisses her. It's not like they stood there making out or anything, it was a quick peck on the lips, but it was just enough to make my blood feel equivalent to molten lava. A slap in the face reminder that she's here with *him*. That he gets the absolute fucking privilege to kiss her any time he wants, when it's all I can ever think about.

I see her eyes cut to me, though she doesn't allow herself to face me completely. Which is probably a good thing considering I am fresh out of fucks to give tonight and would more than likely pull her out of his arms and haul her off to anywhere but here and beg her to just give us a chance. But she keeps her hand in his, and her eyes forward as we make our way to Spurs.

Can this guy just fall off a cliff already?

"How's operation *steal the teacher* going?" Tucker asks, from beside me as we watch Max and Tank spar in the ring that was recently put up at Hall's.

"Please tell me you were not the one responsible for naming you guys' missions?" I glance up at Max and he smirks.

"He was not," he says before taking a swing at Tank.

"But I could have been because I'm *great* at it. And you didn't answer the question." I take a deep breath and cross my arms over my chest.

"I'm not trying to *steal her* so much as trying to show her that she should be with me and not the pair of khakis she pretends to be so taken with."

"What makes you think she's pretending?" Max asks, keeping his eyes on Tank.

"You've met the guy, right? He has the personality of a wet paper towel." Tank snickers and cocks his head.

"I have to say I've had more interesting conversations with my seven-year-old than him."

"Well, that may not be entirely fair to the guy. Hendrix is one of the best storytellers I've ever met," Tucker adds.

"I don't know man. I just feel stuck. What can I do when she's literally dating someone else." I hold my hand out and see Tucker's brows raise.

"Do what I did." He shrugs.

"I'm a little scared to ask but... what did *you* do?"

"Get in the way." I can't help but laugh when he smirks.

"That was the best possible way you could have explained that," Max laughs from the ring.

"Thanks, brother," Tucker says adoringly.

"What the hell do you mean, get in the way?" I'm genuinely confused on if I'm supposed to just stalk her and show up everywhere they go, or if it's more metaphorical. I don't really have the time to be stalking her ass.

"When Taylor started thinking she wanted to date the guy she'd been casually hooking up with at work—after waiting for over a year for her to be ready to date so I could ask her out—I decided she'd know *exactly* how I felt about her and that I was done just being friends. Whether she kept trying to date this guy or not. I let her know where *I* stood."

"I'd ask how that worked out but since you're currently picking out flowers for your wedding, I'll assume it went well," I tease.

"It did, but it took some time."

"Just be straight with her man. The best thing you can possibly do for her, especially after hearing what happened between you two back in the day, is to prove that you're gonna be there for her. And if you really love her, that means being there for her as a friend too, not just as…more. She's got walls built up man—and they may take a while to break down." Max is like the cranky big brother that actually loves you and is full of good advice that could change your life. JJ is a great big brother, but all he's full of is medical knowledge and bullshit.

"Why don't you get up here and show me what you got, hockey star?" Tank says, waving a glove at me.

"Because my coach would chew my ass out if I did anything to get hurt in the middle of the season. Maybe after the playoffs."

"I'll hold you to that." He points a glove at me then he's back to sparring.

Chapter 21

TUCKER

We going Christmas shopping this week or what?

TANK

But there's so many PEOPLE out there.

MAX

I'm with Tank. What happened to good ole online shopping and avoiding all the people cracked out on peppermint mocha and the need to touch every damn thing in a store while Christmas music plays so loud you can't hear yourself think.

TANK

Right? What's with that? It's like they're trying to brainwash you with cheerful nutcracker music so you end up buying way more than you actually need to.

TUCKER

Oh my fucking God Scrooge and Scrooge Junior. Lighten the hell up. Do I HAVE to remind you we're shopping for your families just so you'll stop your whining?

ME

And this happens ANNUALLY?

TUCKER

Yes, and it gets worse every year.

ME

Wait, you guys always shop together for Christmas? How sweet.

MAX

There's strength in numbers.

TANK

Someone's always got your back.

ME

Little scared of this energy, but I'm down. Maybe you guys can help me figure out what to buy Leah.

TUCKER

That's the spirit! 🎄🎅😊🎁

MAX

Someone sedate Cindy Lou Who please.

TUCKER

I always knew I'd be the one to make your heart grow three sizes 😏

TANK

ME

💀

I have to admit, as someone who's been kind of a loner outside of playing hockey, it's nice to have guys that include me in the ordinary shit in life.

Such as Christmas shopping.

Have I ever been Christmas shopping with a group of dudes before? No.

Am I positive it's going to be one of the most entertaining trips to the mall I've ever made? I would bet my entire career on it.

I book it to my last stop before hockey practice, knowing damn well Coach is going to be up our asses, yet again, about not getting lazy just because it's the week of Christmas. That's never affected the way *I* play, but I guess he wouldn't know that on a personal level yet since this is my first year on his team. I'm nothing if not determined to make this my best season yet.

"Oh my god, you weren't kidding. There's so many people out today." My brow lifts to my hairline as the four of us walk into the mall. The guys told me they'd meet me here after practice today, and even though I'm so beat I feel like I could pass out any minute, I'm glad I came. Because I would never miss a chance to see Max and Tank dealing with the Christmas rush at the mall a week before Christmas.

"I fucking told you," Tank groans, turning himself sideways to dodge a shopper that would have run into him otherwise. He gives Tucker a warning look and Tucker must be able to read his expression because he rolls his eyes and speaks next.

"That lady was probably seventy-four years old, brother. She probably didn't even see you."

"We were in her direct line of sight, Tucker. She shouldn't be allowed to drive if she can't see a brick wall four inches in front of her."

"Maybe she has a driver." Max shrugs, shoving his hands into his jacket pockets.

"Whose side are you on?" Tank leans forward to ask him, making me chuckle.

"Okay, so any idea where we're stopping first?" I clap my hands together, swiftly changing the topic of conversation before the two of them end up turning around to leave.

Tucker takes off to look for a second pair of work shoes for Taylor, and what is supposedly the world's softest blanket, while Max stops in front of a store with a full window of coffee mugs. Tank and I hit the LEGO store first to grab a couple of sets for Hendrix, then he manages to find a onesie for Poe that says *my dad's tattoos are badder than yours*. The way this man's face lit up at baby apparel was downright heartwarming. When he dipped into Victoria's Secret I opted for the store across from it to look at candles.

"Good choice, I don't need you knowing what kind of lingerie my wife wears." Tank slaps the side of my arm and walks so confidently into that store I can't help but laugh.

I look around for a while but after smelling a candle that was supposed to be *cucumber* scented, but smelled like straight up wet feet, I left.

"No luck, brother?" Tucker claps me on the shoulder as I'm rubbing a hand down my face in frustration, and I shake my head.

"Why is it so fucking hard to shop for women?"

"It's not really." Tucker shrugs and I give him an expectant glance.

"Please, enlighten me."

"Women are viewed as such complex creatures, and don't get me wrong, some of them are. There are high maintenance and *very* particular women out there that you'd never be able to shop properly for. But you and I both know; Leah is not one of those women. Is she?" I think his words over and catch him raising a brow at me.

"Nah. She's not." I let out a sigh, trying to think of everything I know about her. What she likes and doesn't like and rack my brain for some idea of what to get her. When I glance to the left the answer practically slaps me in the face.

The bookstore.

Leah is the biggest bookworm I've ever known. She reads anything she can get her hands on, from fantasy, to autobiographies, and every funny, dirty, thrilling thing in between. Surely something will pop out at me in there.

"No luck yet?" Max asks as he reappears beside us.

"I think I'm getting an idea."

"Good deal. Glenda said to tell you hi." He nods to Tucker and Tucker's eyes grow wide.

"You saw Glenda? And you were pleasant enough for her to feel confident you would relay a message to me?" Max rolls his eyes as Tucker lays into him.

"Who the fuck is Glenda?" I ask, watching Tank snicker as he walks up behind Max.

"She's the jewelry store lady," Max growls. "It's a long story. What are you getting Leah?" He dismisses the conversation and I nod to the bookstore before the four of us walk in together.

The amount of mouths hanging open and lingering glances are not lost on me. Tucker stops in front of an end cap and points to a sign that reads *Hockey Romance* and barks out a laugh.

"Dude, look, they have a section about you." I roll my eyes and we each pick up a book and thumb through them.

"Oh, shit," Tucker says, rearing his head back and slamming the book shut. "I didn't know they made books dirty like that." He sits the book back down and rubs his hands on his shirt like it he touched something he shouldn't have, and I can't hold back my laugh.

"Yeah, well I'm not too keen on the idea that I get her a sexy book about the sport I play for Christmas. Seems a bit forward, doesn't it?" I glance up and see Max and Tank both staring very hard at a book that I can't see the title of. Whatever it is, they're completely engrossed by it.

I think hard about the book I heard her telling the girls about while we were at the dinner the other night and vaguely remember the name of the author.

I look around for what feels like an eternity but when I have no luck, I grab my phone and search the author's name and find all her books online. I sit on one of the chairs at the bookstore coffee shop, looking through the entire list of books by this woman and when I finally see one that I think—*hope*—she'll love, I order it and finally stand to rejoin the guys. They're going to have to get over the fact that I cheated and ordered one of her gifts online because this is the only thing that I feel even slightly confident she'll like.

"I think I'm gonna grab her a mug and then we can bounce," I announce and the guys regroup around me. They all share a worried glance and I let out a laugh.

"Don't worry, I have a plan. I'm not getting her *just* a mug." Tank whistles and pats me on the back.

"I thought for a second Max was going to lose his spot as the worst shopper." Max rolls his eyes at the comment.

"I got my wife and my daughter matching bracelets as well as the matching slippers and pajamas as requested. I think you're projecting. I'm an excellent shopper."

"So domesticated," Tucker jokes.

"Where the hell did you hear that term?" Tucker scoffs, but when Max raises a brow demanding an answer his face falls.

"Leah. She said I was domesticated when I was baking the other night," Tucker mumbles. I laugh so loud I feel like I'm about to get shushed by an angry librarian.

That's my girl.

"So that was her polite way of saying you're whipped." Tank smirks and now all of us were smiling.

"Hi, did you guys need any help with anything?" a girl in a bookstore apron and glasses asks, looking up at us.

"No ma'am. Thank you though, we were just heading out." I smile at her, and she nods while still staring at us with an endearing smile on her face. She doesn't move though; she just stands there staring at us. I glance over at Tank, and he shrugs.

"You okay there, Becky?" I glance down at her name tag and her mouth pops open, her cheeks turning rosy before she glances down and blows out a puff of air.

"So great... okay, buh bye now." Then she races off in the other direction.

Weird.

I grab Leah a mug that has a worm wearing glasses and reading a book and call it quits. This book better get here in time, or I'm screwed.

Chapter 22

"Happy Christmas Eve, eve!" Shane yells as she walks through the door with her Christmas onesie on. It's been a tradition for as long as I can remember that we wear the most festive pajamas we can find, order in our favorite food from Casa Taco, and watch Christmas movies and just be together on the day before Christmas Eve.

"Get your fine asses in here, we're starving!" Lauren yells from her place next to me on the couch. Lauren snuggles are some of the most precious things you can imagine having in life. She's one of the fiercest, strongest women I know, so when she's comfortable enough to snuggle up to you while wearing a Rudolph onesie that has a butt flap in it—you're in her safe zone.

"Sorry, Enrique wouldn't stop flirting with Ruby."

"Lower your voice, Tank might hear you. Then who will give us free cheese dip." Taylor slaps her hand over Shane's mouth dramatically. Shane jerks away and scowls at her.

"Why would he stop giving us free cheese dip?"

"He can't very well do anything if he's *dead* now can he?" A look of understanding comes across Shane's face.

"Ohhh, right," she laughs. Ruby rolls her eyes and pushes between the two of them, tossing one of the carry out bags on the kitchen table before running over to snuggle the other side of me on the couch.

"Ah, all's right with the world again." I sigh happily.

"Y'all are some bitches if you don't make room for us *right now.*" Taylor wags a finger at us before she and Shane climb on top of us, eliciting multiple groans from those of us underneath them.

"Did everyone get their Christmas shopping done? I mean, it's a little late to be asking *now* buuuut," Lauren inquires, taking another bite of her taco. Everyone confirms that they've completed their shopping, giving little teases about what each girl has gotten the other, then all eyes land on me.

"What about you, Le? You're normally the one that's done first, putting the rest of us to shame," Ruby teases.

"Yeah. I'm all done."

"Okay, but why do you seem so sad about it?" Taylor lifts a brow at me. I give her a knowing look and roll my eyes.

"Because I'm nervous about giving Sawyer his gift. I'm more nervous that he didn't get me anything and then it'll be weird that I got him something."

"Wait, why would that be weird?" Ruby sits up a little straighter, leaning her back against the couch as she looks at me.

"Ugh. How much time do you have?" I groan, throwing my head back on the cushion.

"Pretty much all night. Spill. Why is it weird?" Taylor pulls me up and gives me an encouraging wink.

"I had a thing for him back in high school. Then he dropped me like a senior elective, didn't talk to me for two months, broke my heart—which I couldn't tell you guys about because he's Tay's brother and that's awkward—never told me *why* he left things the way he did, then showed back up ten years later wanting to apologize and act like his world won't spin if I'm not in it." The words fly out of my mouth at the speed of light, though my expression is almost emotionless. I've told this story one too many times to even care at this point.

"First and foremost, holy shit. Second of all, what the shit?" Ruby shakes her head.

"Please fill in some blanks. Like, *when* did he apologize? *How* did he apologize? Most importantly, why do you think his world will stop spinning if you're not in it? And why on earth are you worried about giving him a Christmas present if that *is* true?" Lauren asks, meeting my pace.

"He asked me to meet him in the locker room after I went to the hockey game *without* Jackson—"

"Ow ow!" Lauren hoots.

"Nothing *happened*. He just told me he was sorry for how he left things and assured me our friendship wasn't one-sided. Since, ya know, I kind of freaked out at Thanksgiving and told him that's how it felt. Which would be fine if it was just a simple apology and an explanation so we could move on but..."

"But what?" Taylor looks over at me curiously.

"But it wasn't just a simple apology. I was in there for maybe five minutes, and it was the most electrifying five minutes of my life and all he did was *talk* to me. Not to mention he keeps giving me these looks and saying things that just make me feel like..." I trail off, not sure I want to say the next part out loud. I could chalk it up to misinterpretation, but it's kind of hard to misinterpret *"You've always been mine, lose the boyfriend."*

"Bitch, I swear to god if you don't finish this sentence." Lauren holds her hand up like she's about to slap me. We both know she won't do it.

"Like no matter how hard I try to fight it, or how much I try to convince myself that I hate him for what he did to our friendship, that I'm still going to end up falling for him again. And I can't do that, because when I fell the first time—I almost didn't get back up." I see

Taylor's face fall as a heavy silence falls over the room, and though it only lasts about thirty seconds, with this group it might as well have been an hour.

"Well, I have nothing intellectual to say because my tequila hit about two minutes ago, but let's just see if he got you a Christmas gift first. Then we'll see if he's even worth falling for all over again or not," Shane teases as she flips her ponytail around.

"And remember that we're here to catch you this time, if he's stupid enough not to." Lauren winks at me.

"Not to be a bitch and bring down the mood but like...are you still seeing Jackson?"

"I don't wanna talk about it." I roll my eyes before letting them land on Ruby. Her eyes widen like she's sorry she ever asked.

"That date we went on a couple weeks ago is still rubbing me wrong. Like, for the love of God, be a *man*," I groan, making the girls giggle.

"Okay so I know we've already gone over this—"

"*Twice*," I interrupt.

"But was it *really* that bad?" Ruby asks, making me deadpan.

"When it comes to knowing when to stick up for your date, the man has the tenacity of a wet paper towel." Shane snorts at my remark and when I look over her eyes are already closing. She's got about a minute left in her before she's asleep on this couch.

"Can we please change the subject? Shane will need a recap if we keep going and I just honestly don't want to think about any of this anymore." We all look over to see Shane passed out curled up into a ball so tight I fear she'll lose circulation in her legs.

"Say less babe." We all bundle up on the couch together, turn the TV up and finish our night of Christmas movies in comfortable silence.

Well, the room is silent—my brain, however, is not.

I can't stop my mind from replaying the moments I've shared with Sawyer over the last two months on a loop.

Why him?

Why those moments?

I'm in a relationship with a guy who's perfectly nice—okay, maybe *too* nice sometimes—so why can't I think of the countless dates we've shared and replay *those* on a loop?

Unfortunately, these are rhetorical questions, I'm well aware of the reason.

Because Sawyer Clark has the ability to set my soul on fire by simply looking at me. Something no other man has ever come close to doing.

Chapter 23

Sawyer

You'd think I was carrying one of the world's most precious artifacts in my hands the way I'm handling this book tonight. When it came in yesterday, I let out a sigh of relief that proved just how much pressure I'm feeling over making sure I give Leah a Christmas present she'll love. I'm still not sure she *will* love it. For all I know I heard her wrong that night and I've just gotten her a book she said she hated or would never dream of reading.

I guess I'll find out soon enough.

Taylor and Tucker are hosting Christmas Eve at their house tonight because, outside of my own place, theirs is the biggest. With our parents and Leah's here, it's very…*cozy*. I would have offered to host, but I pussied out over the simple fact that if Leah came into my house and left her scent *anywhere* and things between the two of us didn't work out the way I'm hoping they will—I would have to move.

And I actually quite like my house.

"Sawyer, you okay son? You look the same way you did before the puck-drop your first time in the playoffs." My dad puts a hand on my shoulder and gives me a gentle shake.

Wow, am I really that transparent?

"I'm okay, Pops. Just hoping everyone likes their gifts." I hear him snort next to me and turn to face him.

"I didn't realize she'd turned into *everyone*," he teases.

"Huh?" My brows pull together and I follow his gaze to the kitchen where Leah is pouring herself a glass of wine.

"The good ones always do feel like the *only* one." He gives me a wink just as my mom calls him over to where she's holding Poe by the fireplace.

They'd make the best grandparents.

I wonder if Tot will ever want to have kids?

"Okay, everyone! Find a spot and get comfy. Time to open presents!" Taylor singsongs as she claps her hands together, scooping Hendrix up in a bear hug before showing him where his pile of gifts are.

She'd be a great mom.

"Please tell me you got something other than that worm mug for her," Tank whispers, standing beside me at the back of the room. "I mean it's cute and all but if you're as crazy about her as you say you are—" I cut him off with a glare. "All I'm saying is… I hope she *really* likes coffee mugs." His arms come up in mock defense.

"I appreciate your concern with my gift buying abilities, brother. I got her something else though so you can relax a little." I can't help but laugh when he pretends to wipe his brow in relief.

"Boys, come sit," my sister demands.

Tank falls onto the couch next to Ruby and Hendrix and when I look around the room for a place to sit, as fate would have it, the only empty spot is right next to Leah on the floor. I take a subtle deep breath and wipe my sweaty palms on my jeans before taking my place next to her.

I can see out of the corner of my eye the way her body stiffens ever so slightly, her eyes trained on anything else in the room but me.

That seems fair.

The last two times I saw her I was *not* shy in letting her know how I feel about her—going as far as telling her she should dump the guy she's currently seeing to be with me. I'm not sure how aggressive Tucker meant for me to be when saying I should get in the way, but I feel as though it's safe to say I fully committed to the assignment.

I don't regret it, nor have my feelings changed on the matter, but I can still understand why I may not be her favorite person at the moment.

That's fine with me though. I'm still going to push every button of hers I have access to until she finally breaks and gives me a chance. I wonder if she listened to my advice and lost the librarian yet?

Gosh I missed having big Christmases.

Looking around the room and seeing it filled from corner to corner with our friends and family just gives me that warm feeling in my chest that *should* accompany the holidays. For the last decade I've felt a little empty during Christmas. While traveling for games, Taylor not making it back home as often, and JJ and Blaire being on the road constantly, we haven't had a Christmas like this since—

"This one's for you," Leah says softly, handing me a green and red wrapped present.

The warm feeling that was in my chest just moments ago fades into a dull sadness as I lock eyes with her. Those hypnotic green eyes that I could stare at until I find every shade of green painted in them that makes them pop the way they do. Because it reminds me that the last time we had a holiday gathering this big, was the Christmas after I ruined us.

The smile I had grown so fond of never appeared on her face that year—not in regards to me, anyway—and I think that's what broke me. I knew I'd messed up more than I ever thought possible, and she wasn't inclined even the least bit to hear me out when I tried to apologize.

"Hey, you okay?" The cool brush of her fingertips on the back of my hand has me snapping out of my blast to the past. I look down where my hand is palm down on the floor with her pinky resting over mine and before she can move her hand I lock our small fingers together.

"I'm working on it," I admit honestly. Her cheeks flush and she gives me a small nod, extending the gift she has been trying to hand me. She clears her throat, and her cheeks grow an even darker shade of red.

"This one is from me." My heart begins beating faster, my eyes snapping up to hers once more.

She actually got me something? I thought she still hated me?

The box is one of the smallest I've ever seen but that doesn't change the excitement I'm feeling over knowing she thought of me. When I open the box, my heart damn near explodes. Because there's a keychain of a hockey stick with pink tape around the blade and the number thirteen etched at the top.

"You made this for me?"

"I mean *I* didn't make it, but I designed it, and *had* it made," she giggles. She has no idea what this means to me, and I love her even more because of it.

"Thank you, Dove. I love it." She smiles and turns to the rest of the boisterous room as people continue opening their gifts, and when I see that Leah has opened all of hers, I pull the simply wrapped package from behind me and hand it to her.

"Psst, Leah." Her head whips around, her curls bouncing when they come to a stop. "This one is from me." The look on her face takes me by surprise.

"You got me a present?"

I match her shocked tone. "You thought I wouldn't?"

She gives me a curious glare then takes the package from my hands.

"Uh, be careful, here...pull it from right here." I reach over and find the loose portion of wrapping paper for her to tear from—not wanting her to start ripping and tear the cover. I look up to see her smiling at me and my heart skips a beat.

"Thanks." When the paper is off and she flips the book around, she looks as though she's seen a ghost.

Her features fall and her mouth pops open but before she can say anything Lauren yells, "What did you get?" causing her to turn her focus on the rest of the room.

"Loving Romeo." All the girls stop and look at her.

"From *who?*" Shane squeals excitedly. Leah simply turns to face me, and all the girls follow.

"Sawyer." I know she's simply answering the question asked, but hearing my name on her lips will never not be my kryptonite. No matter the reason it's there.

"Yeah, well I thought I heard you talking about that author when we were all at Spurs that one night, and I remember how much you used to love watching *Rocky* with your dad so I just thought it might be a good choice. She had a lot of books to choose from, so I just took a shot in the dark." I shrug, trying to let her know it wasn't a big deal. It is just a book after all. Even though I couldn't find it in stores it isn't like I had to scour the earth to find it or anything.

She stares at me blankly for another moment then, without a word, she stands up and walks away, taking the book with her. Either she's going to throw it away because it's from *me* or she loves it so much she... I don't know? Needs a moment alone with it? Taylor must see the concern written on my face because she chimes in as the rest of the group goes about opening their gifts and chatting.

"I'm sure she loves it, Moose. You know how she is about books. You did good." She gives me an encouraging smile, but I still get up to check on Leah for myself anyways.

When I walk into the kitchen she's standing in front of the large bay windows, looking down as her fingers trail over a page of the book. I shove my hands into my jean pockets nervously and take a few more steps in her direction.

"I'm sorry if it's not what you wanted. Or if it's something you already have. I wasn't sure which—"

"You really just overheard me mention this author's name at dinner and found the book you *thought* I would want most of hers?" She looks up from the page and our eyes lock.

"I mean...yeah."

"She literally has *so* many books out, and you just randomly chose this one?"

"Yeah, Dove. Look, it's just a damn book. If you hate it I can just get you something else—" Again, she cuts me off mid-sentence.

"But it's *not* just a book, Sawyer. It may sound stupid to you, but it's just another reminder of how well you know me. Even after..." She closes her eyes and lets out a sigh, the same way she always has when she's sad, and I can't help but gravitate towards her. I take a chance and place my finger under her chin to get her to look at me. Surprisingly she doesn't swat my hand away. Her eyes open and lock with mine, and like it does every time Leah looks at me, my heart stops.

"It doesn't sound stupid to me. You have no idea just how good it is to hear I still know you. Even if only a little bit."

"Why?" she whispers.

"Because there's no one else in the world I want to know more than you, Dove. Do you really not care to know me anymore?" The pain in my voice shocks me. I haven't let myself play out the scenario in which Leah wants nothing to do with me anymore. Because the pain that would come with that would be crippling.

"I'm still dating Jackson." She visibly swallows and drops her gaze. I can't help but pick up on the hint of remorse in her voice when she says his name or the involuntary rage that begins bubbling up in my chest at the mention of them being together—but I do my best to push that down.

"I didn't ask if you were with him. I asked if you want to know *me*, Leah. Aren't you even the least bit curious to know why I left the way I did? Why I ruined the only friendship that ever meant anything to me? Why I was stupid enough to let the girl I was *crazy* about slip away from me?" Her eyes snap back up to mine, her pupils flaring as her breath catches.

"What?"

"*That's* my truth, Dove. I was so completely crazy about you; I wanted you in ways I never should have. And I knew I couldn't risk your friendship with Taylor if I fucked things up between us by telling you. So, I left. I tried to forget about you, but the reality is—I haven't gone a single fucking day without wishing you were mine." I take her face in my hands, knowing she just told me mere moments ago she's still with someone else, but fuck I just don't care anymore. I wanted her to be the one to break but it looks like it's going to be me that breaks after all.

"Sawyer, what are you doing?" Her breaths are short and fast. I press my forehead to hers, my jaw set tight as my need for her finally wins.

"I'm not walking away this time." When my lips finally land on hers, it feels like coming home. I know within the first few seconds that I'll never be the same without her. Her hands land on my sides, and when I dip my tongue into her mouth to deepen our kiss, she lets out the tiniest moan and fists my shirt.

My mind is suddenly clear of anything but her.

In this moment there's nothing but us.

Until someone clears their throat behind us.

Leah rips herself away from me like she's on fire and I can't help but feel as though some kind of instant karma is about to play out.

"Um… Jackson's here."

Yup. That sounds about right.

When Tucker takes a step to the side and Jackson pops out from behind the wall, I look down to see Leah's face has turned completely white.

"Surprise!"

Fuck.

Chapter 24

"Surprise!"

"Second biggest one of the night," I mutter to myself through clenched teeth.

"What?" Jackson frowns, confused because he couldn't hear me. I glance up at Sawyer and just before he retreats to the living room, he gives me a wink that—luckily—only I can see. My cheeks heat instantly, and I try to mask it with a smile directed at Jackson.

Tucker slaps Sawyer over the back of the head as they walk side by side across the room and I can't help but smirk when Sawyer shoves him back.

"Oh, I can't believe I actually pulled that off." Jackson walks over to pull me into an embrace, clearly proud of himself for pulling off this *very* unexpected surprise.

"What are you doing here?" I try my best to sound pleasantly surprised but I'm having a hard time focusing on anything but the phantom feeling of Sawyer's tongue gliding across mine.

"I wanted to surprise you!"

"During the biggest family Christmas gathering anyone's ever seen?" I laugh nervously.

"I mean, yeah. I knew you said you'd be here tonight and even if I don't love being here with all your friends, I still wanted to see *you*. Plus, I can finally meet your parents this way." The one part of my brain that was finally starting to work after the hottest kiss of my life, breaks all over again as I process what he just said.

"What did you just say?" Cocking my head to the side I glare at him until he becomes visibly more uncomfortable.

"What? You don't want me to meet your parents?" He frowns.

"Um, no. I want you to rewind to the part where you said you don't like my friends." I don't let my glare waver for even a moment as I cross my arms over my chest defensively.

"I didn't say I didn't like them. I just... I don't know. They're a lot sometimes. But *you're* not! I just like it better when it's just the two of us." He smiles. He actually *smiles* at me.

"What the hell, Jackson?"

"Is that a problem?" His brows knit together, as my eyes widen. He *can't* be serious.

"Uh, yeah. It's a fucking problem. Those girls aren't just my friends, they're my family. If you have a problem with them then *this,*" I wave a finger between us, "isn't going to work."

"Things just seem to work out better for us when they're not around. Don't you agree? We don't have to get along for you and me to be together, do we?"

He truly thinks we can date and just never see my friends? The people I've shared more than half of my life with?

Suddenly my entire future flashes before my eyes and it's only me and Jackson, a closet full of the same pair of khaki pants in bulk, with no other friends in sight.

"Hey, look...if it's really that important to you, I can try again." He plasters a larger-than-life smile on his face, takes both my hands in his and it takes everything in me not to rip them away. He makes it sound like he's doing me some kind of favor—offering to *try* to like my friends. There are just some things you can't force to happen, and if he doesn't love them already, chances are, he never will.

"I don't think that will be necessary. You should go." I take a step back out of his grip and his face falls.

I wait for him to argue and say he wants to stay and make this work or get angry that I'm not letting things go any further simply because he doesn't like my friends. I mean, I'm sure other twenty-eight-year-old women don't come with four deal-breaker best friends, but I'm not other women, and I *do*.

But, of course, he doesn't fight for me to give him another chance. He simply nods and turns to leave. I should have known he wouldn't care. He's way too passive to fight for what he wants. Or maybe I'm just simply not what he wants anymore.

I hear the front door slam and I close my eyes, fighting the tears that are daring to spill out the moment I lift my eyelids again. I take a few deep breaths, trying to compartmentalize everything that's happened tonight so I can at least attempt to appear merry and bright for the remainder of the evening. Then I feel someone's hands on my arms and my eyes fly back open.

My girls.

All four of them are standing around me in the corner of the kitchen, looking on with concern as I blink away the unshed tears.

"You okay?" Shane asks first.

"What was that about?" Lauren nods to where Jackson just made his unnecessarily loud exit.

"I uh, I think Jackson and I just broke up."

"What? How come?" Taylor asks. Even though it feels like the universe is trying to somehow apologize for constantly screwing me over in the relationship department by giving me a glimpse of what it will be like to be with Sawyer the very same night Jackson revealed his true colors as the perfect shade of shitstain, I can't bear to tell them—on *Christmas* no less—that it's because he has a problem with *them*. So, I roll my eyes and brush it off. That's a conversation for another night.

"Something stupid. It's not even worth mentioning." I give them a half-ass smile as they all scoff and start in on the *We never liked him anyways* speeches that come with the territory of defending your best friend's broken heart.

Only I'm not broken-hearted. Things with Jackson had become mundane at best even before he said what he did about my friends. I thought maybe I missed the spark between us because our first—and second—kisses were tainted by Sawyer's presence. But even when Sawyer *wasn't* around, things with Jackson never felt *electric*.

Not the way my friends made it out to be.

Not the way it was when I was kissing Sawyer.

Then, of course, there was the date where Jackson let our waiter ogle me without so much as a care in the world. Now, tonight, him telling me he doesn't like my friends was simply the last straw for me to justify being *done*.

My heart is… fine.

Or at least it is until I look up to see Sawyer standing in the threshold of the kitchen with hurt written all over his face.

JACKSON
MON, DEC. 25 10:00AM

I'm really sorry for how I handled things on Christmas. I really would like to try and get to know your friends better. Please give me one more chance.

MOOSE
MON, DEC. 25 10:05AM

You and I will never be something "stupid" Dove.

How did I go from the girl who's never had a real relationship to THIS?

RUBY
SAT, DEC. 30 1:30PM

NYE at our house this year? We can do sparklers with the babies before they go to bed then watch the park's firework show from the backyard??

SHANE

OMG that sounds perf. We can bring the sparklers!

TAY

Tucker said he's bringing his own fireworks because he's a man and wants to light something on fire. 😌

LAUREN

Can you tell him to bring me a man instead? I'm gonna have to kiss Maverick at midnight at this rate and I'm not fucking happy about it. 🐕 I wanna make out with someone hot. 😢

ME

You could invite Lucifer and kiss him? 💀

LAUREN

I'd rather lick the floor of a school bus.

RUBY

Tank said you're not making out with his dog.

LAUREN

Asshole.

Cece squeals and smiles so big her rosy cheeks look squished beneath her blush pink beanie as she watches the sparklers come to life. Hendrix is running around the yard with one in each hand, dancing and making every shape he knows while Poe just stares blankly at the one Ruby is holding in the hand opposite of where she's carrying him.

It's crazy to think that just a few years ago we were spending New Year's Eve at Chattahoochies, wondering what the hell was going on with Max and Shane after she mysteriously disappeared during the ball drop. Now they're married with a beautiful daughter and two more of our friends have started families. All because the two of them ran into each other one day.

"Okay, Munchkins. Time for bed!" Tank waves Hendrix in from the yard as he grabs Poe from Ruby's hands and gives her a quick peck on the cheek. Max carries a drowsy Cece in after kissing Shane on the forehead and just like that, the dads of the group are putting their babies to bed. I never in my life would have dreamed I would see either of those men carrying their kids to bed at 10PM on New Year's Eve, but here we are.

"Okay, well. I'm gonna take the furry babies in the house and turn *their* sound machine on so the fireworks don't bug them." Tucker whistles for Riley and Maverick to follow behind him, closing the French doors to Ruby's living room behind him once they're inside.

"Isn't it so weird that *this* is how we're spending our New Year's Eve now?" Shane hugs her blanket tighter to her, taking a seat next to me on the outdoor couch.

My mouth pops open as I spin to face her. "Stop. I was literally *just* thinking that. Get out of my brain." She giggles and leans in to rest her head on my shoulder.

"It's so wild. Two of us are married with kids. I'm next in the queue to get hitched, unless one of these bitches decides to elope or something—" Ruby slaps Taylor's arm, cutting her off.

"Bite your tongue. They better not." She leans forward, switching between me and Lauren as she stares us down. "You better not. We may have gotten married quickly, but at least you guys were there for it." She waves a finger between her and Shane.

"And *who* the hell am I running off with, exactly?" Lauren glares at her.

"Me, obviously." I lean over and kiss her cheek obnoxiously loud. We all fall into a fit of laughter but as soon as it's quiet again I hear the faint sound of my phone going off.

I pull it from my pocket, hovering over my phone while wrapped up in my fleece blanket, and I can feel the moment my cheeks turn red. It's the same moment my heart rate picks up to an unhealthy speed.

MOOSE

Meet me at L27 Rooftop Lounge at midnight.

ME

I kind of already have plans. I'm spending NYE at Ruby and Tank's with everyone. I don't wanna just bail.

MOOSE

Please, Dove?

I lock my phone and clear my throat. "Um. So, I kind of forgot to mention something that happened on Christmas Eve." Everyone stops talking and looks straight at me. Their unwavering attention feels like a big ass spotlight, and I do *not* love it.

"What? With Jackson?" Shane frowns.

"Um, no…with Sawyer." I glance around nervously, and Taylor not so subtly squeezes Shane's arm next to her.

"We kind of kissed." Immediately squeals begin to break out around the circle.

"I knew he looked smug and happy when he walked back in the room after being with you. I just thought he'd called Jackson a mean name or something though." Taylor waves a hand in the air.

"Details!" Shane wiggles in her chair.

"I don't know. We didn't have a ton of time to talk but… apparently, he liked me too. Back in high school I mean, and all he said before he did it was that he's not walking away again."

More squeals.

"What happened?"

"What's wrong?" All three guys come running back out the doors, causing the excited noises to come to a halt.

"Leah and Sawyer kissed!" Taylor screams.

"I know, but it sounded like someone was getting their eyes

scratched out." Taylor levels Tucker with a lethal glare as he finishes his sentence.

"It might be you. What. Do. You. Mean. You *knew?*" she asks and the rest of us slink into our seats further to watch his rebuttal.

"Oh, I just… I mean," he chuckles nervously, looking to Max and Tank for help.

"Nope."

"You're on your own, brother."

"Oh, I think Cece needs her Uncle Tucker." He backs into the house and blows Taylor a kiss.

"Mhm, I'll deal with you later."

"Promise?" He wags his brows and winks at her, making her cheeks turn red as she rolls her eyes. Then the guys follow behind him and we're left alone on the patio again.

"So, what does this *meannnn?*" Lauren grins ear to ear as she shakes my arm. I love that about her. Even though she jokes about wanting a man, and being so lonely she resorts to kissing a dog— she's able to be happy for her friends when something like this happens.

"I don't *knowwww,*" I mock. "Jackson fucking showed up and I haven't talked to him since."

"What! Why?" Ruby exclaims.

"Well, he heard me telling you guys that the reason Jackson and I broke up was over something stupid and I think he assumes I meant the kiss."

"But it wasn't?" Taylor narrows her eyes, as if she's now wondering what the stupid thing was too.

"No. But he left early, and I didn't want to explain unless I could do it in person and now—" I pull my phone back out and open our texts, showing everyone the latest one he sent me. "He wants me to meet him at midnight."

Taylor jumps out of her chair and grabs my phone.

Shane stomps her feet on the ground excitedly.

Ruby claps at the speed of light.

And Lauren shakes my arm again.

"You have to go!" Taylor hands my phone back to me and I look down at the lackluster outfit I'm wearing.

"To a rooftop lounge? Looking like this?" I wave a hand down my body.

"Obviously not. You're borrowing something of mine. But your hair is all cute and curly and you can just throw on some blush and mascara because your skin is sinfully perfect." Ruby pulls me from my seat and starts dragging me through the house.

"Wait. Are we sure this is even a good idea?"

"Only one way to find out." She grins at me as we all pile in the house to get me dressed.

Chapter 25

Sawyer

I check my phone again for the millionth time to see if I have any messages from Leah.

Nothing.

I don't know why I thought she would come. She isn't the one to bail on plans—especially not with her friends. Our entire team was put on the VIP list for this NYE party tonight and even though press is my least favorite part of the job, it comes with the territory. I told one of the guys at the door that I was expecting a plus one and gave him Leah's name—in case by some miracle she decided to come—but as the moments tick by, I'm growing less optimistic that she will.

I grab a whiskey from the bar, shamelessly checking the entrance for her *again,* as someone slides up next to me.

"Well, if it isn't *the* Sawyer Clark." I turn to see her standing with her arms crossed over her chest, with a clutch in one hand and a glass of champagne in the other and a playful scowl on her face.

"Alana Townsend. Holy shit. Long time no see." She finally breaks and a huge smile spreads across her face.

"Yeah, that's what happens when you trade, you asshole." She slaps my chest with her clutch and laughs. "Dad was so pissed when he lost you. This season hasn't been the same without you."

I wave a hand dismissively. "Ah, he'll be alright. He has plenty of talent there, he's just gotta utilize it." I wag my brows and she shakes her head, a soft smile playing at her lips.

"I always admired that about you, you know? You never were afraid to let him know how to use certain players' strengths to the team's advantage."

"Ah, what's the worst he could have done, traded me?" I wink at her, and she rolls her eyes.

"Benched you," she teases, tipping her champagne glass up to take a sip. I place a hand over my heart.

"Oof. Talk about not using your players to your advantage." We share a laugh and simultaneously check our watches.

"I better go find Decker. It was so good to see you, Clark." She lifts on her toes to give me a hug.

"You too, Alana. Give Decker my best if I don't catch him tonight." She gives me a nod before disappearing into the masses. I allow myself to check the entrance one last time for Leah, and my heart skips a damn beat when I actually see her.

She came.

She looks drop. Dead. Fucking. Gorgeous.

Her hair is naturally curly tonight, falling around her shoulders perfectly. She has on a fitted, long sleeve, gray mini dress—that makes me want to drop to my fucking knees—and a pair of blue booties that ironically, match the suit I'm wearing tonight. But, the look on her face nowhere near reflects the elation I'm feeling over seeing her. And when I follow her gaze as it leaves mine, I see Alana floating through the crowd.

Of course she saw me with her and is thinking the worst.

When I turn back to her a look of embarrassment flashes across her face, and she spins on her heel headed straight towards the exit.

Um, I think the fuck not.

I rush through the crowd of people to get to her, not caring who I shove out of the way in the process.

When I finally reach her, I wrap my hand around her arm, causing her to freeze mid step. I take another step closer, bringing her back flush with my chest and I lean down so only she can hear me.

"Where do you think you're going, Dove?" I notice as her shoulders square before she turns around with her game face on.

"Just didn't want to interrupt, that's all." She shrugs her shoulders and looks around the crowded rooftop casually. "Thought if you had found someone to hang out with at midnight, maybe I would find someone to hang out with too." Her eyes lock with mine again and she raises a brow. I glance up to find an empty spot in the corner next to us and gently pull her over to it.

"You're cute when you're jealous. You know that?" I smirk at her, letting her know I'm not indulging in her little mind game. Not tonight.

"I am *not* jealous." She rolls her eyes, but her cheeks betray her, turning that perfect rosy shade they do when she's flustered.

"Well, I sure as fuck would be." Her expression softens and those perfect green eyes find mine again.

"Why did you ask me to come here, Sawyer? It looks like you have more than enough people to keep you company tonight." It's not often I see Leah in a vulnerable state. Anyone else might miss it if they didn't know her—but I see it. The way she avoids eye contact, or distracts herself when she asks questions she's not entirely sure she wants the answer to.

I nod to the right. "That's Alana Townsend, she's my old coach's daughter. She's married to Decker Townsend and has been for four years. They have two kids, and she was like a sister to me the entire time I've known her. And if you hadn't shown up tonight. I *would* have left here alone."

"Oh..." I can't help but smirk when she turns pink from her chest up to her hairline. She may have changed in some ways over the last ten years, but she's still my little Dove at her core.

"And I asked you to come here because I haven't stopped thinking about you since I kissed you. I tried to give you space—to come to terms with what happened and how it may have ended another relationship for you. I thought about calling you to apologize but the more I thought about it, the more I realized I couldn't do that."

"Why not?" She frowns.

"Because I'm not sorry. Maybe I should be. Maybe it makes me a horrible person for not feeling bad about kissing you when you weren't mine. But I just—" I run my hands through my hair, frustrated by how many things I want to say to her. That I've wanted to say to her for so long and haven't been able to.

"Fuck, Leah. I need you. Simple as that. I can't get you out of my head and even more, I don't *want* to. So, if that means taking you from someone else without remorse, then so be it." I take her hands in mine, looking at her until I know she's looking at me, and only me. "I asked you to come here tonight because I need to know if you can forgive me. If you think you could ever let yourself trust me again, because I think you and me...we could be something really amazing. Don't you?"

"Maybe," she breathes. I can see it in her eyes, how badly she wants to say yes.

"What's it going to take for you to give me a chance?" I see a glimmer of amusement flicker in her eyes.

"Maybe I want to see how long it takes for you to beg." She lifts a brow in an almost defiant way, with the same glimmer in her eyes and a smirk on her lips. Suddenly all the blood in my body starts traveling south.

Fuck me. I'm helpless with this woman.

"Say the words and I'll drop to my knees and beg like a dog." I close what little space is left between us, running a hand carefully through her curly hair.

"I don't want to get hurt again, Sawyer," she whispers, and it breaks my heart knowing that I've caused her any kind of pain in the past.

"Then let me heal what I hurt and prove to you that I'm not walking away again." Her eyes flick up to mine and she says the single best word I've ever heard.

"Okay."

"Okay?" My heart picks up speed as I confirm that I've heard her right. She nods her head and smiles softly at me. As the people around us begin the countdown to midnight, I take her face in my hands.

"Please tell me I can kiss you, Dove. That I can let everyone here know that you're mine." She bites her lip, and it completely unravels me. My heart is hers, whether she wants it or not.

"Yes, please."

Motherfucker.

My lips land on hers just as the fireworks go off around us. My hands travel to her ass, and I pull her body flush to mine and her arms wrap around my neck. I swipe my tongue across her soft lips, and she parts them, allowing her tongue to dance with mine. While people shout around us, cameras flash, and fireworks pop in the sky, the only thing I can think is—this is how it was always meant to be.

Me and Dove against the world.

I'll be damned if I fuck this up again.

I wrap my arms around her waist and pick her up, feeling her foot pop out behind her as she squeals against my lips. I finally set her back down, allowing both of us to come up for air, and I'm certain I've never been happier than I am right now.

"Since I'm no longer pretending that I hate you, I guess I'll let you know… you look so sexy in this blue suit." Her hands fist the collar of my jacket as she bites her now swollen lips.

"You should see how I look *out* of it." I wink at her and when her eyes grow wide and her cheeks flame, I know I'm going to have the time of my life making her mine—properly.

Chapter 26

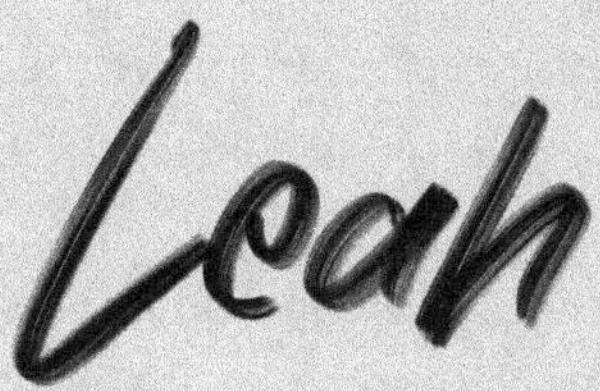

You're fine, heart. Just keep beating. Don't be dramatic.

The image of Sawyer completely naked has infiltrated my mind and I'm now unable to think of anything else. He stands behind me with his arms wrapped around me like a blanket as we watch the fireworks together, and I *still* can't quite believe that we're here.

After all these years, Sawyer and I are actually together. I keep waiting for the alarm to go off and wake me from this dream. But when he nestles his face against my neck and electricity travels down the length of my spine, I know it's real. How could everything I feel when I'm with him be anything *but* real?

"You wanna get out of here?" he whispers against my skin. My heart skips and a nervous energy I wish I could get rid of washes over me.

"Where to?" I hold my breath as I wait for what I feel is the inevitable *"your place or mine"* response.

"Let's go driving." He gives me a smile that takes me back in time. Back to high school when he would make me yell shotgun before anyone else could claim the front seat when we would go driving just to burn gas. Windows down, music up, and laughing until our cheeks hurt.

"Okay." I can feel my cheeks burn as I smile up at him.

He grabs my hand and leads us downstairs, wrapping me in his arms the entire time we wait for the valet to bring his truck around. When the guy comes around to open my door, Sawyer steps around me and stops him.

"I got it, thanks man." He shakes his hand and I see him slip the valet a twenty-dollar bill as a tip. The guy nods and smiles at him gratefully and wishes us a good night.

I think I sometimes forget that Sawyer is a professional hockey player and that they don't make baby bucks like little old school teachers. He's always been just Sawyer to me, but seeing him in this suit tailored to perfection, tipping someone twenty dollars like its loose change and opening the door to his pristine black Ford Raptor makes me feel a little out of my depth.

There's no telling what kind of women he's used to being with either, or what kind of lifestyle he maintains. I have no idea if I'll even fit into his life now the way I might have back when our feelings for each other first developed—and that's a terrifying realization.

We drive around for almost an hour, talking about anything and everything. I tell him about some of my most memorable stories from kids I've taught over the years, and he tells me about some college memories he wished he could have shared with me back when they first happened. He clues me in on the conversation he had with Taylor the night of the hockey game when he threatened Jackson, and it takes everything in me not to pick up my phone and call her to yell at her for not telling me.

I know she was trying to make up for what happened by doing what Sawyer asked and letting him do it himself, so I refrain from yelling at her— for tonight.

We're in the middle of discussing how his season is going, when I bring up the fact that I've kept up with every single one of his games for the entirety of his career.

"You have?" He looks over at me for so long, I'm sure he's going to crash the truck.

"Yes," I reply simply, hoping he'll turn his attention back to the road. He does, but only long enough to pull over on the side of the road and throw the truck in park.

"Every game?" There's a look on his face that I can't quite place, but he sounds confused and...proud? I shrug and nod my head in confirmation. "But I thought..." He blows out a breath and runs his fingers through his hair. I lean back on the headrest and look over at him.

"I still wanted to know you too, Sawyer. It just hurt too much to admit it. That I wanted to be in someone's life that I thought didn't want me there." I chew on my bottom lip nervously as his gaze finds mine.

"Get over here." It's a command more than a request and the deep tone of his voice sends a rush of excitement down my spine. He unbuckles his seatbelt and when I fail to move, he leans over and undoes mine as well. "Now please, Dove."

Oh my god.

"You want me to—" He cuts me off before I can finish asking for clarification.

"Come over here and straddle me." I swallow hard, trying to keep my composure—that I can feel slowly slipping away from me. I have to consciously tell myself to not ask any more questions and just do the simple thing he's asking me to do.

I crawl over to his lap, resting my legs on either side of him as my dress inches further up my thighs. His hands grip my waist, and his eyes fall to my lap where my dress is now only an inch away from exposing the silk underwear I have on, his jaw ticking as he throws his head back on the seat.

"Do you have any idea what it does to me, knowing you wanted me the same way I wanted you all these years?" His hands fall to the slope of my ass, but his eyes never leave mine. The truck is fairly well lit between the lights from the radio and the moonlight filtering in from the windows, allowing me to see just enough of his swimmable blue eyes to know how much he's hurting.

"I think I've got a fairly decent idea, actually." I grin at him, running a hand through his wavy brown hair. I've always loved that Sawyer keeps his hair long. I've imagined what it would feel like to run my fingers through it more times than I can count, so being able to do it now—while sitting in his lap with his not-so-subtle erection pressing hard against his suit pants—feels like a dream I'd gladly never wake up from.

I run my fingers through his hair again, twirling one of the curls before sliding my hands down to hold his face. His perfectly scruffy, gorgeous face. I lean in closer and for the first time ever *I* kiss *him.* His grip on me tightens, making me squeeze my thighs together—or attempt to at least—drawing the sexiest moan from him.

Holy fuck, I have to move or I'm going to ruin *his suit pants.*

I try to pull away in an effort to move back to my seat, but he brings one of his hands to the back of my neck and holds me there.

"No," he growls against my lips and I'm a freaking puddle in his hands.

I can't help but relax against him, loving the way his hands feel on me. I'll deal with the embarrassment of just how much I love this when I finally return to my seat. His hands are in my hair and mine are fisting his suit jacket as our lips move in a way that feels as though they've known each other forever. When he presses his hips forward, pressing his dick against where I'm completely soaked for him, a breathless moan slips past my lips.

He moves his hands to my hips and a little yellow warning flag waves around in my mind.

Shut up, it's fine.

He grips my thighs and for the first time ever I notice just how large his hands are.

God, I bet he could just toss me around like a doll if he wanted to.

His fingertips dance along the hem of my dress, not crossing that line quite yet. His thumb sneaks beneath the fabric and the internal battle I'm having over wanting him to touch me and wanting to ask him to go slow is about to kill me.

"Sawyer," I whisper against his lips.

"Yes, Dove?" With his eyes still closed he brushes the tip of his nose over mine.

"Can we… Can we take things slow?" I can feel my heart in my throat as soon as the words leave my mouth. I don't want this to stop, but I don't want to let things keep going without making it clear what I want.

"I've waited for over ten years to be with you, Leah. I'd wait a hundred more to do anything more than this if that's what you wanted. As long as you're mine." I can't help but giggle at the thought of us being a hundred and thirty before anything more than a hot make out session would happen.

"I don't need a hundred years. I just want to know that this is real. I don't want things to happen so fast and then it be over just as quickly." His eyes meet mine and I realize that my biggest fear just slipped out into the open.

"If it's up to me, Leah. This will never be over. You'll have to demand it before I ever let you go or walk away from you again. And even then, I won't go without a fight."

"Is this really happening? It feels too good to be true—like I'm dreaming," I whisper into the darkness, running my fingertips over his defined jawline. He leans up and kisses me again, brushing a strand of hair behind my ear.

"If it's just a dream, then I pity the fool that tries to wake us from it." He winks at me and I smile back at him.

He looks behind me at the dash and sighs. "I guess I better get you home, huh?"

I turn around and see that it's already 2AM.

"That's fine, but…will you stay a while? Just so we can keep talking I mean. I just feel like we still have so much to catch up on. If you're too tired I understand—"

"I can't think of anything I'd rather do," he cuts me off, smiling as he does. I begin moving to return to my seat—feeling the coolness from the damp fabric between my legs—and stop. "Oh, um… I would just like to go ahead and apologize for potentially ruining your suit pants." His brows knit together in confusion, and I nod, patting his shoulder twice before returning to my seat.

"Oh, fuck me." I peek over at him, but he doesn't look mad. He looks... *Oh.* The animalistic look in his eye stuns me. He just stares back at me, letting his eyes drop to my legs before sinking his teeth painfully into his bottom lip.

"What are you thinking?" I don't mean to ask it out loud—mostly because I'm not sure my heart is ready for the answer—but there's no taking it back now.

"That I can't wait to sink some part of myself between those perfect thighs of yours."

Did I just catch on fire? Because that was the hottest thing I've ever heard spoken out loud.

"Don't worry, Dove. We'll go slow. But you asked and I owed you an honest answer." He smirks at me, and I can't be sure but I *think* he completely breaks my brain. I sit silently in the passenger seat as he reaches over, stopping my heart, as he pulls my seat belt down and clicks it into place.

Then he grabs my hand, kisses my knuckles and keeps our fingers intertwined as he drives us to my house.

Happiest. New Years. Ever.

Chapter 27

TAY

Care to share how the rest of YOUR night went, you gorgeous bitch?!?!

ME

It was fine? I would love to fill you in when I get both of my eyelids open. Why are you freaking out, exactly?

TAY

Sports TEA-V article

I click the link to the article Taylor sent me from one of the hottest sports gossip blogs, shooting straight up in my bed when I see it.

My eyes are fucking open now.

The first picture in the article is a team photo of the Badgers from last night at the lounge, but what has me almost falling on the floor— is the second photo. Because it's a photo of Sawyer and me kissing with fireworks going off behind us. My arms are wrapped around his neck, and his are around my waist, lifting me with one of my feet popped out behind me.

It's actually a really good picture.

But I didn't plan on being on the front freaking page of a gossip column that almost everyone I know reads religiously.

ME

Oh. my. God. 😵

SHANE

BABEEEE!!!! 😍 you should frame that!

RUBY

If the dress is ripped or ruined in some way don't even worry about it 🙂

SHANE

ME

OMG. Your dress is fine & Shane what the hell was that?

TAY

Popping her cherry?

SHANE

Ding ding ding.

LAUREN

Clever. 😏

ME

😳 I feel like I'm texting my kindergarteners.

SHANE

That's concerning. This is much too mature of a conversation for six year olds to be having.

RUBY

Ummmm. Excuse me, how did I not know Le was a virgin???

ME

Probably the same way Sawyer doesn't know. It's never come up. 😵 😬

TAY

Oh, shit.

SHANE

 Ope. My bad babe.

ME

Wait, did you really think I would sleep with him the SAME NIGHT we get together?!

SHANE

Of course not.

LAUREN

Girls night anyone?? Maybe we can discuss how Leah will tell Sawyer she's tighter than Fort Knox but in a sexy way??

ME

Yeah, we're not going to do that...

TAY

Yes we are. Ruby's house after dinner with your parents.

"Mornin' Dove."

Chapter 28

Sawyer

I wake up to the incessant sound of texts *woop-ing* on Leah's phone and I'm immediately annoyed that she's rolled out of my arms.

"Good morning to you."

"Tell my sister and the rest of the spice girls to leave you alone so you can get your ass back where it belongs," I groan, resting my chin on her shoulder as she locks her phone.

"And *where* exactly does my ass belong?" She turns her head, causing her nose to brush across mine.

"With me, of course." I give her a quick kiss before pulling her back flush to my front, burying my face in the crook of her neck. I was worried she may have an issue with me sleeping in my boxers—seeing as how we came straight here after the NYE party I was required to be at and I had no other clothes—but from the way she's pressing her ass against me and purring like a content kitten, I'd say she's fine with it. She smells like vanilla, just like she always has, and it makes me want to taste every delicious inch of her.

You're taking it SLOW, asshole. Pull back.

"You stayed," she whispers, turning to face me. The still sleepy yet soothing tone of her voice sends a rush of excitement down my spine.

"Of course I stayed, wherever you are is where I want to be too, Dove." When she drags her bottom lip through her teeth, I can't help but pull it out with my thumb before leaning in to bite it myself. "What are you doing today?" I force myself to change the course of conversation before I end up doing something stupid.

"Before I answer, can I show you something?"

"Of course." She grabs her phone from the nightstand and taps on the screen a few times before turning it towards me.

"What are we going to do about this?" she asks, a look of worry on her face that I don't quite understand.

"What do you mean? Do you not like the photo?" I take the phone from her hands and examine it closer. It's probably my new favorite picture because damn it looks like she's mine.

"No, I mean, it's magazine worthy, but I just wasn't sure you'd be okay with it." She shrugs, chewing on the sleeve of her sweatshirt. I lock her phone and toss it to the other end of the bed.

"I told you last night that I wanted everyone to know you were mine. I wasn't just saying that to hear myself talk, Dove. I meant it. You're mine now, and I want every damn one to know it." Her cheeks turn rosy, and she smiles at me. "Okay." I lean down and kiss her the way you should kiss your girl on a Sunday morning—sweet and lazy —like you have nowhere else in the world to be. However, when my dick thinks it's his turn for some attention, I pull back to keep myself from even thinking about going for more.

"So...you were going to tell me what we're doing today." I clear my throat and wrap my arms around her, settling into the pillows behind us.

"*I* usually just do boring stuff until I go to dinner with my parents. Then *apparently* we're having girls night at Ruby's after that. Which should be illegal on a work night." Even listening to her talk about her daily plans is fulfilling to me. I truly can't wait to see how she spends all of her time.

"What's the boring stuff?" I run my fingers carefully through a few strands of her hair.

"Laundry. Grocery shopping. Cleaning my house." She looks up at me and rolls her eyes. "I told you—boring stuff."

"Can I do them with you?" She rears back with the cutest frown on her face.

"You want to do my errands with me?"

"I told you; I want to be where you are. If doing the *boring things* means I get to spend today with you, then hell yeah, I want to run errands with you." Her cheeks turn pink, and she smiles so brightly I wish I could freeze this moment and capture it to hold onto forever.

"Take a picture, it'll last longer." She sticks her tongue out at me, giving me the inclination to do just that.

"You know what, that's a great idea." I grab my phone off the nightstand next to me as she begins trying to wiggle out of my arms.

"Sawyer, no! I was kidding. Don't take a photo of me right now I look—"

"Perfect. You always look perfect to me, Dove." She pretends to fight me for the next few minutes while I snap god only knows how many photos, hoping I have at least *one* that won't be too blurry to stare at when I miss her.

"Are you letting me spend the day with you or what?" She bites down on her bottom lip and smiles.

"Fine." She rolls her eyes, swinging one of her legs over my waist to straddle me. "But if you die of boredom, I am not to be held accountable. You've been warned." I push her sweatshirt up, allowing my hands to rest on the bare skin of her hips.

"How could I ever be bored with you?"

I pull back up to Leah's house after going home to shower—and put on something a little more comfortable than the three-piece suit I wore over here last night—feeling more excitement than one man should over spending a simple Sunday with a simple girl.

Simple, but extraordinary.

Extraordinary because she is the only person in the world that has ever given me butterflies, the only person who set up camp in the forefront of my heart and mind and refused to leave—even when all hope felt lost of having her in my life somewhere other than just my imagination. She grabs my attention the moment she enters a room and captivates me in a way that makes me want to get completely lost in her.

Simple because those are the things she enjoys most in life. A beautiful sunset, the way water crashes against a riverbed, or a well written plot twist—simple. It never has taken much to make Leah happy, but that's not going to stop me from trying to give her the whole damn world.

I hop out of my truck, slamming the door shut with my elbow—careful not to spill any coffee—and before I'm even halfway up the driveway I can hear music blasting from inside.

I manage to knock on the door with my foot and hear her yell "Come in!" The music only grows louder once the door is open and I can hear the unmistakable voice of Lana Del Ray.

I make my way through the house, setting our coffee down on the kitchen island before Leah reappears in the living room with a laundry basket in tow. She has on a pair of light gray sleep shorts and a lavender sweatshirt, with her hair still damp from her shower and her glasses perched on her perfect nose.

She smiles at me as she continues to sing along to the song pouring out of the Bluetooth speakers mounted in the corners of her living room. I take a seat on the barstool, crossing my arms over my chest watching as she sways her hips and folds some of her T-shirts. She doesn't let me stay there long before she walks over and pulls one of my hands free, spinning herself beneath my arm. I quickly fall in line, pulling her closer to me, taking her other hand in mine as I spin her around the living room.

Her laugh is so carefree and her smile so content but they both shift into a look of shock when I start to sing one of the verses with her.

I never made it a habit to sing in front of other people, but when I see the way Leah's eyes widen and her mouth pops open, I assume those who have told me that I can were right. I bend down to kiss her, loving the way she stands on her toes to reach me better. I pull her legs around my waist and when her tongue hits my lips, I wrap one hand behind her neck and eagerly let her in.

We stay like this until the song changes and when she goes to pull away it takes everything in me to let her. I swear I could kiss this girl forever and never grow tired of the feeling of her lips on mine.

"You can freaking sing?!" She clears her throat and slaps my chest, clearly amused by this new revelation. She slides down my body until her feet hit the ground again and when she steps away, I turn to grab our coffees off the island with a shrug.

"Eh, can't everyone?"

"Not like *that,* no. You should hear Max on karaoke night," she snickers, taking a sip of her coffee before setting it down on her coffee table.

"Okay, what can I do?" I clap my hands together, raising my brows eagerly.

"Sawyer, you really don't have to do anything."

"Pfft. Are you kidding me? The faster we get all this shit done, the sooner we can snuggle up on this couch and you can read this amazing book to me." She rolls her eyes playfully when I pick up the book I got her for Christmas that's sitting on the coffee table. "Someone really great must have gotten this for you." I plop down on the couch and grin. She begins pulling more laundry from the basket and folding it as I flip through the book, careful not to let her bookmark fall out.

"You really like it though?" She side-eyes me as she shakes out a pair of blue jeans.

"Are you serious? That book is *kind of* the whole reason we're together," she giggles.

"And here I thought it was my charming, good looks and persistence in breaking you and the ferret up."

She frowns. "The what?"

"Never mind." I slam the book shut and turn it around, looking at the blurb on the back.

"To answer your *ridiculous* question, yes. I love it. Laura Pavlov has been one of my favorite authors for forever." I catch the playful smile on her lips when she answers.

"What's your favorite book by her?" Roll my head on the back cushion of the couch and notice the distant look on her face. Like she's thinking really *really* hard about her answer.

"Too hard to pick a favorite or?"

"Always Mine. It's the first book in one of my favorite series." Her answer is clipped as she shakes her head and goes back to folding her laundry.

"Cool. I'll have to read it sometime." I toss the book back on the coffee table and she glares at me. "What's next on the agenda?" I reach into her laundry basket and pull out the first thing I touch, which is—much to my delight—a pair of her underwear.

Not just any underwear though, a pair of black, silk underwear that I now can't stop picturing her in. I clear my throat and see the moment her face goes from focused to panicked. She tries to snatch them from me, but I pull them back where she can't reach them.

"Sawyer, give me my underwear!" She continues reaching for them until she's standing between my legs, and I take the opportunity to pull her into my lap. She squeals as I adjust her legs to straddle me comfortably.

"No chance. Because *these*," I hold them out to the side, still too far out of her reach, "have my imagination running *wild* wondering what you have on under those little gray shorts." Finally letting her grab them from my grip, she fists the black fabric in her hand and levels me with a stare.

"I'm not wearing anything under them right now." Her brow lifts and her eyes fall to my mouth as her tongue peeks out to wet her lips. When she pushes off my shoulders to stand, my hands grip her waist before she can get her feet back on the ground and her eyes snap back to mine.

"I don't believe you." I watch her carefully, waiting for nerves or timidness to make themselves apparent.

Neither do.

Instead, she settles herself back down in my lap. "I guess you'll just have to find out for yourself."

Fuck me.

"Don't tease me, Dove," I warn. Just last night she told me she wanted to go slow, and I have every intention of respecting her wishes. But I'm not the type that has to be told twice.

"What? You're just checking to see if I'm lying or not." The innocent way she shrugs, with the most seductive look on her face, has me hard as iron—which I'm sure she can feel through both of our sweats.

"And if I slide my hands into these tiny little shorts and find that you're *not*. Then what?" Her cheeks flame as her teeth bare down on her bottom lip. "Do you want me to get up and walk away, Dove? Or do you want me to play with that pretty little pussy?" Her lips separate the slightest bit, and I can't stop myself from reaching up to bite on her delicious bottom lip.

"I'm gonna need you to tell me exactly what you want from me." My hands slide painstakingly slowly up her thighs until my fingertips are teasing the hem of her shorts. Her chest rises and falls more quickly now and she visibly swallows.

"I want you to touch me, Sawyer," she whispers, her dark green eyes that have a way of calming my soul locking with mine.

God she's so beautiful.

"Atta girl." I reach beneath the loose-fitting shorts and when my fingertips make it to her hips—without a trace of underwear to be found—I have to catch my breath with the realization that she really wants this.

Wants me.

What really floors me is the way she holds my gaze. While my fingers trail down to her swollen clit, and as they swipe through her wetness her eyes never leave mine. Something primal awakens in my chest that I've never felt before. The absolute *need* to make this woman mine and ensure no one else ever touches her again roars to life. My fingertips tease her entrance and her eyes flutter shut.

"Don't stop," she whispers.

Dammit, she's gonna ruin me.

I push one digit inside her and feel her walls squeeze around me. If she's this tight around my finger, I'm going to have to make sure I take my time with her before I fuck her. Which is all I've ever wanted with her—time. She's biting her lip so hard it looks as though it might start bleeding soon if she doesn't release it.

Reaching up I wrap my free hand around the back of her neck to pull her lips down to mine. She kisses me with fervor as her hips rock against my hand, sending all the blood in my body straight to my cock. God I can't wait to know how she feels wrapped around me. I slide a second finger into her, and she lets out a moan, breaking our kiss.

"You can do it, baby. Just relax. It's just me and you." I can feel the moment she lets me in, and her lips meet mine again. Her walls begin to tighten around me, and her lips slow their movement against mine.

"Sawyer," she pants. When her eyes lock with mine again the look on her face fucking kills me. There's a mix of worry and satisfaction and I don't quite know what to make of it.

"Let go baby. Come for me." She grinds her hips, rubbing her clit against my palm with every movement while chasing that high. When she digs her nails into my shoulders and cries out in satisfaction, it's the most beautiful thing I've ever heard.

Chapter 29

Holy Shit. That just happened. Okay, everything is fine. Just breathe.

Sawyer pulls his hand out of my shorts and just when I think I'll be able to get my heart rate to slow, he sucks the same to fingers that were just inside me into his mouth.

"If you ever want me to touch you, Dove. All you have to do is ask." He leans up and kisses me again, turning my heart into a puddle for him.

I've wanted to know what it would feel like to have this man's hands on me for far longer than I care to admit. I thought I was going to lose my damn mind last night sleeping next to him in nothing but his boxers. I deserve some kind of medal for not telling him to take me in every way he could think of right then and there. Or maybe I'm an idiot for *not* doing that.

When it comes to Sawyer, *complicated* is the best way I can think to describe my feelings. I've never cared for anyone the way I care for him, but the hurt I've felt over him in the past isn't something you get over easily. Sure, it's been ten years since it happened, but I've only recently found out *why* it happened, and it still stings. Even so, I want him more than I want air most days.

His thumbs rub lazy little circles around my thighs as he leans back and looks up at me.

I have no idea what to do now. I still want to take things slow… *ish*, but I can definitely feel how hard his dick is beneath me and *wow*. But I have no idea how to do…*that*. I mean, I know *how*, I don't live under a rock. I just have zero experience and if he made me come with two of his fingers while sitting down—that's kind of a hard act to follow.

"Okay! You ready to get some groceries?" And just like that, he eases all my worries and answers my unasked question. He drums on my ass playfully and helps me stand back up.

"Uh, yeah. Let me go change real quick." I smile, adjusting my shorts that are hanging a little too far to one side.

"I'll take your coffee out and warm up the truck." Then he kisses my forehead and walks out the door. Like he's done this a million times before.

Has he?

Was there someone else he did lazy Sundays with? I mean it's not like I didn't miss out on ten whole years of his life. He could have been married and divorced in that time frame. I mean, sure I probably would have heard about it because there's absolutely no chance Taylor could keep that information to herself, but my intrusive thoughts refuse to acknowledge *that*.

I glance down at the book on my coffee table and smile. I know Sawyer too well to be worried about any of this. No matter how many times I've tried to deny just how well. If I want to know about his past, all I have to do is ask.

I run to my room and throw on a pair of leggings and my favorite high-top sneakers before locking up and heading out to go grocery shopping.

With the guy I've loved forever but only been with for a day.

My life makes no sense to me but I'm just gonna roll with it.

"Regular or barbeque?" Sawyer stops in front of the basket and holds up two bags of chips.

"Neither. Sour cream and cheddar." He places the bags back on the shelf and scans the aisle until he finds the right flavor. "What about you?" I tip my chin at him.

"Barbeque. Duh."

Some things never change.

The Clark household used to have a family sized bag of BBQ chips on hand at all times, just for him. God help the poor soul that touched that bag without asking—it literally had his name on it.

"What are you laughing about?" He nudges my arm, bending down to rest his elbows on the basket handle next to mine.

"Do you remember when you used to write your name on a family sized bag of chips and you would get so pissed if anyone would eat them without asking?" I laugh.

"Yes, because JJ always left it empty and Tot would only leave crumbs and claim she *didn't eat them all,*" he says defensively.

"You always shared with me though." My eyes narrow on him as a memory resurfaces.

"You were the exception." He winks at me and gives my ass a slap before taking my list from me. I stop him before he gets too far down the aisle.

"Hey Sawyer?"

"Yes, Dove."

"Was there ever anyone else? That you did this kind of stuff with?" I'd like to say my nerves are settled as I ask him this in the middle of the grocery store, but that would be a big fat lie.

"Do what? Grocery shopping?" I let out a small laugh because I can tell how serious he is in asking that.

"No. Boring Sundays. You seem… I don't know. Too good at it for it to be your first time?" He lets out a laugh now, and I feel completely ridiculous for even bringing it up.

"While I like the idea that you think I'm experienced," he says with a wink. "No, I've never done the lazy, boring Sundays with anyone before."

"Then why does it seem so natural? The way you can shift from…" I lower my voice and step closer to him. "From what we did on the couch to telling me you're gonna warm up the truck and have my coffee waiting for me?"

"Because it *is* natural to me." I can feel the confusion written all over my face and he takes a deep breath, taking my hand in his. "You're still my best friend, Dove. Being with you has always felt easy to me."

"So boring Sundays are special? Just for us?" I smile, wrapping my arms around his neck.

"Boring Sundays will always be just for us. I promise." He presses a quick kiss to my lips then pats on my butt playfully. "Okay! Last movie that made you cry?"

Sawyer continues our little game of twenty questions while we check everything off my list before heading to the register to pay.

DING.

MOM

Hey sweetheart. Dad and I aren't feeling so well tonight. I'm so sorry. Is it okay if we skip dinner tonight?

ME

Oh no! I'm so sorry you guys aren't feeling good. I'll drop some dinner off for you both and we can pick back up next week. Sound good?

MOM

You don't have to get us anything. Next week sounds great though. 😊

ME

I am bringing you dinner, Mom. Don't argue with me. 🩶 Do you need anything else?

MOM

Okay then. Yes, actually could you pick your dad up some cold medicine? The kind that dissolves in hot water? It always seems to kick this junk the fastest.

ME

You got it. I'm at the grocery store now so I can drop it off in about half an hour.

MOM

Thank you sweetheart. I love you.

ME

I love you too, Mom.

"Everything okay?" Sawyer asks, leaning against the basket handle as he studies me with a worried expression.

"Oh, yeah. Sorry. My parents aren't feeling well. They asked to cancel dinner but I need to grab my dad some cold medicine." I look around the store for a pharmacy sign.

"I hate to hear that. Is there anything else we should grab for them?" My heart swells in my chest hearing Sawyer's concern for my parents.

"I don't think so. I'm just gonna grab the medicine from the pharmacy, I'll be right back."

After finding medicine for my dad, grabbing food from a restaurant Sawyer recommended—because they have a really clean menu which is good for Dad's dietary needs—and dropping everything off at my parents' house, we make it back to my place right around sunset.

"So. How was your day of doing boring things with me? Ready to run back home yet?" I laugh, unlocking my door as Sawyer carries almost all of the groceries he bought for me in one hand. Yes, he bought my groceries, and paid for my parents' dinner—because why not give me one more reason to find him insanely perfect?

"This might just be my favorite Sunday to date." There go those damn butterflies again. Fluttering to life at the sound of his voice, at the idea he enjoyed a lazy Sunday with me. At the way he comes up behind me, after setting the bags on the island, spinning me around in his arms.

"I hear you're free for dinner tonight?" He brushes the tip of his nose against mine, picking me up around my waist prompting me to wrap my legs around him.

"It appears so." My arms drape lazily around his neck, and I smile as his eyes land on my lips.

He walks me over to the kitchen island, setting my ass down on the empty space as the tension in the air grows thicker. He doesn't say a word, he simply runs his hands down the length of my spine, squeezing hard when he gets to my backside before pulling me closer to him. Then he leans in and kisses my neck, licking and biting in a way that has me wet within seconds and sends my mind into a tailspin.

"Dove," he growls against my skin as my head falls back.

"Yes," I whisper pleadingly.

"Can I take you to dinner tonight?" His kisses trail up my jawline and he nips at my ear before standing back to face me completely. When I finally catch my breath and focus on him, he actually looks *nervous*.

"Sawyer Clark, are you asking me out on a date?"

"I am." My heart does a somersault in my chest because I never thought this day would happen. Not in this lifetime at least.

"I would love that." I bite on my cheek to keep my smile from bursting at the seams.

"Alright then," The boyish smile on his face and the strong Tennessee accent in his response has seventeen-year-old me absolutely *screaming* on the inside.

"Let's get stuff finished up here then we can get ready to go, sound good?"

God, I love an assertive man.

I nod in agreement and just like it's been the rest of the day, Sawyer flawlessly transitions from a heated moment to putting laundry away for me like he's been part of this routine forever. Meanwhile, I can't stop thinking about what happened on the couch before we went grocery shopping and wondering if he had the same inclination I did to let it happen again on the island before he asked me to dinner.

As I'm putting the last bit of groceries away, Sawyer comes walking back out of my bedroom with something in his hand, but what really gets my attention is the pained expression on his face.

"What's the matter?" My brows knit together as his head shakes back and forth.

"You kept this?" Now it's my turn to frown. I look down at the blue and yellow hoodie I've had since tenth grade with our school's hockey logo on it and my expression softens.

"Of course I did. You gave it to me." He begins closing the distance between us, coming to a stop right in front of me.

"Even when you hated me. You kept it? You...sleep in it?" The strain in his voice as well as the way he visibly swallows make his emotions clear.

"I never hated you, Sawyer. I just *wanted* to hate you because..." I roll my lips together, unsure if now is the time for this conversation.

"Because why, Dove?" The agony in his face is pleading with me to finally be truthful—with him and with myself.

"Because I never stopped loving you." I've never seen a man get emotional. Not directly at least, and *never* about me. But the way Sawyer's chest is rising and falling with short, quick breaths and the sad joy that's now in his eyes, it's unmistakable.

"You *loved* me?" His voice cracks, making my heart squeeze and my eyes begin to water.

I nod in response. "Well...yeah."

"For how long?" The strain on his voice breaks me in ways I never knew were possible.

"For as long as I can remember," I whisper. "Ever since you first called me Dove." He breaks down, letting his hands cup my cheeks and he presses his forehead to mine.

"Why didn't you tell me?" His voice is soft like a whisper, but full of pain.

"Because we became friends, and I didn't want to lose you. And —" I drop my head, looking down at my socks until he pulls my gaze back to him.

"And?"

"I was convinced you'd never look at me the way I always looked at you. I was just your little sister's best friend for a while, then we were friends, then I was... nothing." I can almost feel my heart breaking all over again as I hear the collapse of our relationship voiced aloud.

He steps back and pulls his shirt over his head, making me breathe a little deeper when I take in his perfectly sculpted, tattoo covered body. He grabs my hands and places them on his ribs, making my face twist in confusion.

"I've wanted you for far longer than you even realize, Dove. I've only seen *you* for over ten years. You engrained yourself into my mind so deeply, that when we went our separate ways, the only way I could make sure I had some part of you with me always, was to etch you into my body as well." When the realization hits me, I look down where he placed my hands, a small gasp leaving my lips when I see it.

An angel wing is tattooed on the left side of his rib cage with the word *Dove* closing one side. I run my fingertips over the scalloped part of the wings, my vision becoming blurry behind my glasses.

"When did you get this?" I ask, wiping the tears with the sleeve of my sweatshirt.

"About a week after Halloween."

"Why this? Why there?" I point to the tattoo again. He smirks as he caresses my cheek with his thumb.

"You were dressed like an angel that night. When the girls left you in the corn maze and we started walking together, you got scared and you grabbed onto me so tight that you left nail marks on my ribs right here. The scalloped part of the wings are the outline of your fingernails. When they started to fade it felt too much like a sign of what was to come. I knew I didn't want them to fade because I didn't want our friendship to either, even though I was pretty certain it would, given the way I was having to avoid you. So, I got them inked in permanently. Your name, well, I should hope that one is obvious." He smirks, but it's a sad smirk—not playful or flirty like the ones I've grown so fond of. I wrap my arms around him, resting my head on his bare chest, basking in the warmth and the wild rhythm of his heartbeat.

"I can't believe we lost so much time." He kisses the top of my head, running a hand through my hair.

"I know. But we're together now. And I'm not losing another damn second with you."

Chapter 30

Sawyer

She loved me.

I don't think I'll ever be able to forgive myself for not handling things differently back then, but I'm sure as hell going to be handling them better from here on out.

DING.

Leah grabs her phone off the counter as texts continue to come in one after another.

"Shit," she whispers, biting on the inside of cheek.

"What's wrong?"

"I forgot I was supposed to go to Ruby's after dinner with my parents tonight." She tilts her head up to look at me, and I can't help but love that she looks a little disappointed about that. Since the alternative was going on a date with me.

"That's right. The should-be-illegal-on-a-work-night girls' night."

"That's the one." She points her finger at me, giving a sarcastic smile. I can tell how torn she is over having to choose between canceling her already established plans and the ones I sprung on her at the last minute.

"Go have your girls' night." My encouragement earns me a scowl from her that makes me laugh. "*That way* I have time to plan some-thing really good for us to do for our first date." Her expression changes immediately, and a warmth appears across her cheeks when she smiles.

"Okay." I lean down and take her lips in mine, basking in the way that this feels more right than anything else ever has. Not even my skates hitting the ice compares to the way I feel when I kiss this woman.

I force myself to pry my lips from hers and grab my keys from the counter before turning to head out. "Tell the spice girls I say hello." I wave over my head.

"Which one am I?" She calls after me, causing me to turn around just as I reach the door.

"Which one is baby spice?" Her face falls into a scowl again.

"Get out of my house." I bark out a laugh when she throws her hand up, directing me to leave.

"Catch you later, Dove." I give her a wink and head home.

Chapter 31

If today taught me anything it's how easily I could get lost in Sawyer. In the way he looks at me, touches me, the way he makes me feel like I'm the only person in the world when we're together. Which is how I ended up completely forgetting that I was supposed to be at Ruby's about ten minutes ago.

When I walk in the door, I can already hear laughter pouring from the kitchen and see Hendrix singing the ABC song to Poe on the living room floor. He says his brother is going to be the smartest baby because he's going to teach him everything he knows—which is everything.

"Having all the fun without me?" All the girls turn to face me when I make it to the end of the island in the kitchen.

"Well, it's not our fault you're *late!*" Shane throws a chip at me with a smile on her face.

"*Sorry*, I got a little caught up."

"How are Loretta and Allen doing?" Taylor asks, popping the top of her diet soda open.

"You *must* stop calling them that."

"And disrespect your mother's wishes? Absolutely not." I roll my eyes and slide onto the countertop, crossing my legs before reaching into the party size bag of chips.

"So, what happened last night?"

"Tell us everything!" Ruby and Lauren say one after the other.

"Well, when I first got there, he was talking to one of the most gorgeous women I've ever seen in my life." I startle when Taylor let's out the *most* dramatic gasp I've ever heard in my life.

"That bastard!" She slams her hand down on the countertop.

"What's a bastard?" We all turn to face Hendrix walking to the fridge to retrieve a juice box, with Tank following closely behind.

"That's what you were before I married your mom." Ruby slaps Tank's arm so hard *my* skin tingles.

"Tank Landry!" she scolds him. He sucks air through his teeth and rubs his arm.

"Jesus, Honey. It's just the truth. You know I don't lie to him." Her argument is an eye roll because she knows he's *technically* right—even though none of us would have said it out loud. Hendrix is the smartest kid I know and his relationship with Tank is one of the most beautiful things I've ever seen. The trust and honesty between those two has created a bond I don't think we'll ever see severed.

"We're going to play LEGO's!" Hendrix announces excitedly, completely forgetting the previous conversation being had.

"Build me something super cool." Ruby leans down and gives him a kiss before he takes off down the hall.

"I will!" he shouts. Tank waves behind his head and follows Hendrix's lead.

"I will kick him in the balls, I don't even care if he's my brother." Taylor flawlessly resumes our conversation.

"It turns out she's his old coach's daughter, she's married and has two kids, and they were just talking, but it still hurts—seeing him with someone else. I almost ran right back out the door." A few of them nod in understanding, waiting for me to continue. "I don't know. Maybe it's just my own paranoia but I just can't shake the feeling that he'll end up leaving again. Or that he just needs to get me out of his system before he moves on to something better." I hang my head, a little embarrassed that I still feel this way. He's done nothing but assure me that things will be different now that the air has been cleared between us, but it's almost an involuntary emotion—associating Sawyer with possible heartache.

"First of all, there *is* no one better for him than you. That's painfully obvious. *Second* of all, I don't think he's just getting you out of his system. You don't hard-launch a relationship like this if you're planning to bail," Shane says, turning her phone towards me. I see the same photo of us from the article Taylor sent me this morning and pay it no mind.

"That's not a hard-launch. It's not even a launch. That whole party was literally just for the press. He didn't have a say in that getting published." I grab a chip and pop it into my mouth, watching as her brows draw together.

"Please take this phone and look again." She shoves her hand out further and I take the phone from her, seeing that the picture is actually part of an Instagram post by Sawyer himself. I read the caption first, *"This might just turn into the best year of my life."*

Hello, butterflies.

Then I swipe to the right and my heart stops. Ruby suddenly pops her head further over my shoulder and screams.

"BITCH WHAT!" Ruby yells.

"What?" - Taylor

"Did he post something else?" - Shane

"Someone show me the damn phone, *now!*" - Lauren

I swipe once more—seeing a photo that I was unaware he took of me looking at popcorn in the grocery store—before handing the phone back over to Shane. Taylor and Lauren are stuck like glue to either side of her trying to see the screen better. Mouths hang open, squeals erupt from all of them, and my cheeks are absolutely flaming, as my stomach twists uncontrollably.

"Talk faster, because if you don't give context for that second photo right the fuck now, I'm gonna pass out," Lauren demands.

Referring to the photo Sawyer took of us in my bed this morning. It's a little blurry, but you can still make everything out perfectly. My wild curls thrown into a bun, me trying to hide behind my sweatshirt sleeves as he has an arm around me kissing my temple.

"Was Fort Knox invaded?!" Lauren gasps.

"Umm... Am I needed for this conversation?" Tank must have some God given gift of showing up during the absolute *worst* moment of conversations.

"*NO!*" We all shout in unison. He rears back and frowns, wiping his hand down his chest as if he's been physically hit by the impact of our answer.

"Y'all are mean when you're together, you know that?" We all burst into laughter as he grabs a water bottle from the fridge and watches in fear and concern as he exits the kitchen again.

"*No*, it wasn't... Not completely at least." You could suddenly hear a pin drop in this kitchen. It gets so silent.

"I'm not gonna scream, I'm not gonna scream, I'm not gonna scream." Taylor closes her eyes and chants to herself.

"I fucking might," Shane argues, leaning forward on her barstool.

"So, he stayed over last night..." Taylor grabs onto Shane's arm like she might fall over—even though she's sitting down. "But nothing happened. We just got back late and talked and he...*stayed*." I shrug with a grin creeping its way across my lips.

"Awwww!" They sing together.

"*Anyway*... He asked if he could spend the day with me, so I said yes, and... I *may* have not put underwear on after my shower, and he *may* have found out. In a *very* climactic way."

"I've never been so happy in my life," Lauren coos, grabbing my head and pulling me to her chest.

"I can honestly say, me neither." Genuinely happy looks come from every single one of my friends and my heart feels full.

"I hope you know you could have fucked that man eight ways to Sunday on the same night you had your first kiss, and we would be nothing but happy for you," Ruby assures me, pulling my mind back to the fact that I still have to find a way to *tell* Sawyer I've never slept with anyone before.

"Random hockey player, he's just a random hockey player," Taylor whispers to herself, making me narrow my gaze at her.

"It's how I keep things separate so I can indulge in these moments with you without remembering it's my *brother* we're talking about." She makes a fake gagging face and I roll my eyes at her.

"Well, I appreciate the support, but I still have to *tell* him I've never been with anyone before and hope he isn't bothered by it."

"Look, I'm not claiming to be an expert on men, nor am I one, but I have a really strong feeling that he'll be more than okay with it." I give Ruby all my attention as she speaks.

"Guys like the idea of being your first, they're weird and possessive that way. But *that man*? He's so obsessed with you it's impossible to imagine him being anything but elated by the information."

"How do you figure that?" I ask, skeptical of her assumption.

"Because I've had a front row seat to the way he looks at you for the last three months. I don't know *how* these bitches never picked up on it. But if he's been looking at you like that for as long as he says he's been. It's not going to be a problem. I wouldn't even sweat it."

This kind of conversation may seem unnecessary to some—or inappropriate to those who don't know what it's like to have friends you can say literally *anything* to—but this is our dynamic. We share what's on our minds and what's happening in our lives, and we always walk away feeling better about things afterward.

Which is exactly how I feel now when leaving Ruby's tonight.

After getting in my car, I pull my phone from where I left it in the cupholder and see a tag on Instagram from Sawyer—making those same butterflies from before awaken all over again—as well as a text message from him.

MOOSE

Now there's no mistaking who's girl you are. 😏

ME

Feeling a little possessive are we?

MOOSE

No. Not a little. Very.

My thighs clench together as an ache forms between my legs for him.

That's never happened before…

No shit, Sherlock. You've never been with him before.

MOOSE

If you're waiting for me to apologize. It's not gonna happen. Get used to being mine, Dove. 😌

ME

I think I can get on board with that.

MOOSE

Atta girl.

Sweet Jesus, I'm wet.

Before I even put my car in reverse my phone goes off again.

TAY

Post Fort Knox convo we forgot to ask you about…
You guys wanna do Broadway this weekend? Do
our out on the town night early this month before
house hangs start??

ME

Sounds good! Let me know what time and I'll see if
Sawyer is free.

TAY

I love her dramatic ass.

Chapter 32

Sawyer

I tried like hell to stay awake last night so I could call Leah when she got home but staying up until after 3AM on Saturday night has me fucked up. I barely got my eyes open enough to reply when she texted me back last night, and I was out like a light within minutes of our conversation ending. So, with my five o'clock alarm going off right now it's taking everything in me not to throw my phone across the room.

I silence it with a groan and push myself out of bed to get on with my day. After getting a run and a quick workout in, I take a shower before dressing in my Badgers hoodie, a pair of blue jeans, my old Yankees cap and running shoes and I'm out the door by six. Which is a new personal best for me.

TUCKER

Congratulations, I think you're married now.

attachment of NYE photo

TANK

Wow. He beat you to it. 🤭

MAX

Are we sure Taylor actually even likes you at this point?

TUCKER

I have reputable proof that she does 😏

ME

I will remove myself from this group chat so fast if you start talking about your sex life with my sister.

TUCKER

TANK

ANYWAYSS... Looks like you got your girl then? Congrats man.

ME

You are the most in touch with your feelings group of guys I've ever met you know that? And thank you. Just gotta keep her now.

TUCKER

That's because we're all in therapy. We're some healed motherfuckers who learned how to express their feelings. 🧘

MAX

Are you doing their commercials now or something???

TANK

Max is still new to therapy. You'll have to ignore him.

ME

No no. I like Max's vibe. Don't try to change him.

MAX

Nah, they're right. I need some healing too. But don't worry, I'll still be an asshole. For you. 🥺

ME

What the fuck is happening?

TUCKER

Are you guys coming this weekend?

ME

Is WHO coming to WHAT?

MAX

They're like one day into this Tucker, she probably isn't TELLING him what they're doing yet...

TUCKER

Fair. We're going out this weekend. Hitting up Broadway. You should come.

ME

If Leah's there, I'm there.

TANK

whipped GIF

ME

"Iced mocha latte!" I slide my phone into my back pocket and grab the Bruman's cup from the counter, smiling at Clara before darting out the door.

ME

Mornin Dove.

DOVE

Good morning to you. 😊

ME

Hey, what time do you usually head to work?

DOVE

I should be leaving now but as luck would have it, I can't find my keys. 😉

ME
Perfect.

DOVE

Huh??

I pull up by her mailbox and throw my truck in park before rushing up the front porch stairs. *Why the hell am I nervous?*

I knock on the door and a few seconds later, it's swung open and everything in my mind goes quiet. How does she always look so damn beautiful?

"Mornin' Dove." I smile at her as a pleasant look of surprise washes over her face.

"Good morning to you," she repeats the same response she gave me over text. "What are you doing here?"

"Freezing my balls off if you don't invite me in." Normally the cold doesn't bother me. I mean, I *do* have a career where I spent most of my time on *ice*. However, it's a whopping twenty-eight degrees outside today with a *breeze* and my hair is still damp from my shower.

"Of course, come in!" She swings the door open wider, ushering me inside. As soon as it closes behind her and her coffee cup is safely on the entry table, I pull her body into mine. She lets out the cutest little gasp just before my lips land on hers and I can feel her smiling as she melts into me. I wrap her legs around my waist, not only because it settles our height difference, but because I need to have her as close to me as is physically possible. I place a few light kisses to her lips, one after another, and she lets out a content laugh.

"Since you're no longer freezing your balls off, what are you doing here?" My head falls back in laughter, planting her feet firmly on the ground again.

"I wanted to bring you some coffee before you head into a full day of handling kids that are still riding the Christmas high." I turn and grab her coffee cup from the table and present it to her. "Plus, I'll take any excuse to see my girl." I wink at her and the apples of her cheeks heat as she smiles up at me.

"Is there anything wrong with you? Like, at all?" She glares up at me.

"What do you mean?"

"You are like, frighteningly perfect. You do boring Sundays with me; you show up with coffee." She glances at the label and laughs. "My *favorite* coffee. You had no issue telling me exactly how you felt about me, no matter how many times I told you to leave me alone—"

"Well, that was never gonna happen, so..." I shrug playfully, making her smile. But it only lasts a second before it falls along with her gaze as it drops to her feet.

"Do you do this for all the girls you date?"

"Of course not. This is all for you." I smile and brush a strand of hair behind her ear.

"How many people *have* you dated before?" She still won't meet my eye, and that fact along with the questions she's just asked me doesn't sit right with me.

"Define *dated*." Her eyes snap up to mine and the urgency behind it worries me. "I never really dated anyone, but I did have my puck bunny phase just like every other college hockey player."

"So, you've just..." Her lips fall into a frown as she waves her hand around. "Oh, well hey, that's fantastic. For you, for them. For everyone really."

"Dove..." My brows knit together as she becomes slightly frantic, looking around the room.

"Shoot, look at the time, I really better go. Don't wanna be late."

"Dove?" I try getting her attention again, but she goes on ignoring me.

"Oh look! My keys." She grabs them out from behind a plant sitting on the table next to us and pulls her jacket and bag off the hooks on the walls.

"Leah!" My voice is as firm as I can make it without shouting trying to get her attention but her eyes just fall closed. "What is going on?" I plead with her to tell me.

"Sawyer, I really need to go. Can we talk later?" When she looks up at me again her eyes are glossy, and my heart physically aches to know what happened to put her in this state. I want to argue and say I won't leave here until I know what's wrong so I can fix it, but I know she really does need to leave now to get to work on time.

"Of course. Call me later?" It kills me to say, but I don't have a choice. She nods and reaches up to kiss my cheek, holding the door open for me to leave first.

I stay in my truck, watching her lock up and pull off down the road, all the while replaying our conversation over and over again.

What the hell did I say?

I just wanted to bring her coffee and see her before work, but I feel like I somehow ruined her day before it even had a chance to start.

My focus is complete shit the rest of the day. I went home and laid on my couch, staring at the ceiling replaying my morning until it was time for me to get up for practice.

"Wherever your head is, Clark, get it back on before tomorrow's game. You're a hell of a good defenseman but you played like shit today."

Tell me how you really feel, Coach.

"Will do."

"Everything good man?" Matty grabs his stuff from the locker next to mine.

"Yeah, just a little distracted." I check my phone again but still have no messages or missed calls from Leah. It's past five at this point so I know she's done at school.

"Would this have anything to do with that gorgeous new wallpaper of yours?" Matty smirks, nodding to my phone. It's face up with a picture of Leah and me from the other morning.

"Yeah. It'll be alright. I'll see you guys tomorrow." I stand and gather my things, not in the mood to discuss what's going on in my head with anyone but Leah.

I pull up to her house and park in the same spot I was in earlier, wearing the same exact thing I wore earlier because I've been unable to function like a normal human being ever since I left here this morning. When I notice her car isn't in the driveway I begin to worry.

It's nearing six o'clock and though I'm sure she could be out with the girls, at her parents' house, or literally doing anything else she wants—my brain only knows how to go straight to the worst-case scenario. Just as I'm grabbing my phone to call and check on her, she pulls into the driveway. I breathe a sigh of relief, but it's quickly followed by the same feeling of worry I've had all day that she may not even want me here.

Too fucking bad, cause here I am. And I'm not leaving until I know she's okay.

I hop out of my truck and run over to take the box she's just pulled from the back seat from her hands.

"Let me help with that." When she smiles up at me it instantly relieves some of the tension I'm holding in my shoulders.

"Thanks." She's quiet as we walk up to the front door, and all the way inside to the island. "You can just set that on the ground there." I do as she's asked and when I stand back to my full height she looks as nervous as I feel. Her arms are crossed over her chest as she avoids looking me in the eyes. All I want to do is pull her into me and fix whatever is wrong.

But I have to know what that is first.

She glances at the door and her brows draw together. "Have you been here all day?" That makes me laugh.

"No, I left shortly after you did." She nods in understanding. "I came back straight from practice because I didn't like how we left things this morning. I just wanted to make sure you were okay." I test my luck and reach for her arms, and she lets them fall, allowing me the opportunity to take her hands in mine.

"So, are you? Okay?"

"Yeah." Her voice is small, like she's hiding from the question.

"Really? Because you practically threw me out the door this morning." I laugh, hoping to break some of the ice around us.

"I'm sorry. I just… I don't know how to do this, Sawyer." She runs her hands through her hair, putting distance between us again as she walks around the kitchen.

"Do what? Be with me?" When she finally stops on the other side of the island, she looks up at me, her face red and looking like she's on the verge of tears.

Shit, is that really it?

"Do you not want to be with me?" My heart is holding on by a thread waiting for her to answer. I'm not quite sure what I'll do if she says she doesn't.

Die, probably.

"Of course I want to be with you! I just… I don't know how to *be* with you because I've never *been* with anyone before." She rolls her eyes, swiping angrily at a tear that has fallen.

"That doesn't make sense to me, Dove. You were with *Jackson*— and for far too fucking long might I add." Saying his name instead of one of the many alternate things I've called him over the last three months is challenging enough, picturing her with him is pure torture.

"I've never *been* with anyone, Sawyer." Her words come out slower, more emphasized and I feel like a fucking idiot when it hits me. I close the massive distance between us—because fuck that right now —and stop only when I'm towering over her.

"You mean—" I stop myself briefly, ensuring I don't make her feel uncomfortable when I clarify. "Leah, are you still a virgin?"

"Yes, I'm still a virgin." My heart acts like a complete fool as feelings of joy, guilt and pure shock fight for dominance over the situation.

"Yesterday, when you came for me…" I glance over to the couch, then back at her. Her face turns a bright red and I know the answer before I even ask the question. "How far *have you* gone?"

"I only ever kissed someone. Until you." My heart feels like it's going to bust through my chest cavity and do a damn victory lap around the block. "So excuse me for being a little embarrassed by my inexperience since the guy I'm dating could probably fuck his way through every sorority house in Massachusetts if he wanted to." I struggle to hear anything past the fact that she's still a virgin.

Knowing that I'll be the first person to experience that with her sends an elation soaring through me that I don't care to contain. But I still hear the worry in her statement, and it makes me wonder if that's part of why she pulls back with me. Outside of what's happened in the past, when we do finally steal moments alone and it feels like things are going well, she clams up the moment any kind of spark passes between us. Until this morning, at least.

"Is that why you pull back with me sometimes? Because you're worried about your lack of experience?"

"Among other things…" she admits, letting her gaze fall once again to the floor.

"What other things?" She finally looks up at me, tipping her chin with a confidence I find wildly sexy on her.

"Honestly, Sawyer. I am scared you're going to leave me again. That if I let my guard down, you'll take what's left of my heart and leave me in pieces." *Shit.* "The fact that I won't compare to the other women you've shared your life with is just an added worry that joined the mix a mere twelve hours ago."

"I am the farthest thing from perfect, Dove, but I hope you know I will never stop trying to make up for the way I've hurt you in the past. I want to do boring Sundays with you—*only you*—and bring you your favorite coffee before work just so I can kiss you. I want to plan the perfect first date for us because if there's anything I want to get right in life, it's this. *Us.* I want all of it with *you.* No matter how many women I've been with in the past, I've not *shared my life* with any of them, because *you* are my life. *You're* the entire reason I traded to the Badgers and moved back to Nashville. Because I knew if there was even the slightest chance in hell you could be mine, I had to do whatever possible to make that happen. You are incomparable. Nobody is you, Leah, and nobody but you has *ever* had my heart. If anyone gets left in pieces this time, it'll be me, because the only way this ends is by *you* walking away. I told you I'm here to stay. You just have to let me in." She swallows hard and I watch her expression carefully. An unsureness still flickering in her eyes.

"You traded just to be with *me?*"

"Of course I did." My brows pull together as if that question could only have one possible answer.

"You say so many beautiful things, sometimes it's hard to know if you're real or not." I pick her up and place her on the island beside us, taking her face in my hands before letting my lips crash into hers. My hands tangled in her hair and hers fist my shirt as our lips dance together like they were only ever supposed to be with each other. Her hands move to my chest, resting perfectly still over where my heart beats wildly in my chest—only for her.

"This is the realest thing I've ever felt in my life. The only thing I've ever been sure of. I want you to be mine, Leah. Completely, fear- lessly mine."

"Then I'm yours, Sawyer. Completely and fearlessly."

"Atta girl."

Chapter 33

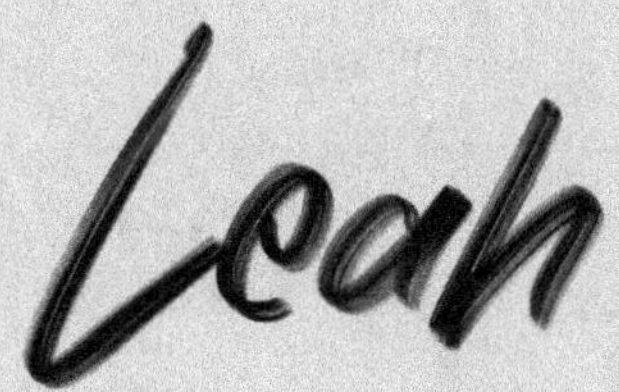

I never knew how exhilarating it would be to voice my concerns about being with Sawyer, *to Sawyer*. I feel so much lighter. Like I'm walking on air. Although, that could also be from the way Sawyer is kissing me like he'll die if his lips aren't on mine right now.

That motherfreaking 'atta girl' is going to bring me to my knees for him, I already know it.

I know I can't live my life scared of being hurt by him, especially not when he's here telling me he'll do everything he can to prove to me that he won't. That would just be stupid on my part, and I've never thought myself to be a stupid woman.

"Hey, what are you doing this weekend?" I ask, breaking our kiss.

Sawyer clears his throat, clearly stunned by the abrupt stop. "Umm. Going out. Broadway, I think?" I rear back and he laughs.

"I've been inducted into the guy's group chat. They informed me about it." He shrugs.

"Holy shit. You got in with the grumpy bunch?" He barks out a laugh and it's one of my favorite sounds to date.

Seeing Sawyer smile is one panty-melting thing.

Hearing him laugh? Fills my heart to the brim.

"Well, seeing as how Tucker is going to be my brother-in-law soon, and I kind of recruited Tank's friendship shortly after I met him, it wasn't too hard." I can't fight my smile knowing how well he's getting along with my best friend's husbands—and one's soon to be husband.

"So, you're not busy then? No games, or big parties to be at?" I tease.

"Nah, games are tomorrow and Thursday, and I don't go to parties unless it's mandatory. Not quite my scene." He presses his forehead to mine, a playful look in his eyes.

"You're away for tomorrow's game, right?"

"Yes, don't remind me," he growls, burying his face in the crook of my neck making me giggle when he keeps nuzzling like he can't get close enough.

"Why?"

"Because I can't take you with me," he mumbles into my hair then leans back and looks at me. "Can I?"

"No!" I giggle louder, making him groan in disapproval again.

"Then I'm staying here tonight." I feel my heart stutter and Sawyer smiles against my neck. "I just wanna spend time with you, Dove. Don't go overthinking it on me."

"I wasn't," I lie.

I was one hundred percent over thinking it.

He leans up and grabs my thighs, giving them a reassuring squeeze.

"I am going to do this right for you, I promise." He pulls one of my hands to his lips and kisses the top of it, simultaneously giving me a wink.

I stopped imagining what my first time sleeping with Sawyer would be like a long time ago. Then I stopped picturing sleeping with anyone all together, too put off by the idea of being with anyone but him in that way. So, I know no matter how it happens, it'll be perfect because it'll be with Sawyer—and I don't see how that could ever not be right.

We end up ordering pizza, letting the TV play in the background and talking until I can barely hold my eyes open. Then he carries me to bed, strips down to his boxers and slides in next to me.

I'm woken up by the sound of Sawyer's voice saying my name. At first I can't tell if I'm still dreaming or not, so it takes me a moment to realize I'm hearing him in real life. The rasp to his sleepy, already deep seductive tone has me wetter than I already was from said dream.

"Leah," he says again.

"Mmm," I groan back. "What? I'm sleeping," I mumble.

"Dove, if you don't stop grinding your sweet little pussy on my dick in your sleep, you're not going to be getting much more of it." His arms are wrapped tightly around my torso, and his lips are brushing over the shell of my ear and that's when I realize I am latched onto him like some kind of horny koala bear.

Someone just bury me under this house, please.

"I am so sorry." I barely slide my leg over an inch before his hold on me tightens.

"Don't you dare fucking move."

"But I thought—" He releases me just enough to let me lift my head to look at him.

"You better have been dreaming about me." His voice is so sexy he could probably *talk me* to the finish line at this point.

"Well, it wouldn't be anyone else that's for damn sure." I'm grateful for the low lighting in my room because I can feel how red my cheeks have gotten.

God it's like I have some kind of illness around him where I can't *not* blush at everything he says or does. He flips us over so I'm on my back and he's hovering over me, slowly sliding his hand down towards my sleep shorts.

"How wet am I going to find you if I slip my hand in these little shorts of yours, Dove?"

"Slip it in and see,"

Bitch, what did you just say?

Fuck it, here we go.

I bite down on my lip, still riddled with nerves but trying to remain calm. I want this with him, I want it all with him. I just have to step into my confidence about it.

He slides his hand up the loose shorts, finding me without any underwear—again.

Am I doing it on purpose? Yes. Yes I am.

When he slides a finger inside me with ease he groans and presses his forehead to mine.

"Do you want me tonight, Dove?" My heart pounds and my pussy aches for his touch.

"Yes," I half whisper, half whine.

"Tell me how. What part of me do you want?" I see the muscle in his jaw tighten as he stares back at me with a fire burning behind his gorgeous blue eyes. Not ready to say it out loud yet, I run my fingertips over his lips—realizing just how soft they are to the touch.

"You want me to eat your pussy?" I bite into my bottom lip and nod. "Then say it with that beautiful voice of yours." He frees my lips from the hold of my teeth, and I almost pass out from how fast my heart is beating.

I can't do it. I can't do it. I can't do it.

"I want you to eat my pussy."

Holy shit, I did it.

"Thank fuck." He leans down and captures my lips with his, moving his hand back down to my shorts to untie the drawstring. Once it's undone, he slips his hand into the waistband and teases me further. Running a finger—then two—through the wetness between my legs before rubbing my clit. He better get down there fast because I'm already about to come apart.

"Sawyer, please?" He nips at my neck then descends down my

body. Pulling my shorts from my legs and discarding them to god only knows where.

"I got you, baby." His hands caress the sides of my hips as he kisses the inside of my thigh, taking a deep breath just inches away from where I need him to take the edge off. Then he gently glides his tongue through my lips and growls in a way that quiets everything else in my mind but him.

"You taste so fucking sweet; I may never come back up for air." Then he goes back down, and I die in the most lovely way. Every flick of his tongue, every kiss, every time he sucks me into his mouth with the perfect balance of firmness and tenderness, I let go a little more. Then he slides his fingers inside of me, curling them to hit every pleasure point he can, and I completely fall apart. Hands tangled in his hair, hips grinding against face, and one final *"Atta girl, come for me, baby"* and I'm met with the most mind-altering orgasm I've ever experienced.

It starts in my legs and travels all the way up to my nose, as he savors every last bit of my release. Even after I'm on the descent of my high and he slides his fingers out of me, he wraps his hands around my thighs and continues gently licking and kissing every inch of me in a way that gives me a feeling so foreign I wouldn't dare try to dissect it in my current state.

He wipes at his chin, then crawls back up my body until our eyes are locked. "Was that as good as your dream?" I wrap my hands around the base of his neck as he smirks at me.

"You're better than anything I could ever dream of." The playfulness disappears and he leans down to kiss me—slow and deep, letting his tongue explore every inch of my mouth it can reach—sending a fresh wave of desire between my legs.

"I'm completely addicted to you, Dove."

The feeling is mutual, Moose.

Chapter 34

Sawyer

DOVE

Good luck tonight hockey star

ME

You sure you don't want to just quit your job so you can make it to all of my games?

DOVE

Why do I feel like you're serious?

ME

Why would I joke about that?

DOVE

Sawyer!!

ME

Catch you later, Dove

DOVE

You better 😊

"That's what I'm talking about! Let's fucking go!" I can't contain the adrenaline running through me any longer when Matty slaps the tie-breaking shot into the net right before time runs out. We all tackle him and celebrate yet another win making it an undefeated season for the Badgers so far.

Just as I'm walking back to my locker from the showers, I hear my phone go off, smiling when I see the photo of Leah and I lighting up the screen.

DOVE

What an assist. 😓

ME

Were you able to watch?

DOVE

Sure was!

ME

They let you watch a game during a parent-teacher conference?

DOVE

attachment 1 image

No way.

I click on her contact and put the phone to my ear. It only rings once before her voice fills the line.

"Hey there hockey star."

"See, that sounds so much nicer coming from you than when Tucker says it." I smile when I hear her laughing. "You're here?"

"I am. Our meetings ended a little earlier than expected so I ran home and changed and then came straight here." That gives me an idea.

"What are you wearing?" The guys start hooting and hollering, acting like complete idiots—the way men do in locker rooms.

"How scandalous of you to ask," she teases. "Why don't you come find out."

"Oh, I intend to. Come down here and wait in the hallway, I'll be ready in ten."

"Ready? For what?"

"Our first date, what else?" I smirk when the line goes quiet. "Ten minutes."

"Okay, bye." She hangs up and I dress in the suit I showed up in tonight instead of the clothes I was *planning* on leaving in. Exactly ten minutes later I'm walking out of the locker room with my bag slung over my shoulder, and when Leah comes into view I come to a halt. She is wearing a blue dress that makes me want to blind anyone else who's had the absolute privilege of looking at her in it.

The peasant style sleeves are long and flowy, gathering around her wrist more tightly, while the skirt is layered and dangerously high on her thighs. She has on some gray booties with it, and I physically cannot pull my eyes away from her.

"You okay there, Moose?" She blushes and my feet finally start working again.

I stalk towards her, dropping my bag a few feet away from where she stands, and when I finally reach her, I wrap my arms around her ass, careful not to lift her dress when I pick her up, and kiss her. She wraps her arms around my neck and kisses me right back and it isn't until some of the guys start to exit the locker room, starting with their shenanigans, that our kiss breaks.

She bites down on her bottom lip and buries her face in my neck, giving me a sense of pride. Knowing that she's mine and that she finally feels comfortable and safe with me is a feeling I won't ever take for granted.

"I'm better than okay. And you look absolutely breathtaking tonight." I finally put her feet back on the ground and she grabs the collar of my suit jacket, taking me in.

"Back at you. I can't decide what I like you in more, your uniform, your suit or your boxers." She raises a brow, causing my dick to follow suit.

"Want me to let you see option number three again? To help you make a final decision of course." I wink at her, and she playfully rolls her eyes. "Ah, maybe another time then, I've got better plans for us tonight anyhow." I wrap my arm around her, grabbing my bag from the ground as I lead the way to my truck.

When we pull up to the restaurant Leah's eyes light up. It's notorious for being booked out for months but they're also known to have the best drinks in Nashville and if there's one thing I've learned about Leah—and the rest of the girls—it's that they can appreciate a good mixed drink.

"Are you serious? This place is impossible to get into!"

"I may or may not have a standing reservation here." I shrug, and her eyes grow wide.

"How rich *are* you?" I bark out a laugh, unbuckling my seatbelt and she mirrors my movement.

"Oh, come on now, I was sure you didn't care about that stuff." She shrugs at my teasing tone as I get out to round the truck and help her out.

"I don't," she says simply, lacing her fingers through mine as I walk a step ahead of her the whole way up to the entrance.

"Good evening Mr. Clark, your usual table?"

"Yes, Maggie. Thanks so much." The hostess smiles and leads us through the quiet restaurant to the table in the far-right corner.

"I live a modest life; the way Momma always told me to when I made it big. I make smart investments, only spend what I need, and when I do decide to splurge, I make sure it's on important things. Your money goes a lot further that way." Leah nods in understanding, propping her elbow on the table as she studies me.

"You are never going to stop surprising me, are you?"

"I sure hope not." I wink and lean in to kiss her but before I can, we're interrupted.

"Leah Gates?" A voice I don't recognize pulls Leah's attention away from me, her eyes widening as her mouth pops open.

"Joshua Miller?"

I look up to see a guy standing by our small, round table, the look of joy on his face matching Leah's which immediately pisses me off. I spent long enough trying to convince her she should be with me instead of the weasel, I'm not in the mood for any more distractions.

I take the opportunity to grab the back of Leah's chair and pull it seamlessly closer to mine, placing my hand on her leg somewhere between her knee and the bottom of her dress. Never breaking eye contact with the guy. Though he doesn't take his eyes off of *her*.

Motherfu—

"I can't believe it. I mean, what are the chances I'd run into you after all these years?"

My jaw is clenched tight, trying to keep myself from asking who the fuck this is and how the fuck they know each other. Especially when she pops out of her seat and rounds the table to give him a hug.

"I know! Oh my gosh, it's so good to see you." I grab her hand and pull her back into my lap. Startling the guy and causing Leah's head to whip around to look at me.

"Who's your friend, Dove?" I shoot a charming smile—my press smile, as I like to call it—to the guy to ease some of the growing tension.

"Sawyer, this is Josh. We went to college together. He went to Peru after graduation to teach and—I still can't believe you're here!" she says, shaking her head in disbelief. Josh just nods at me with an awkward grin on his face.

"I'm so sorry, I'm so rude. I'm just still in shock. Josh, this is my boyfriend, Sawyer. He—"

"*The* Sawyer?" His eyes widen and even though she's not facing me, I can see Leah turning red. *So, she talked to him about me?*

"The one and only." I extend my hand and Josh shakes it firmly.

"Wow. I mean, that's great. I'm really happy things worked out for you, Le." I internally growl at the nickname. How fucking close were they?

"Thanks Josh. It was really good to see you." She smiles sweetly.

"Yeah, I better let you two get back to it." *Josh* waves and waltzes further into the restaurant. Leah, however, becomes eerily still.

"*The* Sawyer?" I question, "Care to explain that?"

"Um...no?" She tries to stand but I place my hand back on her thigh, though this time my fingertips have disappeared beneath the fabric of her dress. She's hidden behind the tablecloth so no one can even see where I'm holding her, but I still see the way her head swivels around the restaurant.

"Dove?" She sighs and her eyes lock with mine.

"Josh and I met in college, and we became fast friends. He was honestly one of my *best* friends while I was there." I attempt to ignore the blood thumping in my ears.

That time should have been ours.

"You already had friends." I'm aware I sound completely insane right now, but I told her I was a jealous motherfucker—and I meant it.

"Who were all away at different colleges..." The look on her face as well as the ultra-slow pace of her words tells me she's aware she's reiterating something I already know.

"Anyways, he ended up catching feelings for me that I didn't recip-rocate. I told him I didn't feel the same way and felt comfortable enough to tell him *why*—which is where you come in. He was really understanding, and it was so close to graduation that we didn't really have time for it to become awkward before he left. This is actually the first time I've seen him since he asked me to go with him." She casu-ally stares out into the restaurant, meanwhile my heart falls through the seat of my chair.

"He did what?"

"What?" Her eyes meet mine again, and her brows pull together like she's trying to figure out what she missed.

"He asked you to go with him to *Peru?*" My heart is back and beating so hard it's almost painful.

"Oh, uh... Yeah." Now it's me looking around the restaurant, but mostly to keep myself from spontaneously combusting.

"How close were you two, exactly?" Every word feels like acid on my tongue.

Her head tilts to one side. "Sawyer, come on. That was *years* ago. You know I haven't been with anyone—"

"Hop up, Dove." I pat her hip and her face turns to sheer panic.

"No," she argues. I pick her up and move her from my lap, grabbing her hand as I walk us outside. I made a promise I wouldn't walk away again, and I don't want her misinterpreting this as me doing so, but I can't fucking breathe in this restaurant right now. If I don't get out soon I *will* be making a scene.

When we make it outside the cool air hits my lungs, and I relish in the way it allows me to pull in a full breath. Leah follows behind me until we're stopped in front of an alley, far enough away from the crowd gathered outside the restaurant.

"Sawyer what the hell is going on?" She crosses her arms over her chest, and I run a frustrated hand through my hair.

"Oh, I don't know, Leah. I just found out that some guy thought the two of you were close enough to ask you to go live across the world with him, so—"

"But we *weren't*," she argues, her voice low but shaking.

"Really? *He* apparently thought you were!" The idea of her being that close with anyone else pisses me off—but not at her. Not even at the other guy. At myself.

She wasn't in my life during those years because of *my* decisions, and the realization that she could have ended up with someone else, living in another *country* with them, makes me want to go back in time and knock the shit out of twenty-year-old me.

"But we *weren't*, Sawyer. We weren't!" she shouts back now.

All I can do is shake my head. She runs her hands through her hair as rain starts falling around us.

"God! This isn't fair, Sawyer. You don't get to be upset about me having a *friend* in college, when you got to go around fucking anyone you wanted to during that same time. You didn't see me throwing a fit over *that* when I found out, did you?"

"That's different. Those girls meant nothing to me! I never saw a future with them. I never even saw a tomorrow with them. It was just a stupid way to blow off steam and fill a void. This guy clearly saw a future with you!"

"But *I* didn't see one with *him!*" she shouts, taking my face in her hands, my chest heaving with every breath I take.

"Don't you get it, you idiot? I have only *ever* been able to see a future with *you!* I couldn't get you out of my head. No matter how hard I tried, you were there, Sawyer. You've lived in my mind and my heart since the moment I met you. No one compares to you. I. Am. *Yours*. So don't let people from my *past* make you think I'm not!"

"Say it again." I grip her hips, letting my fingers dig into her skin as the rain begins falling harder.

"I'm yours, Sawyer." Her thumbs caress my cheeks, a gentle comparison to the fierce way our words have been coming out and my lips come crashing down on hers. Our kiss is needy and desperate to make each other understand just how in this we are.

"Take me home, Sawyer," she breathes against my lips. "Let me show you how yours I am." The heart that was once beating twice its normal speed stops at her words.

"Are you sure?" My eyes lock with hers and she nods.

"Yes."

Completely abandoning the plans I had in store for the evening, I kiss her one more time and take her home.

Chapter 35

ME

Ruby, I need your help. I need it as fast as possible and with as few questions as possible.

RUBY

Hit me with it.

ME

I need you to tell me the basics of how to give a good blow job.

RUBY

I am honored that you came to me for this.

Okay, first and foremost. Hide your teeth. No room for those bitches in a blow job. Lots of spit. Like, don't bother trying to clean up, it helps. Use your hand at his base by his balls to pump while you work some serious magic with your tongue. Flatten to take him further, swirl to play with the tip, that shit drives them wild. And lastly… Ask him to teach you how.

ME

Thank you, but uh, why? You just told me everything.

RUBY

So he can teach you how to give HIM a BJ. Specific to his wants/needs. This way you go in prepared, but he can also tell you things he wants.

ME

Duh. You're the best.

Chapter 36

Sawyer

"Are we going to your house?" Leah asks from the passenger seat with her fingers intertwined with mine.

"We are. Is that okay with you?" I glance over and she smiles softly and nods.

We pull into the driveway, and she stays surprisingly quiet the whole drive up. I watch her face closely, curious what she's thinking.

"Wow." Is all she says, and I can't help but smile.

We're parked on the circle drive right by the front porch of the massive farmhouse, and as soon as she steps out of the truck her eyes dance around, taking it all in.

The porch wraps around both sides of the house and there's a swing hanging to the left that my mother would be proud of—perfect for watching the sunset.

The black exterior is accompanied by walnut stained columns, shutters and a double front door. There is floor to ceiling windows all around the house to allow for the most natural light but have automatic shades for convenience inside.

When we walk through the door she stops taking in her surroundings and instead, turns to *me*.

"Sawyer," she whispers.

"Yes, Dove?" Our voices echo in the open space.

"I'm a little nervous." We're still soaked from standing outside in the pouring rain when I wrap my hands around her arms.

"If you've changed your mind—"

"No," she cuts me off quickly, but doesn't say more.

"I'm going to take care of you, Dove. Do you trust me?" I dip my head, catching her gaze.

"Yes,"

"That's my girl." I shoot her a wink to help ease her nerves, and she smiles up at me. "Turn around." Tipping my chin to direct her, she turns and faces away from me.

Her breath catches when I step closer, brushing her hair away from her neck before I press my lips there. She tilts her head, opening the space for me to explore further. I run my hands along the wet sleeves of her dress before reaching for her zipper and my fingers begin sliding it down. She takes a deep breath when I stop at the end of its path and my lips leave her skin. I slide the sleeves down her arms, and her dress hits the floor with a wet *plop*.

I stand back and admire the way her ass fills out the blue lace underwear that match the bra she has on—that I'm sure her breasts are perfectly poured into.

"You wear this for me?" I run my finger beneath the clasp of her bra, toying with the idea of popping it off. She turns her head, looks up at me over her shoulder and nods.

Fuck.

I lean down and kiss her because it's impossible not to.

Guiding her to face me again, I drop to my knees, and she sucks a breath in. Staring up at her, I smirk before unzipping one of her booties and pulling it from her foot. Trailing kisses along her thigh before taking her other foot in my hand and repeating the motion.

When I'm back on my feet her hands find the collar of my suit jacket and she slides it off of my shoulders, keeping those intoxicating green eyes locked on mine as it hits the floor, and she begins fumbling with the buttons on my shirt.

She has no idea how many times I've imagined this very moment.

When my shirt is discarded on the floor with my jacket, her dress and shoes, she starts at the belt I'm wearing, and my cock reaches a record breaking hard.

I never knew how intimate having my pants removed could feel, but the way she's looking at me while she undresses me makes me feel more connected to her than I've ever felt with another person.

I kick my shoes off and she slides my slacks down my legs, looking up at me once she's on her knees and fuck if I've ever seen anything more beautiful. She stands back up, looking at me with such anticipation and desire in her eyes I can't keep my hands off her for another second. I scoop her up and her legs immediately wrap around my waist as I head towards my bedroom. Burying my face in her neck, I breathe her in and squeeze her tighter. On que she runs her fingers through my hair, and grinds her pussy against my abs.

Throwing the door to my room open, I walk over to the dresser and set her on the top of it, expecting her to look around the space, but her eyes stay locked on me.

"Just tell me to stop if you change your mind or want to slow down, okay?"

"Okay." She nods, wrapping her hand around the back of my neck, pulling my lips back to hers. My hands grip her thighs when her tongue slides across my lips and she presses herself closer to me. I reach the side of her lace underwear and rip them at the seams, eliciting a small gasp from her before letting the fabric fall out of the way, allowing me to slide my fingers inside her.

As soon as I do, she moans and bites down on my lip, causing me to let out a moan of my own. I pump my fingers in and out of her, curling them to hit her sweet spot as she paws at me like she can't get enough. Finally, she pulls her lips from mine and I am rewarded with the sweet sound of her little pants.

"Sawyer, oh god!" Her hips rock in rhythm with me, and as soon as my thumb presses against her clit and my fingers curl inside her, she comes apart. Letting her arousal completely soak me, her nails dig into my arms as her climax hits and it awakens the animal inside of me that is absolutely *starved* for this woman. I pull her from the dresser and walk to the king sized bed in the middle of the room.

The remnants of her underwear fall to the ground and once we reach the mattress I sit with my back to the headboard, letting her straddle my lap. She bites down on her lip when I let my thumb run over the floral detail of the lace on her bra. My hands sneak around her back and release the clasp, pulling the straps from her shoulders before the fabric is laying on my chest and her perfect, full breasts are finally on display for me.

"Fuck." Her cheeks are rosy, her tits heavy with desire, and her perky nipples are begging for my attention. "You are perfect." I grip her waist, pressing my painfully hard cock against her, the arousal from her first orgasm soaking through my boxers. I take my time pinching and sucking each of her nipples into my mouth, trying to get my fill of her in every way possible.

Truth is, I'll never get my fill. She's already become a drug for me, and I'm a willing addict.

I kiss her from her chest to the slope of her neck before tilting her head so she's looking at me again.

"Lift up on your knees." She does as instructed and I slide down until my head is flat on a pillow below me.

"What are you doing?" she giggles, her legs being spread wider to allow for my shoulders to fit between them.

"I want you to ride my face." Her mouth pops open then snaps shut again.

"Uh, I don't— What do you mean?"

"I mean, sit your sweet pussy right here." I gently pull her up once more to line her entrance up with my mouth. "And ride my face the same way you were riding my hand when I had you falling apart on that dresser a minute ago and come down my throat."

"You have a filthy mouth." Her cheeks flame red as she's looking down at me.

"Dove, you haven't heard the half of it." I try to gently pull her down, but she flexes her muscles and keeps herself hovering above me.

"You're gonna suffocate!" she argues.

"Then let me die fucking *happy*." I pull her down and this time she falls into place with a gasp when my tongue slides into her. The animalistic groan that comes out of me must encourage her to relax a little because as my tongue glides from her entrance to her clit, she starts grinding her hips and without prompting, grabs onto the headboard. I reach up and play with her tits, pinching and rolling her nipples as little moans of pleasure fall from her lips.

"Fuck, Sawyer, *fuck!*" Leah cries out, riding my tongue like it's her sole purpose on earth.

When she looks down at me, I shoot her a wink and she comes down my throat with my name on her lips. She rides out every wave of her orgasm and I relish every moment she's seated on my face. She slides down my body—allowing me to sit upright—her cheeks flaming, and her expression sated, a vision of absolute perfection. I brush her hair back with my hands, taking her lips in mine.

"Lay back for me, baby." I rub the tip of my nose over hers when her eyes fly open.

"Wait!"

Chapter 37

"What's wrong?" Sawyer pulls back with his eyes trained on mine.

"No, nothing is wrong, I just. Before we—" I let out a frustrated breath.

Just fucking say it, Leah.

"I want you to teach me how to give you a blow job." I try to look as confident as I *miraculously* managed to sound, but I can feel my cheeks betraying me when they flame. The devilish smirk on his face makes my pussy ache even though I've already come twice in the last ten minutes—stupid whore vagina.

"You want to suck my cock, baby?"

Ohhhh my god.

"Yes… If that's okay with you." I tip my chin up but the growl he lets out has me ready to hit my knees.

"Alright, up." He slaps my ass and we stand next to the bed.

He is the sexiest man I've ever had the pleasure of looking at. His body is sculpted to perfection, every single muscle toned in a mouth-watering way. His ink covered skin is tan and scarred from years of ice related accidents and his blue eyes are a striking contrast against his dark brown hair. I could stare at him forever.

He has yet to remove his boxers in front of me, which I'm just realizing is extremely unfair since I'm standing here in my birthday suit. But I'm sure I'll be just as impressed by what's *down there* as I am with the rest of him.

"On your knees, Dove." I swallow hard, kneeling in front of him. He is unmistakably large, and I'm suddenly worried my previous confidence was misplaced. "Go on. Take them off for me," he commands, noticing the way I'm staring with wide eyes at his length hiding behind the black fabric. I hook my fingers into the waistband and slide the fitted boxers down his muscular hips, suppressing the squeal that threatens to escape me when his cock springs free.

Oh my damn.

My eyes shoot up to his, slightly panicked, but mostly exhilarated. He wraps one large hand around his shaft and pumps his length a few times. Then he guides my hand to take over.

"Open your mouth wide and stick out your tongue." I do as he says and line him up with my mouth. "Mind your teeth and relax your throat." I relax my throat, letting it open wider as I think about how I'm supposed to not let my teeth maul him. Just as the tip of his head lands on my tongue, he reaches down and gently pinches the bridge of my nose between my eyes. All I can do is lift a brow to question him.

"Helps with your gag reflex," he smirks and my pussy clenches around nothing. "It's going to get really messy, and that's a good thing. The more spit that's dripping down your chin, the better. So don't go worrying about being proper with it, alright?"

Cock sucking for beginners—who knew it'd be this fucking hot?

I take a deep breath and suck him into my mouth, letting the precum that had gathered on his tip slide down my throat. I swirl my tongue around his tip, letting the groan that leaves his chest and the intense look in his eyes encourage me. I suck him as far down my throat as I can, releasing only long enough to take a breath before I do it again.

When I wrap my lips around him and start to take him faster, his hand comes around the back of my head, his fingers tangling in my hair. With my hand around his base, my tongue teasing him and my lips and throat working together to take as much of him as I can, I can feel the tension in his grip.

"Just like that, baby. Yes." I've never heard a man groan with such satisfaction before but that along with sucking him off has me dripping wet for him. He's just beginning to guide my head at a steady rhythm, then he pulls back, and I'm left empty.

My heart beats a little faster, wondering if I did something wrong or hurt him somehow, but before the thought can even take root in my mind, he pulls me up to him.

"The first time I come for you isn't going to be down your throat, Dove. Get on the bed." I turn to crawl back on the bed when I feel a hand come down on my right butt cheek. I sit down and face Sawyer, who is stroking himself again, making my whore of a pussy ache for him.

"Lay back,"

Oh my god, okay. It's happening. It's…it's not happening.

Sawyer wraps his hands around my thighs and pulls me to the end of the bed, leaning down to bury his face between my legs again.

"I thought…" I lean up on my elbows to look at him.

"We are baby, but I want to make sure you're soaked and ready for me. So it won't hurt so much,"

Won't hurt so much. Oh boy.

I close my eyes and let the feeling of Sawyer's mouth on me and fingers in me distract me from my own mind. His kisses against my clit feel like magic, and when he finds that one sweet spot, he pulls me over the edge for the third time—allowing me the pleasure of hearing just how wet I am now. He sucks off his fingers, then wipes his chin before kissing all the way up my stomach until he's hovering over me, eye to eye.

"Are you ready for me?"

"Yes." He leans down and kisses my nose before standing up and opening his nightstand drawer.

He pulls out a box of condoms, opening the brand-new pack and for some reason that brings me a sense of peace—knowing they haven't been used yet. He tears one of the packages with his teeth and spits the foil out as he rolls the latex down his shaft. Then he grabs a small bottle of lube, pouring some onto the tip and spreading it out evenly. I tilt my head and he smiles at me as he rejoins me on the bed, spreading my legs to settle himself between them.

"I felt how tight you are, Dove. I'm doing everything I can to make this feel as good for you as it's going to feel for me."

Goodness, he really is perfect.

I pull his lips to mine and he lines himself up to my entrance. My chest grows tight with anticipation as I look down between us, just as his head presses into me.

"Breathe for me, Dove. You can take it." I let out a breath, feeling myself relax around him. "Atta girl, just look at me, baby." My eyes lock with his and when he notices me gripping the bed sheets, he grabs my hand, locking his fingers with mine.

He leans down and whispers in my ear. "Just a few more inches." He kisses right beneath my ear, sending a shiver down my spine. "You're doing so well." His kisses travel down my neck, the electricity from his lips easing the burn from between my legs. Then I feel it, the moment I've taken all of him. The magnitude of this moment hits me full force and tears involuntarily spring to my eyes. He slides out gently, before pressing back into me. It hurts less the second time— my come mixed with the lube he used helping him to slide in with ease now.

"Thank you. For giving me this moment with you, Dove." He leans down and kisses me, and I almost think I'm dreaming. That this can't possibly be happening, after all this time. After imaging this for so many years then mourning the thought of it never becoming a reality after having my heart broken by him leaving.

"Are you okay?" I nod in response. "Can you take a little more?" The pace he's keeping feels like a tease now that I've adjusted to his length, and I'm more than ready for more.

"Yes." With a satisfied smirk, he pounds into me harder, each thrust of his hips hitting a spot that has me craving even more. He releases one of my hands and wraps his arm around my waist, pulling my hips off the bed to slide a pillow under me, before taking my hand in his again.

Holding my hands while he takes my virginity might just be the thing that makes me fall in love with him the most.

Thrust.

Oh, FUCK!

Thrust.

"Oh my god, yes!" I cry out. His pace is punishing in the most delicious way, but his attentiveness is as gentle as ever. His thumbs caress my hands as my orgasm begins to build. My eyes roll back as my body presses into him.

"Eyes on me, Dove. I want to look into those beautiful green eyes while you come on my cock." My mouth falls open with a silent scream as my orgasm rips through me.

When I can't force my eyes to stay open any longer, they flutter shut and he kisses me. Soft but firm—urgent and desperate to be connected in every possible way we can be. He releases my hands to be able to grip my face, moaning into my mouth as our kiss deepens and I think my heart bursts wide open. Completely at his mercy to be broken again but trusting that it will be safe. Then he pulls his lips from mine, slams into me once more and finds his own release.

"*Fuck*, Leah."

Chapter 38

Sawyer

There are some memories you'll hold onto forever. You know, the ones that stick around no matter what else in life you end up forgetting. Tonight, with her, is a memory that will outrank every other memory I've held onto in the past.

Seeing the vulnerability in her eyes, hearing the way she cried out my name, *feeling* her wrap around my cock like she was tailor made just for me. I'll remember this night in every lifetime.

When her eyes open and a tear spills out, my heart constricts in my chest.

"Don't cry, baby." I reach up and wipe her tears with the pad of my thumb, still buried deep inside of her as her green eyes shimmer.

"I'm sorry. I don't mean to ruin the moment—" She rolls her eyes in an effort to keep more tears from falling.

"Look at me. Nothing could ever ruin this moment. What's the matter? Talk to me." I caress her cheek, keeping my hands on any part of her I can.

"I just... I—" She takes a deep breath, rests her palm on my cheek and smiles at me. "I'm so happy it was with you, Sawyer." The tears start falling into her hair and this time she makes no effort to stop them.

"Me too, baby. I don't think you'd even believe just how much."

She smiles up at me. "Deep breath." I slide out of her and she inhales sharply. When I look between us there's the slightest evidence of blood staining the inside of her legs. "Stay right here, I'll be back." I kiss her lips softly and disappear into the master bathroom to dispose of my condom and turn the shower on.

I lift her from the bed and carry her into the large washroom, setting her feet down next to the toilet. "I'll grab us some towels." Giving her some privacy to pee, I close the door to the small space and grab three towels from under the sink, placing them on the small wooden table right outside the shower door. A moment later I hear the toilet flush and the door opens. I waste no time walking back over to grab her again, picking her up as a beautiful laugh escapes her.

"What are you doing?" I open the door to the massive walk-in shower and put her feet down, letting the hot water hit her back before brushing her hair behind her ear.

"Taking care of my girl." I don't think I've ever seen so much love and trust in someone's eyes before, but when I look into hers—there's no one in the world I've ever wanted to protect more than this girl in front of me.

Dipping my head to take her lips in mine, I feel the same damn butterflies that I felt the day I realized I had a thing for my little sister's best friend—the only woman to ever have this effect on me. I cup her face in my hands and hers lay comfortably on my sides as we stand under the stream of water, letting ourselves get lost in each other.

With one final peck, I instruct her to turn around, taking my time to run shampoo through her hair. Every little moan that falls from her lips while I massage her scalp makes me smile even harder than the one before. I do the same with the conditioner—remembering the *very* detailed instructions my sister gave me for washing curly hair when I made the mistake of mentioning getting some things for Leah to have at my place. I don't know why I still tell her things, honestly.

Then I grab the vanilla body wash, rubbing my hands together until it becomes foam before washing every inch of her perfect body.

Starting at her shoulders, I massage them gently as her head falls back with pleasure. I lather her back, arms, chest and stomach—taking my time with her breasts because they're fucking works of art. Then I add a small amount of wash to my hands again before lowering to my knees.

"Spread your legs for me." Her cheeks turn red but she doesn't argue. She doesn't just widen her stance though, she lifts her foot onto the bench behind me, giving me the most glorious view of her pussy.

My pussy.

I lean forward, gently kissing her there before forcing myself to stay on task. I wash the inside of her thighs, ridding it of the blood, cum and lube mixture, careful not to let the suds get too close to her entrance. Then her hands slide gently through my hair, playing with some of the long locks.

"Thank you, Sawyer." I hear her sweet voice and my eyes shoot up to lock with her tear-filled ones. I place her foot back on the ground and stand in front of her, wrapping my arms around her until my soapy hands are resting on the small of her back.

"For what, Dove?" I press her closer to me, feeling like I can't possibly get close enough to her right now.

"For being better than I could have ever dreamed. I'll never forget tonight or the way you've cared for me."

"Tonight was the best night of my life, Leah. I won't forget it either." She reaches up with her hands around my neck and kisses me like she has all the time in the world. When she finally pulls away, she pushes my chest, walking me back until the back of my claves hit the built in bench.

"Sit." She nods behind me, and I do as she's asked. Then she reaches for the shampoo on the shelf opposite of where I've placed hers and she squeezes it into her palms.

"What are you doing?"

"I'm taking care of my man." She smiles at me, and I realize—I would rip my heart from my chest to give it to her. To show her just how fucking much she owns me.

The second her fingers begin working the shampoo through my hair I exhale in a way that feels like it's taking all my worries with it. In this moment, there's nothing more important than the girl that's washing my hair, and the fact that she calls me hers.

She pulls the shower head down from behind me, fumbling with it until she figures out how to turn it on. "Head back." She smiles when I comply, and I close my eyes as the water and her fingers work to rid my hair of the suds.

Fuck, this feels good.

Once the shower head is back in place, I wrap my hands around the back of her thighs and pull her closer to me. Kissing from her stomach up to her breasts. Her fingers twist through my hair as I flick my tongue over one of her nipples, causing it to harden immediately —then I do the same to the other. I leisurely palm one of her breasts, pinching, sucking, *enjoying* every second of my mouth on her body. I grab her legs and lift her to straddle my lap, continuing like this until she starts to slide herself over my cock that is hard for her again— because how could it not be?

"I want you again," she whispers against my lips and my dick jumps in excitement.

"Are you sure?" I lean back and catch her eye.

"Are you telling me no?" A devilish smirk plays on her lips.

"Oh, that'll never happen." I stand with her still wrapped around me, shutting the water off before I walk to the room, dripping water all over the damn place.

And I absolutely do not care.

I lay her down on my bed and take a moment to stand back and just stare at her. Wondering if this is really happening or if I'm dreaming it all.

"You okay there, hockey star?" She leans up on her elbows, letting water fall from her teardrop tits.

"You're going to bring me to my knees one day, Dove." She pulls her bottom lip in with her teeth, smiling at me with a brow raised.

"Prove it." I tilt my head at her. "Get on your knees for me, Sawyer." Her playful smile is gone, in its place is a nervous look of anticipation—as if she's wondering just how far I'm willing to go for her—and fuck if I wouldn't do anything she damn well asked me right now. I take a step forward and hit my knees, then I grab her legs and pull her to the end of the bed and before she can so much as gasp, I bury my face between her legs.

The moan it elicits from her has me struggling to be as gentle with her as I intended to be tonight. I want to fucking devour her—to throw her around this bed and show her just how fucking badly I've wanted her all these years—but I won't go there unless she asks for it. My fingertips dig into her thighs as I suck her clit into my mouth, lapping up every drop of sweetness she releases when her orgasm hits.

"God, yes!"

"I'd much prefer you scream *my* name when you come, Dove." I taunt, standing to hover over her. She blushes and smiles at me, wiping her thumb across my face.

"So messy," she teases.

"So delicious." I dip my head, letting my nose caress her neck, inhaling the scent of *her*. Her back arches off the bed, pressing her body against mine as she hums in the most satisfied way. I stand to grab another condom from the drawer, quickly rolling it on so I can rejoin her.

"How do you want me?" Her question causes me to pause.

"What do you mean?"

"Well, I don't intend to just be on my back every time we have sex. I thought you might want to... I don't know, try something different this time?" My dick pulses of its own will as my mind speeds through every position I've imagined taking her in.

"There's not much I haven't thought about doing with you, Dove.

I'll fuck you any way you want me to." Her legs squeeze together, and I hope she decides on something soon.

"What's your favorite?" I don't really want to mention what position I've preferred to use with other women, so instead…

"I have pictured you riding my cock more times than I could even begin to count. So I can stare into those pretty eyes, and watch those perky tits bounce, and watch you come apart wrapped around me." My fingers glide through her hair, gripping it to turn her gaze to mine. "What do you say, Dove? You wanna learn to ride?" She nods her head eagerly.

"Yes."

"Atta girl." I kiss her quickly before situating myself against the headboard. "Climb on."

She straddles my lap and looks at me, awaiting further instruction. It's kind of fun being the one to teach a teacher.

"Now grab my cock and slide on at whatever pace feels good for you."

"I want it to feel good for you too," she says shyly.

"Baby, if my cock is inside you—no matter where or how fast it gets there—I can assure you, I feel fucking fantastic." She grabs my shaft and lines me up to her entrance.

If she had any idea what the feeling of her *hand* wrapped around me did to me, she wouldn't be concerned with how fast she lets my cock inside of her. I watch as she takes all of me, inch by inch without so much as a pause, until I'm filling her to the hilt. The moment I'm all the way in she lets out a gasp the same moment I suck in a sharp breath.

"Now what?" She gently rocks her hips against me, trying to find friction in our new position.

"You can move your hips like this." I grab her waist, rocking her back and forth to allow her clit some attention. "Or you can bounce like this." I guide her up and down my length, noting the way her breaths pick up as she bites so hard on her bottom lip that I fear it may draw blood.

I think we have a winner.

I stop guiding her, keeping my hands on her hips as she bounces up and down, her pussy squeezing me just as tight this time as it did the first. I knead her ass, putting to memory the way it feels when it's bouncing as she rides. I bring one hand around to rub circles on her clit and her movements falter—only for a moment before she finds her rhythm again.

"Sawyer, I need…"

"I got you, baby." I thrust into her, grabbing her hips with both hands. "Play with your pussy." I expect some kind of argument out of her, but she reaches down and begins rubbing small circles over her clit as I rail into her.

"Fuck, Dove, you're taking me so well."

"Sawyer, oh shit!" Her walls clamp around me and while she's still riding out her orgasm, I flip her on her back. I continue thrusting into her, not missing a fucking beat as she continues to come on my cock.

"Your pussy was made for me, Dove," I practically growl, feeling my own release just moments away.

"Fuck! Yes!" she screams, as her orgasm hits even harder than before. Her entire body is writhing beneath me when I find my release.

I rest my forehead on her shoulder, trying my best not to collapse all of my body weight on top of her. I've never felt this with anyone before. Sex is great, sure. Sex with Leah is fucking life altering. I don't know how I survived ten years without her, and I know damn sure I'd never survive another ten without her.

"Sawyer," her fingertips are softly trailing over my back while I'm still seated comfortably inside her.

"Yes, Dove?" I pant.

"I love you." I lift my head to see her watery eyes locked on mine and the sweetest smile on her face and another moment gets seared into my memory.

"I love you, too, Leah. I can't remember a time I haven't loved you."

Chapter 39

Waking up in Sawyer's bed, with his arms wrapped around me, knowing that last night actually happened—the sex *and* the full vulnerability of telling him I loved him—feels like all of my dreams have finally come true.

"Mornin' Dove," he rasps, kissing the top of my head as I lie next to him, tracing the tattoos on his chest. Our naked bodies mold to each other like missing puzzle pieces and I haven't even the smallest desire to move from this position today.

"Good morning." I smile up at him and he immediately pulls me in for a kiss.

"How are you feeling this morning? Are you sore?" I noticed the ache between my legs before I even moved this morning, but it's an ache that I welcome and quite honestly, crave more of.

"Yes." His brows knit together in concern. "But it just makes me want you even more." His tongue swipes across his bottom lip, then a look of panic flashes through his eyes.

"Shit, what time is it?" He shoots up to look at the clock. "You're going to be late!" He stops when he sees me smiling at him instead of throwing myself into a panic to match his.

"I'm not going to work today." I shrug.

"You're not?" He raises a brow at me.

"I may have texted last night to let them know I would be taking today off." He smiles at me in a way that sends my heart fluttering.

"And when did you do that, exactly? Because if I remember correctly, you were pretty occupied most of the night." He wraps his arms around my waist and buries his face in my neck, causing goose-bumps to immediately cover my skin.

"I did it on the way here," I giggle. He rears back and looks at me. No playful remarks made about me calling into work because I was getting laid the night before. He just—looks at me.

In one swift motion, he pulls me onto his lap and begins planting kisses all along my neck as my fingers tangle in his hair. One small rotation of my hips and he would slide into me with ease.

"What do you want to do today, Dove?" He rubs his hands along my back lazily, and I would be fine with doing *this* all day.

"Well, if I don't have coffee in the next ten minutes, you're not going to like me very much."

"Coffee, got it. Let's go." He reaches up and kisses me before pulling me up and planting my feet on the ground. He pulls on a pair of black sweatpants and runs his fingers through his hair before putting his old Yankees cap on backwards. Then hands me his Badgers hoodie.

"There are hair ties and some clips as well as a new toothbrush in the bathroom drawer." I raise a brow at him as I slide the hoodie over my head—that fits me like a dress.

"You know, I thought the curl specific shampoo and conditioner were a coincidence but…" I trail off, hoping he'll inform me why his bathroom is stocked with items he clearly doesn't need.

"I bought stuff for you to have here." He shrugs. My mouth pops open but no words come out for a solid ten seconds.

"Why?"

Genius question, Leah.

He smirks at me and walks over to wrap his hands around my waist.

"Because when you finally said yes to giving us a chance, I knew we would end up here one day and I wanted you to have everything you'd need."

"You're the most thoughtful person I know, Sawyer Clark." I smile up at him.

"Only for you, Dove." He kisses me once more then squeezes my ass. "You want a quick tour before breakfast?"

"Um, absolutely I do."

After wetting my hair to tame some of the frizz—because *oh my god*—I throw it haphazardly into a claw clip then we walk around the farmhouse style mansion Sawyer lives in.

There's about six other bedrooms not counting his, one with all his hockey memorabilia, a few that are actually guest rooms, then there's the last room that's been completely transformed into what can only be described as a mini library. There are bookshelves on every wall—some full, some with only a few books, and some still completely bare—with the most heavenly looking reading chair tucked into the corner next to the floor to ceiling windows that face the expansive backyard.

"This is probably my favorite room." I stare out the window as he walks up behind me, wrapping his arms around my waist.

"Well, I should hope so, it was made for you." I turn around and see a boyish smile on his face.

"What do you mean?"

"Come on, Dove. You think I would buy claw clips and shampoo for you, but *not* have a room designated just for your books?"

"I— I honestly don't know what to expect from you anymore. You surprise me at every turn."

"Good," he whispers against my lips, pressing his gently to mine before standing back to his full height. "Why don't you spend some time with the books, and I *know* you want to try out the reading chair. Then come down when you're ready." I can't help but smile at how well he knows me, and I nod in agreement. I see every single one of Laura's books lining one of the shelves and pick up Always Mine, flipping through to read over some of my favorite scenes, until I smell coffee brewing and abandon the books to join Sawyer in the kitchen.

When I walk in, I see Sawyer spreading something onto a bagel and my stomach begins growling. I'm not sure which thing is turning me on more though, seeing Sawyer making us breakfast, or the smell of the coffee.

"Hey there, beautiful."

Hello, butterflies.

"Hey handsome." I saunter over to him and wrap my arms around his waist as he continues plating our food.

"Try this." He lifts one arm, turning in my grip and holds the mini bagel to my mouth for me to take a bite.

"Oh my god," I mumble with a mouth full. "What is that?"

"Cinnamon butter." I moan as I savor every bit of the taste.

"I loved making cinnamon butter when I was little. I never could get the ratio right though," I say after finally swallowing the bite.

"Well, problem solved. They make it for you now." He winks, pressing his lips gently to mine.

Being kissed by Sawyer will never get old.

I begin walking around the kitchen, taking in the massive space. I told myself no matter how badly I wanted to let my eyes roam around last night, that I would stay focused on *us*. Because the second I get distracted, there's usually no saving me.

The kitchen is the same size as my kitchen and living room combined, with an island the size of my car in the middle of it. The cabinets are a light natural wood, complemented by off-white marble countertops. The island base is painted the most gorgeous pine-green color that I can't stop staring at, and black appliances with gold hardware top it all off.

"Can you grab some creamer out of the fridge? Second shelf."

Sawyer points to the refrigerator but as soon as my fingers wrap around the handle, something catches my eye and I stop to stare at the magnet hanging perfectly at eye level.

"Dove, you okay?" I feel Sawyer stop behind me—his presence sending an undeniable heat through my whole body. "You like it?" he asks, causing me to finally turn and face him.

"I completely forgot about that photo," I admit, fighting the tears that have formed in my eyes. He pulls the magnet off the fridge and lays it face up in his palm.

"I have looked at this picture of us every day since it was taken, holding out hope that one day you'd look at me like that again." I dry my eyes and look again. It's the picture Taylor took of us on Halloween night my senior year. Sawyer is wearing my angel wings and I'm in his denim jacket, staring up at him like he hung the damn moon.

"I'd been looking at you like that for years, you just never noticed." A sadness swirls in my chest as the magnet pops back onto the door.

"I hate that we never caught each other staring. Maybe life would have been a whole lot simpler if we had. But—" He pulls his hand around, with another magnet facing up. "I have to believe that where we ended up is exactly where we were meant to be all along. I just had to stop waiting for fate to bring us back together and do it my damn self." I choke out a laugh as I stare at the new photo magnet he's holding.

This one is the picture he took of us in my bed the morning after he stayed over the first night. Ten years later and I'm still looking at him the way I always have. He tilts my chin up with his forefinger.

"I love you, Dove. I always will."

"I love you too."

BANG. BANG BANG. BANG. BANG.

"Moose! Open this fucking door!"

Is that?

"Is that my sister?"

"How many other people with that pitch call you Moose?" I narrow my gaze at him, making him snap a finger gun at me.

"Right." He turns to walk towards the door when she starts yelling again.

"Your girlfriend is MISSING! Get your ass up and ANSWER THE DOOR!" she screams, causing him to turn around with a devilish smirk.

"Please go answer the door." He shoots me a pleading look, and I tilt my head at him.

"Are you serious?" He folds his hands like he's begging. "Sawyer, I'm not wearing underwear!" I whisper shout at him, as if Taylor could hear me over the crisis she's currently having on the front porch.

"I don't think that's really going to matter unless you're planning on straddling her."

"MOOSE!"

"Okay fine!" I walk over to the door and take a deep breath, shooting one final eyeroll in Sawyer direction. He looks so fucking giddy about this I have to fight to keep from smiling about it.

I swing the door open, and Taylor lets out a loud groan. "Fucking fi—" Her mouth hangs open, her words dying on her lips when she sees me.

"Hey, Tay. Everything okay?" She lets her eyes rake over me in her brother's hoodie, my hair a mess and bare from the waist down—though she can only see from a little above my knees down—and she screams.

"Oh my god, and now I'm deaf." I hold my fingers to my ears as Taylor storms through the front door. Taking in the mess of clothes right inside the threshold.

Oops. Forgot about those.

"I think I'm having a heart attack." She holds her hand to her chest and tries to take a deep breath. "Oh my god!" Her other hand flies to her eyes and I look behind me to see Sawyer with those delicious looking sweatpants slung low on his hips as he leans against the wall with amusement on his face.

"This is *my* house, Tot. You're just lucky we're as dressed as we are." I shoot daggers at him, but he winks at me and suddenly I wish we *weren't* as dressed as we are.

"Did you need something?" I turn to face her, and both of her hands fall to her hips.

"Um, *yes!* I need to know why my best friend's phone is going straight to voicemail, why her car was still in her driveway well after eight o'clock on a Friday morning when she's never taken a day off work unless she was *dying,* and why my tree of a brother didn't answer *any* of my 911 texts about it." She looks between the two of us and when I meet Sawyer's eye again, he's looking at me like he's replaying last night, and I can't help the blush that washes over my cheeks.

"I uh, took the day off work, Uber'd to the game last night, left with Sawyer, then I stayed here last night which is why my car is at home, and I honestly don't know where my phone is." I glance around and see it sitting on the floor next to my dress. Likely dead as a doornail.

"And what's *your* excuse?" She stares past me at Sawyer.

"My phone is on do not disturb."

"Why?!" The room is silent for a moment before Sawyer speaks again—but not before he walks over to wrap his arms around me.

"Because I wasn't to be disturbed last night. Isn't that right, Dove?"

"I am feeling so many things right now I can't even begin to land on one emotion," Taylor says almost robotically.

"Try," I encourage as she looks between the two of us. Then she narrows her gaze on me.

"Yay for the invasion of Fort Knox!" She claps excitedly, quickly followed by her finger being shoved in my face. "Don't you ever let your phone die again, I thought you were getting crazy murdered somewhere." Then she pulls me into a giant bear hug. Going through the five stages of grief in a very shuffled way at lightning speed is kind of Taylor's specialty.

"Since you're alive and well, I expect to see both of you tomorrow night on Broadway. If you can manage to get dressed and out of the house long enough to grace us with your presence." She shimmies her shoulders and winks at me, then stares blankly at Sawyer before closing her eyes.

"Random hockey player, he's just a random hockey player," Taylor chants as she shakes her head and walks back out the front door, leaving Sawyer and I staring after her.

"I don't know why the things she does still surprises me after all these years," he says after we hear the engine to her car start and the tires begin rolling down the gravel driveway.

"Well, she wouldn't be Taylor if they didn't."

Chapter 40

"For the love of God can we skip line dancing tonight? If one more person gets into an *almost* fight, I'm going to have to ban them indefinitely," Lauren demands as we all congregate on the sidewalk that is bustling with people—per usual.

"If we do not walk into a building soon, I will go the fuck home," Max says, his eyes never landing one place for long.

"How's therapy going, buddy?" Sawyer asks from his place behind me. Max growls in response.

"Let's just go into the saloon here and get a drink and then we can decide where we end up next." Tucker leads the way as we all file in behind him like kids on a damn field trip.

"Oh my god, I love this song." Lauren starts swinging her hips as the live band begins to play a Teddy Swims song. When she points to me mid lip-synch and takes a step back, she bumps into someone and turns to apologize.

"I'm so sor—" Her apology falls short, and she tosses her hair behind her shoulder. "I'm so sorry your new prescription doesn't seem to be working. You should really get that fixed."

Damn Lauren. Who the hell—

"Maybe it's you who needs glasses, then you'd be able to see how many of your clients are falling into my lap every day."

Oh my god.

"Who's the friend, Lauren?" Tank asks, sliding up next to her all protective big brother like, earning a glare from the guy I can only imagine is Fitz.

"Friend is a stretch. We just happen to work in the same office, unfortunately," she scoffs as Tucker joins the conversation.

"Oh, is this Lucifer?" Tank asks, causing Lauren's head to snap over so quickly I fear it might turn completely around.

"It's *Luther*," Tucker corrects. "We played Topgolf together once—" his head tils, likely realizing this is in fact, *not* Luther. "Didn't we?"

"Um, no. We did not," he answers Tucker matter of factly. "Lucifer, really?" He walks closer to Lauren, whispering something in her ear before exiting the building without another word to anyone.

When she turns around to face the group again, the girls are all a mess of wide eyes and mouths hanging open, while Tank and Tucker simply shrug and begin a conversation completely unrelated to just calling a guy *Satan* and mistaking him for an entirely different human being all together.

"I hate that guy," Lauren bites out through her teeth before tossing back the rest of her drink.

"I have missed *so* much, haven't I?" Sawyer leans in and asks, making me laugh.

"More than you can even imagine." I take a sip of my margarita, the strawberry and tequila hitting the spot.

"Let me have a sip," Sawyer says, nodding to my drink. We're practically having to yell over the music playing, as a few of us sway to the songs flowing through the room. I hand him my drink and he takes a big sip, keeping the straw to the side with his index finger.

"You're getting another one, this is mine now." He winks at me, taking another long pull from the glass.

Who knew a man with a fruity drink could be so damn sexy?

"Karaoke time, bitches!" Shane squeals, as Max has his arms

wrapped protectively around her. Then we pay for our drinks and head down the street to the karaoke bar.

By some miracle we end up sitting in a corner booth that fits our entire group—barely—as the guy on stage finishes his very off-key rendition of *We Are The Champions*. What a wild pick for a karaoke song if you ask me, but to each their own.

"Okay! Who's going first?" Shane asks, looking directly at Tucker.

"Why do I always go first?"

"Probably because Max sounds like a cat drowning in a barrel and I'm trying to give my wife a break before she ends up pregnant again." Tank winks at Ruby, then looks over at Sawyer.

"You sing, Moose?"

When the hell did he start calling him that?!

"You ever gonna not call me that, Tank?" He immediately starts shaking his head.

"Nope. No chance."

"Fantastic."

"Oh, he sings," Taylor says with a big ass grin on her face. My eyes shoot back over to Sawyer who has his jaw clenched now.

"No, I don't," he argues.

Umm. Liar.

"Whatever. You may only be able to sing the one song, but me and your shampoo bottles heard you loud and clear almost every day during my senior year. You actually got kinda good at it."

What song?!

I can clearly recall him singing with me in my living room the other day and my stomach and pussy flutter in unison when I remember just how dreamy he sounded. Even over the insane volume I had the speakers on.

"Sawyer, you don't *have* to sing. We just come for fun." A very *un*-invited Tank head appears right beside me, interjecting himself further into our conversation.

"Uh, if you've got the pipes, you have to sing. It's a rule." I fight the urge to visibly facepalm.

"Fuck it, I'll go first." Sawyer claps his hands against his jeans, kisses me on the cheek and walks to the front with Tucker and Tank.

"Oh my gosh, is he actually going to sing?" Lauren whispers, leaning in closer to Taylor and me.

"I really was just trying to give him a hard time, but I mean... I guess so." She shrugs. I'm watching with anticipation as he stands up on the small stage and the drunken audience starts yelling and clapping.

"Go Badgers!" One guy yells as the MC gets the music ready, earning a fist pump to the air from Sawyer.

"Number thirteen, have my babies." A woman in the crowd yells, making me want to throat punch her *immediately*.

"Oh, um. No. Thank you," Sawyer says into the mic. When his eyes find mine and he gives me a *yikes* look, I can't hold in my laugh.

Then the music starts.

I think for a minute it might just be a coincidence, but when he winks at me and Shane pipes up from beside me, I start thinking differently.

"Oh my god, Le. It's *your* song." The song I've been obsessed with for years. Well, the performance by Heath Ledger in my favorite movie is at least.

"You're just too good to be true. Can't take my eyes off of you. You're just like Heaven to touch—" And my heart completely leaps into my throat. He dances across the stage, making a big show out of it, and even runs into the crowd, getting down on his knees to sing directly at my feet at one point. When the song ends and the entire bar erupts in applause, he's still down on his knees in front of me, and without caring who's watching, I take his face in my hands and kiss him. I'm pretty sure I hear Max *woof* from behind me and I pull away before I end up laughing directly into Sawyer's mouth.

"I've never been able to keep my eyes off of you, Dove."

Have my *babies' number thirteen, damn.*

Chapter 41

Sawyer

"I feel like I'm imposing on a sacred tradition, are you sure it's okay that I'm here?" I glance out the window of my truck, taking in the surroundings of Leah's parent's home.

"Sawyer Clark, are you *nervous*?" she teases.

"I can confidently say I have only ever been nervous about things that concern you," I tell her, earning one of those heart stopping smiles of hers.

"How does this concern me? It's just dinner with my parents. Unless you end up punching one of them in the face or mentioning anything about our sex life, I'll still like you when it's all said and done."

And now I'm picturing her naked. Fantastic. Let me just walk into her parents' home with a hard-on for their daughter. That would be swell.

I sigh and lean my head back on the driver seat. "The last time I saw your parents was at Thanksgiving. Not my best moment, if you recall."

"Sawyer, that was months ago. They've probably long forgotten about it." Leah grabs my hand reassuringly, but I roll my head to look at her.

"Really?"

"I mean, probably not, my mom has a scary good memory. But

come on, it's going to be fine." Her laughter fills the cab of my truck, easing a bit of the nerves I have.

"Okay. If you say it'll be fine, it'll be fine. But I did tell Tank where I am tonight in case I don't come out alive."

"The two of you as friends does *not* shock me." She leans back in her seat observing me.

"Oh yeah? How come?"

"I can't explain it. It just…makes sense."

"Whatever you say, Dove. Now let's go before they get suspicious." She rolls her eyes as I hop out to open her door for her.

So far no one has reprimanded me for my tone at Thanksgiving, and I'm still alive so I'd say things are going well. Loretta asked me about hockey and my travels, Allen only chiming in when he questioned my stats. I get the feeling he isn't my biggest fan, but he's been polite. I'm all but eased of my nerves when he clears his throat and grabs his jacket.

"Let's go for a drive, Son."

This is where I die…

"Hey, that's *our* thing," Leah pouts, getting the warmest smile from her dad in return.

"Don't you worry, Sweetpea. You know I'm always just a call away and the truck is ready to go." As I walk out of the den I shoot Leah a worried look, but she simply shrugs and encourages me to go. If *she's* not worried about my safety, then I guess I won't be either.

When we step into the garage, I see a blue and white '86 Chevy Silverado in pristine condition.

"Hop in." I do as I'm told, and we sit silently as he makes his way down the road.

"Nice truck. You had it long?" I ask, trying to break some of the tension in the air.

"Got it the year Leah was born. My old truck was a mess, and I needed a safe way to get my baby girl around." I nod and see him glance at me out of the corner of his eye.

"She's a beauty." I'm referring to the truck, but he takes the opportunity to change the course of conversation.

"She is. Listen, Sawyer…" His southern drawl makes me smile. "That girl is my entire world—outside of her mama, of course—and I watched her fall in love with you, then I watched her get her heart broken by you."

"Sir, I—"

"I don't need all the details. What's happened between you two, is just that—between you two." I nod my head and listen. "I saw tonight how much she cares for you. I've never seen that girl light up the way she does when she's with you. Even as kids when the two of you were just friends, but even more so now. The light coming from her smile tonight is damn near blinding." He looks over again to ensure I'm keeping up—I am.

"Don't you let that girl lose her light again. If you're in this, you better be so far in that you can't even see the way out anymore. Don't you let my little girl's heart get broken or so help me, I will hunt you down and ruin your life."

"I understand sir. I'm not walking away again." He nods his approval. "And with your blessing, I'd like to marry your daughter someday, sir." He stills in his seat, not taking his eyes off the road.

"Your daughter makes me happier than I've ever been in my life. I never want to be without her again, I told her that the only way that would happen is if she demands it." This makes him smirk, then he wipes at his eyes and clears his throat, cluing me in to his emotions on the matter.

"I'm afraid there's never been anyone I thought was better suited for my daughter than you, Sawyer. You have my blessing, for whenever you make good on it." We come to a stop back in their drive and I notice the way I'm sweating an embarrassing amount.

Just as I'm about to open the door, his hand falls to mine. When I meet his eye, I see the sincerity beneath his aged stare.

"I mean it. You take care of her."

"Yes, sir." With one final nod he pats my hand, and we return to the house with Leah and Loretta, and when she looks up from the TV and smiles at me, I see my forever.

"Everything okay?" Leah stands and walks over to me, and it takes everything in me not to pull her in and let my lips land on hers in a way that is *not* suitable for her parents' kitchen.

"Everything is great, Dove. I promise." Her shoulders relax and her smile softens even more, and I begin counting down the minutes until I can take her home.

Fuck tomorrow for being Monday.

Chapter 42

TAY

Are we going to talk about the fucking marriage proposal of a karaoke performance my brother did for Le this weekend orrrr?

ME

IDK ummm are we going to talk about the interaction with HOT BOY FITZ at the saloon?

SHANE

Ooohh. Tough choice, but I'm gonna have to go with Leah because what the FUCK?! You didn't tell us he was a glasses wearing HOTTIE?!

LAUREN

I'm friend-divorcing anyone who calls him hot. I hate him.

RUBY

Is there a possibility for re-marriage in the future? Asking for a friend… 🙈

ME

You remember what Mama Loretta says about the line between love and hate, don't you Lu?

LAUREN

Just because you fucking catapulted over to the love side, does NOT mean I'm going to. There isn't even a love side with him?! Just a deep abyss of hatred. Are you and Moose getting married or what?! I'm with Tay. That was some next level in-love shit.

ME

I told him I loved him.

SHANE

What?!?!?!

TAY

SCREAMING

RUBY

WHEN!!!!!

LAUREN

ME

Umm… after we had sex?!

SHANE

WHAT?!?!?!?!

TAY

SCREAMING HARDER

RUBY

I'm so proud.

LAUREN

I'm passed out on the floor. Bitch, EXPLAIN YO SELF.

ME

I showed up at his game Thursday when meetings ended early. He took me out, we ran into Josh (you guys remember Josh?) Anyways, we yelled at each other in the rain then I told him to take me home (for activities) and… he did.

LAUREN

I need to re-hydrate so I can cry more tears.

RUBY

Fucking legendary. Yelling in the rain before sex? That's movie worthy shit right there.

SHANE

I think Max might take me to the hospital soon if I don't stop hyperventilating.

TAY

Why isn't this happening over margaritas?!

ME

Because it's seven o'clock on a Monday. You nocturnal ER zombie.

TAY

That's fair. On that note. Goodnight beauties.

MOOSE

attachment 1 photo

My heart stops when I see a photo of a shirtless Sawyer with gray sweatpants on, holding a book in his lap. I click on the photo and zoom in, letting out an audible gasp when I see what he's reading.

Always Mine by Laura Pavlov herself.

Before I can reply he texts me again.

MOOSE

Hmm… friends since childhood, he gives her a cute little nickname, dude has long hair and is built like a… what was that? A Greek god?? I'm seeing a lot of similarities to us in this book, Dove. Any reason this one is your favorite??

Busted.

ME

Total coincidence I guess. 😇

MOOSE

Suuure. You've always been mine, Dove. I'd say our story is one for the books too.

ME

Happily ever after?

MOOSE

I thought that was a given. 

Someone get a mop because I'm a fucking puddle.

Chapter 43

Sawyer

I'm pretty sure I've entered the stage of our relationship where I want to do nothing but be with her twenty-four-seven. I hate when Monday comes around, and she has to be at work all day and I hate when I have away games and she can't be there with me. I do, however, love that we've spent every night together since the night she told me to take her home. We've split the time between my place and hers, but I'd sleep on the grass in the bitter cold as long as I got to have her by my side—and you know, we didn't freeze to death.

I've just landed from our game in Boston and am racing against the clock to make it home to shower and get ready before Shane's birthday celebration at Taylor's house tonight. The guys may make jokes about it, but I don't mind having Leah tell me what we're doing. It makes me feel like I'll get to spend the rest of my life hearing her tell me all the parties and plans we're meant to attend—and knowing we'll be going together makes it all worth it in my mind.

No more longing for her from across the room.

When I finally reach the house, my heart begins to race when I see Leah's car parked out front. As soon as I step out of the truck, she runs out of her car to greet me, jumping into my arms and wrapping her legs around my waist.

"I missed you," she whispers into my neck.

Music to my damn ears.

I inhale as deep as my lungs will allow and kiss her neck. "I missed you too, Dove." When she finally pulls back, I reach up and kiss her, letting my lips reacquaint themselves with hers.

"What are you doing here?" I ask, after several parting kisses before planting her feet back on the ground.

"I wanted to be here when you got home. I thought we could ride to Taylor and Tucker's together." I wrap my arm around her shoulder as we walk up to the house.

"I'd love that. I just gotta shower and get dressed first." After tossing my keys on the counter I turn to see her cheeks burning red.

"Okay." Is all she says, but I can almost hear the wheels turning in her brain.

"Care to join me?" I wrap my arms around her from behind and lean in closer, nipping at her ear before she turns to me with sheer enthusiasm in her eyes.

"I don't need a shower though."

"But *I* need *you* in the shower."

Her teeth sink into her bottom lip, and she smiles. "Can't argue with that."

I stand up and slap her ass, leading her down the hall to the bathroom. "That's my girl."

Needless to say, after spending forty-five minutes in the shower with Leah, we're late to Shane's birthday gathering. And I do not give a single fuck about it.

Cece is walking around babbling into her Minnie Mouse phone, Poe is bouncing in some contraption on the floor by Ruby, and Hendrix, as always, is right in the middle of the guy's huddle. Some of the girls are chatting and mixing drinks when we finally make it to the kitchen.

"Catch you later, Dove." I wink at her as she joins them, and I mosey over to where the guys are sitting around the table playing cards.

"Go-Fish." Hendrix smirks from his place at the head of the table.

"How's it going over here?" I nod to Max and fist bump Tucker and Tank.

"Hendrix is wiping the floor with us, as usual," Tucker grumbles, making Hendrix wag his eyebrows at me.

"At Go-Fish?"

"Don't even ask dude, he and his mom are wizards or something because they are undefeated at this stupid game," Tank explains.

"Alright then." I glance over at Leah, somehow pulling her attention straight to me, and she winks at me.

God, I'm so in love with her.

I smile at the gesture then we both turn our attention back to our surrounding groups.

After singing happy birthday and eating some cupcakes, someone turns the music to a slightly above a background noise level as we sit around the living room talking.

"How's everything been at the Veterans Center, Tank?" I was sure that questions would make him perk up like a puppy, but instead he lets out a sigh.

"Things are good I guess; we're just trying to find a couple of more donors so we're able to keep things running smoothly at *both* locations. The old building is needing some major maintenance repairs right now and as much as Asher and I have tried to manage on our own, we just have to get some outsourced help at this point. Not to mention needing to be able to keep up with the supplies we need replenished on a regular basis."

"How much are you guys looking at needing for long term upkeep?" I ask, tapping Leah's cup to ask for a drink. She giggles when I take a sip of the margarita before handing it back to her.

"I haven't really sat down to calculate a long-term number, but

right now we're needing around ten grand to cover the HVAC alone."
I whistle in response.

"Tell me about it. These residents deserve the best, man. They fought for our country and some of them have lost so much, the least they deserve is a place with people who are going to take good fucking care of them." Ruby rubs his arm to comfort him. "Sorry, it's just—" he scrubs a hand down his face. "They just deserve more. It's fucking outrageous that athletes make as much goddamn money as they do, while people who have defended our country are barely making it by. While serving *and* once they're out." The room falls silent, and it takes a moment before Tank's eyes fall shut.

"Shit, man. I am *so* sorry. I didn't mean—" he instantly begins apologizing, but I'm not the least bit offended.

"Don't apologize. I completely agree with you. You guys do deserve way more than what you're given. Excuse me." I stand up and make my way to the kitchen, shooting a text off before I feel hands wrap around my waist.

"Hey, you." Leah kisses a spot on my back before I turn around to face her.

"Hey yourself." I lean down to kiss her lips.

"Tank means well. He's just used to being around guys that...*get it*. You know?"

"I do. I'm not offended. I meant it, I agree with everything he said," I assure her with a kiss to the forehead.

"I know this may not be the kind of night you're used to having but thank you for coming anyways."

My brows draw in. "What do you mean?"

She shrugs and looks back towards the living room.

"I don't know. The intimacy of these little parties, the conversations about work. I just... I don't know what you're used to doing. If it's all glamorous nights out at fancy clubs and talking about hockey 24/7—" I can't help but laugh, making her stop and look at me with mock annoyance.

"Baby, I love nights like this. The only thing I could want more than this is being home alone with you. But I like hearing about the Veterans Center, and what's going on with the bar expansion. I enjoy annoying Taylor any chance I get and getting to do all of it with you in my arms. I've never really liked night clubs and have had *plenty* of hockey talk to last me a lifetime. There is nowhere I'd rather be, I promise." She smiles up at me as Shane yells for someone to turn the music up from the living room.

I wrap Leah's legs around my waist and begin dancing with her, making her head fall back in laughter until we're both singing along to the lyrics and deliriously happy.

Chapter 44

Taylor

I'll never forget the night Sawyer told me how I'd interfered with him telling Leah how he felt about her. I felt sick over it for days, and if they'd never worked things out and wound up together, I'm not sure I would have ever forgiven myself for it.

I noticed a few times when we were growing up that Leah would look at him like she saw him as more than a friend, but I never said anything about it for two reasons.

One, it could have just been a crush—the simple fact that she thought my brother was cute—and nothing more.

Two, if she had wanted me to know she liked him, she would have told me.

When he left for college after our senior class party that year, I noticed how Leah acted differently when he *did* come back around, but I genuinely had no idea why. And for fear of putting myself in the middle of whatever had happened—or not happened—between them, I let it be. It makes sense now, how when I would talk to Sawyer and mention things that were happening in my friends' lives, he always had more questions about Leah than Lauren or Shane. When she graduated college, he asked what her class ranking was. When she got her master's, he asked if she planned to do more or if she just wanted it as a backup. His eyes always had a little extra spark when her name would come up. I was just too stupid to realize why.

Seeing them now? In their own little world, dancing around my kitchen together, completely in love and obsessed with each other. It just feels right. I'll forever be grateful that they found their way back to each other. There's nothing I love more than seeing my best friend and brother truly happy again. The way they *always* were when they were together.

Chapter 45

Sawyer

Seeing my girl in the stands never gets old.

She looks gorgeous as always, but her outfit tonight is killing me. Leah has always preferred dresses over any other clothing choice—something I began noticing around the same time I started using hot pink tape on my hockey stick—and while I was always able to appreciate her sheer beauty and the softness behind her that her dress choices accentuate, I now appreciate those things *and* imagine what she's got on underneath.

We're on the ice doing warm ups and the way her eyes are glued to me during my groin and glute stretches gives me a little extra encouragement to make my movements nice and slow for her. When I shoot her a wink her cheeks blaze red and I'm glad my hardening cock is well hidden under all this gear.

Once we're up and taking some practice shots, one of my favorite KISS songs comes on and I begin singing it to myself and dancing around the ice like a complete lunatic. The cameraman finds me in no time and when I see Leah swaying her hips and singing along with a couple of the girls, I get the inclination to give my girl a show.

I skate over to the glass by her just as I mouth the words *"I was made for loving you, baby. You were made for loving me,"* then I blow her a kiss, and the camera pans to her, and she blows me one back.

Damn straight. Now everyone knows she's mine.

"Did you forget to put the blades on your skates today, bender?" I laugh, skating past one of the opposing team members that can't seem to stay upright to save his life tonight. We're up by four with only three minutes left in the last period and my adrenaline is at an all-time high. I'm not one hundred percent sure if it's because Leah is here tonight, but I would be lying if I said I haven't felt the impact of her presence during games here lately.

That adrenaline is working in my favor until the guy snaps back at me, and I lose it. "Must be weak from fucking your girl all night."

Why must some people be so ignorantly disrespectful?

I toss my gloves and skate right up to him, landing a punch that I pray knocked a couple of his teeth loose, and I'm immediately escorted to the penalty box.

I hope he chokes on a few Chiclets for that one.

After the game ends, I avoid any contact with that player—for fear I might actually try to kill him—and sit in the locker room trying to calm down after my shower as everyone around me starts to head out. When I'm the last one standing, I grab my phone and shoot off a text to Leah.

ME

Get your ass down here. Please.

DOVE

Omw.

Knock. Knock.

"It's just us, Dove." She steps in the room and closes the distance between us.

"Hey, are you okay?" She places her hands on my shoulders as I'm sitting on the bench by my locker. I run my hand along her arm, from her wrist, to her shoulder and back down again.

"I am now." I pull her down to sit on my lap, taking her lips in mine with an urgency she must sense.

"Hey, talk to me. What happened?" she whispers, letting her fingertips glide over my jaw.

"Nothing," I try to argue, but she knows me better than that and doesn't let it slide.

"Sawyer."

"Some guy pissed me off talking shit on the ice, so I've got more rage and adrenaline coursing through my veins than I know what to do with. I'm sorry." I rest my forehead against hers, as she hums.

"So, what I'm hearing is that you need an outlet? Some way to let all that rage and adrenaline out?" Her voice is all tease, causing me to rear back and look her in the eye. "Cause I could help with that." She stands up from the leg I'd pulled her to sit on and straddles me instead.

"You know I'd never say no to you," I remind her.

Her slender fingers run through the back of my hair as she presses her body tight against mine and dips her tongue into my mouth. The growl that vibrates through my chest perfectly reflects how I'm feeling inside. I grab her ass as she begins rocking back and forth in my lap, causing my dick to stir with excitement. She moans into my mouth, dropping her hips again as she slides over my cock.

"Stand up," she whispers, biting my bottom lip before removing herself from my lap. She pulls me up by the hand before dropping to her knees in front of me.

"What are you up to, little Dove?" I raise a brow as she smirks up at me in a sinfully beautiful way.

"I'm sucking my boyfriend's cock in a locker room, of course."

Holy shit.

She pulls my sweats down, letting my aching cock spring free. When she wraps her lips around the tip, her eyes meet mine and she fucking *winks* at me.

"Fuck, baby," I hiss through my teeth as she sucks me all the way down. She bobs her head back and forth from base to tip a few times before taking me so far back I can feel her throat closing around me.

I reach down and pinch that same spot on her nose and her glossy eyes look up in appreciation. When she takes me back again and her tongue swirls around me, I feel like I might come apart right this second. Then she wraps a hand around my base to work together with her mouth, letting out a hungry moan and I couldn't possibly hold back the groan that comes out of me if I tried.

"Hmm, you like that, don't you?"

"Dove, if you keep this up, I'm gonna come all down your throat."

"Then come for me." She sucks me back down, and my mind explodes at the same time I shoot cum straight down her throat. She flawlessly swallows down every bit, and I pull her to stand, still hard as fucking iron for her.

"You are so fucking sexy when you take control, baby." She pulls her bottom lip in, her eyes practically sparkling from the praise. "But it's my turn now." I pull my sweats back up around my waist, slide my hands up her dress—hooking my thumbs into the string of her silk underwear and pull them down around her ankles.

"I do like how you look on your knees for me, baby," she purrs.

Fuck, she's killing me tonight.

"Hold onto the shelf behind you." I nod to my locker, and she reaches above her head to grab onto it. Then I wrap her legs around my shoulders and bury my face in her sweet pussy. My hands are digging into her smooth skin, her dress is pushed up around her hips and the sweet little moans she's giving me with every flick of my tongue make me never want to come up for air.

"Yes, Sawyer. Right there." She grinds her hips in rhythm with me. "Don't stop. Don't stop," she begs.

I wouldn't fucking dare.

She reaches her climax with the sweetest cry of my name on her lips and I savor every last drop of her.

"Sawyer," she whispers, looking down at me. I slide her legs off my shoulders and stand up to face her.

"Yes, Dove?"

"Please fuck me." My cock is basically trying to find a way back out of my sweatpants on his own at this point.

"I don't have a condom here, baby."

And I want to kick my own ass for not at least having one in my wallet.

"Are you clean?" Her question takes me by surprise.

"Yes?" I narrow my gaze at her, and she rolls her eyes, clearly misreading my tone.

"Well, you know *I* am. I've only ever been with you," she explains, but what I'm having trouble with is not completely falling apart that this is about to happen.

"Are you on birth control?"

"Yes, why?"

"Because once I'm inside you bare, I don't think I'll ever want out." My lips are on hers as I wrap her legs around me. Her legs lock into place allowing me the chance to pull my sweats down to free my cock. After running a finger through her lips to ensure she's wet and ready for me, I line myself up to her entrance.

"Breathe for me, Dove. Let me in." Her whole body relaxes when she lets out a sigh and I slide into her, with nothing between us for the first time. The loudest moan I've ever heard leaves her lips when I do, and I have to hold myself back from absolutely railing her against this locker. I ease into her a few more times, and her hot pussy accepts every inch readily.

"Fuck baby," I bury my face in her neck, breathing her in and biting down on her neck before kissing away the sting from it.

"God, Sawyer, you feel so good. I need more."

"Anything you want, baby." I grab onto her ass and thrust into her, making her scream my name so loud I have to cover her mouth with my hand.

"Shhh. We don't want to have to stop, do we?" She shakes her head. "You gonna be quiet if I move my hand?" She nods.

"Don't stop. Please, don't stop," she whispers pleadingly.

"Atta girl. Let me feel how much you love getting fucked by me, Dove. Soak my cock with your cum baby." I pull the top of her dress down and suck her nipple into my mouth, making another beautiful cry fall from her lips—though I can tell she's *trying* to keep quiet.

"Such a good girl."

I pull the other side of her dress down, sucking the other nipple into my mouth, sinking my cock into her harder with every thrust.

"Sawyer, I'm coming!" she cries, digging her nails into my shoulders as she milks me for all I'm worth.

"That's my fucking girl," I grunt through my own release. I spill every drop into her as her walls clench around me. She pulls me into a kiss that completely stops time around us, and I don't think life will ever get better than it is right now with her.

"Fucking you, Dove. Feels like coming home." She giggles and presses her forehead against mine, running her fingers through my hair the way I love.

"You feel like home to me too, Sawyer."

"I love you so much."

"I love you, too."

Chapter 46

MOOSE

Hey beautiful, how do you feel about a second first
date?

ME

With you? I feel good about it.

MOOSE

I'm not going to ask about the clarification about it
being with me, but I'll come pick you up at 6.

ME

What should I wear?

MOOSE

A dress.

ME

That's equally very specific and very vague. 😑

MOOSE

I love you in dresses. But I'm not picky, so wear
what you feel good in. See you tonight. 😊

ME

See you tonight. 🤍

I love you in dresses.

Well, watch me never wear anything else again.

I rub my hands over the dress I'm wearing, which is undoubtedly one of the sexiest pieces of clothing I own—which is probably the reason I've never worn it before.

I purchased it a couple of years ago and I immediately threw it in the back of my closet after trying it on because it was *pushing* the limits of my comfort zone.

I've never liked having attention drawn to me, preferring instead to fade into my surroundings rather than be the one people noticed. It's different with Sawyer though, I feel a new sense of confidence when I'm with him. I *want* to draw his attention and know he can't take his eyes off me.

So instead of slumping my shoulders and folding my arms to try and hide from my appearance, my shoulders are back, my head held high, and I feel hot as fuck.

I hear a knock at the door and my heart skips a beat. I glance at the clock on my dresser and notice it's six o'clock on the dot. I grab my black strappy heels and slide them on before rushing to answer the door.

"Evenin, Dove."

Oh, fuck me. He looks delicious.

He's wearing a pair of cropped navy-blue slacks and a white button down shirt—that both fit him like a second skin—with a pair of white sneakers. The top few buttons of his shirt are undone, showing off the tattoos on his chest, and the sleeves of his shirt are rolled up to his elbows.

When I finally meet his eye after my lustful inspection of him, I see that he's doing the same with me. That hungry look in his eye that makes me weak in the knees is on full display as his eyes rake over my body.

"You are breathtaking, baby." He takes my hand in his, turning me under his arm before pulling me into him.

"You're one to talk." My hands fall to his chest as he bends to kiss me and, as always, I melt into him.

"You ready to go?" I nod my response, grab my purse from the hook inside the door and lock up before he escorts me to his truck.

"Sawyer, I love you, but why are we at the grocery store?" I turn to face him, a little paranoid that I've severely over dressed for the occasion.

He simply smirks back at me. "I'm cooking you dinner tonight, but I wanted you to help me pick what to make."

"You can cook?!"

"I can. Let's go." He winks at me then comes around to open my door. We walk through the store looking like we're headed to a black-tie event while getting everything we need for Sawyer to make parmesan chicken.

"People are staring at us," I whisper in his ear, as we stand staring at the wall of cheeses.

"Can you blame them?" he whispers back, wrapping his arms around me. "You look absolutely heart-stopping in that dress." He kisses my neck. "But *I* can't wait to see you out of it." He kisses the same spot again as goosebumps spread across my arms and down my legs.

"Found it!" I say, pulling the parmesan cheese off the shelf before turning back to him. "Let's go."

He raises a brow and teases me. "You in a rush, Dove?"

I take a step closer to him, running my fingers lightly over the exposed part of his chest as I look up at him with the most seductive look I can conjure up. "Yes."

Two can play this game.

"Yeah, okay let's go." He throws the bag into the basket and grabs my hand, rushing us to the checkout line.

"When did you learn to cook?" Sawyer finishes plating our food, taking it over to the table as I follow behind with the wine we picked up. The small laugh he breathes out makes my curiosity grow even more.

"So, it was my first year playing with the Bears. We were on a winning streak and decided we should all go out and celebrate. I think I got more wasted that night than I had ever gotten in high school or college put together. The next morning, I was so hungover I knew I needed to eat something to absorb all the alcohol and either make it come back up or settle it." I grimace at the statement as we begin eating.

"Anyway, I made it to the kitchen of my apartment and was rifling through the cabinets like a starved raccoon and tried to make something with the stuff I had on hand—which was some hot dogs, *beer* and ramen."

"Oh, god."

"I decided after that day that, *one*, I would never get that drunk again, and *two*, it was time to call Mama and ask her to teach me how to cook for myself."

"Why didn't you just order food in or something?"

"I had thrown my phone off a two-story building the night before, apparently." My mouth hangs open as he raises his brows. "*Yeahhh*," he whispers.

"Moose! What the hell?" I ask through my laughter. His cheeks turn red and he shakes his head, as if he's trying to rid the memory. "Sounds like you had some good times back then."

"Eh, it was alright, I guess. I made many story worthy memories, that's for sure." He never meets my eye as he continues eating the *delicious* dinner he's made us.

"What about you, Dove? What was the craziest thing you ever did?" He finally looks up and my face falls. "Oh, come on, I just told you I tossed my phone off a building because I was so drunk. Yours surely can't be worse than that."

"You're right. Because I've never had a crazy drunken night. At least none that you weren't a part of." My cheeks heat when a memory of us getting a little too tipsy in high school resurfaces. I was *sure* he had caught me practically undressing him with my eyes while we were having game night in one of our friends' basement one night. I stopped drinking Smirnoff after that.

"Doesn't have to be a drunken night. Not everyone makes as horrible of decisions as me," he teases. "Any crazy parties or pranks you pulled in college?" I roll my lips and shake my head. He folds his arms over his chest and sits back in his seat, narrowing his gaze on me.

"Yeah, my Dove never was the crazy party girl type. Too sweet and pure of heart for all that shit."

"Is that why you call me that?" I tilt my head, trying to figure out why in the world I never asked before. I just blindly accepted it because I liked that it was something only Sawyer called me. He leans forward, placing his elbows on the table as he laces his fingers together.

"You know, it's funny. When I first called you that it was because I thought it was fitting—I associated it with the pure, innocent soul you were. But then I found out what doves truly represent and knew I'd picked the right name for you."

"What do they represent?" I frown.

"Doves are often a symbol of peace, freedom…and love. The three most accurate things I could use to describe how I feel when I'm with you." I stand up and round the table, causing Sawyer to sit back in his seat. He pushes the chair further away when I place a hand on his shoulder, and when there's enough room, I place a leg on each side of his hips and sit.

"Is that so?" I ask, running my fingers through his hair.

"It is. I've never felt as at peace as I do when I look into your beautiful green eyes," he brushes his fingertips down the length of my arm.

"As free as I do when I'm with you—" He presses his lips to my neck.

"Kissing you." Kiss.

"Touching you." Kiss.

"When I'm inside of you," he whispers in my ear, sending electricity racing down my spine. Then he leans back and looks me in the eyes.

"And I've never loved anyone the way that I love you, Dove. No one has ever come close, and no one else ever will."

Chapter 47

Sawyer

"Hey Dove?"

"Hmm?" Even her little hum of a response sounds sweet.

Her body is pressed against me, with one of her legs draped lazily over mine while she traces her fingertips up and down my chest.

"Why did you wait?" Her fingers stop and her head pops up so she can look at me.

"To have sex?"

"Yeah. I just mean… I know you said you and that Josh guy didn't date but…was there ever anyone else?" She lets out a sigh that makes me wish I could take that last bit back. I don't think I want to know if there was someone else she wanted that with. She's *mine* now. That's all that matters.

"Yeah. There was someone else. He was the only guy I ever really thought of that way and when it didn't work with him the way I had hoped it would, I just kind of… I don't know. Lost the desire?" She shrugs. "So, I dated. But when I would think of sleeping with anyone but him it never felt right." It suddenly feels like there's a boulder on my chest, and I feel like a fucking idiot for even asking the damn question in the first place.

"Who was the guy?"

"Sawyer?" I can't quite pinpoint the tone of her voice, but I can tell she's wondering why I'm asking. She sits up straighter in the bed, letting the sheet fall to showcase her perfect body.

Smooth skin.

Full breasts.

Pussy that only I've ever had.

So why do I keep torturing myself over who was in her past?

Because that Josh guy showing up really took you by surprise and you need to learn to let things go.

"It was you." Her words confuse me, before I can fully process them.

"Me?"

"You honestly didn't know?" I shake my head.

Should I have? I guess I could have assumed as much after knowing how we both felt back then, but a teenage crush is different than waiting your whole life to have sex with someone.

"Sawyer, I didn't just have a crush on you when we were younger. I had fallen in love with you. You had more of my heart than I ever realized I had given you. I daydreamed about what it would be like to be yours almost every day—to the point I felt a little creepy if I'm honest." We both let out soft laughs, then she continues. "I wanted you to want me back so badly, and when you left, I never thought of anyone the same way I'd thought of you."

"And now?" She frowns at me, sliding onto my lap.

"What do you mean *and now*?"

"Do you still only think of me?"

"Why are you asking me this? Have I done something to make you think differently?" I begin shaking my head before she even finishes.

"No. I just can't stop thinking about that guy showing up and how he wanted to take you away to another country. I just..." *Fuck, I hate this.* "You say you're worried I'll walk away again, and I've assured you that it will never happen. But I'm scared too, Dove. Because what if you realize I'm not the guy you fell in love with all those years ago? That if who I am now isn't what you want anymore. What if one day you wake up and decide you don't love me, but it was the idea of me you fell so hard for. You're my future Leah, my forever. The only life truly worth living, is one with you in it. So what if—" She presses her finger to my lips, gripping both sides of my face and kissing me. Kissing me as if I'm it for her, as if she's promising not to disappear from my life, like I've begun to fear she will.

I always knew I was a jealous motherfucker, but I didn't realize how ill I truly felt at the thought of not having her anymore.

"You're not the boy I fell in love with in high school, Sawyer. You're the man who came back for me. I've fallen in love with *this* version of you tenfold. I'm not walking away either. I promise." I wrap my arms around her tighter, burying my face in her chest, breathing her in, hoping that I can somehow tether her soul to mine. Then she wraps a hand around my length and without warning, she slides herself onto me.

"Fuck, baby." I growl, sucking in a breath through my teeth as she bites down on her bottom lip.

"I. Am. Yours." Every word comes out in sync with her sliding up and down my cock. "Only. Always. Forever." Then, as she continues to ride me, she pulls my lips to hers, sliding her tongue across my lips and I feel it.

The tethering of our souls.

Only. Always. Forever. Mine.

DEVON

My man. I'll tell my boy to add you to the list with a plus one.

ME

Thanks Dev.

DEVON

No sweat. Maybe you can get the other g-pa's out of the house for the night.

ME

Who the hell are the g-pa's???

DEVON

You know, you, Matty, Javi… All settled down and happy and shit. Just like my grandpa.

ME

Nice.

DEVON

Tell them to come. See you tonight.

ME

You and Lyss wanna go to Fr33style tonight?

MATTY

What the hell kind of name for a club is that?

ME

Dude, I have no idea. But I wanted to take Leah out and Dev said that's where they'd be.

MATTY

Did he put you up to asking me?

ME

Yes, but I was going to ask you anyway. If I'm gonna survive this night with Devon there, I'm gonna need you there too my guy.

MATTY

Fair enough. I think Lyss wants to go so we'll meet you there. Tell Dev to add us to the list.

ME

Will do.

"Tell the grumpy bunch to leave you alone. Your muscles move every time you type and it's disturbing my sleep," Leah grumbles from her place tucked beneath my arm.

"It's not the grumpy bunch, but I'm sorry for disrupting your sleep." I kiss the top of her head and she finally looks up at me.

"Then who was it?" She hides her face to yawn then looks back up at me.

"Devon and Matty. How do you feel about going out with some of the team tonight?" She perks up a little more.

"Really? Where? How come?" I can't help but laugh at her nervous, yet excited questioning.

"Yes really. A place called freestyle, and because I want you to have one night that can at least resemble a *party girl* night but this way you get to do it with *me*." Her eyes soften when she realizes my motivation behind taking her out tonight.

"You're giving me a party girl night?" She pokes her lip out in a fake pout.

"Only if you want to go. If you've passed that phase, then I can tell Devon to take us off the—"

"I wanna go," she cuts me off, looking at her dress on the floor. Then her face falls. I'm not sure why because when I recall the way it was basically ripped from her body last night, my face lights the fuck up.

"What's the matter?" My fingers rub along her back, watching as her nipples harden from my touch.

"I don't have anything to wear."

"What are you talking about? I have seen you in countless outfits that made me want to do the same thing to them that I did to that dress last night."

"I'm sure I can find something." She smiles and wraps her arms around my neck, kissing me in thanks.

Chapter 48

"We're not going," Sawyer says from his place on my bed when I walk out of the bathroom.

"What?" My eyes grow wide, and my movements freeze in shock.

"Let's just stay home and see how many different positions I can put you in while you're wearing that skirt." I roll my eyes when he gives me a devilish smirk. Then I turn to look in the mirror again.

"Should I change? It's too much, isn't it. I should wear something else." I look in my full-length mirror and begin messing with the zipper on my skirt when he rushes over to stop me.

"Don't you dare take this skirt off." He plants a kiss on the spot right behind my ear that makes my brain swim.

"Is it too short? What if—"

"Stop right there. Look." He nods to the mirror, standing behind me like a shadow.

"Forget where we're going, and that anyone else is going to be there. How do you feel? In what you're wearing right now, with it being just me and you." I drag my eyes away from the reflection of his and take in my appearance again–from the booties I'm wearing, to the black bouncy skirt, to the corset top, all the way to my hair and makeup—and I smile.

"I feel...good, confident, kinda sexy." My cheeks heat at the small admission.

"*Very* sexy," he corrects. "Then keep it on. I know how to fight, baby, I didn't spend half of last season in the penalty box for nothing. So, if you're comfortable in this when it's just the two of us, then I'll make you feel like we're the only ones there." He winks at me, letting his hands glide down over my hips.

"Sound good?" I'm practically panting when his fingers tease just inside the hemline of my skirt.

"Yes," I breathe the word out, trying to keep my composure as he kisses and bites on my neck.

We may never make it to this club...

We make it to *Fr33style*...eventually, and I can't get over the surreal feeling of being out—*at a club*—with Sawyer.

"Sawyer Clark." Sawyer gives his name to the bouncer, keeping his hand wrapped protectively around my waist as we pass the line that is so long it disappears behind the back of the building. I glance around and see girls eyeing him, whispering and giggling as they take him in.

I can't blame them; I'd be doing the *same* damn thing if I were them. Hell, I *was* them for so many years. I look up at him and he gives me a flirty wink, and I can't help the satisfaction I feel knowing I'm his. I'm no longer the girl wishing he'd look my way and fantasizing about him in the most secret parts of my mind.

Now I'm the girl that he loves, that he's brought to a club to help her live out a missed college experience and the one he's scared to lose—and that knowledge is empowering. Which is why their whispers and ogling don't make me feel insecure like they once would have, but they make me feel that much more confident.

I reach up on my toes and plant a chaste kiss to his cheek, but he pulls me in to kiss me harder, taking my breath away when he does. It only lasts a moment, but it still has the power behind it to consume me.

"Enjoy your night." The bouncer says, releasing the rope from in front of us.

I look over my shoulder at the girls who have their mouths hung open and crushed expressions on their faces and shoot them a wink before turning to walk into the building, with Sawyer's hand on my ass.

"You're a naughty thing, aren't you?" he whispers in my ear, sending chills racing down my spine.

"I don't know what you mean," I feign innocence, but he pulls me into him harder, demanding every bit of my attention to be on him.

"Go ahead and play innocent, baby, but I'm *all yours.*" He leans in, letting his lips brush along the shell of my ear. "And it makes me hard as fuck knowing you want to remind the world of that." He nips at my ear before kissing me in a way that leaves no room for question about who he belongs to.

"Damn dude, looks like you should have just stayed home," someone says, interrupting our world muting kiss.

"Matty, so glad you guys could make it." Sawyer greets him and that's when my eyes find Lyssa's.

"Hi, long time no see." Lyssa smiles, leaning in to hug me. "Hey there, Cowboy," she greets Sawyer and I feel his grip tighten on me.

I had almost forgotten how much of an ass I'd been about her—to myself of course—when I thought she and Sawyer were dating.

"Lyssa, good to see you again." He nods politely to her, then just as Matty claps his hands and opens his mouth to say something, someone else appears from seemingly nowhere.

"Do my eyes deceive me?" The brightest smile spreads across the guy's face as he wraps his arms around both Sawyer and Matty's shoulders. "Whatever you two beautiful ladies did to get these two out tonight, thank you." He unwraps his arms and places his palms together giving Lyssa and I both a slight bow of thanks. Our eyes widen at each other as we both try to hold back a laugh.

"Devon, this is my girl, Leah." Sawyer winks at me, causing my cheeks to blush immediately. "Leah, this is Devon."

"Pleasure to meet you, Beauty. I have to bounce, but I do hope you enjoy your night." He winks at me before walking away and I can't help but notice Sawyer's jaw tightening as he raises a brow at him.

"Let's sit, yeah?" Matty interjects, holding a hand out to guide us further into the club. For the first time since walking in, I take in the space and my eyes widen as I try to adjust my vision.

All the tables and booth seats are stark white with neon lights lining every inch of them. The dance floor surrounds a small platform where people can go up to dance—though it's currently empty—and the bar covers the length of the far-left wall with at least four bartenders working it. There's a big ass restroom sign with an arrow on the very back wall and to the right is the massive DJ's table.

We make our way over to a small circular booth and slide in, Lyssa and me in the middle with Sawyer and Matty on the outside.

"We'll grab the drinks, be right back." Sawyer kisses my cheek and stands up while Lyssa tells Matty what she wants from the bar.

I'm guessing Sawyer is confident in my drink choice since he didn't ask me?

"So!" Lyssa chirps. "Like I said before, long time no see." She shifts in her seat to tuck her feet beneath her bottom.

"Yeah! I've been to a couple of home games, but I guess our seats are like, insanely far from each other, maybe?" I laugh and she nods.

"Yeah, I'm usually on the upper level with Matty's mom and sister."

"Ah, that would be why. Me and my friends are down closer to the ice."

"Well, we'll have to make sure we steal you away during the playoff games. I need someone to stress eat with." She rolls her eyes, tucking a strand of blonde hair behind her. "Matty's mom basically fasts during games and his sister is concerningly calm when he plays."

"Mental," I say sarcastically.

"Right?!" she laughs in response. "I knew we'd get along well. I'm glad we came out with you guys tonight." A wave of guilt rushes into my gut that I can't help but feel *ridiculous* about.

"I have a confession."

"Uh-oh. Why do I feel like this isn't the juicy kind?" I laugh as she leans in closer to me.

"The first time I met you, wasn't the first time I'd *seen* you."

Her brows pinch together. "*Okayyy.*"

"I'd been out at Knockin Boots one night—on a date, actually—and saw you and Sawyer dancing together. Then I saw you guys *leaving* together and I pretty much hated you immediately. So, when I was talking to you in the hallway that day, I was trying to find out if you two were dating. Then you called him Cowboy and I'm so used to only hearing couples giving each other cutesy little nicknames that I was all but convinced you two were together, and seeing as how he'd just had a *very* close proximity conversation with me in the locker room, I was basically simmering with rage." The anxiety I'm feeling over explaining this to her vanishes when she throws her head back and laughs.

"Oh my god, that is the best story ever."

"It was…*so* embarrassing when I actually confronted him about it. I thought I was some badass by calling him out on his bullshit and then it came back to bite me in the ass when I wound up looking jealous."

"You were *so* jealous." Lyssa tilts her head at me, and I can't help but laugh.

"I was *so* jealous. I mean freaking look at you. Who wouldn't be?" I wave a hand up and down bringing attention to how hot she is.

"Well thank you, but you're downright *stunning*. This hair alone makes me wish I could hate you," she sighs dramatically. "Unfortu-nately, you're delightful as hell. Looks like I'll just have to be in love with you instead."

It's amazing how much she reminds me of the rest of my friends.

"Hey now, none of that." Matty slides in next to her and she rolls her eyes at him.

"You were all worried about her being swept up by my dancing, but it turns out it's my girl she's taken with." Sawyer sets a drink down on the table in front of me before wrapping his arm around my shoulder.

"Lyssa and I are in love; you will just have to get over it." I reach a hand out and she takes it in hers and kisses the top of it. I pucker my lips to blow a kiss in her direction and wink—leaving both guys speechless. Then Lyssa and I burst into laughter.

After about three vodka cranberries, two strawberry margaritas— that Sawyer was not shy about taking massive sips from—and two tequila shots later, Lyssa and I are on the dance floor giggling, singing and swaying our hips to the music.

"Come with me," she yells, and I follow blindly behind her. Next thing I know, she's pulling me up on the platform with her. "That guy kept bumping into my ass, this way we're untouchable." She's still yelling as the song changes, and when "Down On Me" by Jeremih starts bumping through the speakers it feels like I'm back in high school all over again. Only this time, I have this newfound confidence and a shit ton of alcohol to encourage me to actually dance to it.

"Oh my god, I love this song!" she screams.

And then we turn into complete whores—and it's the most fun I think I've ever had.

We bounce and grind and shake our asses on each other like we've known each other forever and when she bends over to twerk her ass in front of me, I give it a good smack and we fall into a fit of laughter.

"Hell yeah!" I hear someone shout from the crowd.

"Sexy as fuck!" someone else yells.

I begin looking around the room and when I can't tell where it's coming from, I settle my gaze on our table, only to see Sawyer and Matty both heading in our direction.

I've seen Sawyer in pretty much everything—his hockey uniform, a three-piece suit, a hoodie and jeans, boxers, *nothing*—but it never fails, I find new things to love about him in every single thing he wears. Tonight, for instance, he is in a pair of dark-blue jeans, green and black high-top sneakers, a black T-shirt that hugs him in *all* the right places, and a black ball cap that is getting turned backwards as he gets closer to the stage.

Aaaand I'm wet.

Just when I think they're going to rip us from the stage—throwing us over their shoulders and hauling us out of here—they step up onto it with us.

He pulls me into him, my back flush with his front and his hands slide down to my hips as he begins rocking his with mine to the music. I reach up, letting my hands fall comfortably around the back of his neck as we move together. While swaying my hips, I turn in his grip and we keep moving while he sings along, looking at me like he could absolutely devour me.

"Bathroom, now," he growls into my ear. I lean back to see the hungry look in his eyes and nod as we make our way towards the far wall. When we bypass the lines to the restroom I wonder if there's some sort of VIP one I am unaware of.

Holy shit, there is.

When Sawyer sees the confused look on my face he smirks and answers my unasked question. "This is Devon's brother's club. We get a bit of special treatment here." He punches in a four digit code to the keypad on the door, the light turning green with a click as it unlocks. Then he pulls me in behind him, slamming the door shut once we're inside.

He pulls me to him and his lips come crashing into mine with desperation. I wrap my hands around the back of his neck as he lifts my ass up onto the sink counter, spreading my legs to step between them. His lips move down my neck all the way to the neckline of my corset, my hands tangling in his hair as my head falls back, savoring the feeling of his lips on my skin.

Our eyes meet again when his hands disappear beneath my skirt, and I nod eagerly, lifting my hips so he can slide my underwear off. Then he hits his knees, wrapping my legs around his shoulders as he pulls my ass to the very edge of the counter. My mind feels so light from the buzz of the alcohol that my body is more relaxed than I think it's ever been. It doesn't take long before he's bringing me to the edge of my first orgasm.

"Sawyer, I'm gonna come," I whisper as my head falls back on the mirror. Almost as fast as I can get the words out, I make good on my word. My legs wrap tighter around him as he continues kissing and sucking my clit, devouring me like the animal I've discovered he is.

Then he's on his feet again. "Can you stand?"

Um, probably the hell not.

I feel like I'm having an out of body experience as I watch the sexiest man I've ever laid eyes on undo his belt and free himself from his boxers. I manage to slide off the marble and land on my feet—thank god.

"Turn around; hands on the sink." My thighs squeeze together at the command. I turn around and place my hands palm down on the cool surface. Then he wraps his hands around my waist and pulls me back, pressing my back down as he flips my skirt up. My breath is caught in my throat as I watch his muscular arms flex as he puts me where he wants me.

"Breathe for me, Dove." I take a deep breath in, but before I can completely release it, he slams into me, and I cry out in pure plea-sure. I welcome the warmth and press my ass further into him, loving the stretch from his cock and the way he always manages to hit that sweet spot that makes me see stars.

His grip on my hips is as unrelenting as every thrust into me, and his eyes remain locked on mine through the mirror the entire time.

"You know, you asked me once before what my favorite position was," he growls, slowing his pace.

Teasing me.

Torturing me.

"I always preferred this position because I could imagine it was whoever I wanted if I wasn't looking them in the face." My eyes snap up to his in the reflection.

What the fuck? Why is he saying this to me? And why now?

"Wanna know who I always imagined?"

"No. I would like you to stop talking about other women and fuck *me,*" I snap. This makes him smile so devilishly that my pussy squeezes around him. He growls and gives me a warning look. Then he leans over, kissing the back of my neck until his lips are at my ear.

"I imagined it was *you.* Always you. Only you." I'm not really sure what to make of this new information. I should probably be appalled —that he did that in the first place *and* that he's decided to bring this up *now*—but I can't manage to feel anything but blissful satisfaction. He must see it on my face because he stands back up, confidence painted all over his face.

"I'll only ever fuck you like this if I get to see your pretty face while I do. No more pretending—because I've finally got you."

"Sawyer, please." I whine, needing more from him.

"Please what, Dove?"

"Please fuck me harder."

"You are so pretty when you're begging, baby." He gives me what I want, railing into me until I'm gripping the counter so tight my knuckles are turning white.

"Right there, Sawyer. Oh! Don't stop." He pulls me up, bringing my back flush to his chest as he reaches around, gently massaging circles onto my clit until I'm moaning uncontrollably. "Sawyer." His name falls off my lips as a pant. He is dominating my body unlike ever before and I can barely stand from the orgasm building in every inch of my body.

"Louder for me, Dove." All at once he thrusts into me, flicks my clit and bites down on my neck, sending me into the abyss of orgasms.

"Sawyer! God, yes!" The most powerful one I've ever experienced rips through me, making my knees almost buckle. Sawyer wraps his other arm around me, keeping me upright as he chases his own release.

"Atta girl, scream for me baby."

As if I don't know how to not to, I let out one final scream of pleasure and he spills inside of me.

"Fuck, Dove!" I can still feel him pulsing inside me, as I watch him bury his face into my neck. He lets out a moan, gently kissing my neck before he pulls out of me, letting his cum drip down my leg. He tucks himself back in his jeans, righting his belt before grabbing a napkin to wipe my leg. Then he grabs my underwear from the floor, but before I can take them back he nods to the toilet and I roll my eyes.

Is it weird I find it so hot that he thinks of all *the post sex care details?*

Chapter 49

Leah

TAY

Leah!!!! Where the hell have you been?

That's a fair question. I have spent the last two months completely consumed by Sawyer. They've flown by so quickly I didn't even realize spring break was next week until one of my students mentioned going to the beach this weekend.

ME

Your brother's bed.

SHANE

😂💥

RUBY

Hell yes.

LAUREN

You asked for that one, Tay. Where the hell else would she be?

ME

😇

TAY

HOW AM I SUPPOSED TO PRETEND HE IS A RANDOM HOCKEY PLAYER IF YOU DIRECTLY ADDRESS HIM AS MY BROTHER?!?!?!?

SHANE

Stop shouting babe. It'll give you wrinkles faster.

LAUREN

True statement.

RUBY

I'll be a raisin before 40 at this rate.

ME

I'm sorry. I'm sorry. Have I missed a lot?

TAY

No, I'm being dramatic. I just miss you guys. I've had a shit schedule lately anyways.

SHANE

I've been busy getting my next exhibit ready to ship to Hugh and chasing Cece around. Nothing to miss here.

LAUREN

I'm not even adding to this convo because yall think my problem is hot and I'm still mad about it.

RUBY

Poe is rolling over now. Other than that, not much to report.

ME

I went to a club and danced with a girl I thought was dating Sawyer earlier this year. We're in love now.

RUBY

You and Sawyer or you and this HARLET?

TAY

You tramp!!!

SHANE

Divorce. Immediately.

LAUREN

How could you do this to us?

ME

I think you guys would really like her. Her name is Lyssa, she's dating Matty.

TAY

Oh I've met her before! She is really nice.

RUBY

You switched sides really fast.

ME

Should we invite her to girls night?

SHANE

Sure. Margs for six, coming right up. 🦢

I've just finished sending a picture of my feet propped up on my desk and sent it to Sawyer asking if it's spring break yet, when I hear someone knocking on my classroom door.

Knock knock knock.

God, that was the saddest knock I've ever heard.

I look up from my desk to see Jackson standing in the doorway and my stomach twists uncomfortably. He has actively avoided me for the last two months and I can't say I've minded it. The way things ended with us left no sorrow in my heart or mind for this man.

"Hey, can we talk for a minute?" He takes a cautious step inside my classroom, and I straighten my posture.

"Sure, come on in." I wave a hand in front of me and he walks a little further in, sitting on one of the small desks. "How can I help you, Jackson?" My tone is nothing short of professional, and while I believe that to be the best course of action here, he must disagree. His brows knit together, and he looks at me with a sadness in his eyes that makes me want to roll mine so far back in my head that I can't see him anymore.

I refrain from doing so.

"I don't know if you got my text or not, after Christmas, or if you did and you're just ignoring me."

Ugh, is he serious?

"I really am sorry for what I said. I didn't want things to end like that between us. I didn't want them to end at all. We had something so good up until then. Didn't we?"

Um, no.

"Jackson," I lean forward, folding my hands together on top of my desk. "Do you like my friends? Yes or no."

"I said I would try—"

"Yes. Or. No." He lets out a sigh that tells me this whole conversation is a huge waste of time.

"I like *you*, Leah. In the grand scheme of things, does it really matter if I like your friends or not? I can really picture a future with you."

I can too, and it's freaking terrifying.

"Is that so?" A new voice joins the conversation and I look over to see my six-foot-four, perfect hockey star of a boyfriend filling the doorway. His posture is rigid and intimidating, his head is tilted and the most beautiful bouquet of wildflowers I've ever seen is in his hands. His eyes drag from Jackson over to me with a stoic look in his eye. "Why do so many people seem to think they have a future with you, when they so clearly do not?" His features completely relax when I smile at him.

"Sawyer, what are you doing here?" I am up from my seat and rushing over to him leaving the conversation that was happening with Jackson when he showed up in the dust. He glances at Jackson again, a look of disdain in his eyes when he does, then his gaze softens when it's back on me.

"I wanted to bring my girl some flowers, give her something *almost* as beautiful as her to look at—" he stops and leans down to whisper in my ear low enough that Jackson can't hear him. "Until you get home and can watch yourself come apart around me." He leans back up and winks at me, making my cheeks heat instantly. He hands me the bouquet and I breathe them in, they smell just as lovely as they look. Then Jackson clears his throat, reminding me of his very unwelcome presence.

"Your girl?" I turn around, seeing that he has stood up and has his arms crossed over his chest. He looks so *small* in comparison to Sawyer, it's almost laughable that he's trying to make himself look intimidating. "Aren't you the same guy that flew off the handle when I kissed said girl in question." He smirks and I can't hold my eye roll back any longer. I hate awkward encounters such as this, but I am *not* here for the dick measuring contest that is about to break out in the middle of my kindergarten classroom.

"The very same," Sawyer answers, shoving his hands into his front pockets. He's keeping himself more composed than I'd expected, but that may be *because* he's in a kindergarten classroom. Jackson turns a worrisome shade of red as he scoffs. Narrowing his eyes as he looks between Sawyer and me.

"Was this why you broke things off with me? It wasn't the stupid friend thing; it was because of this date ruining asshole?"

"No, Jackson. I ended it for exactly the reason I told you."

"Sure, Leah. Whatever you need to tell yourself to feel better." He gives me a look so condescending it makes me want to throw something at him. When he makes it to the doorway, Sawyer grabs my waist, moving into the classroom with me to move out of Jackson's way.

"Just remember, she *was* mine first." Jackson brushes past him and Sawyer stops him with the back of his hand.

"Oh, weasel. She was *never* yours." Jackson frowns at Sawyer, then looks at me—possibly waiting for me to correct him—then nods.

"Good to know," he mumbles, pinning me with the same distasteful stare as before.

"You know what, Jackson. Maybe it did have something to do with Sawyer, because if I'm being completely honest—which I always am—I felt more with him during one kiss than I did with you the entire time we were *"dating"*. But that still doesn't change the fact that I would *never* be with someone who tried to have a relationship with me and keep our life completely separate from the one I have already established as well as the people in it. Nor does it give you the right to stand here and disrespect me just because we weren't compatible, and your feelings are hurt over it." His face goes completely red, and he scoffs his final goodbye.

"Have a nice life."

I *almost* feel bad, until I remember how truly awful he is as a person.

Yeah, I don't feel bad at all actually.

"I don't like that you see that guy every day," Sawyer growls.

"Me either," I sigh, letting go of some of the pent-up aggression towards him. Then I smile as I turn my attention completely back to Sawyer. "So, you really just wanted to bring me flowers?"

"Well, not entirely..."

When I finally got back to the group text after Sawyer stopped by, we managed to throw together the world's most last-minute girls night that even Lyssa was available to make on such short notice—which just felt like a miracle.

We're all sitting around the island at Lauren's house with take-out containers covering every inch of the counter as I finish telling them about Sawyer's visit at school today.

"Oh my gosh, he asked you to go with him?!" Shane squeals.

Sawyer ended up asking me to go to his away games with him this week since he knew I'd be out of school, and I think that might just be the most romantic thing ever.

"Yessss. They're playing in Minnesota, and he said he really wanted to take me somewhere special while we're there."

"That is so romantic, I can't wait to hear all about it." Lyssa squeezes my hand before taking another sip of her margarita. "Holy shit, Leah. You weren't lying, this is the best margarita I've ever had." Shane takes a very humble bow, and we all start to laugh.

"I don't know how you're not drinking one yourself." Lyssa adds, pointing to Shane. I frown when I realize she's right. Shane hasn't poured herself one yet and the pitcher is almost empty.

"I was wondering how long it would take someone to notice." We all look like meerkats when we realize.

"Are you pregnant?!" Taylor screams. Then Shane pulls an ultrasound out of her back pocket.

"OH MY GOD!" We all begin screaming and sobbing in unison.

"Congratulations!" Lyssa tells her, joining our little group hug.

"Thank you, welcome to girls' night," Shane laughs.

"They're pretty much all like this," Lauren says. "Dramatic, I mean. Not someone being pregnant at every one of them. That would be insane." She waves one hand around as she explains, wiping the tears from her eyes with the other.

"Let's not wait to have girls' night for so long anymore. We *clearly* missed more than Shane let on," Ruby says in an accusatory tone.

"Well, I wasn't going to let it slip in a *text*. I needed to hear the joyful screams." We all break from the group hug.

"Are you guys waiting to find out what you're having again?" Lauren asks, as we all use napkins to dab our tears away.

"Yep! Just like with Cece." She slides the ultrasound onto the counter, leaving it there for us to look at while we keep chatting.

"When do you guys leave, Leah?"

"Tomorrow, actually. I'm supposed to stop by my parents' house tonight to see them before I go. I feel like I haven't seen them in *years*," I groan. I've missed them more than I could ever accurately describe.

"Well get out of here then. Tell Loretta and Allen I say hello."

Taylor grins at me and I roll my eyes. She's fully taken on the task of calling them by their first names like Mom told her to on Thanksgiving and it is *so* weird.

I pull up to my parent's house and hope my dad hasn't already gone to bed. It's just past nine so I'm hoping maybe he stayed up if he knew I was coming. I walk in and head straight to the living room to see my parents both sitting on the couch together, even though Dad has his arms crossed over his chest and is doing *the dad sleep*.

You know, when they're in an upright position but are passed the hell out. That one.

"Hiiii," I sing out softly.

"Hey sweetheart. Allen wake up," Mom greets me first then elbows my dad in the side. He doesn't get startled or jerk awake, his eyes simply pop open, and he scans the room until he sees me.

"Hey Sweetpea. Good to see you." He pushes himself up off the couch and walks over to wrap me in a hug.

"Hey daddy, it's good to see you too. How are you?"

"Oh I'm right as rain." He gives me a playful shake and I smile at him.

"How about you? You good?"

"I'm really good," I assure him.

"No drives necessary then?" He grabs his keys from his pocket and spins them around his finger, making me realize he's still in his street clothes and not in his pajamas like he *always* is at this hour.

"None necessary, but always appreciated." I lean up on my toes and kiss his cheek, pulling him in for another appreciative hug.

"Maybe we'll go just for fun when you get back next week, huh?"

"Sounds like a plan."

"Good, I wanna hear all about this new exciting life you're living."

He gives me a wink and kisses my head. "Alright, your old man is going to bed. I love you Sweetpea."

"Love you, Dad."

"Love you, Lettie." He calls to my mom, who is still snuggled on the couch knitting.

"I love you too, dear."

I hope Sawyer and I stay in love for as long as they have.

I kick my shoes off and join Mom on the couch, snuggling under my blanket like I always do.

"Fill me in, Honey. What have I missed?" I let out a sigh, thinking about all the things I've done over the last two months—that I can comfortably share with my mother.

"Everything, and nothing." She laughs like she understands. "How is that possible? How does life feel so different but still the same?" She looks over at me, placing her project in her lap as she takes my hand in hers.

"I'm sure if you took a step back and really looked at it, you would see just how much your life has changed since you fell in love. It's just that your life with Sawyer is your new normal so it feels natural, almost as if nothing has changed at all. And *that* is a truly beautiful thing to experience."

Does everyone's mom just know everything about everything or is it just mine?

"I love you, Mom."

"Oh, I love you too, Sweetheart." She leans over and kisses the top of my head. "What time do you need to leave?"

"I'm in no rush." She returns my smile when I answer.

"Then grab that remote, get Aaron Hotchner on the TV and make some popcorn."

"Yes ma'am."

I love coming home.

Chapter 50

Sawyer

"Go stand over there!" I point to the giant sculpture of a cherry on a spoon. "Should I pretend I'm popping it?" I wag my brows and Leah's eyes turn the size of saucers when she slaps my chest with the back of her hand.

"Sawyer Clark!" she scolds me before running over to pose in front of it, sticking her tongue out to look like she's licking the cherry.

We stop at every sculpture in the garden taking photos, but my favorite is the one of us in front of the bronze *LOVE* sign.

"This place is so cool. I'm so glad you brought me here." Leah smiles as we walk hand in hand towards the parking lot.

"And I started with the *least* interesting place first. We still have two more stops to make while we're here." I smile and catch a playful look from her. "But this is all for today. Let's grab some food and go back to the hotel for a bit before the game tonight." I wrap my arm around her shoulders and pull her closer to me to kiss the top of her head.

Leah is fast asleep on my chest, curled up in my Badgers hoodie with a pair of black sweatpants while sitcom reruns play on the TV in our hotel room, but I couldn't sleep if I wanted to. I have been wanting to show her my favorite place in Minnesota ever since…well, ever since I found it if I'm honest. I wanted to call her that same day and show her but as we all know that wasn't going to happen. But ever since she told me she'd give us a real chance; I've been dying to bring her here.

My alarm starts to go off letting me know it's time to head to the rink and I see her face immediately scrunch in disapproval.

"We just fell asleeeep," she whines.

"I know baby, we'll have plenty of time to sleep when we get back tonight." I kiss the top of her head and gently shake her arm. She pushes to sit up in the bed, letting out a yawn and stretching before letting her hand plop down on the bed beside her. When she picks up her phone from the table beside the bed, she looks up at me with a frown.

"The game isn't for *hours*."

"Correct."

"Would you be super disappointed if I text Lyssa to see if we can ride there together? That will give me a little more time to get ready." She gives me a pleading smile. Lyssa found out Leah would be at this game and managed to move her schedule around to be here too, or so I was told. Which I think Leah was really excited about so she wouldn't be in the stands alone.

"Could I ask you something first?" She perks up a little more and crosses her legs.

"Anything."

"Well, as I'm sure you know from the simple fact that I've used the same color tape for my stick for over ten years, that all athletes have their game day rituals?"

"Yeah, like not washing your socks or wearing the same underwear," she explains, as I bob my head from side to side.

"Yes, but none of mine are nasty like that."

"I just meant, yes. I'm aware," she laughs, shoving my shoulder for teasing her.

"Well, I want you to become part of my game day ritual."

"Seriously?" There's a glimmer in her eyes as she asks, and it makes the nervous shake in my hands settle down a bit.

"Hell yeah, seriously." She bites down on her lip and smiles.

"Yes! Of course I will. I would love to! But what should it be? Or do you have something in mind already?"

"Not necessarily, but it could be anything. Showering together, getting coffee, dancing, you coming early with me to watch me warm up..." I trail off as I continue thinking.

"Let's do it then!" She jumps up from the bed, holding her hand out to help pull me up.

"Which one?"

"All of them." She shrugs, like the answer couldn't possibly be anything else.

"You're amazing you know that?" I smile, pulling her closer to wrap my arms around her.

"Get naked, hockey star. We have a shower to take." Then gives me a quick peck on the lips, pushes out of my arms, and strips off her sweats with me hot on her trail.

I check my phone before heading to the ice for warmups and see a text from Leah saying she and Lyssa are grabbing drinks before heading back to their seats.

"Hey man, I'm really glad our girls became fast friends. Lyssa really needed someone like Leah," Matty says from where he's starting his stretches next to me.

"Well, I'm glad to hear you're happy about it. Because when she became friends with Leah, she got four bonus friends too." I give him a playful warning look.

"So I heard," he laughs. "It's good." The tone of that last sentence hits a little different, but before I can ask if everything is okay I hear *her*.

"Have my babies' number thirteen!" I snicker at the remark, remembering how someone said that while we were out not too long ago. Leah looked like she wanted to scratch that girl's eyes clean out of her head. When my eyes land on her, time stops around me—the way it only ever does with Leah— because she's wearing a pair of skin-tight blue jeans, a gray beanie over her loose, wavy hair and she's pointing to her back. Where on a bright-green jersey are my name and number. She must have had Lyssa bring it for her so she could surprise me, since we came here early together.

"Yes ma'am," I yell back. When she turns around with the brightest smile on her face, I return it with my own and give her a wink. She takes her beer from Lyssa, and they head back up the steps to their seats and I'm left wishing the game was over before it ever starts.

We're tied with only ten seconds left in overtime, with the puck way too close to our net for my liking, when someone takes a shot that ricochets into the air. Swatted to the ground by their center, I pick it up and take off down the ice with Javi and Matty on either side of me. I pass to Javi, who takes his shot—blocked by the goalie who sends it right to my blade—and I slap it into the net right before the buzzer sounds. The noise from the crowd is deafening as the team piles in on us to celebrate.

As soon as I'm out of the locker room and round the corner, Leah is running full sprint towards me. She jumps into my arms and wraps her legs around my waist, and I pull her lips down to mine.

"That was amazing!" The elation on her face is everything I've dreamed of for my entire career. Having not just *a girl* that loves me by my side and excited about a game like this one, but having *the girl*. The one I always wished would love me back and be proud of what I'm doing. "Are we celebrating?"

"Hell yeah we are." I kiss her again and slap her ass before placing her feet back on the ground.

"Where are we going?" I wrap my arm around her and bring my lips down to her ear.

"The room."

"I thought for sure you'd want to go out and celebrate. That last play was incredible." I press the keycard to the door and the light turns green.

We barely make it through the door before I drop my bag on the floor and wrap her in my arms, pinning her to the wall. Her eyes fall to my lips as her breaths pick up in speed.

"You know what will be more incredible? Burying myself inside of you while I watch you come apart with my name on your lips *and* on your back." Those green eyes finally land on mine, and she nods impatiently.

I drop to my knees and make quick work unlacing her sneakers, pulling them off before unbuttoning her jeans. I slide them down her legs, kissing a path up her bare skin. I rub my nose teasingly along her clit, inhaling her scent because I can't get enough of her. I have never starved for someone the way I starve for her. I take advantage of the fact she's wearing lace tonight, rip her underwear from her hips and kiss her everywhere I can—along her thighs, her hips, her stomach, her clit—if I never did anything else but kiss this woman, I'd consider myself lucky.

"You're soaked for me, Dove." I slide my tongue along her slit, moaning in satisfaction and savoring her sweet taste. She reaches down and tilts my chin up to look at her and it's one of the hottest things I've ever witnessed.

"Sawyer, I need you inside me," she whispers.

"You are so gorgeous when you tell me what you want." I stand up and wrap her bare legs around my waist as she begins unbuttoning my blue dress shirt.

She finishes about the same time I set her ass down on the dresser across the room and she slides the shirt down my arms, letting it fall to the floor. I have my belt off and pants down within seconds, standing in only my gray boxers, which my dick is already peeking out of.

She runs her hand along my length, sliding her finger over my head bringing it to her lips to lick the precum from it, causing my hunger for her to deepen. She slides my boxers down and pulls out my cock, stroking me as her eyes stay locked on mine.

"Spread your legs wide, baby." When her knees are as far open as they'll go, I pull her to the very edge and sink into her. The way she holds onto me, letting her nails dig into my flesh as she welcomes me with a moan is absolutely electric.

Her touch, her sounds, her taste—everything about her pulls me deeper and deeper into her orbit. I'm no longer my own, I am hers—heart, soul, and body—every fiber of my being exists for her.

And I've never been fucking happier.

"Harder," she whispers, sending my heart racing with excitement. I grip her tighter, railing into her harder, as I see my name on her back through the mirror on the wall above the dresser.

"You look so sexy with my name on your back, Dove. You look more like mine tonight than you ever have before."

"I am yours. Only. Always. Forever." A wicked smile spreads across my face.

"Mine," I growl just before our lips collide. I can feel her tightening around me, her back arching as she chases her release. I lean back to slide a hand between us with plans of playing with her clit to send her over the edge, then she stops me.

"Flip me around." I frown slightly. "So you can see your name on my back and still watch me scream your name." The devilish smirk she gives me almost does me in.

"Fuck, I love you." I kiss her once more before pulling her down from the dresser, flipping her around so her hands are flat on the surface and she's facing the mirror. The gasps when I slide back in, biting her lip as I rub her clit.

"Yes, right there." Her eyes fall closed. "Oh, I'm gonna come."

"Eyes on me, Dove," I demand, leaning over to kiss her neck the way she loves. "Let me see that pretty face when you come for me, baby," I growl into her ear just as her eyes find mine in the mirror.

"Atta girl."

"Oh! Sawyer, yes!" she cries out. Her pussy squeezes around me, milking me for everything I'm worth, and a moment later, I find my own release.

She stands up, pressing her back to mine, caressing my cheek with her hand as she watches us in the reflection.

"You are everything I've ever wanted, Sawyer Clark."

"You're everything I'll ever need, Dove."

I run a warm bubble bath for her in the suite's jetted tub—that she demands I join her in—and spend what feels like an hour holding her, kissing her, touching every perfect curve of hers and forging them to memory. That way, when I'm old and gray I'll still have the memory of what it feels like—falling in love with her right now.

Chapter 51

Sawyer

"Where are we going if we need *snacks* for the drive there?" Leah asks as we walk through the candy aisle of the gas station.

"I told you, it's a surprise." I kiss her temple and she rolls her eyes.

"Fine. But how man—" She stops when her phone starts ringing. "Oh, it's my mom." She smiles, swiping across the screen to answer. "Hey Mom." I scan the shelves as I try to decide what I want to take for the trip when Leah *psst*'s me over to her. "We're just grabbing snacks before we go to some secret place Sawyer wanted to show me. What's up?" She sticks her tongue out at me and holds her bag of nerd clusters out for me to take from her, but before I can take them, they fall to the ground. I bend to scoop them up and when I look at her again, my blood runs cold.

"What do you mean? Is he okay?" Her eyes begin to water immediately, and her lip is quivering furiously as she hunches over with her hand covering her mouth. "No no no no no, please no!" The hand holding her phone falls to her side, and I grab it before her cell can hit the tiles.

"Leah, what's wrong? What happened?" Her body is completely limp in my arms as she sobs. Nothing she says is comprehensible, so

I look down and see the call is still connected. With a pit in my stomach and a lump in my throat I pull the phone to my ear.

"Mrs. Gates? It's Sawyer." I hear her sniffle and clear her throat.

"Hey, Honey. Do you think you could get Leah back home?"

"Of course. We'll be on the next flight out. Is everything okay?"

"Allen had a stroke. He uh, he didn't make it." She is trying to be so strong right now, but her voice breaks at the last minute.

I wonder if there's anyone there with her.

Leah lets out another soul crushing wail and I clear my throat, trying to force my composure back into place.

"I am so sorry, Loretta. We'll be back as soon as possible."

"Thank you." I hang up the call and sit our snacks on the shelf closest to me, wrapping my arms around her as tight as I can without crushing her, trying to bring her some kind of comfort.

Does that even exist?

Comfort right after finding out one of the most important people in your life isn't going to be there when you get back home? Not in the way you want them to be, at least.

Fuck!

"Come on baby, let's go home." I scoop her up, walking her out to the car and buckling her in before heading back to the hotel to pack and book the next flight out.

She doesn't say a word the entire way back home. She goes between crying and staring blankly out the window. From the car, to the airport, to the plane, until we land back in Tennessee. I wrap my hand around hers when we get into the truck, but she doesn't move an inch until we pull up to her parents' house. Then, for the first time since her phone rang this morning, she looks at me.

"Your mom is here. I thought you'd want to be with her, but—"

"I do." Her voice is so raspy from crying and refusing to drink anything. It breaks my heart hearing the pain she's in. I hop out, open her door and she takes my hand to get down, then pulls it away and wraps her arms around herself.

"I'll probably stay here with her tonight," she says, looking down at her feet.

"Of course. I'll come by in the morning to check on you both. Come on, I'll walk you up." She lifts her head, tears immediately streaming down her face when she does. I wipe them away with my thumbs and her eyes fall closed.

"Please go home, Sawyer." Her voice cracks.

"What?" I rear back, confused by her request.

"I can't do this. Okay? I can't." She shakes her head, her sobs shaking her whole body.

"I know, baby. I'm so sorry this happened but I'm right here, okay? I'm not going anywhere." She lets me wrap my arms around her and press a kiss to her forehead, but the moment ends just as quickly as it happens.

"No. You don't get it! I don't want *you* here, Sawyer!" she yells, frantically running her hands through her hair.

"What?" My chest tightens and my brows pull together in confusion. She looks away from me, with tears and snot streaming down her face.

"I can't look at you without thinking about *why* I wasn't here. Why I wasn't here for *months* before that. I missed out on so many chances to be with him. Because I was with *you*."

"Baby, you couldn't have known this was going to happen. You can't *not* live life just because of what may or may not happen."

"But it *did happen*. It *did!* And now he's gone, Sawyer! My dad is *gone*. I'm never going to hear him call me Sweetpea again or take me on a drive when you break my heart, or try to get me to sneak him a cookie after dinner before he checks—" she sucks in a few deep breaths and I can tell she's about to have a panic attack. "*Whyyyy!*" she tries screaming, but there's too much strain on her voice to allow it so it comes out a pained whisper.

I blink away the tears that have formed in my eyes and pull her into me. She may hate me right now, but she needs me just as much.

"Breathe for me, Dove. Please, baby. You've gotta breathe." She isn't. She can't. The grief is consuming her.

"Breathe with me." I take a deep breath in, letting it out on a three count. Then I take her face in my hands with tears streaming down both of our faces.

"Breathe. With. Me," I command, taking another breath just like the last, only this time, she inhales too. We do this a few more times until she's breathing on her own again.

"I'm not walking away from you, Dove. I told you I wouldn't and I'm not. I can't. I told you you're going to have to demand it or be the one to walk away." She shakes her head, sniffling as more tears fall.

"Then I am. I have to." I take a few steps down the walkway, running a hand through my hair as I try to keep my heart from shattering.

"No. Please, baby. You promised. You promised me you wouldn't walk away either. Please don't do this, I can't lose you. Not again, not after I just got you." My voice shakes with every word.

"That was before my *dad* was *gone*, Sawyer! I don't want to see you right now. Why can't you just understand that?"

"Because I love you," I whisper.

There's as much pain in my voice as I know there is in her heart—and I know the pain in mine could never compare—but that doesn't change the fact that when she turns around and runs into her mom's house, she rips my heart out of my chest and takes it with her.

MOM

We just landed. We'll be there soon. Thank you for letting us know.

ME

You're welcome. Leah is staying with her mom. They'll probably both be there.

MOM

When will you be going back? We could wait to go with you.

ME

You should go without me. Leah doesn't want to see me anymore.

MOM

What happened Sweetheart?

ME

She blames me for not being there when it happened.

MOM

Oh, Sawyer. You know that isn't your fault. She's just hurting and needs time to grieve. Don't give up on her.

For the first time in my life, I feel like giving up is exactly what I should do to make things right with her.

Chapter 52

"Mom!" I run into the house and straight into her arms.

"Hey Sweetie." She tilts her head, and I can see that her eyes are puffy from crying, but she's putting on a brave face.

"What happened?" I sob, wrapped in her arms with mine squeezing her so tight I'm afraid I might break her. Hanging on this tight is the only thing that feels right at this moment though. Like if I keep her connected to me, there's less of a chance she'll disappear too.

"Why don't we sit?" She keeps a tight hold on my hand as she leads us to the couch. I instinctively grab the blanket I always curl up in and pull it into my lap. She lets out a sigh and my heart sinks.

"Your father had a mini stroke about a month ago."

And then it falls completely into my stomach.

"What? What do you mean? Why didn't you tell me? Why didn't *he* tell me?"

"Sweetheart." She places her hand over mine where I'm picking anxiously at the string on the blanket stitch. "You were out there, living your own life, falling in love and having all the experiences a twenty-eight-year-old woman should have—"

"SO?! You still could have told me that Dad wasn't doing well. I would have made sure I was here more," I sob, yanking my hand from hers to wipe the tears angrily away from my face.

"Leah, your father didn't want to tell you. He went to his doctor afterwards and he said that we were doing everything we should be doing to keep him healthy but that these things just happen sometimes." I know she's trying to make me feel better, but it's not working. It's making me feel worse, actually.

I should have been here.

Whether I knew my dad was in ill health or not, I should have made time to see them.

"Your dad was so proud of you, and so happy to see you happy, we didn't want to worry you unnecessarily over something we have no control over." She wipes a tear from my cheek and caresses it with her thumb. I lean into her touch and let my eyes fall closed.

I can't be mad at them. They're the best parents I could have ever asked for. They were putting my feelings above theirs—like they always have—and making sure I had a good life.

So why am I still mad at them for not telling me?

"I understand," I assure her.

"You know how much we love you, right sweet girl?" I nod and roll my lips to keep from breaking down again.

Of course I know that. It was the one thing they always made sure of.

"There you go, Sweetpea. You're getting it."

"Daddy look! I'm doing it all by myself!"

The old home video plays on my TV for the hundredth time while I sit on my couch, surrounded by tissues, and take out containers that are half full because I haven't wanted to eat anything. I close my eyes and let more tears fall down my face, listening to my dad encourage me as I learned to ride my bike without training wheels for the first time. I'm met with visuals of us riding in his old Chevy with rock music playing, the windows down, and the flavor of the day ice cream in our hands. Mending my broken heart one ride around town at a time. Only now my heart is irreparably broken, and it's because the one who had mended it so many times before, is gone.

Knock knock.

"Le? Open up. We're here to help you get ready."

I don't want to go.

I don't want to accept that he's really gone or have to say my final goodbye. It's not goodbye. I'll never let the memory of him go, he will always be a part of me because *he* helped shape me into the woman I've become.

I don't want to have to get up and answer the door.

I don't want to accept that I'm going to have to live the rest of my life without him.

A few more soft knocks sound at the door and I drag myself off the couch and across the room to unlatch the deadbolt. Taylor is standing front and center and as soon as I see her my chest aches, but when I see the tears in her eyes and a Bruman's cup in her hands, I completely crumble.

The girls manage to pull me through the process of getting ready for my dad's funeral, all without saying more than was necessary.

"We won't leave your side, okay? You can do this." Shane kisses my cheek and I nod in appreciation. She knows what this feels like. Losing her parents right after high school put her in a really dark place, and I finally know what that place feels like.

The whole service happens like background noise to me. My focus stays on the portrait of my dad next to the urn on the table surrounded by family photos. When we're leaving the church, I can hear the whispered condolences and people gently rubbing my arm in an effort to comfort me.

When I make it outside to the sidewalk a breeze blows through and I take a deep breath, trying to clear my mind. It's officially spring now—the perfect driving weather.

Though if I tried to drive myself anywhere right now there's a good chance I would end up in a ditch or embedded into a large tree. I haven't completely focused on a single thing outside of home movies in almost a week.

Then I feel it. The sudden chill from someone's eyes being on me. I turn robotically, scanning my surroundings until I see him. Standing in the distance with his hands in his suit pockets, looking almost as broken as I feel.

He came.

His chin lifts slightly when he notices me looking at him and I realize I'm actually *looking* at him. His sapphire blue eyes full of pain, his perfectly sculpted shoulders hung in despair.

Broken.

"You ready sweetie?" Ruby links her arm with mine, startling me, causing a tear to fall down my cheek when I turn to face her.

I was crying?

When I look over my shoulder Sawyer has disappeared and the focus I had gained, only to look at him, fades away.

Knock knock knock.

I'm headed back to the living room from grabbing another pint of ice cream from the fridge—double chocolate chip, Dad's favorite— when the sound takes me to the door instead.

I don't intend to open it, but I head that direction anyway. Sliding down the wall beside it I can hear my friends on the other side of the door.

"She hasn't responded to any of our texts. We don't even know if she's alive at this point."

"She's grieving, it's a lot to endure—especially by yourself."

"Exactly! She shouldn't be alone. We should be in there with her."

I love them so much. I just can't be around people right now. Not even *my* people.

"Leah. Sweetie, we wanted to check on you. We don't have to stay or anything, but can you just let us know you're okay?" Shane's voice filters through the thick wooden door.

Of course I'm not okay. But I'm alive. Unless you count dying from a broken heart. In which case I'm a walking corpse.

More tears begin falling down my face as I remain silent.

"Le, baby girl. I'm about five seconds away from busting this door down. Please. Just any sign of life? Knock once if you need us and twice if you're okay but want us to leave."

Lauren.

The one who has been my other half for most of our younger years and still was well into adulthood.

Knock. Knock.

I can hear a collective sigh from them, but I know they're not leaving any time soon. They sit on the other side of the door silently for almost half an hour. Sipping what I assume is coffee since I can hear someone shaking the ice in their cup about ten minutes later. They don't even talk to each other. They're just here. Then when they get up to leave, they say I love you through the door, and leave.

They're still here for me, even when I won't let them be here for me. And that's why they're my best friends.

I've used more PTO at work in the last few weeks than I have any other time in my entire teaching career. I'm not even sure what today is. I know it's April, but beyond that I don't really care. I turned my phone off the day after Dad's funeral when my mom told me that she was heading to her and Dad's favorite campsite and wouldn't have reception. I knew she wouldn't need me, and I put on a brave face to convince her I would be equally as fine.

I'm not.

I'm as far from fine as one can be before ceasing to exist at all, and

I don't know how to get back. Back to the life I was just beginning to thrive in and undo the damage that's been done. Losing my dad was an unchangeable, unpredictable tragedy—and by far the worst news I've ever received—but losing Sawyer was a self-inflicted and unnecessary one.

I thought it would hurt less if I didn't have a reminder of the pure joy and all-consuming love I was feeling while part of my heart was leaving the Earth.

Because *that's* what Sawyer really is to me. Not the awful reminder I accused him of being.

He makes me happy and has given me experiences I never even dreamed I would have before being with him. He makes the pain of our past seem nonexistent, because he reminds me how much he loves me every chance he gets.

At least he used to—before I made the choice to walk away.

Something I had promised I would never do.

Something I should have never done.

When the series finale of *Gilmore Girls* comes to an end—again—and previews begin playing for shows I may want to watch next, I snap out of my trance to look for the remote. I've officially broken my record for days between hair washes because I can't remember the last time I even showered.

I find it tucked into the couch cushion, start the show over from episode one, and sink deeper into the cocoon I've created around me, breathing in the collar of Sawyer's hoodie, hoping there will still be some trace of his scent on it to help lull me to sleep—something else I haven't done since I returned home from Minnesota.

Chapter 53

Sawyer

I haven't spent much time at Chattahoochies since moving back. It's no doubt the coolest bar I've ever been to, with the Viking aesthetic, the old school jukebox in the corner, and the reserved table for fallen soldiers. Max really did something unique with his bar. This is the first place I've come to outside of games—that I literally have no choice but to be at—since Allen's funeral.

"You motherfucker." I turn to see Tank walking over to me with an unreadable expression. He's either about to hug me or pummel me and it's frightening that I can't tell which it is.

"Hey to you too, Tank." He strides over and sits down on a barstool next to me as Ruby places a soda in front of him. He gives her a wink then turns to face me.

"It was you, wasn't it?"

"What are you talking about?" I try not to give away that I know exactly what he's talking about, but I never did perfect my poker face. He shakes his head and lets out a small laugh.

"I don't know what I ever did to deserve having a friend like you show up in my life, but you've just made more of a change for these people than you may ever know."

"I wish I could do more, if I'm honest." Hearing Tank talk about his work and knowing the impact it makes, the real change he's trying to achieve at The Veterans Center, is admirable.

"I'd say a four-million-dollar donation is plenty, you beautiful Moose. However, if you ever get bored with figure skating with a stick, I'd be happy to put you to work." I force out a laugh that fades almost immediately and I finish off my whiskey.

"How are you doing man?" He gives my shoulder a squeeze and I plaster on my mask and nod.

"I'm alright." He studies me closely and takes a deep breath.

"I'm always here man, if you need to talk." Tank may wonder what he's done to have a friend like me in his life, but I wonder the same thing about him. He, Max, and Tucker all have been so accepting and some of the best friends I've made ever since I got here.

"Thanks man. I appreciate that."

TOT

Are you going to pull your head out of your ass and go take care of your girl or what?!?! She's hurting Sawyer, where the FUCK are you?

ME

Taylor, don't start. I'm losing my fucking mind not being with her right now. Where the fuck do you think I want to be? She made it clear she didn't want to be my girl OR see me anymore. So I'm staying away like she asked, even though it's killing me. That's where the fuck I am, Tot.

TOT

We both know she'll always be your girl. She's just hurting right now, Moose.

ME

I know she is. And knowing I'm the reason for that hurt is the ONLY reason I'm staying away. Please make sure she's okay. Okay? Can you do that for me?

TOT

I'll do my best. I promise.

I love my house. When I moved back to Tennessee, I hoped that I would be here indefinitely, so I made sure to pick a place I would want to call home when I turn old and gray. I'd be lying if I said I picked aspects of this place that I thought Leah would love too. Like the porch swing where we could watch the sunset, the huge kitchen where we could host holidays or birthday parties, and the built-in bookshelves on every wall in the room she calls her mini library.

Called her mini library.

I bought this home with every intention of sharing it with her. Some may say it was foolish, and I might even believe them now. But I knew that was how it was meant to be.

I still know it, deep down.

But I also know it's likely no longer a realistic dream. Because even though my heart still only beats for her, with every pump of life I ache. To see her, to be near her, to inhale her sweet scent and feel her soft skin on mine. To look into those calming green eyes and see that smile that lights up my entire damn life.

Things I'm beginning to accept will never happen again.

I toss the magnet down on the counter and run my hands through my hair, grabbing my shoes to take a walk.

When I reach my mailbox, I see my dad's truck pulling onto the gravel road and my brows knit together.

"Hey Pop, what are you doing here?"

"At your house or in the state?" he laughs.

"Both, I guess." I offer a small smile and he squints at me.

"Hop in, I'll give you a ride back up to the house." I open the door and place my mail on the dashboard, slamming the door behind me. "How you been, son?"

"Fine, Dad." He nods but doesn't say anything else. We ride back up to the house with nothing but the sound of gravel beneath his tires filling the truck. When we reach the circle drive, he parks the truck and cuts the engine.

"Is that so?" *Here we go.* "How's Leah?"

"You'd have better luck finding that out from Tot, Dad."

"She said she hasn't spoken to Leah since Al's funeral. Her phone has been off." My heart starts to race with panic. Why the fuck didn't she mention that when she text me? Has no one talked to her since the funeral?

"Maybe she's with her mom." I try to find an explanation that will end this conversation, so I don't have the inclination to go bust down her front door and check on her.

"Loretta went to the campgrounds. I doubt Leah is with her there." My heart squeezes so tight it feels like I can't breathe, because all I want to do is call and see if she's okay.

But her phone is off.

I could just go by her house and check on her.

She doesn't want to see you; she probably wouldn't even answer the door.

Or worse, she'd slam it back in your face when she saw you.

"What are you doing, Sawyer?" Dad's voice breaks me out of my thoughts.

"Sorry, zoned out I guess." He snickers at that.

"With Leah. Why are you sitting on your ass when your girl is hurting?"

"She doesn't want to see me, Dad." I clench my jaw to keep from snapping at him. It's not his fault no one really knows what happened between us.

"I doubt that's true," he says calmly, staring out the window at the house.

"Well, it is. She blames me. For not being here when it happened. For missing so many Sunday dinners because we were together," my voice shakes. "She hates me, Dad, and honestly, I can't even blame her. I consumed so much of her time, and I didn't think twice about it."

"When did she tell you this?" His face is pulled into a frown, and I can't remember a time I ever saw my father look pained on my behalf.

"When we got back from the airport. I took her to her moms, and she said she couldn't look at me without remembering why she wasn't here with him. You asked how I am? I'm fucking miserable Dad. That's how I am. All I want to do is be with her, but I'm the reason she's hurting so damn bad, so what good would it do?" He sits back in his seat and is quiet a minute before he speaks again.

"Grief has a really ugly way of throwing people into the darkness. It eats you up and causes you to lash out. That's why the first two stages are denial and anger. Do you love her, Sawyer?" I look at him in surprise. I thought it was painfully obvious to everyone how much I love her.

"More than anything."

"Even after she said what she did, you still love her?" I know this is leading somewhere, but the insinuation that I would ever *stop* loving her still angers me.

"I would love her even if she lived her life loving someone else. She's it for me, Dad. She's always been it for me." I try to swallow past the lump in my throat, fighting the pain that lives permanently in my chest at the thought of her.

"Then go get your girl, son. Because the fourth stage isn't one she needs to go through alone and I have a feeling she might be in it. She may have given up, Sawyer—she's allowed to feel hopeless after what's happened—but you're not. So go get her."

"I will, Dad." I shake my head and he pulls me into a hug. I hold onto him for dear life, knowing that what I'm doing right now isn't something to be taken for granted.

"Don't forget this." Dad hands me my mail as I'm stepping out of the truck, and when I look down, my stomach hits the ground.

A letter from Allen? Why would he send me a letter?

Once my dad is gone, I sit on the front porch steps, staring at the envelope for what feels like forever before I finally get the guts to open it. When I do, I see another envelope enclosed—addressed to Leah. I set it to the side and unfold the paper that is addressed to me.

SAWYER,

YOU TOLD ME RECENTLY THAT YOU HAVE PLANS TO MARRY MY DAUGHTER SOMEDAY. IN THE EVENT I AM NOT HERE TO TELL HER MYSELF, I HAVE WRITTEN HER A LETTER THAT I WANT HER TO READ WHEN YOU FINALLY DO POP THE QUESTION. WITH THE WAY YOU TWO LOOK AT EACH OTHER, I FEEL CONFIDENT I'LL BE ABLE TO TELL HER ALL OF THESE THINGS MYSELF BECAUSE I DON'T SEE YOU WAITING MUCH LONGER TO PUT A RING ON HER FINGER, BUT JUST IN CASE, I AM LEAVING IT IN YOUR CARE—— JUST AS I AM LEAVING HER.

TAKE CARE OF MY BABY GIRL, CLARK. SHE IS THE SINGLE BEST THING TO EVER HAPPEN TO ME AND LORETTA. SHE SHINES BRIGHTEST WHEN SHE'S LOVED, AS MOST WOMEN DO, AND I'VE NEVER QUITE SEEN HER SHINE THE WAY SHE DOES WHEN SHE'S WITH YOU. IT'S NOT LOST ON ME WHY YOU CALL HER DOVE, AND I DON'T THINK THERE'S ANYTHING MORE FITTING YOU COULD HAVE CHOSEN TO CALL HER, BUT DID YOU KNOW THAT DOVES HAVE AN UNNATURAL ABILITY TO FIND THEIR WAY BACK HOME? NO MATTER HOW FAR THEY GET, THEY FIND THEIR WAY BACK. I THINK THAT'S WHAT HAPPENED WITH THE TWO OF YOU. SHE FOUND HER WAY BACK TO THE PERSON WHO FELT LIKE HOME.

ALRIGHT. THAT'S ENOUGH OF THE MUSHY SHIT FOR ME. GIVE MY GIRL HER LETTER WHEN THERE'S A RING ON HER FINGER.

ALLEN.

P.S. — I'M NOT GETTING ANY YOUNGER HERE.

Tears are streaming down my face so fast I'm sure I'll have stains on the paper I am holding, but I can't hold it in anymore.

I miss my girl.

I hate that I've been sitting around here instead of being there for her—taking care of her, helping her through her grief.

As if the universe sent both of our dads to kick me in the ass, I dart into the house, tuck the letter from Al safely into my mail slot, then grab my keys before sprinting to my truck. My eyes are still misty from my tears, that I don't even notice another vehicle in my driveway until I hear a door slam just as I open mine.

"Hey thirteen." A cold chill shoots down my spine and my head snaps up. I'm sure I'm hallucinating when I see Leah standing next to her dad's old Chevy in my Badger's hoodie and a pair of white sneakers. Hallucination or not, I waste no time running to her. The way I should have run to her weeks ago. I wrap my arms around her small frame and lift her off the ground, feeling her entire body relax when I do. "Sawyer." Her voice shakes against my neck and my arms squeeze her even tighter.

"Hey Dove."

"I'm sorry for just showing up here. If you were going somewhere I can–" Her voice is tight as I reluctantly place her feet back on the ground.

"I was headed to *you*, baby." Her eyes water and her lip begins to quiver.

"You were?" I nod my head as tears begin to fall down her cheeks. "I need you, Sawyer." A sob rips through her, shaking her entire body and she falls into my chest.

"I'm right here baby, I've got you." I kiss the top of her head, letting my own tears fall into her hair.

"I'm so s-sorry," she chokes out.

My heart is aching, but in a *good* way?

She came back to me.

"Welcome home, Dove." She looks up at me with those mesmerizing green eyes so full of pain. Pain that I couldn't even begin to understand but will do everything I can to ease.

"Can I take care of you, baby, the way I should have been doing all along?" I cup her face in my hands and the faintest smile appears on her lips as she nods.

"Yes, please."

I scoop her up and carry her inside, taking her all the way to my bathroom before I set her down on the counter. Her face is still expressionless, much like it was on the plane ride home a month ago, but she's *here*. For that, I'm grateful.

Sliding the shower door open I turn the water on and kick my shoes off before returning to her. I start by bending to untie her shoes, placing them gently to the side and tucking her socks into them.

"Arms up." I stand back up and wrap my hands around the hem of the black hoodie. Her eyes meet mine, shimmering with the slightest bit of life as she reaches her arms up over her head. I pull it off and am met with the view of her perfect breasts, completely free of any restraint, and a pair of boyshort style underwear. My jaw clenches as I try to control the blood rushing to the one place I need it *not to* right now.

I offer her my hand to help her down from the counter and she accepts. When her feet are on the ground I bend to my knees once more, pulling her underwear down her legs and kissing her stomach before standing back up. She watches me closely as I pull my shirt over my head, tossing it to the side before unhooking my belt and sliding my jeans off.

When I take her hand and walk her into the shower, she lets her eyes fall shut as the warm water beats down on her back, soaking her untamed curls. She looks like she's lost weight and from the looks of her hair when she showed up, I'm not sure when she last showered.

I should have been there. Or at the very least made sure someone else was.

The same pain from before hits me in the chest, but I push it away and try to focus on the fact that she's here now.

I grab her shampoo and lather it in her hair, the sigh she releases makes some of the tension in my shoulders disappear as I rinse it out and do it again—knowing she needs a little more maintenance right now than usual.

Then I do the same with the conditioner before grabbing the body wash from her shelf. I squeeze a generous amount in my hands and start with her shoulders, watching as the wash lathers into thick suds as I rub it along her back, wishing I could kiss every inch of her and tell her how sorry I am and how much I love her.

I wash her entire back all the way to her ankles and when she turns around, I'm unsure if she would rather do this herself or if she's okay with me doing it. Then she reaches for my hand and places it on her chest, and I have to take a deep breath to ground myself. My cock is hard as iron and aching for her touch, but I'm praying she somehow doesn't notice. My heart races at painful speeds as I wash her breasts, stomach, between her legs and down to her feet. I turn her around to allow her to sit on the built-in bench, dropping to my knees to take her feet in my hands, massaging each one thoroughly.

"Sawyer."

"Yes, Dove?"

"Why do you still have your boxers on?"

Ah, fuck.

"Because I wanted to take care of you, I didn't want you thinking I had any other intentions."

She frowns. "You want to take care of me?"

"Of course I do." My brows pinch together as I place her feet on the shower floor, rubbing my hands up and down her calves.

"Then lose the boxers." My expression morphs into surprise at her request. I was worried she wouldn't even want me touching her right now, so I definitely didn't expect *this*. "Please, Sawyer. I've done nothing but *hurt* for *weeks*. I have hated myself for walking away from you and making you think I didn't want you just because my heart was broken, but I couldn't pull myself out of the fog long enough to tell you as much until today. I just... I need you Sawyer. I need all of you because I love you, and I need to know that you still love me too." The pain in her voice breaks me.

"Nothing in this world could keep me from loving you, baby."

I spread her legs, allowing the needed space for me to move closer, cupping her face and pressing my lips to hers. Her mouth opens and I dip my tongue inside, tasting the saltiness of her tears and I don't waste another second making her question how deep my love for her is. I break our kiss to stand and slide my boxers off, kicking them to the side before pulling her up. I pick her up, wrapping her legs around my waist and pressing her back gently against the tiles on the wall as I kiss her in a way that surely proves my love for her.

Then she reaches down and wraps her hand around my length, my heart skipping a beat as she lines me up to her entrance. She sucks in a breath, and I quickly realize she's holding it in. It's been a while since we've been together, so I have no doubt she'll have to take some time to adjust.

"Breathe for me, Dove." She exhales and I bury my face in her neck, kissing, biting, licking, as I slowly slide into her. Her nipples harden and press against my chest while I kiss the sensitive spot behind her ear.

"Almost there baby, let me in," I whisper as she relaxes and drops her hips, taking the rest of me so beautifully. I thrust into her, slow but firm, as sounds of pure satisfaction vibrate through my chest.

I lean back and look at her, seeing the tears spilling over her eyes and stop.

"What's wrong? Are you hurt?" I begin to pull out, but she tightens her grip on me to stop me.

"I just missed you so much, please don't stop," she cries, with a smile on her face. "Fuck me like you love me." Holding her up with one arm behind her back, I grab her face gently with the other as I begin again.

"I love you, Leah. I have *always* loved you. I am yours, baby. Only. Always. Forever." I wrap both of my arms around her, holding her body close to mine as I pound into her, our lips dancing with one another the way they always do.

We stay this way until our lips are tingling, our bodies spent, and the very last wave of our climax has subsided.

Chapter 54

No one tells you how hard it is to pull yourself out of the darkness that grief throws you into. One moment you're living life, in love and on your way to a new place with the person who makes you happiest, the next you're feeling your world crumble around you, and then—without warning—you're staring at a blank TV screen, wondering what the rest of your life will be like if you don't get up.

I miss my dad; I'll never stop missing him because he was the best man I'd ever known. Learning that he left his truck to me—no doubt because that's where some of our best memories were made—caused me to break down all over again. That thought was exactly what led me to the image of Sawyer—the *other* best man I've ever known—and I knew if I didn't go to him, I would lose him forever too.

Before I knew it, I was in the truck driving to his house. Completely unshowered, in the same state I'd remained in for several days, because I simply couldn't do anything else until I knew whether or not he still loved me. After the way I'd blamed him for my absence the last few months of my father's life and for my not being here when he passed, the cruelty of those remarks would warrant his never wanting to speak to me again.

Luckily, the things my grief allowed me to believe were the

farthest thing from true. Sawyer didn't stop loving me or wish not to speak to me anymore because of what I had said to him. He simply stayed away because that's what I had asked of him. Because if there's anything I've learned about him in the last few months, it's that he would do anything to make me happy.

"Your hair smells so good." He presses his nose to the top of my head and inhales deeply.

"You picked a really good shampoo. I could never afford that brand. Why do you think I shower here more than my own place?" I look up at him and smile and he watches me—like I'm the most precious thing in the world to him.

I'm in one of his black T-shirts and a pair of underwear I'd left here and he's in nothing but a pair of boxers while we lay in bed together.

"Hey Dove. If you don't want to talk about it, we don't have to, but...do they know what happened? With your dad?" My heart sinks at the thought but I'm sure he's been curious—I know I would be. I have no idea what my mom has told people, if anything at all.

"He uh, he had a stroke—not the one we knew about, he had one before that—and it was what they've decided to call a *mini stroke*, so they didn't think they had anything to worry about. But then he had the second one and..." I trail off and he doesn't press any further.

"I am so sorry, baby." I glance up and his brows are raised, then he looks at me and his features soften.

"Thanks," I say softly, letting the warmth of his skin comfort me as I will my heart to pull back together.

"Are you hungry?" He caresses my cheek with his thumb, changing the subject as if he knows that's exactly what I need.

"For the first time in weeks, yes actually," I answer honestly.

"Italian, Mexican or Pizza?" he asks, and I feel like I could eat my favorite dish from each place right now.

"Yes," I giggle, trying to think of a *real* answer to give him, but he has other plans.

"All of them it is." He winks at me as he picks his phone up and places our order, and I bury my face deeper into him. The cedarwood scent from his body wash fills my senses and I feel my eyes growing heavier with every passing minute.

Just as I think I may fall asleep; I'm shocked back to full attention.

"Move in with me, Dove." I sit up in the bed and look down at him—taking in the gorgeous smile on his face and the content look in his eyes. I'm confused at first by my lack of push back, but no one has ever felt more like home to me than him. Which is why coming here today has made me feel better than anything else has even come close to in the past few weeks.

"Okay."

"What? That's it? No arguments?" He looks at me surprised.

"Did you *want* me to argue with you?" I raise a brow at him, and he laughs.

"Not at all." He pulls me into a kiss, and I instantly melt into his touch. "When can we move your stuff in?"

"Tomorrow? If we're not moving furniture, it should all fit in the back of your truck." I shrug.

"You're being very agreeable about this," he teases.

"That's because I want this too. Nowhere has ever felt more like home to me, Sawyer." His expression grows more serious.

"You mean it?"

"With my whole heart." He pulls me back down and tucks me beneath his arm, kissing my temple, cheek and jawline multiple times in a row until I'm in a fit of laughter.

"So...he left you the truck?"

I smile to myself. "Yeah, he did."

"It suits you." This man has an indescribable way of making my heart feel completely full.

"I think so too."

"Hey Dove."

"Yeah?" I lift my head to look up at him, surprised to find a nervous look on his face. He hasn't looked like this since we went to Sunday dinner at my parent's house.

"When you're feeling up to it I would really like to take you back to Minnesota. There's still somewhere I really wanted to take you, but I don't want to rush you. Just—let me know when you're ready."

"Okay." I'm not sure how it'll feel being back in the place where I found out about my dad dying, but I know he would have a fit if I stopped living life and going on adventures just because I was sad. That was the whole point of the truck rides, afterall, to remind me to keep going and that heartbreak didn't have to be the end of the road.

Who knew my dad was such a deep man?

ME

Hi.

TAY

Hiiii bby.

SHANE

Hey there sunshine.

RUBY

I thought that was you Shane? But hello to you too missy.

LAUREN

BABY! YOU'RE BACK!!!!

ME

I have a change of address for you guys.

TAY

If it's not in the state of Tennessee, you WILL be able to hear me scream from wherever you are.

ME

Current Location

TAY

Oh, thank god. 🐻

SHANE

Where is that?

TAY

Moose's house.

LAUREN

Yayyy! 😊

RUBY

Damnnnn. Look at that place. I know where we're having girls night from now on.

ME

Did you just Zillow his house?

RUBY

Duh.

LAUREN

I've taught you well.

SHANE

Why have we never been there before?

TAY

Well, I have. Almost caught a show after the invasion of Fort Knox too. 🙈

SHANE

WHAT!?!?!?

LAUREN

You KNEW and you didn't TELL US??!?!

RUBY

Wait, what kind of show? 👀 because...

TAY

If you say that's my brother I stg.

RUBY

That's your brother.

RUBY

Oops. Sorry. 🤐

LAUREN

LMAO. 🤣

SHANE

Okay but can we fr do girls night there next?

ME

I missed you guys. 🤍

SHANE

🤍

TAY

We missed you more.

RUBY

Agreed. 🤍

LAUREN

🤍🤍

ME

One more thing. We're headed to the airport so I'll catch up with you when I get back.

TAY

What?!

SHANE

Where are you going!?

LAUREN

You're playing with my anxiety too much.

RUBY

Have a safe flight! 🛫

"Hey Dove, we're landing," Sawyer whispers, as I feel the plane descending. It's crazy how his presence alone helps me to sleep better. No one sleeps well on planes, but I just got some of the deepest sleep I've had in the last two weeks, simply because he's here.

"I can't believe we did this." I lean over and giggle like we're a couple of kids cutting school and could be caught any moment. I'm not used to spontaneous adventures like this—but I sure could get used to them.

"What is life if not one great big adventure?" Sawyer smirks over at me and my heart flutters.

The whole time we're deboarding the plane, getting a rental car, and driving to wherever we're headed, Sawyer is mostly quiet. He will turn and give me a smile or bring our joined hands to his lips to kiss the top of mine, but something just feels...*off*.

"Here we are." When he puts the car in park, I pull my eyes from him and look out the windshield. My mouth hangs open when I see where we are.

"Oh my god." Sawyer climbs out of the car, coming around to open my door before offering his hand to help me out as well.

We walk hand in hand until we're at the very top of Split Rock Lighthouse. Due to the fact that Sawyer gave the security guard a nod and it was returned with a smile and them stepping to the side to allow us to pass, I assume it's okay for us to be here after closing.

"Sawyer, this place is amazing." I marvel as we look out over the water. He wraps his arms around me from behind, warming me from the cool lake's breeze.

"I found this place during my sophomore year of college, and the first thought I had was, *Leah would absolutely love it here*. It felt like it belonged on a book cover or something. I don't know." He shrugs. "Anyways, I would visit here frequently and imagine a day when I'd get to bring you here. I *also* imagined we'd visit my favorite local coffee shop first and I could impress you with my expert ordering skills and get you a coffee that would make you fall in love with me." My body shakes with laughter at his confidence.

"But this visit is going to be a little different than all the ones I planned back in the day." I rest my head on his shoulder, looking up at the night sky where the full moon is shining so brightly it's like the earth's own nightlight.

"Oh yeah? Why's that?" His hands slide out from around me and the warmth from his body pressed against mine is gone. When I turn around, he's down on one knee with a little velvet box in his hands.

"Because I'm going to ask you to marry me instead." Then he pops the box open and I have to fight back the urge to scream.

Oh my God I'm turning into Taylor.

"Sawyer—"

"Dove, let me stumble through this really quick then you can say whatever you need to say. Because if I don't do this now, I might throw up." I choke out a laugh through my tears and nod for him to continue.

"Leah, I have loved you from the day that I met you. Not in the same way I love you now, of course, but I loved the way you carried yourself. You were quiet but sure of yourself, you were smart beyond belief and loyal to your friends and you lit up a room with your smile without having to utter a single word. As we grew up, you became one of my very best friends and I would have chosen you over anyone else if ever given the ultimatum. Because even before I realized it, you and I were meant to be. Then you brought me hot pink tape for my hockey stick one night and winked at me, and like a switch being flipped, I realized I would do *anything* to have you do it again. I fell in love with you through the years and I thank my lucky stars you've fallen for me too." I can't see through my tears anymore but that doesn't stop him.

"If the last few weeks taught me anything it's that I don't want to spend another day without you, for the rest of my life. So, will you do me the honor of being my wife and promise to never stop coming back to me? No matter what life throws at us?"

"Yes! Sawyer, Only, always, and forever. YES!" I rush the words out and he slides the ring I can't even see onto my finger before picking me up and spinning me around with his lips on mine—where they belong.

"There's something else." I let out another strained laugh.

"What else could there *possibly* be? You've already asked me to move in *and* marry you in the last 24 hours." He takes a deep breath and pulls an envelope from his inside jacket pocket. I look down and see my name scrawled on the front, but it's not Sawyer's handwriting —it's my dad's.

"I haven't read it, but he sent me one too and told me when to give it to you. Which I thought was strange until you told me he had a stroke prior to the one that took him… Um, I'm just gonna let you open it now." My brows knit together but I refrain from asking any questions because I doubt he has the answers for them anyways. I rip the envelope open and pull out the letter, his handwriting alone making my throat feel tight with emotion.

Hey Sweetpea,

If you're reading this letter then it's safe to assume two things.

1. That boy has some sense and finally put a ring on your finger.
2. That I'm not there to celebrate with you in the flesh.

I'm sorry for that second one, babygirl. Just know that even if I'm not there, I'm never really gone. I'm up in heaven celebrating that my little girl found her way into the arms of the one man I've ever been confident could take proper care of her. (Besides your old man, of course.)

The night you brought Sawyer home, I took him on one of our rides (I'm sorry I had to leave you home for that one) but I needed to make sure he knew how lucky he was to be in your life. You are the single greatest accomplishment in my life. You are smart and beautiful and kind and wise beyond your years, and I will always be proud to be your dad. I'm not sure if he'll tell you this or not, but Sawyer told me his intentions to marry you, and I gave him my blessing right away.

You are so deserving of a life full of love and happiness, and to be with someone who helps your light shine even brighter than it ever has before. I just know you lit up the whole universe with your smile when he asked you to be his wife. Don't you worry, I'm sure I saw it.

I wish you a lifetime full of adventure, laughs that make your stomach ache, and new memories that you can hold onto for an eternity. And since I'm gone, I want you to think of me any time you see the moon, because you were always my sun baby girl— the absolute light of my life.

I love you Leighann Gates. (Future Mrs. Clark I suppose) You will always be my sweetpea.

Love, Dad.

"Thanks, Dad," I whisper to the moon. Feeling a little more of my heart mend as I hold his letter close to my heart.

"You okay, Dove?" Sawyer asks, pulling me closer to his chest. I nod my head and sniff back my tears.

"Yeah. I'm gonna be."

"Can I give you one last thing?" He asks hesitantly. I'm not sure if my heart can possibly take any more at the moment, but the look on his face tells me it's important so I nod in agreement, and he reaches into his jacket pocket again.

Those things must be bottomless.

Then he opens another small box with the most beautiful necklace sitting inside.

"Sawyer, you *just* gave me the most magnificent engagement ring I've ever laid eyes on. You did not have to do this," I tell him, feeling spoiled in a way I can't quite fathom.

"This isn't just any necklace. It's uh…" He frowns then clears his throat. "Did you know they make custom jewelry from cremation ashes?" My eyes jump up to his from looking at what I *thought* was a pearl/diamond stone of some sort.

"You didn't." My voice is strained as tears come rushing back to the surface again.

"I asked your mom if she would be okay with it, and she was more than happy to allow me to have this made for you. I actually got one made for her as well…"

"Sawyer, this is the most thoughtful thing—" My emotions get the best of me and I'm unable to finish my sentence. He takes the necklace from the box and puts it on me, allowing me time to process the moment.

"Thank you, Sawyer."

"I just thought he should be here for this."

I don't know what I ever did to deserve this kind of love.

Chapter 55

Sawyer

"My sister is going to kill me for doing this a thousand miles away from her."

"If we listen really closely, we might be able to hear her scream when she sees it," Leah teases as she places her left hand on my chest with the water in the background as she holds her phone up to take a photo of her engagement ring. The smile on her face as she types away warms my heart. She's beautiful, in every single way, and she's *mine*.

Only. Always and Forever.

She sucks in a deep breath and turns around to press her back against my chest as we await the responding texts.

TAY

I'm gonna fucking throw up. 😭

SHANE

AHHHHHHHHHH! SHE GONNA BE A WIFEY?! 🧎‍♀️ 🕊️

RUBY

😭 Congratulations bby!! What a ROCK! 😍 🥹

> LAUREN
>
> If you elope I'm kicking Sawyer in the balls. But also, OMFG I'M SO HAPPY FOR YOUUUUUU!!!! 🐻 🖤

> TAY
>
> If you get married before me I will NEVER hear the end of it from Tucker. 😰

"Hmm, eloping. There's a thought," I think aloud, catching a sassy side eye from my future wife.

"Nice try. Lauren *will* kick you in the balls. Taylor would probably try to shave your head and I'm not sure our parents would ever recover from the betrayal."

"You always were the smart one." I kiss her forehead, loving the way her eyes flutter closed every time I do. "Shouldn't you tell your mom too?" I look down and frown.

"Well, I figured I'd tell her once we got home."

"Because you trust Taylor not to have it on the front page of the newspaper by tomorrow morning?" She lets out a loud, beautiful laugh.

"A *newspaper?*" I tickle her sides as payback for mocking my outdated quip.

"You know what I mean." I bury my face in her neck and begin kissing her there repeatedly as she giggles.

"Fair enough. We could try to call her?"

"Let's do it." She pulls her phone back out and dials her mom via FaceTime. It rings twice before the line connects and Loretta comes into view.

"Hey, Mom." Leah smiles so big it's hard to miss the fact that she's sitting on information.

"Hey, Sweetheart, is everything okay?" She adjusts her glasses as the lamp on the end table next to her lights up the screen.

"Yeah, everything is fine. Sawyer and I took a little spontaneous trip to the place he wanted to bring me last month." She turns the camera around and shows her the lighthouse, turning it slowly towards Lake Superior as her mom squints to take it all in.

"Wow, it's lovely there!"

"Isn't it? He sure has an eye for beautiful things, doesn't he?" She turns the camera to me and places her hand on my chest much like she did with the photo she sent to the group chat.

"Yes, he sure—OH! OH MY GOODNESS! HE DID IT? HE PROPOSED?!" The line fills with emotional excitement and Leah turns the camera back around, putting us both into frame as she continues flaunting her ring to her mother.

"He did!" Their smiles are identical as they look at one another.

"Congratulations baby girl! Sawyer, you did good sweetheart," she says, giving me an encouraging wink.

"Thank you, Loretta, I'm glad you approve."

"You two have a fun night celebrating." She gives Leah a knowing look and I can't help but chuckle when Leah's face turns bright red.

"*Mom!*" Loretta rolls her eyes playfully at her daughter.

"I love you, sweet girl. When will y'all be back home?"

"We fly out in the morning so I'm back in time for my game," I answer, knowing Leah doesn't know that yet.

"See you both tomorrow."

"Bye Mom, I love you."

The line goes dead, and Leah lets out a sigh.

"Your parents next?" I groan, wishing we were a thousand thread counts deep into celebrating our engagement. "Really? If you thought Taylor would tell *my mom,* what makes you think she hasn't already called *yours.*"

"I really hate when you're right." I lean down and kiss her, hoping it'll sway her enough to change her mind.

It does not.

"Make the call, Moose."

"Fine, but as *soon* as we hang up this phone, I am taking you back to the hotel," I lean down and nip at her neck. "And I plan on keeping busy until our plane takes off in the morning."

"Call them faster," she breathes, and I smirk knowing I've gotten her worked up.

"Sawyer?" My mom says when the line connects.

"Who else would it be, Ma?" I tease as she turns the light on in the kitchen.

"Well, smart ass, you've never FaceTimed me at this ungodly hour before, I just wanted to make sure it was you. Are you okay?" When she slides her glasses on and sees Leah her face lights up a little more. "Leah! Hi sweetheart. What a pleasant surprise."

"I'll pretend that didn't hurt." Mom waves me off and I laugh. "Where's Dad?"

"He's just on the deck smoking a cigar. Why?"

"Can you call him over?" I love that my mom doesn't ask questions or start analyzing why I need both of them on FaceTime in the middle of the night.

"Tony! Come here, Sawyer is on the phone." Dad comes into the frame and notices Leah straight away.

"Hey there young lady. It's good to see you two together." He winks at her, and she smiles brightly.

"Thanks, sorry we're calling so late." She scrunches her nose up apologetically.

"No worries, it's never too late to call home." I pick Leah's hand up and kiss it, angling her ring finger at the screen.

"SAWYER ANTHONY CLARK!" Mom screams. "DID YOU ASK THAT GIRL TO MARRY YOU?!" No wonder Tot acts the way she does—she comes by it honestly.

"I did." I'm smiling so big my cheeks hurt.

"And she said *yes*?" My dad teases as my mom continuously slaps his arm and screams.

"Of course I did, who could say no to this hair?" Leah matches his wit, running her hand through the brown waves and he smiles.

"Well, I'll be..." Dad's smile grows wider and he swipes at his eyes. Meanwhile my mom is a blubbering mess, wiping her eyes repeatedly to clear her vision.

"Congratulations to you both. Leah, sweetheart, you have always been part of this family in my heart. I am just so happy it's going to be official now." Mom sniffles as tears fill Leah's eyes.

"Thanks, Mama Marilyn. I love you." Leah sniffles now too.

"Oh, I love you more, sweet girl." Mom's lip quivers and Dad wraps his arm around her and pulls her over to kiss her temple.

"We did good, Honey."

"Goodnight Mom and Dad, I love you."

"Love you too, Son."

"Love you, baby boy." I roll my eyes playfully at my mom's comment. She has no idea her *baby boy* is about to do unspeakable things to his future bride.

We hang up the phone and as soon as it's back in my pocket Leah looks up at me.

"I was promised there would be hotel sex." She smiles devilishly, sending waves of excitement through my whole body.

God, I love this woman.

Chapter 56

ME

What are you guys up to?

LAUREN

It's cute that you act like you don't know we're sitting outside your house waiting to tackle you and look at that ROCK!

TAY

Seriously though, Sawyer couldn't have hidden a key under a frog or something? It's actually hot today.

SHANE

Remember when you were complaining three short months ago about freezing your tits off? Let's just savor the breeze while we have it.

ME

You do realize you could just say these things to each other face to face right? Since you're all together?

RUBY

True. BUT then we'd feel bad for leaving you out.

ME

So thoughtful.

"I'm not sure why I expected a quiet moment after we arrived home." Sawyer looks over at me and winks. My cheeks grow warm at the action, then he pulls our intertwined hands to his lips, pressing a kiss to mine and I melt in my damn seat.

"Get used to it, hockey star. This is what the rest of your life is going to look like. Just add a few husbands and a flock of children to the mix." I laugh as we draw nearer to the house.

"I'd hardly call three kids a flock." My eyes grow wide, and I can hardly bite back my smile.

"Shane is pregnant again," I blurt out. The shock hits him full force and he whips his head around to face me.

"No way! That's amazing. Are they excited?"

"Why don't you ask for yourself." The girls are all standing on the front porch, shifting on their feet impatiently as he puts the truck in park. Just before I open the door, he stops me.

"Hey, Dove."

"Yeah?"

"I love you." My heart leaps every time I hear him say that. I reach over to cup his face in my hand.

"I love you, too." He gives me a chaste kiss then nods for me to join the girls. They run over to me, wrapping me in a group hug and my heart overflows with joy.

"We missed you so much," Lauren whispers, brushing my curls out of the way.

"I missed you guys too." I try to swallow past the lump in my throat and take a deep breath. "I am so thankful to have friends that don't give up on me—even when I start to give up on…well, everything else."

"You know we're here 'til the end, babe," Shane says, giving me one of those calming smiles she's mastered.

"Okay okay, let's see this *ring!*" Ruby begins clapping excitedly. I hold my hand up and there's a collective gasp as they all stare at it, taking turns moving my fingers around to watch the sun reflect off it.

"Oh, that is stunning." Lauren is the first to speak, clearly impressed by Sawyer's choice. It's the most breathtaking piece of jewelry I've ever laid eyes on—a simple, but *radiant* marquise diamond set on a thin, rose gold band that looks almost like a vine.

It's very...*me*.

Taylor quietly breaks away from the pack and runs over to Sawyer, throwing her arms around him—clearly taking him by surprise—but he doesn't miss a beat wrapping his arms around her and squeezing her back. I can't hear what either of them are saying but they nod, and smile and he kisses the top of her head before she runs back over to us.

Sawyer walks up behind me, squeezing my waist as all the girls look on with adoring expressions.

"As much as I want to steal my future wife from you all so I can get some sleep before my game tonight, I am willing to share her— just this once."

"Oh my god, we have another possessive husband in the group," Lauren complains in an obviously playful way.

"Shane, congratulations on the new addition. I'll be sure to tell Max the same the next time I see him." Shane holds her bump-less stomach, smiling at Sawyer.

"Thanks, Moose."

"Catch you later for our rituals, Dove," he whispers in my ear before kissing my neck and heading into the house.

"I am so sorry I didn't get to see this happen sooner." Taylor's smile is pained as she stares straight at me.

"I'm not. Our story is happening exactly how it was meant to. In the end I got the guy *and* my girls. Nothing could be better than that." I grab her hand and she rests her head on my shoulder. "Now let's go inside and break in the blender and Sawyer's *super* fucking comfort- able sectional with a *proper* girls...uh, day, I guess?" I laugh, realizing it's ten o'clock in the morning.

"Mimosas!" Shane yells, pulling a bottle of champagne from her bag. "Or ya know, orange juice for the one that's expecting," she laughs.

I never thought I would leave my little old house. I enjoyed adding my own personal touches to modernize it, while keeping the house mostly in its original state, but living with Sawyer felt right from the moment he asked me to move in with him. Never mind the fact that approximately ten hours later he asked me to be his *wife*, so moving out of my own house would have been inevitable anyways.

"This is the last of it." Sawyer emerges from my bedroom holding a box in his hands labeled *books*. "You sure you're ready for this?" He looks around the empty living room with me.

I take a deep breath in. "Yes. This house served me well while I was here, but starting a life with *you* in our own house? I'm more than ready for that." I smile up at him and he places the box on the island, pulling his phone from his pocket and scrolling through it for a moment before placing it on top of the box.

"How about one last dance before we go?" His smile sends my heart into a frenzy, and I accept the hand he has offered me. Then he pulls me into him, and we dance. Spinning me, dipping me, holding me close, much like we did on our first lazy Sunday together, and I can't wait to have a million more days just like it with him.

MAY 31ST - TAYLOR'S BACHELORETTE PARTY.

"Peen pasta?!" Taylor squeals as Shane walks out of the kitchen with a casserole dish of alfredo covered penis pasta. "What a full circle moment." She holds her hand over her heart dramatically, making us laugh.

"It only seemed right." Shane sets the dish in the middle of Lauren's massive coffee table, passing out bowls and forks to each of us.

"Leah, no comment on the girth of the pasta this time?" Ruby teases, and I stick my tongue out at her.

"Well, I—"

"If this is in any way going to lead to you talking about my brother's penis, please don't," Taylor gets out over a mouth full of food.

"Does saying I can just appreciate the girth now count? Cause if it counts, I won't say it." Taylor scrunches her nose at me.

"It counts." We all burst out laughing as we carry on eating.

"I can't believe you're going to be gone for a month!" Lauren whines. "Well, a cross country road trip for a honeymoon *does* require more time than flying somewhere exotic." Taylor tucks a piece of Lauren's hair behind her ear in a comforting way.

"Are you saying you'd rather be flying somewhere exotic?" I ask.

"No! Not at all. On the road is where I fell in love with Tucker. I'm actually really excited about this. We're going to try and find all the best waterfalls in the country." She smiles to herself and it's freaking contagious.

"I'm so happy for you, Tay." Shane reaches over and hugs her neck.

"Okay, okay, enough mushy stuff. Let's do something fun. Who wants to trash talk our exes?" Taylor raises her brows.

"Yesssss." We all laugh and begin going on about the shitty things they did or said before finding a man that put every other one to shame. I watch Lauren carefully as we all talk, noticing the way she seems to be holding herself back from the conversation a little. She's seemed different lately—quieter than normal—almost as if her mind is so loud, she can't hear anything else going on around her.

"You okay?" I nudge her arm with my elbow as Taylor and Shane are arguing over why Shane ever dated a guy that wore a sweater vest to the beach. Her brows knit together, and she shakes her head.

"Yeah, just distracted, I guess." Then she offers me one of her fake smiles and I know that's my cue to leave it alone for now. So, I pull her a little closer and snuggle into her, finding a bit of relief in the fact that she nuzzles back into me too.

"All I'm saying is, when you're at the *beach* and you see a guy that looks like he got lost on the way to the library, maybe don't let him have your number?"

"Oh. My. *GOD*. I'm literally pregnant with my second child. Could we maybe let it go?" Everyone, including Shane, bursts into laughter.

JUNE 1ST - WEDDING DAY.

Taylor was determined to plan the perfect wedding—not wanting to follow in the footsteps of Shane and Ruby and have a wedding literally days after getting engaged—and today has proved that her efforts were not in vain. The girls and I *of course* helped when opinions were asked for, but I'm convinced Taylor will plan her own funeral well before she's gone to ensure it goes over perfectly.

God help us if it doesn't because this bitch *will* haunt us.

After moving into the home Tucker built for them—on over ten acres of land—she had a vision of what their wedding day would look like at their own home, and she has brought it to life exceptionally well.

The aisle runs from their sliding back doors—that take up the entire back wall of their house—all the way to the arch Max and Tucker built together. Red rose petals line each side of the aisle runner that has been staked into the ground to ensure the wind doesn't blow it away, with lanterns at the end of each row of white folding chairs.

Further down the yard there's an entire reception tent set up complete with a dance floor, DJ booth, twinkle lights and centerpieces to correlate with the red roses and lanterns used along the aisle.

Tucker, Max, Tank, and Sawyer wait at the end with the justice of the peace while friends and family fill every seat. The groomsmen are all dressed in black tuxedos with white shirts and black neckties, while Tucker has on a bow tie to set him apart.

As for Taylor, well she's one of the most stunning brides I've ever seen in my life. Her red hair is styled in the most beautiful up-do, with her vail tucked into the low set bun and a few wavy pieces framing her face. Her dress is another level of gorgeous, the ivory gown has spaghetti straps, a corset style bodice with a full tulle skirt covered in lace floral details.

"Why the fuck am I nervous? It's been a year, it's not like he's changed his mind," Taylor nervously rants. "Right? You don't think he's changing his mind, right?" She looks at me with panic in her eyes.

"Babe, I'm pretty sure he'd have to be at the morgue to not be at the end of that aisle when you walk down it." She nods her head so quickly I'm scared her hair might fall.

"Right, okay. You're right. I mean. It's Tucker. He almost killed two of my exes in one night. I'd say that's pretty committed."

"You alright in there, Darlin'?" Tucker's voice filters in through the door and Taylor gasps.

"Tucker! You can't be up here. It's bad luck!" she scolds him, pushing me in front of her to shield herself.

He lets out a low laugh. "I'm not coming in. I just wanted to come check on you. You were uncharacteristically calm this morning, just making sure it didn't catch up to you."

"It didn't."

"It did," Taylor and I say in unison.

"Traitor," she whispers in my ear before moving out from behind me.

"Darlin', there is *nothing* that is going to keep me from marrying you today, nothing that could ruin this day, and nothing that will ever change the fact that I want to spend the rest of my life with you. Alright? Take a deep breath, and I'll see your fine ass down the aisle."

Taylor visibly relaxes, tilting her head in awe as she smiles at his words.

"I love you, Tucker."

"I love you too, baby." Tucker's footsteps fade down the hallway from their bedroom and Taylor takes a cleansing breath.

"Okay, I'm ready."

Chapter 57

Hendrix Landry has *way* too much swagger for a seven-year-old child. The way he struts down the aisle while holding Cece's hand is a true testament to just how much like his father he really is. Lauren goes out after the two of them, then me, followed by Ruby and Shane before Tay makes her grand entrance with Tony—my future father-in-law.

As soon as it's my turn to walk down the aisle, I find Sawyer's eyes on me. He shoots me a wink and I can feel my cheeks burning—and it's not from the summer sun.

When I scan the rows of people, I almost trip over my own two feet when I see a familiar face in the crowd. I keep my eyes ahead, as the instrumental for "One Man Band" plays until the rest of the bridal party is in place at the front.

"Lauren," I whisper behind me, keeping a smile on my face so no one knows how badly I'm freaking out right now.

"We're not doing this right now," she says through her teeth as she too smiles, with her eyes trained on the doors where Taylor is going to emerge at any minute.

"Fine. Then we'll do it later." I raise a brow at her, and she shoots me a flirty glare.

"Stop flirting with me, Le, you'll make Sawyer jealous." She nods to where he has a brow raised in our direction and when I turn back to her, she shoots him a playful wink and he shakes his head at us.

"Whatever is wrong with you two, you better cut it out, she's about to walk out," Shane whisper-scolds us, making us immediately go silent and turn to face the doors.

I think after watching *27 Dresses* enough times we all collectively agreed that watching the groom's face when the bride is walking down the aisle is one of our favorite parts of weddings as well. So, after getting a glimpse of Taylor and Tony, we all turn to look at Tucker.

He is doing his best to hold it together, but the man is full on sobbing, the purest form of love gleaming from his tear-filled eyes as his bride makes her way to him. I steal a glance at Sawyer who is also red in the face, sniffling back tears as he watches his little sister walking down the aisle. Then he meets my eye and shoots me a wink and I can't help but imagine what our wedding will be like someday.

But today isn't about us...it's about them.

"Who gives this bride to be?" the officiant asks.

"Oh, she makes her own choices, her mother and I just support her in them." The crowd erupts in laughter at the very on brand comment made by Mr. Clark.

He kisses her temple then Tucker takes his place next to Taylor as Tony joins Marilyn on the front row.

I continue watching Tucker, wondering if it's hard for him to not have either of his parents here. He and Tank don't talk much about their mom, but I know their dad was a big role model to both of them. My heart sinks knowing my dad won't be at mine and Sawyer's wedding and that we won't be able to share a father daughter dance together, but I know he'll be smiling down on us even still.

"The couple will now exchange the vows they have written for one another."

TAYLOR'S VOWS

Tucker,

You came into my life by happenstance and while it may seem harsh, I've never been more grateful for a friend's failed relationship (sorry Shaney) that ended with us doing shots at a bar with the most gorgeous bartender I'd ever laid eyes on. The moment you called me Darlin' for the first time the chemistry between us was absolutely electric. And even though I turned you down at first, I will never be able to express to you how grateful I was that you didn't give up on the idea of us. You gave me the time I needed to finally get over the heartache that left me jaded and against the idea of love, you didn't hold back in telling me how you felt about me, and it's that bold vulnerability that finally lifted the veil I had hidden behind and showed me you were who I was meant to be with all along. Your friendship comforted me, and your love healed me in ways you may never fully understand. You are my best friend, my soul mate, and the one person I want to see at the end of every day. You fill my life with so much love and adventure and I can't wait to take on the world with you. I promise to never try to cook without your supervision, to be vulnerable with you even when it's hard, and to always be a safe space for you to land when your mind takes you to difficult places. I promise to love you, encourage you and support you in whatever dream you chase next. I promise to never forget what it feels like to fall in love under a waterfall and that you understand me better than anyone else. For the rest of my life, I am yours and I will love you in a way that proves just that.

TUCKER'S VOWS

Taylor,

If there was ever a time I was glad I knew how to make a proper key lime martini, it was the day you walked into Max's bar. All fiery attitude and a challenge in your tone. I was intrigued from the moment I saw you, and as our friends began to fall in love, I was falling in love with you too. You are unlike anyone I've ever known. Bold, loyal, strong, beautiful from the inside out, and there's not a single thing about you that I haven't fallen in love with through the years. I know I gave you a hard time about you taking so long to plan our wedding, but I would spend all of my lifetimes waiting for the chance to call you my wife. You understand me, you comfort me, you challenge me and encourage me to do the things that I love and above all you let me love you. Even when it was hard to let me in, you took a chance on us, and I will be eternally grateful for the life we've gotten to start together because of that. I promise to support you, protect you and defend you, but to let you do it yourself when you feel as though it *is necessary to do so. I promise to always come home to you and that I won't try to keep you out of my hardships, but to let you in and work through them with you, as husband and wife. I promise to make you key lime martinis and bake cookies when you're having a bad day, and that at the end of the day you know how loved, wanted and respected you are. I promise to never let you forget that you have become my favorite person in the entire world. For the rest of my life, I am yours as well Darlin'. I have been from the moment I laid eyes on you.*

Taylor was a freaking genius putting tissue in the middle of all our bouquets.

"By the power vested in me by the state of Tennessee I now pronounce you husband and wife, you may now kiss the bride."

When Tucker kisses Taylor it's a magazine worthy moment—the sun setting beautifully in the background, him holding onto her like he can't keep his hands off her and the smile on her face as he continues to kiss her repeatedly.

The wedding party begins walking out behind them, Shane and Max, Tank and Ruby, and then Lauren and I on either side of Sawyer.

"I can't wait to marry you, Dove." He smiles down at me.

"Get in line, hockey star. She was mine first," Lauren teases from the other side of him, puckering her lips at me to irritate him further. Sawyer is so used to our shenanigans I'm certain he isn't the least bit affected by us at this point.

"Yeah, well…she's mine now."

"Excuse me, bitches. Is Lauren here with Devil Hottie?" Taylor finally makes her way over to us after greeting other guests as we're standing at the bar that is set up in the corner of the reception tent.

"Girl, I know, I almost tripped walking down the aisle when I saw him," I whisper and her eyes go wide, hungry with need for more details.

"I thought for sure someone had put something in my drink this morning and that I was hallucinating."

"What are we talking about?" Lauren's voice hits my ears and Taylor looks over her shoulder to see Lauren standing with her arms crossed over her chest.

"We're *talking* about you being here with the guy you claim to hate! Are you sleeping with the devil, Lu?" Taylor drags her over into our little huddle, demanding information.

"Seriously Tay, *this* is what you want to talk about at your *wedding reception?*"

"Piping hot tea is the *best* wedding gift you could possibly give me. Pour it." She taps her fingertips together like some evil cartoon villain.

"There's no tea. I *may* have mentioned during a very low, very rage-filled moment that I didn't want to come to your wedding alone and he offered to come with me." She shrugs and our mouths pop open.

"As an arch nemesis does, *naturally*," Taylor says sarcastically, proving that Lauren's explanation makes zero sense.

"Could the arch nemesis bother you for a dance?" Luci—Fitz's voice stuns us all silent and Lauren's face turns red. She shoots daggers at all of us before turning to him and taking his hand.

"Is this the part where you grab the cake cutter and bring me to my demise?" He laughs at Lauren's comment and oh my *god*, if she's not sleeping with him maybe she should be.

"That girl has some serious mother freaking explaining to do when I get back from my honeymoon." Taylor points to the dance floor.

"We have to wait a *month* to find out what the hell this is all about?" Ruby asks.

"Yes, there will be *no* tea pouring while I'm gone. I will not be deprived of the opportunity to see this story unfold. Or unravel, depending on whether or not they actually hate each other," she mutters the last bit and I can't help but snicker.

She returns to the dance floor with her dad for their father daughter dance and my heart absolutely bursts when I see Marilyn ask Tucker if he would like to dance for the mother son portion. He spins her across the floor, bringing the biggest grin to Marilyn's face as he swipes a tear from his eye over her head so she can't see. She really is one of a kind, that Marilyn.

"Hey sweetheart, I think I am going to head out." My mom grabs my hand and I pull her in to hug her.

"Be safe and let me know when you're home. Do you need a ride? I know you don't like driving at night."

"Oh, I'll be fine. I just got my new glasses and the headlights on my car are working just fine." She gives me a wink and I laugh, rolling my eyes at her sassiness.

"I love you. Talk to you tomorrow."

"I love you too." She takes one step then stops and turns to face me again. "You're going to make the most beautiful bride one day, LeighAnn. I am so grateful you chose the love side of that line."

"There's a fine line between love and hate, LeighAnn, make sure you know what side you're on before you lose him again."

"Me too mom." I smile at her, and she nods before leaving the reception.

Chapter 58

Sawyer

"Can I have this dance?"

"I don't know, *can you?*" Leah teases, taking my hand as I lead her to the dance floor.

"I knew dating a teacher would eventually come back to bite me in the ass." Her head falls back in laughter as we sway to the music.

"Are you having a good time?" She sighs and looks up at me, my soul immediately relaxing when those green eyes land on mine.

"I am. Today was so perfect. Taylor really outdid herself."

"Tot has that *I can do anything* gene. There's not much she hasn't accomplished after setting her mind to it." I watch as she and Tucker dance together, laughing, smiling, so in love that it's sickening. Or at least, it would be if I didn't relate to that very same feeling so damn much.

"You're not wrong. She's a force to be reckoned with."

"So, any thoughts on when you want to do all of this and become my wife?" Her cheeks turn red and the smile on my face is instantaneous.

"I mean, it'll probably have to be next year. I don't really think planning a wedding during the school year would be the smartest decision." I press my forehead to hers and groan.

"Fine." I kiss the tip of her nose and she smiles.

"Maybe we can plan it for July next year? Just in case you guys may make it through the playoffs again. That way you have at least a *little* time to breathe before we get hitched."

"Whatever you want, Dove. Just as long as by the end of it you're officially my wife." I lean down and capture her lips in mine to keep from telling her what I've been planning to do after the finals this year. "You wanna get out of here?" I whisper in her ear, not missing the way goosebumps break out over her arms.

"We can't yet. We still have to do the sparkler send-off." Her voice is heavy with regret and desire. I look around the room to see people still going strong mingling, dancing, and eating cake. No way is that send-off happening in an acceptable time frame.

"Come with me." I take her hand and lead her off the dance floor.

"What? Where are we going?" she squeals, looking behind her before I throw her over my shoulder and stalk towards the house. "Put me down, Moose!" She slaps my ass and I slap hers back.

I walk into the restroom next to the laundry room—that is thankfully set apart from the rest of the house—and put her down on the counter.

"Why are we in here?" She fixes her hair, staring straight at me.

"You remember my first day back, during my welcome home party and you came in here to hide from me? When you brushed past me and put that ticket back in my pocket, I wanted to pull you into this bathroom and show you exactly why you should be mine." Her cheeks grow rosy, and her chest rises and falls more visibly with every breath.

"That would have been a little irrational, don't you think?" I smirk at her teasing tone.

"Hmm. Agree to disagree." I pull at my tie, loosening it from around my neck until I can undo the top few buttons of my dress shirt.

Her nipples are becoming more visible behind the fabric of her dress, making me grow more impatient by the second. I step up to her, pulling her dress up past her knees, spreading her legs to step between them as I lean down and kiss her. Her hands are on my sides immediately, gripping my shirt as my tongue dips past her lips and explores her mouth. She tastes like champagne and mint and I'm already desperate for more. I drop to my knees and move her dress up further, being met with nothing underneath.

"Dove, care to tell me why you're not wearing any underwear under this dress?" I growl, shooting her a curious glare.

"I didn't want a panty line?" She shrugs. Then she runs her hand through my hair and smirks. "Plus, it just gives you quicker access to me. So really, it's a win-win." She bites on her lip, and I swear I would drop to my knees for her if I wasn't already on them.

When the silk fabric of her dress is up around her waist I dive right in, splitting her with my tongue and letting a moan escape from deep within my throat as the first taste of her truly hits me.

"Delicious." I take my time, licking and sucking on every inch of her perfect pussy, driving her closer and closer to the edge but not letting her go over just yet.

"Sawyer, please."

"I'm not done, Dove. Your pussy is fucking addicting." I dip my tongue inside her, before licking her from entrance to clit, over and over until her legs are shaking.

"Right there, yes. Don't stop." I do exactly as I'm told, and I keep my same pace until she's squeezing her perfect thighs around my head and coming on my tongue.

"Atta girl, you did so good." I stand and quickly free myself from my dress pants, pressing the tip of my cock through her soaked entrance. I sink into her, loving the way her warmth welcomes me in.

"God, you feel so good." I thrust my hips. "Just like coming home."

"Oh, yes!" Her hands wrap around my neck and her head falls back as sweet sounds of pleasure fall from her lips.

"Lean back and grab the sides of the counter." She does as she's told, and I lift her hips from the sink, driving myself even deeper than before and eliciting a scream that makes my dick pulse with excitement.

I continue like this until her moans become so loud, I have to pull her towards me, letting her ass hang off the edge of the sink, wrapping an arm around her waist to steady her and placing my other hand around her mouth.

"You know I love it when you scream for me baby, but I'm not done yet and I would hate to have to stop. Not when your pussy is milking me so. Fucking. Well." She moans into my hand when I sink into her harder with every word, causing a smirk to sneak onto my lips.

"Now, play with your pretty pussy while I rail you properly." I remove my hand from her mouth and hers disappears between us, rubbing circles on her clit as I fill her completely with every thrust.

"Sawyer, don't stop. I'm gonna come," she pleads breathlessly. My hands grip her hips tighter as she reaches her climax.

"Don't move baby, I'm close." She remains as still as possible while her climax washes over her, until she leans forward to bite down on my shoulder in an effort to keep herself quiet and that fucking does me in. I bury myself as deep inside of her as I can and empty every last drop of my release into her.

"Now you get to spend the remainder of your best friend's wedding with her brother's cum dripping down your leg. Tsk, you naughty little bridesmaid." Her pussy squeezes around me and I groan from the sensation.

"And you get to spend it with her best friend's cum on your tongue. But I doubt either of us really gives a damn, do we?"

God, I love it when she's feisty.

It's game day, but not just any game day. It's the freaking Stanley Cup Finals, and I've never felt more ready for anything in my life. Ever since we went to Minnesota, Leah has been part of my game day ritual. We shower together, grab coffee, and she picks a song from my game day playlist and we dance to it—whether it's in a hotel room or our own home—then she comes to the rink early with me while I get my head right for the night. She knows how important it is to me to stay consistent with it and the smile on her face the whole day is downright contagious.

"You sure you don't want to try any of mine?" She holds her iced mocha latte up to me and I raise a brow at her. "Wait, does the *kind* of coffee you get stay consistent too?"

"Yes ma'am," I wrap my arm around her and take a sip of my Americano.

"Oh! Noted. You can *not* try any of mine. You have to stay sharp today." I kiss the top of her head as we walk down the sidewalk away from Bruman's and the scent of her vanilla body wash overrides the coffee scent and floods my senses. She looks breathtaking today in her fitted green dress and white converse, her glasses perched on her perfect nose while her curls air dry in the summer breeze.

"You have no idea what it means to me that you're part of this now." She stops in the middle of the sidewalk and turns to face me.

"You have no idea what it means to *me* that you wanted me to be."

"Are you kidding, Dove? I want nothing more than to fill every single bit of my life with your presence. To know that no matter where I go, or what I do, you'll be by my side through it all."

"Only, always, and forever." She reaches up on her toes and kisses me, and if I could freeze time to capture this moment, I would. Though I hope the rest of my life is filled with nothing but time stopping moments with her. "Give me your phone." She holds her hand out and wags her brows mischievously at me.

I hand it over and she punches in the code, tapping the screen before beginning to scroll. She chews on her lip as she hums.

"What, now?" I ask, looking up and down the moderately busy sidewalk.

"Live a little, thirteen." She winks at me and turns the volume up on my phone as the same KISS song I sang to her at one of my games begins filling the space around us. "Are you going to dance me around this sidewalk or not?" She sets both of our cups down on a nearby concrete ledge and I smirk at her.

"I'd dance with you anywhere baby." Her laugh fills the air as we spin and dip and even break out some old line dancing moves on the corner as people around us go about their day. Some people stop to watch—even going as far as recording us on their phones—but to me, it's just the two of us.

Chapter 59

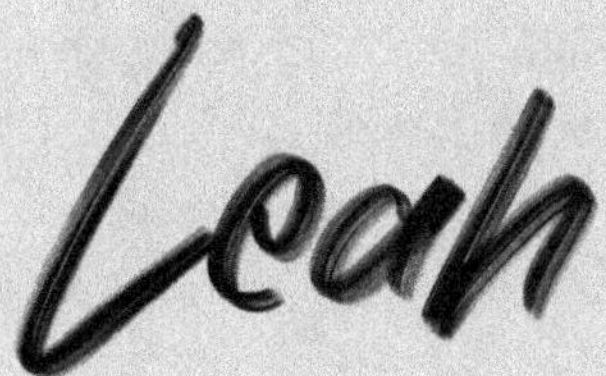

Nine months.

That's how long it took for my life to change in more ways than I ever dreamed possible. When Sawyer came back to town, I imagined I would spend the rest of my life completely miserable—trying to shove feelings I had no business having for him into the deepest depths of my mind. Lucky for me he got tired of waiting for fate to do her damn job in bringing us back together and did it himself. I have never felt happier than I do right now—surrounded by all our friends and family at the final game of the Stanley Cup Finals, as the love of my life plays his freaking heart out on the ice.

When Sawyer told me he wanted me to become part of his game day routine it felt like the deepest expression of love. Game day rituals are no joke for athletes, and especially not for Sawyer—I picked up on that when he started using the pink sports tape every game after I brought him his senior year of high school. That was the game he scored his first tie breaking goal and after that it was pink sports tape on the stick, or he wasn't playing at all.

I've got on my jersey with the number thirteen and Sawyer's name plastered on my back, and I can't wait to show him the new matching green lingerie set I have on underneath it. Lyssa is standing next to me with Matty's jersey on, munching nervously on a bag of popcorn, meanwhile I couldn't eat anything even if I wanted to.

I found out I am *not* a nervous eater, I'm a nervous drinker.

We've filled an entire row with people here to support the guys and it's been the most high energy game of the season. It's four to three in the last minute of the third period with the Badgers in the lead and both teams are *fighting for it* tonight.

The clock starts running down with less than a minute as the puck travels closer to our goal. The other team takes a shot and I hold my breath, but Devon blocks it and sends it right to Matty. He and Sawyer take off down the ice—fifteen seconds on the clock—they're passing it so fast I can barely keep up and as soon as Sawyer takes a shot, it hits the net and the sirens go off.

"OH MY GOD!!!!!" Lyssa and I scream like mad women as we jump up and down together. The entire row is exchanging hugs, high fives and Marilyn and Tony have tears in their eyes as they watch their son achieve one of his lifelong dreams.

The Badgers are all jumping on each other with helmets flying everywhere and then a few moments later I hear someone beating on the glass and look over to see Sawyer standing at the edge of the ice.

"What are you doing?! You should go celebrate."

"I love you, Dove. I couldn't have done this without you," he yells, then he pats the spot on his ribs where my tattoo is, and my eyes begin to water.

"I love you too! Now go celebrate with your team. I'll meet you out there!" He skates back over, and his coach runs out on the ice and celebrates with them.

I think I finally get why he's so worked up after games. I don't think I've felt this much adrenaline pumping through my body—ever, actually.

When the game is over, and the cup has been presented—each player gets their photo taken and has the chance to raise the cup—before the locker room party begins. I only stay a few minutes after they let family members in, opting to leave and tell Sawyer I'll meet him in the hallway, so I don't get bombarded with anymore champagne soaked hugs.

The moment I see him, I take off and jump into his arms. His hair is wet from him showering and he's back in his suit looking like a damn dreamboat when he wraps his arms around me and squeezes me so tight it's like we're the only two here.

"I know I already told you this, but you were amazing tonight," I whisper into his neck where my face is nestled. "How does it feel?"

"Indescribable." His smile is the same today as it was when we were kids. Much more mature now, of course, but the very same one that sent butterflies into a frenzy in my stomach and made it almost impossible to look anywhere but at him. The kind of smile you want to look at forever.

"Are we celebrating with anyone tonight?" I ask him, unsure what the proper protocol is for when your team wins the Stanley freaking Cup.

"The guys wanted to go out for drinks, but I told everyone else we'd do dinner one night at our place if that's alright with you? You feel up for going out tonight?" I love how he's always so considerate of what I want to do and what I'm comfortable with.

"Of course! I'm going wherever you are my love." He hums his approval of the nickname, and we head out for drinks with the entire Badgers team—I'm curious to see what bar is going to house all of these men and their plus ones comfortably.

We pull up to *Fr33style* and find out the entire place reserved for an after party just for the team. The lights inside are lit up green and white to match the team's colors, there's a huge banner hanging up in the back that I'm assuming someone had made just in case tonight ended with a win, and the bottle girls are all wearing cropped Badgers shirts and shorts that look more like underwear.

"There you are!" Lyssa squeals, approaching us from within the crowd. "Matty and the guys are waiting for you by the banner for another picture," she tells Sawyer, linking her arm with mine.

"I take it you're in good hands, I'll be back." He gives me a wink and disappears.

"I can't believe they did it," Lyssa sighs, watching as the guys get in position.

"I freaking can, this is the best season I've seen Sawyer have in *years*. The Badgers absolutely killed this year."

"I can't wait to see how they do next year! It's going to be so fun having you there to freak out with. I think next year may be Matty's last," she whispers, and my eyes grow wide.

"You think so?" She nods her head and smiles while her gaze is fixed on him.

"Yeah. We want to start a family and Matty always said he wanted to be home for all of it, he doesn't want to miss anything, and I think we're ready."

"Lyss! That's so exciting. I really hope everything works out for you guys the way you want it to." I pull her in for a hug and she swipes away a tear.

"Ugh, look at me I'm already all emo about it. Can you imagine pregnancy hormones on top of this?" She rolls her eyes and blows out a breath, making me laugh. A loud burst of laughter catches my attention from across the room and Lyssa and I both glance around for the source until I see where it's coming from.

One of the bottle girls with the number thirteen on her micro top is rubbing Sawyer's arm and tossing her long blonde hair behind her shoulder. Sawyer's tight-lipped smile and the way he has his hands shoved into his pockets tells me that he's just trying to be polite, then his eyes meet mine and they widen like he needs saving—the same way they did that night at karaoke when someone yelled for him to have their babies.

No, I will not be forgetting that woman hollering at my man any time soon.

"Excuse me, Lyssa." I plaster an aggravated smile on my face and she notices.

"Ooh, go get your man, honey." She waves me off and I do just that. Weaving through the crowd I walk over until I'm right by Sawyer's side.

"Am I interrupting?" I smile sweetly as the girl looks me up and down.

"Sweetie, buckle bunnies aren't welcome tonight, sorry." A vision of me slapping the extensions out of her hair flashes through my mind then I narrow my eyes and remember who the hell I am.

"Oh, so how did you get in?" I feign innocence and tilt my head as if I'm truly curious. She glances at Sawyer and recomposes herself.

"Well, as you can see," she points to the thirteen on her shirt. "I'm assigned to be this hunk's bottle service tonight, but I'd be happy to find someone to escort you out." Wow, she's got balls, I'll give her that.

"That won't be necessary, I'll be finding someone else to serve me and my future wife tonight." Sawyer wraps a hand around my waist and pulls me into his side, leaning down enough to capture my lips with his. My hands find their way to his hair, and I let my fingers weave through the soft locks.

"Oh, I am so sorry, I didn't realize." She tries to save face from the previous comment she made, but it's too late for that.

"That is because you simply didn't care to. Have a good night." Sawyer grabs my hand and leads me through the crowd until we reach the bar.

"One strawberry margarita and one whiskey neat please." He orders our drinks and wraps his arms around my waist, kissing along my neck until I'm tingling from my cheeks down to my toes.

"What are you doing?" I ask, leaning my head back on his shoulder.

"We are going to have one drink, we're going to dance a little bit, then I'm taking you home, Dove."

Chapter 60

One drink turned into two, a little bit of dancing turned into us almost shutting the place down, but the night still ended the way he promised it would—with him taking me home.

"I think you calling me your future wife was the hottest thing I've ever heard." I turn to face him as he pulls into our driveway.

"Just wait until I get to drop the *future* part. I'm gonna tell everyone that will listen that you're my wife. We'll have to travel to every country and province within our reach just so I can say it to more people. *This is MY WIFE,*" he raises his voice as he practices his line to the windshield. I can't contain my laughter and he squeezes my hand tighter.

"Falling in love with your best friend is truly underrated."

"Is that so?" His eyes meet mine as he parks the truck and cuts the ignition off.

"It is. You have always been the funniest person I know; we can joke around and be comfortable with each other because it feels so natural, but then—"

"Then?" he presses.

"Then you wink at me, or smile at me from across a room, or

touch me and my entire body ignites. You're the only person who has ever made me want *more* than friendship."

"You're my best friend too, Dove." I smile when he pulls our hands to his lips, placing a kiss in the same spot he always does. "Which is why I can't wait a second longer to tell you this. Especially with the insane week we have ahead of us with the parade and what not." My heart skips and the smallest hint of anxiety settles in the pit of my stomach.

"Okay…" I brace myself for whatever it may be, and even though my mind wants to go to the worst-case scenario, I truly have no idea what could be coming out of his mouth next.

"You remember the night we went to Taylor's house for Shane's birthday?"

"Yes?"

"After talking to Tank, it just made me realize that the work he is doing at *The Veterans Center* is so underappreciated and *majorly* under-funded. So, I talked to my accountant, and I donated four-million-dollars to the center." My eyes practically bug out of my head.

"*Four-million-dollars?* Sawyer that's…that's amazing." I can barely contain my joy knowing how much that money is going to help up there.

"That's not all."

"Oh, okay. What else?"

What else could there possibly be?

"I'm going to volunteer there during off seasons whenever I can. At the beginning of the season, I thought it might be my last, that I would finally hang up my skates. My heart just wasn't in it anymore, but I realize now that's because I was on a more important mission to make you mine. Ever since we've been together and you've been at my games, it put that fire back in me that I'd been missing for a lot longer than I even realized. But I still feel like I could do more to help out there when I'm not on the ice, you know?"

Sawyer Clark. Hockey god. Future husband. Man of endless surprises.

My mouth pops open but I don't think I have any words left.

"Say something," he encourages.

"I'm trying. My brain is out of words." He laughs and it helps break me out of my buffering phase.

"I just wasn't sure how you would feel about it since it will be my first off season since we got together, and we're engaged now and you're out of school for the summer. I just don't want you feeling like we won't have enough time together while I'm gone but… I don't know, Dove. I just felt like I needed to do it. Ya know?" I climb over to straddle his lap like I did the first night we went driving together.

"You are by far the most incredible man I know. You are so kind, you are always thinking of others, you never stop trying to go above and beyond and I don't think I'll ever stop falling in love with you. Was Tank excited?" I ask, curious how I've not heard about this until now.

"I don't think I've ever seen that man smile so hard. It was both unsettling and beautiful." I burst with laughter, remembering just how much work Tank put into healing and bettering himself to get to where he is today. His humor definitely reflects that of his brother more now, but he still has his broody/grumpy streak much like Max. I believe Sawyer and Tank were destined to be friends.

"We are going to have the rest of our lives together. I promise to tell you if I start missing you too much, but as long as you're coming home to me every night, I don't see this being a problem."

"The only way I'm not coming home to you, Dove is if there's no more breath in my lungs." I lean in and press my lips to his, teasing him until he's grabbing the back of my head, controlling the pace of our kiss. I finally pull away and whisper against his lips.

"Take me in the house, I have something I want to show you." He wastes no time opening the door and carrying me inside placing my feet on the ground right inside the foyer. I kick my shoes off and his brow raises.

"Please tell me it's you naked." His head falls back pleading.

"Not quite." I wink at him, unbuttoning my denim skirt and letting it fall to the ground. His jersey fits me like a dress when it isn't tucked into anything, so I take my time pulling it off over my head. When it's discarded on the floor next to my skirt, Sawyer's gaze is so heated I can almost feel it searing into my skin as he takes in the sight of me.

He begins discarding his clothes, starting with his gray suit jacket quickly followed by his black dress shirt. Then he's in nothing but a pair of gray slacks and it's just as hot as every other damn thing I've ever seen him in.

"You look absolutely delectable in that, Dove. Such a shame I'm about to rip it to shreds to get to you." He snatches me up and I wrap my legs around his waist, but instead of taking me to our room, he takes me to the kitchen instead.

His face is buried in my neck—kissing, sucking and biting causing chills to run down my spine—as he sets me on the massive island countertop. Pulling my breasts out from behind the lace he takes one in his mouth as his hand teases the other before switching to give each one equal attention from his soft lips. Then he leans up to kiss me, gently laying me on my back and ensuring I don't hit my head on the marble before kissing his way down my body. He inhales just as the tip of his nose hits my clit and he groans.

He teases me by swiping his hot tongue along the fabric of the lace bodysuit and nibbling on my most sensitive area. Then, without warning, he rips the lace right down the middle, allowing for more than enough access to where I'm aching for his touch. Without the barrier in our way any longer, he licks nice and slow from entrance to clit driving me absolutely crazy.

"God, you taste like *mine*." I'm convinced his mouth must be magic. Every time we're together it feels as though he's known my body forever. How to make it respond to his every touch. Before I know it, he's bringing me to my first orgasm of the night at record speeds before I'm pushing to sit up—earning a look of confusion from Sawyer.

"My turn." I slide down off the counter, turning him so that his back is pressed against it instead. Then I drop to my knees and undo his pants, pulling them and his boxers all the way off. Just looking at him and knowing what he'll feel like when he's filling me completely makes my pussy clench around nothing.

"Fuck you look good on your knees for me." I wrap my hand around his length, giving it a gentle tug before licking from his balls to the tip.

"I'll look even better when I'm choking on your cock, don't you think?" I spit on the tip and notice how his mouth pops open before I take him all the way down my throat.

His hands grip the edge of the counter and the way his knuckles are turning white gives me an extra boost of confidence. I refrain from swallowing to keep him nice and wet, then with my other hand I squeeze his balls and he mutters *fuck* under his breath.

"You're so good at sucking me off, baby." I moan at his praise and take him as far back as I can. He reaches down and pinches the bridge of my nose between my eyes. "Open your throat for me so I can fuck your pretty mouth properly." I hold on to the back of his thighs as he thrusts—completely intoxicated by the way he looks when my mouth is wrapped around him. Then he pulls out of me and lifts me off the ground.

"There's only one place I want my cum going tonight." His lips cover mine, hungry and desperate as his tongue dips into my mouth before he pulls away. "Turn around and hold on tight." I turn and face the island, gripping the counter as he bends me over. He slides two fingers through my lips then sliding them over my clit so I can feel how wet I am for him.

"Atta girl, wet and ready for me." Then he thrusts. He slows his pace only to lean over and plant kisses all over my back, causing the waves of pleasure I'm already feeling to intensify.

"More," I plead. He thrusts twice more then I'm left empty only for a moment as he turns me around, pulling me up by the legs before sliding in again.

"I needed to see that pretty face." My head falls back with a moan as he returns to the beautiful, punishing pace he had set before.

"Don't stop, Sawyer. I'm so close,"

"I wouldn't dare, baby." With every thrust of his hips, I fall deeper into the euphoria that *is* being with Sawyer. He makes me happier than I've ever been, and seeing his ring on my finger while he brings me pleasure only he can, makes me want to be his in every way possible as officially as possible. He presses his thumb to my clit with the most delicate and perfect pressure and I let go, soaking him with every drop of my orgasm.

"Sawyer!" I scream, as he empties himself inside me, pulling me closer so there is no space left between us. With every breath he takes his chest presses harder against mine, allowing me to feel his heart-beat against mine.

"I don't want to wait to become your wife. Marry me, Sawyer. Marry me tomorrow, or next week, or next month if we have to wait that long, but marry me sooner, please?" He looks into my eyes, gently cupping my face with his hands as he smiles back at me.

"I think those are the most beautiful words I've ever heard spoken. Are you sure?"

"I've never been more sure of anything." I nod in assurance.

"Then let's get married." He smiles and my soul completely melts into his. In my mind, Sawyer and I were one from the moment we first kissed. Now we're just making it official.

Epilogue

Sawyer

The entire last week has been absolutely wild. Winning the Stanley Cup is a much bigger deal than winning any ordinary game—as I'm sure anyone would imagine. The locker room was covered with champagne and the smell of predetermined bad decisions right after out victory, the after party that night had an energy like none I'd ever seen before, and don't even get me started on the fucking parade. Having Leah by my side through it all only made it that much sweeter. I'd *thought* we'd have everyone over for a celebratory dinner the night after we won, but I severely underestimated the celebrations that would be had this week.

So tonight, the dinner table at our house is packed with our family and closest friends, to *finally* celebrate the Badgers win at the Stanley Cup. It just so happens it was my night to have the cup, so it's currently full of ice to keep our champagne cool.

"Umm, Moose, hey," Taylor whispers, bending down next to me as everyone around the dinner table mingles. I chose to hire caterers for tonight since there are so many people, that way we're all able to enjoy the evening without having to serve ourselves.

"What is it, Tot?" I whisper back.

"Not that I'm not *loving* the black-tie attire—and the caterers were a super nice touch so your victory dinner isn't potluck style, but—"

She smiles and begins talking through her teeth. "Who's the rando sitting by Mom and Dad?" I glance over and smile.

"A friend."

"I mean, as long as we're not about to turn into a massive breaking news article, I'm good with it."

"I'm confident there are at least three people here who would drop Hank before that happened."

"Riiight." She looks down the table where Tucker, Max, and Tank are sitting. "As you were." With her evening gown floating behind her, she makes her way back down to her seat and Leah leans over and squeezes my thigh.

"Better get to it before someone asks Hank what he does for a living." She lifts her brows and nods me along.

"I suppose you're right." I stand and raise my water glass, tapping it with my fork.

"Can I have your attention please?" I clear my throat when all eyes turn towards me.

"You've had it since you made that winning shot, son." My dad says, easing some of my nerves as laughs spread across the table.

"It's no secret that I achieved one of my lifelong dreams of winning the Stanley Cup last week. I've been playing hockey since I was old enough to hold a stick and the time, effort, and sacrifices made by both of my parents will not go unnoticed. Mom and Dad, thank you. For taking me to practice, for not getting *too* mad at me when I busted a window…or two, while slapping biscuits around the yard, and for never letting me give up on my dreams. *Any* of them." My dad gives me a sly smile and I tip my glass to him.

"But winning a game is simply that. One win. One game. One moment—that I will, of course, be proud of and remember for the rest of my life—but in the end, it is fleeting. Something else happened this season, something much bigger than winning a game. I finally got my girl. I would have never ended up in Nashville, playing for the Badgers if it wasn't for this woman right here and my undeniable need to be where she was. As many of you know, I asked Leah to marry me recently—and she accepted." I smile down at her, and her cheeks grow rosy as people yell and clap around the table.

"Dove, I know I let too many years pass before growing a pair and telling you how crazy I was about you, but I will be grateful for the rest of my life that you finally gave me a chance to apologize and prove to you just how much you mean to me—how much you've always meant to me." I take a deep breath and face our guests again. "So, thank you all for coming tonight, for what you *thought* would be a celebratory dinner for the Badgers' victory." The room goes quiet and people look around to see if the other knows what the hell I'm talking about. Then I grab Leah's hand and motion for her to stand.

"Leah and I are getting married—*tonight*."

"WHAT?!" Taylor and my mom scream at the same time as the other girls gasp and the guys' faces are full of supportive surprise.

"Hank, thank you for coming to officiate. Dove, I'll let you and the girls have a moment and I'll meet you at the altar." I kiss her hand and she looks at me with such love in her eyes I'm almost tempted to give her a five minute clock to be ready to walk down the aisle. "If everyone else would follow me, I'll show you to your seats for the ceremony."

"I'm gonna strangle you with your own jockstrap," Taylor growls at me and I bark out a laugh.

"How about you just go on your long ass honeymoon tomorrow instead and leave me the hell alone?" I smirk at her and watch as she breaks, unable to hold back her smile.

"I love you so much, Moose. I am so *so* happy for you."

Taylor and I haven't had many moments like this since high school. We've always been there for each other, but Taylor is the kind of girl that is going to take care of herself more times than not. Once she became an adult and really came into her *don't fuck with me* attitude, there wasn't much need for a scary big brother anymore. She *was* the scary one.

But ever since I've been back and mended things with Leah—and she found out why I had avoided her for so long in the first place—

I've seen the softer, more vulnerable side of Taylor again. So instead of pulling away first, I hold onto her until she's ready to let go. Embracing every moment I get to hug my sister, silently reminding her that I'll always be here when she needs me.

"Tay, come on!" Lauren shouts from the stairwell. Then they disappear upstairs to help Leah get ready. She spent the entire day yesterday with her mom, shopping for a wedding dress to suit our last-minute timeframe, and by the way she was absolutely glowing when she got home, I can't wait to see what she's picked.

Twenty minutes later I'm told they're ready to get things started and my palms begin to sweat. At the last minute one of the servers' ushers Matty and Lyssa to their seats and the music begins to play.

"Wildest Dreams" by Taylor Swift played by violin actually kills.

Tank stands next to me, followed by Max, Tucker, and Hendrix. It's crazy how these people already feel like family to me—plus you know, now they actually *are* family. Shane and Cece walk out first, followed by Taylor then Lauren and I know she's not far behind. My heart beats so hard in my chest it feels like it's fighting against my ribs to get to her.

"Breathe dude," Tank mumbles from beside me, prompting me to take as much air into my lungs as I can. Thank God I do, because when I see her descending the small steps on our back porch, it takes every bit of my remaining breath away. Everyone stands to watch her walk down the small aisle and I can't take my eyes off her.

Her hair is in its natural curls—I wonder if she wears it like that so often now because she knows how much I love it—pulled into a low bun with her veil tucked into it, and *the dress*. It's strapless, fitting her like a second skin around the bodice with a full tulle skirt that looks like it's made from the softest cloud known to man. The necklace I gave her is around her neck and small pearl earrings are in her ears.

Simple.

Stunning.

Timeless.

Just like the bride that wears it.

Tears fill my eyes, and my throat feels tight as I fight back the emotion that is daring to pour out of me. Her mom kisses her cheek and I step beside her, taking her hand in mine.

"Hey, Dove," I whisper as the music begins to fade.

"Hey, Moose." She smiles at me and it takes everything in me to not lean over and kiss her.

"You may be seated." The officiant goes through his part of the service—Leah and I repeating what he tells us when he tells us to—but all I can do is stare into her eyes as golden hour illuminates my favorite color of green, grounding me into this moment.

"Have you prepared your own vows?" Hank asks and Leah smiles and nods. "Whenever you're ready." He nods and Lauren hands her the paper she was carrying with her small bouquet.

Sawyer

Eighteen years ago, I was put in a study group that landed me in the Clark household. I met some of my very best friends during a class project and little did I know, the middle schooler that waltzed through the kitchen yelling about a bag of bar-b-q chips would come to be one of those best friends too—and even more, my soulmate. You understood me more than most people, you never hesitated to protect not only me, but the rest of the spice girls as well, and you were the reason I started to love hockey. If I'm being honest, I only loved hockey because it gave me a reason to talk to you. My feelings for you grew every time we were together and what was nothing more than a crush for so many years, soon turned into a friendship you could build a life around. You became the one person I could see myself happy with for the rest of my life, and then I lost you. Don't worry, this story has a happily ever after. Because I never again loved someone the way I have always loved you. I tried to hate you, for many of our years apart, but the moment you walked back into my life, I knew I was only fooling myself. You have had more of my heart than you ever realized for much longer than even I knew. Today, in front of our friends and family, I promise to never walk away from you or the life we are starting together, no matter what life throws at us. I promise to cling to you and allow you to help me through the hard things and to always be there for you to cling to as well. I promise to always remember our game day rituals and to never stop dancing with you. I promise to be by your side, supporting you in any and all new adventures you see us going on in the future and I promise that no matter how deeply we fall in love, that you will always be my best friend. From the moment you first called me Dove, I have been yours, and yours I will remain.
Only, always and forever.
I love you.

Leah

My bride, my best friend, my soul mate, and in a few short moments, my wife, standing here today, committing the rest of my life to loving you is the only ending I ever saw for us. I have loved you more years than I haven't and knowing that I get to spend the rest of my life falling more in love with you, with your mind, your smile, those eyes…it is the greatest honor to be the man you wish to call your husband. I have felt many things in my life—the adrenaline from winning my first hockey game, relief in knowing I would be playing for the Badgers when it was time to trade, and the gut-wrenching despair of thinking I'd lost my best friend due to my own horrible decision making. But the things I have felt that are now seared into my memory—falling in love, kissing my soul mate, knowing the exact moment my soul became tethered to another—are all things that I have experienced because of you, Dove. My heart beats for you, and only you. I would give up every other accomplishment I've ever made in life if I still got to marry you at the end of it all. So, today, I promise to love you through every heartache that you may endure, and order take out for lazy days in bed when we need to recharge. I promise to keep you grounded when you feel as though you may lose touch with reality and show you that for as long as there is breath in our lungs, that we have a life worth living to the fullest. I promise to always come home to you and dance you around our kitchen. And to never miss an opportunity to remind you that you are all of the very best parts of me. My heart, my soul and my happiness are at their best when I am with you, as they always have been and will remain to be. Only, always and forever, I am yours, LeighAnn Clark. Only, always and forever.
I love you.

"By the power vested in me by the state of Tennessee, I now pronounce you husband and wife. You may now kiss the bride." And boy do I kiss the hell out of *my wife.*

"Ladies and gentlemen, I present to you, for the first time ever, Mr. and Mrs. Sawyer Clark." I hold our hands up in the air as we run down the aisle, hearing the photographer snapping away when we stop at the end for one more kiss.

"What do you want to do now, *wife?*" I smirk as Leah bites down on her bottom lip.

"Have my babies, Thirteen." She smiles so bright that the setting sun pales in comparison to her.

My only. My always. My forever.

My Dove.

The End.

Acknowledgments

To my parents, Keith and Karen—the Marilyn and Tony / Loretta and Allen of my own life—I love you more than words can say, (which is a big deal seeing as how I write them for a living.) You both have always been the most loving, supportive and encouraging parents a girl could dream of having. You raised me to be kind, respectful and to love Christ above all else, leading by example every day and I can't thank you enough for that. The life lessons, Saturday mornings cleaning the house with Elvis playing, gymnastics meets, and family vacations you both made possible will never be forgotten. Your love and support throughout my writing career has meant more to me than you could ever imagine. Thank you for giving me a childhood worth remembering and an adulthood worth cherishing. I love you both with all of my heart.

To my husband, as always, who didn't make it through this book until it was actually completed. Thank you for loving my words and being the most supportive partner through every story. For all the nights you let me hide away to write and for never letting me give up. I'll never stop thanking you for simply allowing me to live my dreams. I love you to infinity and beyond.

To Kate, without whom the hockey in this story would have been absolute garbage. Thank you for being by my side and never holding back when you think I could do better. Your honesty, friendship and company are what helps me get through every release and I love you forever for it. (And I mean, *of course* the covers, interior formatting, and design for ALL of my book merch- but that's a give, I hope.)

To Keri, my PA who has made my life tremendously easier this year. I love you. Your unhinged alpha comments, your undying support, the way you so effortlessly master the tasks I give you when my brain just completely fries on me. You're a total rockstar and I am so eternally grateful to have you in my life and on my team.

To Erica, who made my heart soar with every comment you left on this manuscript as you edited. I can't believe someone even came close to taking Tucker's place but I am honored you thought so highly of this book and these characters. I am so grateful for your friendship and the chance to work with you every release. Can't wait to squeeze you again!!

To my sweet friend, Laura Pavlov, I cannot thank you enough for allowing me to portray my own love of your books through the writing in one of my own. Always Mine was the first book I read that made me fall in love with your writing and the worlds you create, and Loving Romeo makes me think so much of my own dad and how we used to have Rocky movie marathons together when I was younger. You are such an inspiration to me and I feel so very lucky to know you.

To my ARC and Content teams, you guys come through every release and blow me away with your love and support for these characters. I am so lucky to get the chance to continue writing this series, and I truly don't think that would be possible without you guys and your sharing of my books. So THANK YOU!!

To the readers who have been here from the beginning, and those who have just found me through this release. Thank you for taking a chance on my books. I do hope you enjoyed the story; that you found laughter, healing, or relatability in some aspect, *or* that you simply had a good time as you read. I can't wait to share with you what's coming next.

More From Sarah

Waiting for Sunshine (Nashville Nights 1)
Grumpy x sunshine
Workplace Romance
Military MMC
Grief Bonding

Waiting for Healing (Nashville Nights 2)
Friends to Lovers
Road Trip Romance
Only one bed
Navy Seal + ER Nurse

Waiting for Redemption (Nashville Nights 3)
Marriage of Convenience
Former Marine + Bartender
Second Chance
Single Mom

Trigger Warnings

18+ explicit romance
Alcohol Consumption
Death of a family member